THE
LOST GOSPEL
OF
LAZARUS

RICHARD ZIMLER

THE
LOST GOSPEL
OF
LAZARUS

ABOUT THE AUTHOR

'**Richard Zimler** is a present-day scholar and writer of remarkable erudition and compelling imagination."
—The Spectator

Photo by Alexandre Quintanilha

Richard Zimler's eleven novels have been translated into twenty-three languages and have appeared on bestseller lists in twelve different countries, including the UK, United States, Australia, Brazil, Italy and Portugal. Five of his works have been nominated for the International Dublin Literary Award, the richest prize in the English-speaking world, and he has won prizes for his fiction in the UK, America, France and Portugal.

Richard has explored the lives of different branches and generations of a Portuguese-Jewish family in four highly acclaimed historical novels, starting with *The Last Kabbalist of Lisbon*, now in development as a major film. He grew up in New York and since 1990 has lived in Porto, Portugal. For his contributions to Portuguese culture he was awarded the city's highest distinction, the Medal of Honour.

www.zimler.com
@RichardZimler

GLOSSARY OF HEBREW NAMES USED IN
THE GOSPEL OF LAZARUS

One of my initial objectives in *The Gospel of Lazarus* was to give back to Jesus and Lazarus their Judaism. After all, we are given no indication in the *New Testament* that Jesus ever renounced his faith. Quite to the contrary, he is shown to be very familiar with the Old Testament and, on occasion, quite eager to fulfil its prophesies. In short, I wanted to characterize him as what he must have been – a charismatic Jewish mystic, healer and preacher. But how could I free myself – and readers – from nearly two thousand years of Christian philosophy and related iconography? One of the strategies I used to was refer to him and all the other main characters by their Hebrew names – the names that they would have used in their daily lives in the Galilee and Judea. In the case of Jesus, this meant calling him Yeshua. In keeping with Jewish tradition, his family name became "ben Yosef," meaning "son of Joseph." The original Hebrew name of Lazarus would have been Eliezer. But in my tale he has spent extensive time in the Greek city of Alexandria, so he also comes to think of himself by his Hellenic name, Lazarus. In the same way, Mary, Jesus' mother, becomes Maryam. Saint John, the author of the only Gospel to mention Lazarus, becomes Yohanon.

We know from Greek, Roman and Jewish sources that diminutives and nicknames were also common at this time, so I also used that option on occasion. For instance, Lazarus' sister Maryam becomes Mia.

For me, this strategy worked extremely well. Once I knew the two main characters as Yeshua ben Yosef and Eliezer ben Natan, I was free to see them and all the other New Testament figures with a new eyes and place them inside the Jewish traditions of their homeland. I hope that the reader will find this strategy liberating as well.

Place names are also generally given in Hebrew. In a few cases, however, I have maintained the modern equivalents so as not to cause confusion. For instance, Lazarus' homeland remains the Galilee and does not change to HaGalil. A full glossary of foreign terms follows the text.

English (Christian) Name	Hebrew name
Jesus	Yeshua
Lazarus	Eliezer
Mary, sister of Lazarus	Maryam (or Mia)
Martha, sister of Lazarus	Marta
Mary, mother of Jesus	Maryam
Joseph, father of Jesus	Yosef
John the Apostle	Yohanon
Judas Iscariot	Yehudah of Kerioth
Mary Magdalene	Maryam of Magdala
Nikodemos	Nicodemus
John the Baptist	Yohanon ben Zechariah
Caiaphas the High Priest	Yosef Caiaphas
Annas, former High Priest	Annas ben Seth
Jeremiah, Lazarus' son	Yirmiyahu (or Yirmi)

In death, we never much resemble who we were in life, for all the mystery is gone.

Lazarus ben Natan

A history made of *ifs* – such is the life of mortal men.

Lazarus ben Natan

I

How great is the distance between the sunken-cheeked, leaky-eyed old man writing to you now and the swallow-quick eight-year-old he once was? According to the calendar, it is fifty-seven years. Yet, according to my winged heart, it is the nearly-nothing time it takes for me to close my eyes and alight in Natzeret . . .

Dearest Yaphiel, the time has finally come for me to tell you of your long-secret place in my life – which means, in turn, that I need to tell you of the man you asked to meet when we were last together.

Of Yeshua.

He is our *aleph* and our *taw* and every letter in between, for he is the gift-giver who brought us together.

If I find the courage, my grandson, then I shall also ask you a favour that I cannot ask of anyone else.

I am perched on the mat in my bedroom. It is the twelfth of the month of Tevet, long past the second watch of night, and in my window is a watchful moon.

It is the sixty-seventh year since Rome's conquest of Zion, and Augustus is our emperor.

When I finally fall back to sleep, I dream that the Lord is a blood-red eagle with a purple crest and jet-black eyes. Standing at the corner of our roof, He gazes out towards the spray of sunrise on the horizon with a stern and wary expression, as if all the world depends on His vigilance.

I want to touch him, but fear of His sharp, powerful beak forms a fist at my throat. Still, I venture a first, tentative step, and, when He – the Eagle-God – shows no anger, I ease closer. On coming to His side, I kneel down and reach out with the cautiousness of a boy who has already witnessed a number of executions. I make the movement of my hand into a whisper of greeting – the proof of my goodwill and righteous intent.

With a graceful bow of His head, the Lord leans towards me, granting me permission. I trace the tips of my fingers across the cool, firm, silken plumage of His back. The feel of him – so compact and forceful – makes me shiver. Tilting His head, the Lord's dark eyes catch mine and ask a question.

'Eliezer,' I tell him. 'Though my father calls me Lazarus.'

He blinks to show me He has understood.

At that moment do He and I pass through an invisible gate? We seem to reside now inside our own time and place. Only a decade later will I find myself able to shape my feelings into words, and they will be these: our silent complicity has created an island for the two of us, and around that island is all that I once was – and all that I shall never be again.

Then, a shift . . . I am standing on the defensive wall around Natzeret. The Lord is perched on my right shoulder, His gnarled, rust-coloured talons gripping me tightly.

Invaders will come from across the Jordan River, and we must all be ready to fight. That is the meaning I take from the urgency of His gaze towards the bronze-coloured dawn spreading over the Galilee. As I scan the silhouette of hills around our town, searching out the archers and spearmen of a foreign army, a tendril of flame unfurls on the horizon. Soon it is joined by others, which makes me understand that I have erred in my judgement – the still-hidden sun has not yet announced its return; the enemy is setting fire to our orchards.

With a cry of battle, the Lord takes wing. A few moments later, while soaring above the flames, He is transformed by their heat, growing tenfold in size and tenfold yet again.

All too soon, however, He disappears over a ridge of flaming hills in the distance. Around me now is a sea of fire and smoke.

'Come back!' I cry out in desperation. 'I don't want to die here!'

A man's voice behind me calls out my name. 'Eliezer, I am the gate you seek!' He shouts.

The voice is familiar, though I shall be unable to identify it for many years. Before I can turn to see who it is, hands push me forward. Falling, I am engulfed by the flames.

And yet I am not burned. And I do not die. I tumble through the conflagration until I find myself flying through a bruised red sky. I am clothed in silver feathers.

Yerushalayim rises up before me.

The Phasael Tower . . . I decide to perch at its rim to assess the enemy's strength, but as I alight there . . .

Through that metamorphosis of emotion that marks us for ever as the children of Havvah and Adam, my powerful wingbeats become the leaping heart of a Galilean boy who awakens to find himself in his bedroom, naked, bathed in moonlight, wondering how – and why – he became a God with wings.

2

I must speak to you now of the week that changed my life and sent me into exile here on Rodos – and that brought you into our family. Try if you can to imagine me as the widower and father of two young children that I was then – a man who had celebrated thirty-six birthdays with his family and friends.

One afternoon, I awaken to a confusion of faces unknown to me, lit by the harsh saffron-coloured light of a dozen night-lamps. My heart recoils from so many strangers, and my first thought is that I must quickly make an appeal for mercy. But I do not utter a word; I remain a pair of blinking, terrified eyes waiting for clues that will reveal to me the nature of my predicament.

Out of habit, I speak the Lord's words to the prophet Yirmiyahu inside my head, *Be not afraid of them, for I am with you and shall deliver you.* And yet, raucous shouts from somewhere unseen make me flinch – and wish to run. Rushed whispers soon reach me as well, but I am unable to comprehend them. The tense, insistent beating in my chest sways me from side to side, and my throat is as dry as sand.

Deep underground – that is where my scattering thoughts seem to have sought refuge.

A long-haired youth holds up a torch and leans towards me, studying me with moist and troubled eyes. His tunic is ripped along the neckline.

When I gaze past him, I find butterflies of shadow fluttering on a ceiling of pale stone. The heavy, sweet, humid scent of myrrh fills me with each of my laboured breaths.

They've taken me to a cavern, I think. *I must try to discover what they want of me before I speak.*

A small woman with a drawn face and curious, deep-set eyes leans towards me. She holds a small square of fabric over her mouth and nose, and she peers at me as though endeavouring to solve a complex calculation. She says something unintelligible – in Latin, perhaps – and lifts her brows in an attempt to prompt my reply. I wonder why she doesn't address me in Aramaic – or in Hebrew or Greek.

She must be a foreigner. The others, too. And yet nearly all of them wear Judaean dress.

To my left a stooped old man is weeping, his tallith draped over his shoulders. Beside him is a tall long-limbed woman – forty years old, I would guess – clutching a woollen mantle to her chest as if it might jump from her and scamper away if she were to ease her grip. She has the stricken face of a lost soul who has seen too much, and the collar of her peplos is torn. The small scar on her chin – in the shape of a crescent – seems familiar to me.

Something furry folds into my right hand. A mouse? Could I have been taken to a den of wild animals and vermin? I am unable to turn my head to get a look. Below my racing pulse stirs the hope that the little creature will not bite me.

Yaphiel, you might think it comic, but I later discover that the hand of an old friend can feel exactly like a shivering mouse under certain peculiar circumstances.

My shoulders are gripped from behind, and I am pushed into an upright position. The long-haired youth and the woman with a crescent scar unfold a coarse linen cloth that has been wrapped around my chest and legs. Do I fall asleep while they work? I next remember the tearful old man covering my naked sex with his prayer shawl.

A wooden ladle is held to my lips by a slender man in a camlet cape and hood. He is patient with me, this stranger with generous and powerful hands, and I gulp at the next ladle he offers me, and the one after that, and . . . After a time, I split into two persons: an exhausted being desperate to slake his thirst and a distant and curious observer wondering why such a simple act has become so difficult.

After I have drunk my fill, I notice an amber necklace around my neck. Its beads are a milky yellow. When I try to grip it, tremors strike my hand again.

Help me.

My voice will not come, but the long-haired boy reads the desperation in my face and lifts up the necklace for me to see. Could it be the one my mother always wore?

'Give him a look at the talisman!'

A woman's emphatic voice prompts him to show me a roundel of parchment that has also been hung around my neck. Four crude figures are designed on it, graced with oval Egyptian eyes. Their angelic names are written above their heads: Mikhael, Gavriel, Uriel and Rafael. Underneath them is a quote from the Psalms in the handwriting of a child: 'No disaster shall befall you, no calamity shall come upon your home. For the Lord has charged His angels to guard you wherever you go.'

A flute melody – a Phrygian tune, plaintive and mournful – calls me towards sleep, and the slumber inside me is warm and abundant, like a gently swaying sea.

Some time later, the man who helped me drink kisses me on the lips. He has taken off his hood. He has red and swollen eyes.

He has been grieving, I think, and I wish to ask him if a friend of his has died, but I am still unable to find a voice.

He caresses my cheek. '*Shalom Aleikem, dodee,*' he whispers. *Peace to you, beloved.*

He knows Aramaic, which is a comfort.

Stubble coarsens his cheeks, and his shoulder-length brown hair is in a tangle. He shows me a weary but contented smile.

He would like to let himself go and laugh the exhausted laugh of a man who has been weeping, I think.

The mist of forgetfulness inside me clears at that moment, and I recognize him. Yet he looks older than I remember him – and spent in body. Could he be ill?

When I reach up to him, intending to test his brow for the heat of fever, he grips my hand and kisses it as if we had been lost to each other for years. 'I answered you in the hiding place of thunder,' he says, which is how we have greeted each other since we were boys. It is a quote from our favourite verse of Psalm.

Where are we? I shape this question with my lips – at least, that is my intent – but for some reason I fail to make myself understood, and Yeshua shows me a puzzled face. 'You'll be yourself again soon,' he tells me. 'All of us will help you.'

I scan the countenances around me and count them – fourteen. Standing on each side of Yeshua are my old friends Maryam of Magdala and Yohanon ben Zebedee. Yohanon has had his thick black hair clipped so short that he appears to be wearing an Ionian skullcap. He smiles encouragingly at me through his tears.

Maryam's kohl-ringed eyes look bruised. She is wearing her saffron-coloured robe – a gift from Yeshua – though it looks too large and cumbersome on her. Behind her – dressed in an elegant toga, pinching his nose – stands Nikodemos ben

Gurion, one of Yeshua's benefactors. He peers at me as if I might be an impostor. Could I have changed in some way that makes me seem another man?

At the back, taller than all the others, are my Alexandrian cousins, the twins Ion and Ariston. Ion, the bolder of the two, waves at me and grins in his boyish way.

Maryam draws my glance from him when she raises her hands and blesses me. I spot a wine-coloured design of the zodiac on her palm and aim to ask her about it, but all that emerges from me is a dry ratcheting sound.

At length, I grow anxious to find my mother and father, but they do not seem to be with us.

I know that I am crying only when I taste salt on my lips. The long-limbed woman – whom I now recognize as my sister Mia – takes my hand and places it over her face, breathing in deeply on the scent of me, though she soon starts coughing. When we were children, she used to say that I smelled like warm barley bread. I remember that now, and my name, but many other things still escape me. Might we have all gathered together for my father's funeral?

'Where are our parents?' I manage to ask her in a hoarse whisper.

'Everything will be all right,' Mia replies. 'You mustn't worry yourself.'

She puts her arm around the old man next to her. 'Grandfather Shimon risked leaving the house to be with you,' she tells me in a cheerful voice. She points then to the small tired-looking woman holding a piece of fabric over her mouth. 'And Marta is here, of course. Many friends have come. And your son and daughter.' She summons my children to her with a wave.

Nahara is trembling. She looks as she does when she has been chased out of sleep by thunder. Yirmiyahu, her older brother – the long-haired youth with anxious eyes – lifts her up to me.

Nahara throws her arms around my neck. Blessed be the kindness of the Lord; as she sobs, I still the shaking in my hand long enough to comb her soft brown hair, though my touch only makes her cry harder.

If I'm unable to calm her, then Leah will . . .

Before finishing my thought, I recall that my wife's life ended six years before, at the same moment that our daughter's began. My mind also locates my parents' graves in a suffocating corner of my memory I rarely visit.

'I'm sorry I'm so weak,' I whisper to my daughter.

As she sobs, Yirmi eases her despair with endearments, then leans down and presses his lips to both my eyes, which seems his way of linking the three of us together – and an extremely mature gesture for a youth who only reached manhood a few months earlier.

Yeshua returns to me then. He places his hand on top of my head and presses down, as he does when he wishes to heal a supplicant. '"The season of singing has come,"' he quotes from the Song of Shelomoh.

He begins to chant, and I flow towards his voice, which I know as well as my own, and, when he lifts his hand from me, I follow its absence beyond the borders of my flesh, and I am in the air now, held aloft by the sound of his words in Hebrew, and I remember my father telling me that our ancestors gather around us when we intone our hymns, and . . .

'Do you think you can stand, *dodee?*'

Yeshua's question brings me back inside my body. I shake my head, for I am unable to feel my legs.

'But you know now who I am?' he asks.

A silly memory makes me grin. 'Sometimes a teacher and sometimes bitter trouble,' I whisper.

It is an answer I invented when we were students in order to put him in his place when he grew too full of himself. It is a play on words: *morah* means bitter trouble and *moreh* means teacher.

I expect Yeshua to laugh; instead, he speaks to me in a downhearted voice. 'No, I'm the one who pushed you off the wall and into the talons of the Lord of the Sky. Though maybe I . . .' Before he can complete his sentence, his eyes flood with tears and he squeezes my hand. 'Can you forgive me for coming too late?' he asks.

Too late for what? I wonder.

3

Beware of men who see no mystery when they look at their reflection.

It was my father who told me that. He was speaking of a tyrannical Roman prefect at the time, but he believed that all of us are changed for the better – become more humble, at the very least – when we recognize that our identity tends to slide away from us every time we strive to catch it. And if the 'I' who directs our actions is not fixed and permanent, then how can we ever be certain of who we are and what God has asked us to do?

After my cousins lift me on to a wooden bier and carry me into the daylight, I realize I had been lying inside one of the rock-cut tombs just off the road north to Anathoth.

Yeshua and Maryam, walking together, lead our small group out of the necropolis towards the road south to Bethany. Bread and fruit have been left before many of the entrances to the tombs, summoning clouds of flies.

When my grandfather lifts the back of my head to slip a small cushion underneath, I ask him why I was brought here.

'So you remember nothing, my boy?' he questions.

'No, I don't think so.'

My son raises a palm frond over my head to shade me. 'What's your last memory, Father?' he asks.

With my eyes closed, I see myself seated on a mosaic of a bird, surrounded by the tools of my trade. 'I was repairing the floor of our courtyard,' I reply. 'I think it was this morning.'

The boy grimaces as if I have given him bad news.

His aunt Mia eases him out of the way. 'We'll talk at home, Eli,' she says. 'Just rest for now.'

'At least tell me who died and whose tomb I was in.'

'The tomb belongs to Nikodemos.'

'But he's right over there.' I lift my hand and gesture towards him; he is walking ahead of us, alongside Shimon bar Yona, another of Yeshua's close friends.

'Yes, that's him,' Mia agrees, but she says nothing more.

Frustration makes me wish to shout, but my words come out as a desperate croak.

My sister calls to Yeshua. 'Speak to my brother,' she tells him, which confirms my earlier suspicions that he has been directing this conspiracy against me.

My old friend comes to the left side of my bier, as though to counterbalance the emotional weight of my sisters, who walk on my right. 'Lazar, just be patient. All will be clear in a little while,' he tells me, using his childhood name for me to win my compliance. He pats my arm and implies with his constrained expression that he'd prefer to talk to me only when we have a chance to be alone.

Fortunately for him, I am too weak to argue. Also, an unruly throng has gathered around us, and Ion and Ariston have found themselves forced to thrust their way forward through tightly packed clusters of men and women who stare and gape at me.

The crowd soon parts for a tall man with tight hyacinth curls in his fair hair, a style favoured by the Judaean aristocracy, for they are ever eager to imitate our conquerors. He wears a porphyry-coloured robe embroidered at the collar with golden thread. An armed bodyguard walks beside him.

'I've been warned about you, Yeshua ben Yosef!' the man snarls, and he glares at my old friend as though cursing him in his mind.

At the time I thought that this interloper was simply an angry stranger, but it occurs to me now that news of what had happened to me in my tomb might already have reached the Temple. If so, then he might have been a messenger sent by the High Priest to dissuade Yeshua from using his healing powers again in so astonishing a manner. Indeed, that possibility seems a likelihood now.

'May peace yet find you on this beautiful morning,' Yeshua tells him, holding up his hands to show that he carries no weapon.

'We'll have peace when you and your companions return to your homeland!' the aristocrat retorts.

Yohanon steps beside Yeshua. 'What exactly were you told about us?' he asks.

'That you would bring your evil sorcery to Judaea, and that your sinister words –'

'I cast no spell,' Yeshua cuts in. 'It was the Lord who chose life for my friend.'

The man spits by Yeshua's feet. 'And yet a filthy stench accompanies you everywhere. All who stand downwind of you and your friends know that the Lord has abandoned you.'

'Stop wasting our time and step aside!' my grandfather shouts.

The unpleasant Judaean tells him to mind his own business in an imperious tone and turns again to Yeshua. 'If you didn't steal this man out of the arms of death, then who did? Give me the name of the necromancer who would play at such dangerous games!'

'*Ehyeh-Asher-Ehyeh,*' Yeshua answers.

'So you insist that your trickery is the work of God?' the man says with a sneer.

'No, you've misunderstood me. What I'm saying is something different – that the Lord has reminded us today of the profound and hidden things in our world and His.'

The stranger gives no indication that he recognizes these words as coming from the Book of Daniel, which gives me to believe that he is ignorant of scripture – though I realize now that he might have wished to keep us from guessing that he was in league with our priests.

'Not even a heretic like you could believe that God wishes for cadavers to take to their feet and prowl our streets!' he declares.

'All I know is that the Lord has brought my friend back to us. And I'm grateful.' Yeshua smiles down at me – his eyes moistening – and he again cites Daniel, but this time, only to me and in a whisper, as though to tell me that he and I shall soon need to broach difficult and secretive matters: '"The Lord knows what is in the darkness, though the light dwells in Him."'

At the time, I see no particular importance in Yeshua's focus on the Book of Daniel.

'Do you really expect me to believe that the Almighty is working through a Galilean peasant?' the quarrelsome stranger demands.

Yehudah of Kerioth steps beside Yeshua. 'Enough of this silly argument,' he says to the aristocrat. 'We've got to get our friend home. Can't you see that?'

'Who is it you think you're addressing, young man?'

'I'm addressing a man who ought to let us get on our way!' Yehudah replies in a seething tone. His green eyes are lit with rage.

The stranger's bodyguard unsheathes his sword, but Yeshua pleads for calm, then takes the arm of our belligerent enemy and leads him a few paces away. As I watch them conversing in lowered voices, a barefoot tyke with a much-soiled face, reeking of filth, manages to squeeze between my two sisters. 'Was an *ibbur* inside you?' he asks me in an eager voice.

Before I can find out why he would pose such a silly question of me, an old woman with a squashed and wrinkled face grabs Ion's arm. 'Let's have a good look at him!' she cackles.

When the crowd surges, my cousin loses his grip on the front of the bier, which lands with a thud on the packed earth of our roadway. I tumble off but do not suffer anything more painful than a bump on my shoulder thanks to the quick reflexes of my son, who cushions my fall.

The crone shakes a filthy rag at me, spraying a greasy liquid over my chest and face. 'Now we're gonna see what you are!' she shouts.

Later, my sister Marta, who has long studied the curious arts in a secret circle of local women, will speculate that the fluid was designed to reveal my true form as a demon and that the old woman probably expected me to sprout horns and a tail.

As Mia wipes my face, the sunlight presses like hot metal against my closed eyelids. Thankfully, Yirmi soon has me shaded again with his palm frond, and my cousins lift me back on to my bier. This time, I feel Ion's strong grip around my ankles, which means that sensation is returning to my legs.

Marta spreads my shroud over my belly and legs as a protective covering.

After Yeshua comes back to us, he tells me in an apologetic voice that he has to leave me again for a short while. I quickly lose sight of him, and it is while I am looking for him in the multitude that a sumptuously dressed woman carrying a strand of pearls in her hand asks me if her servant might be permitted to slice off a piece of my shroud.

I am at a loss as to how to reply, but Yohanon intervenes. He speaks with the woman in hushed tones, then comes to me. 'Her eldest daughter is a leper,' he whispers behind his hand. 'She believes that even just a thread of your shroud might cure her.'

So it is that I give my permission for her servant to take a piece.

Yeshua's forearm is bleeding when he returns to me. I ask him about it, but he tells me it is of no importance. He parts the crowd by waving his staff before him.

Just before starting off again, Mia smears ewe's fat on my lips, which must be crusted and cracked, for her fingertip comes away with blood. Judging from the low angle of the sun, it is late afternoon. Swallows are slicing through the air above us, playful and exuberant, possessed of all the energy and grace that I now lack.

All these clues from nature tell me that it is springtime, and, as we enter Bethany, the dusty streets overflowing with pilgrims remind me that Passover is at hand – and the reason that my Alexandrian cousins are with us.

It seems to me that our pilgrims have begun arriving in Yerushalayim earlier and earlier in recent years. Or did I somehow miss the start of Passover? When I ask my grandfather, he pats my hand reassuringly. 'No, my boy, our Seder is still a week away.'

Sitting in a donkey cart by a clothing stall in the marketplace is a young mother with plaited hair, her baby at her breast, and seeing them together reduces my thoughts to a single lost hope: *if only Leah were able to meet me at our door and explain to me what has happened.*

4

On reaching home, I discover that my legs are still unsteady, so my cousins carry me to the alcove that serves as my bedroom, ease me down on to my mat and prop me up with cushions. Marta insists on going to the courtyard to heat up some lentil soup for me, though I tell her I am not at all hungry. After Mia helps me slake my continued thirst, she sets about removing the grime from my face with her strigil, but my skin feels as if it has been burned, and her scraping, no matter how gentle, makes me shudder.

My friends have brought myrrh from the tomb in which I awakened, but its funereal scent sickens me, so, to mask the peculiar stench that accompanies me now, Yirmi and Marta gather wild roses and strands of jasmine and lay them on my table, shelves and clothes trunk. Mia scatters the potent incense she makes of charred thyme leaves around the perimeter of my room.

After Yeshua requests some time alone with me, he lowers my reed blinds around us. My feet have turned to ice, so he covers them with his cape. The squealing laughter of my daughter playing in our courtyard seems the world's way of reassuring me that all will soon be as it was, but my heart – spinning outward towards my fears – gives me to believe that whatever has befallen me has changed me for ever.

Kneeling, Yeshua holds the back of his hand to my forehead and tells me in a pleased voice that the heat of creation is returning to my flesh. When I fail to respond with a smile of relief, he sits with me. 'Talk to me,' he says, taking my shoulder.

'I feel as if you and the others have left me behind with Pharaoh. Nobody will tell me what's happened.'

'You had tertian fever for a week. Mia said that she and Marta piled every cover they could find on top of you, and yet you still shook with chills. You had troubling visions as well. You told everyone you were trapped in snow on the top of Mount Sinai.'

I am unable to recall any wintry summit, but when I lower my gaze, a feeling of entrapment returns to my arms and legs. And I see a bearded man kneeling before me. He wears the long robes and cylindrical hat of a Persian. His eyes are uneasy, and his hand movements are awkward and agitated. Is it dread that I see in his face?

'Did the Baal Nephesh send a friend to look after me?' I ask Yeshua, using the title of esteem that my parents long ago gave our physician, who grew up in Babylon.

'No, your sisters told me that he was away. I don't know who recommended the healer who came to see you.'

'But someone came. I remember him – a Persian with a beard.'

'Apparently so. Marta told me that he brewed herbs for you to drink.'

I recall a bitter taste in my mouth. 'What did he give me?'

'She didn't tell me.'

I call through my curtains to Mia, who presumes the right to eavesdrop on my private conversations. And since I long ago ceded this point to her, there is no need to pretend otherwise.

'The visitor was a Persian named Kurush,' she tells me. 'Lykos recommended him.'

Lykos is the Baal Nephesh's assistant. 'What cure did he prepare for me?' I ask.

'A decoction of vetch and willow bark.'

'It tasted terrible. Did it do any good?'

'For a time. But then you grew weaker.'

The effort she makes to fight away tears makes me raise my hand and bless her for looking after me.

Once Mia is gone, Yeshua continues his explanation: 'Your nephew Binyamin found me preaching near Pella. He asked me to return to you. But I . . .' His expression grows worried.

'What is it?' I ask.

'I waited two days before coming here. I feared we might quarrel again.'

'I don't remember any quarrel.'

'The last time we were together, we argued about my plans to defy the priests.'

As he tells me of our disagreement, I recall growing fearful for his safety and pressing him too vociferously to refrain from challenging the authority of our Temple officials. I am about to apologize when he says, 'Can you forgive me for taking so long to reach you?'

Tears squeeze through his lashes, which summon my own. 'How could I not forgive you?' I say.

'I need to hear you say the words aloud,' he tells me.

'I give you all that you might ever ask of me – including my forgiveness.'

My throat is desperately dry again, so we retreat into silence while I gulp down more water. At length, he stands up and goes to my window. I sense he needs to look into a world beyond our concerns. With Yeshua, there has always been the danger of his descending into too deep a chamber inside himself and never again emerging.

On turning back to me, he takes a deep breath. 'Your sisters told me you died while I was making my way here,' he says.

'I don't understand.'

'You stopped breathing. Apparently you were dead for two days.'

He clearly believes the truth in what he is telling me, so I do not laugh. When I taste blood in my mouth, I realize that I have nibbled away some crust from my lips.

My old friend studies me closely. I expect him to speak within me, as he sometimes does when voicing his thoughts aloud might endanger or compromise us, but he says nothing.

'My sisters told you this?' I ask.

His eyes grow glassy. 'Yes, they said your fever worsened and that you became so weak that you were unable to move. Mia said she was rubbing your feet with oils when felt the tremor of your soul leaving your body. She checked on your breathing, and there was none.'

'Given that I'm here now, she must have been mistaken.'

'Marta confirmed that you were dead.'

'That . . . that's very hard to believe.'

'Yet that's what happened. You were gone, and then you returned to us.' He nods as if no other conclusion is possible. Echoing the Psalms, he says, 'As you know, I have always filled my quiver with the unlikely and improbable.'

That's true enough, I think, *and yet* . . . 'Are you certain?' I ask.

After he confirms that I was dead, I imagine the man I'd been only a moment before standing behind me, observing me, unwilling to come forward and join me. I am tempted to turn to face him, but I hold up my hands instead, and I open and close them, testing what it feels like to be alive. I study my calluses, which are thicker than I remember them, and, as I listen to my hesitant breathing, questions that I suspect I shall never be able to answer begin rattling inside my mind: *How can I still be here? Has every part of my soul returned to my body? If this is possible, then what is . . . ?*

'Lazar, you need not walk this path alone,' Yeshua says. 'And together, we shall –'

I have not told Yeshua to be quiet in at least a decade, but I do so now, because what has happened is beyond my grasp, and I sense that it always will be, and all I want to do is find a plot of land inside my mind where I can bury what I now know and continue where I left off a few days earlier.

After Yeshua sits down beside me, I recall what a little boy asked me as we made our way home from the necropolis. When I turn to my old friend, he opens his arms to welcome my words – and to assure me that he took no offence at my requesting silence. 'If I were an *ibbur* inhabiting this body,' I tell him, tapping my chest, 'then I wouldn't be me – I wouldn't have any of my memories of you or my sisters or anyone else.' Speaking to myself as much as him, I add, 'It's obvious that I'm here in the flesh. But if I had died, then I'd have surely been . . .' I stop speaking because what I was about to say has vanished from my mind.

Marta carries in a bowl of steaming soup before Yeshua can address my apprehensions. She puts it on the low table by my mat and gathers up the protective talisman I'd removed from around my neck, which makes me realize what ought to have been obvious – that she made it for me.

'Eli, stop talking – you need to eat,' she says in a concerned tone.

Could you simply hug me and listen to my fears? I ask her in my mind. Aloud, I say, 'It's very kind of you, Marta, but I don't think I can eat a thing.'

She crosses her arms over her chest, ready for a fight, so I take a first sip and tell her it is delicious.

'All of it!' she warns.

'Of course, Marta, but it's too hot at the moment.'

She looks at Yeshua as if I am being difficult and says, 'Make sure he finishes it.' Eyeing him suspiciously, she adds, 'And don't you dare eat it for him!'

Yeshua smiles at how well Marta understands the two of us – and because he believes it will gratify her. I can tell from his expression that he is hoping, too, that she will go back to our courtyard without further delay, but he has miscalculated; his acknowledgement of her wit and intelligence only serves to irritate her, and she asks him what he means by his smile, and to free himself from that glare of hers that is like a boot on your chest, he tells her that it was meant to be appreciative and nothing more. To get her to leave, he asks her to bring him a cup of wine. The instant she is gone, he closes his eyes and shakes his head, recalling, most likely, how Marta has created tangled complexities for us many times in the past. As though to comfort himself, he reaches for my bowl of soup.

'Don't!' I snap. 'I might not be completely cured!'

'No, I told you, you're perfectly fine now,' he assures me. After taking a sip, he drizzles some water into the broth to cool it and hands the bowl to me with a solemnity that seems at first to be misplaced.

I want to continue speaking of my feelings to him, but my panic has turned into too tight a knot at the back of my throat. I hold my face in my hands.

'"Arise and eat, for the journey has been too great,"' Yeshua tells me. It is a quote from Elijah.

From the seriousness of his expression, I realize that sharing our food is a ritual that he believes will help me, so I take a long sip of the soup while holding his gaze. On handing it back to him, I whisper the instruction from the prophet Yeshayahu that Yeshua gives to those who wish to help him in his work: '"Share your food with the hungry and open your homes to the homeless."'

Exchanging scripture with my old friend restores a measure of comfort to me. I realize then that I am dripping with sweat. *Perhaps God meant this to happen, and I am exactly where I ought to be,* I think.

And yet a tremor shakes me when Marta returns to my alcove with a bowl of *charoset* and Yeshua's wine. She sets the paste of almonds and dates down on my mat. 'You've always been able to eat more sweets than anyone I know, so give this a try,' she says.

After my sister hands Yeshua his cup of wine, he thanks her and brushes her arm affectionately, hoping, no doubt, to win back her good graces, but she pulls away from him and shouts at him to leave her be.

Yaphiel, my beloved, now that I am at an age when rumours about my moral failings and those of my sisters can do me little damage, I shall tell you a secret: both of your great-aunts were caught in a sandstorm while they were crossing the desert of adolescence, and the sandstorm was Yeshua. As for their younger brother, I shall leave it for you to decide how he fared in that same dizzying and – as it turned out – life-altering tempest.

'The colour is returning to your face,' Yeshua tells me when we're alone again. 'Do you want me to go on speaking to you of what happened when I returned to you?'

After I nod, he takes a quick sip of wine and presses his hand over his heart, as he does when seeking the approbation of the Lord for what he is about to say. 'As soon as I arrived in Yerushalayim,' he tells me, 'I went straight to your tomb. I rolled aside the stone blocking its entrance with the help of the others. Your sisters pleaded with me to stop. Marta even started cursing me – she told me she'd never forgive my wickedness, as she called it.' In a conspiratorial whisper, he adds, 'Her insults drew a crowd. And I knew I was behaving badly. But I also knew I needed to see you again. After I removed the sudarium from your face and wiped your cheeks and eyes, I kissed you, and the emptiness in your expression . . . the departure of all that had made you who you were . . .' Yeshua rubs a tense hand back through his hair and takes a steadying breath. 'I was crushed. I found myself high up on the edge of a cliff, and that cliff was all I'd failed to do for you. As I apologized for coming too late, you came to life in my mind, as you'd been when we were last together, and I asked you if you would forgive me.'

'Did I?'

'You wouldn't reply to me. So I placed my hands on your chest and began to recite a lamentation over you, and I'm not sure what came to pass, but my voice became a wind carrying me far from myself.' Yeshua holds his hands over his head to give thanks to the Lord. 'Ahead of me, in the distance, rose up the shimmering walls of the Palace of the King,' he continues. 'I shed my cloak and tunic and sandals, since they were no longer needed, and, as I passed through the central gate, I spoke a verse from the Psalms, and then . . . then I discovered that I was back in the tomb, standing over you.'

'Which verse did you recite?' I ask.

'"Although you have made me see troubles, many and bitter, you will restore my life again; from the depths of the earth, you will again bring me up."'

Yeshua starts to sing the familiar melody, but a hissing sound from the courtyard draws his attention. At the window, he finds my daughter chasing Gephen, our cat, whose name means grape vine.

'Tell Nahara to leave the poor creature alone!' I say in too impatient a voice.

Yeshua passes on my message more softly, then leans down into the courtyard and whispers encouragements to Gephen, who leaps on to the sill beside him. I nibble on the *charoset,* which tastes sweet and soft – and like all the Passovers I have ever celebrated.

Once Yeshua has our cat cradled in his arms, his eyes close and his breathing slows. He does not speak or move for some time.

When his eyes open again, he rubs his hand over his face and looks down at me questioningly.

'You were telling me about seeing me in my tomb,' I say.

'Yes, and I looked at you for a long time, lying there motionless, wrapped in your shroud. And I heard a voice speak your name and say, "You shall return to me."'

'Whose voice was it?' I ask.

'The one we hear when we have joined the Lord.' He fixes me with a challenging look. 'No, it didn't matter whether the voice was God's or my own, for at that moment we were together on the heavenly chariot.'

I voice no protest, since I have long been accustomed to Yeshua's mode of speaking.

As soon as he puts Gephen down, the cat bounds to me and climbs on to my belly. His front paws reach up to my chest, and he shows me a determined look, as though I have become the wall that he must jump over to reach his goal. I pat his bottom encouragingly, thinking, *Yes, it is your affection I need right now*, and, in a single bound, he is up on my shoulder and scratching his soft white face against the stubble of my cheek, so that his musty scent – of earth and weeds, along with a faint trace of blood – is inseparable in my mind from the next question I pose to Yeshua and the rest of my conversation with him.

'And then what happened?' I ask.

Yeshua tells me that a red-glowing presence entered the room, and, when an image of me appeared in his mind, he realized it was my soul and that it had descended through the *Sha'ar ha-Rahamim* of the heavenly Yerushalayim into our world to reclaim my body, and, as soon as it crossed the borders of my flesh, my right arm twitched. 'And when I took your hand, your eyes fluttered open,' he says, shaking his head, still amazed by my revival. Gephen races to him and curls luxuriously around his ankle, asking with the slow curve of his back be lifted into our visitor's arms, so Yeshua gathers him up and cradles him again against his belly. 'Some of the others gasped and cried out,' he continues. 'Mia spoke to you first, but you didn't understand her, so I raised my hand over you and blessed you, and your mouth opened and you tried to speak, but your soul had not yet resumed command over your voice.' He kneels beside me and takes my hand. 'I held you tightly while you put on again the garments of your earthly body lest you come to feel a stranger in a strange land.'

5

Unfortunately, I am given no time to ask Yeshua any more questions about my return to life; my children are unwilling to wait any longer for reassurance that my soul has found its way back to my body.

Once Nahara has absorbed enough of my kisses to put the depth back into her large moon-bright eyes, and after her elder brother has had a chance to tell me – sunken-voiced – about his two sleepless nights of orphanhood, my sisters inform me that it would be inexcusably impolite not to welcome the rest of our friends and family into my room.

Holding Nahara's slender fluttering chest in my tight embrace, I make no reply; I am silenced by how her little body is being shaped by the unstoppable will to grow – and by how close I came to losing my chance to watch her and her brother become adults. All that seems important now is that I remain with her and Yirmi.

'Well?' Marta prompts.

I caress Yirmi's cheek to show my sister what my words may fail to convey and say, 'For now, I just want to be with my family.'

'Oh, Eli, stop making a fuss,' she replies. 'You only need to give our guests a quarter of an hour.'

'A miracle!' Yohanon calls out as he greets me. He raises his fist in triumph, as though I have now been conscripted into his sacred battle against the idol-worshippers who rule the Land of Zion.

As I munch on the warm matzoh that Mia has handed me, my guests speak in reverent tones of the proof of God's omnipotence that they have seen this day – proof that everyone in the room witnessed except for me. Yehudah, Andreas and some of Yeshua's other disciples cast expectant looks at their mentor, eager to hear how he will characterize my return from the dead, but he pretends to be busy with Gephen, who crouches on the windowsill, preparing to launch himself into the courtyard. Maryam of Magdala kneels beside me, and the scars on her right cheek – four deep furrows only partially hidden by the drape of her hair – seem sad reminders of the wounds we give ourselves. She asks me in her welcoming, Galilean-accented voice to join her and her companions in a prayer.

Barukh ata Adonai Eloheinu, melech ha'olam, she'asa nisim la'avoteinu ba'yamim ha'heim ba'z'man ha'ze.

Blessed are You, Lord our God, King of the Universe, who performed miracles for our ancestors . . .

After we sanctify our King with this benediction, Yeshua helps Nahara retrieve her wooden top, which has skittered under the table fronting my oaken trunk. 'As for what Lazarus has been through today,' he says on standing back up, 'I would only say this: "He who restrains his lips often shows great wisdom."'

His friends' ardent *amens* make it clear that they respect his wishes, though I suspect that a number of them are secretly disappointed that he has nothing more to say. As for me, I see

Yeshua's silence as his way of drawing the Lord's attention from me.

You see, Yaphiel, when Yeshua and I were twelve, he nearly drowned in the Jordan, and his mother always believed that it was because he had been so deep in communion with the Lord that he had waded out into the current without recognizing the peril. Once he was safe on the riverbank – and after he and I had had a chance to dry off – she gathered him up into her trembling arms and gripped my hand so hard it hurt. 'Always remember, my children,' she told us, 'there is such a thing as being *too* near to God. And too closely watched by him.'

While I am resting, my cousins Ariston and Ion entertain me with the latest tragi-comic escapades of their father, who has always been the insatiable satyr in our family. Mia soon joins us, and I discover that the rip she had made in the neckline of her chiton has now been sewn. While the four of us converse about the wonders of the main Jewish quarter in Alexandria, I find myself studying Yohanon and Maryam. They whisper together beside my window, and the way they avoid my gaze gives me to believe that they are debating how they might best make use of my resurrection. The truth I would tell them if I could do so without their censure is this: I have no awe-inspiring story to tell anyone who would like to hear of Yeshua's mastery over death. I cannot even say what the afterlife looks like. For I did not see any. I did not return to my body with any prophetic message ciphered in my mind or engraved on my hands. Either my soul was denied admission to Paradise or nothing of what transpired there adhered to my memory.

Or worse; after we die, nothing of who we are survives.

This heresy constricts my breathing and seems to cover me in a netting of shame. Ion helps me drink, and my sisters begin to fuss over me, but I wish only to retreat into solitude.

Terrifying words from Genesis sound inside me even as I speak to my sisters: 'You are dust, and to dust you will return.'

The cold sweat pouring down my neck and back is a betrayal of everything I have ever believed, but I lie to my family and friends about what is wrong with me; I blame my legs, which are indeed stiff and painful. Marta insists that I need air and light if I am not to fall ill again, so Yeshua and Yohanon help me into the courtyard.

I sit on cushions that my grandfather brings me and smile brightly in order to convince him and all the others that I am myself again. But I feel as I did while rushing home through Samaria one winter afternoon when I was nineteen, when the miles of darkening forest around me sent an arrow of terror shooting through the top of my head and I became aware that I had made a misguided and possibly fatal turn somewhere behind me.

When Yeshua joins me again, he tells me that he must accompany his disciples to their inn. My disappointment in him is like a door closing, because I realize that he will soon become burdened by the duties of his ministry and leave me on my own to contemplate the whys and hows of death and resurrection.

I try to hide my despair, but, when my old friend reaches for my shoulder, I moan aloud. He places his callused, woodworker's hand flat against my chest and promises to return after supper. 'Listen to me, Lazar,' he says. 'While I am away, don't be tempted to run – just walk slowly and carefully ahead.' Altering a verse from the Psalms, he adds, 'Though you walk through the valley of the shadow of death, you will fear no evil, for I am with you.'

6

In a dream I have had many times since fleeing Bethany, I see Yeshua wade into the brook that nourishes my garden here on Rodos and vanish below its surface. I call his name, but he will not return. I only know that he has become the brook when I notice that it is no longer flowing down to the sea but up into the clutch of pine where I walk when I wish to make believe that I have returned to our homeland.

Calm is the stream that loves both its banks and the lands it will never reach.

That one-line poem came into my mind one morning last year after I awakened – dejected and lonely – from the dream. It made me realize that I – unlike the streams and rivers or our world – will never find lasting peace. And that I do not want to.

Creatures who mourn. If the Lord should ever ask me to describe how we are distinct from the bats and lizards and all the other myriad creatures of the sixth day, that is what I shall tell Him.

Perhaps the wounds in Yeshua's ankles and wrists will finally become mine when I am near death. If only he had granted my final wish!

I shall tell you something about my old friend that his followers rarely mention, though to me it was the most obvious of all his gifts: when you were with him, he made you certain – through the ease with which he hooked his arm in yours, the empathy in his dark eyes or even one of his boyish jests – that being with you was exactly where he wanted to be. He belonged wholly to you – even if it was just for a quick exchange of greetings. And, because he was yours, you were his as well.

'When you make two into one, you will enter the Kingdom of Heaven,' he used to tell me, and whenever he repeated that wisdom – whether to a friend or a stranger – he meant it as an invitation.

You see, Yaphiel, his hands were always open.

He taught me that a single act of compassion – a hand of blessing on a leper's brow or a kiss upon the foot of a crippled child – can change the direction of a life.

I have found that most men and women huddle behind their own heartwalls and only rarely peek outside. We spend thirty, forty, fifty years or more not seeing one another.

But he looked and saw.

He taught me this as well: when you meet a person, pay close attention to his first words and his last. Often, he will tell you then what it is he is looking for – and how you may help him.

'The wisdom of the Lord has two faces, and one of them we cannot see,' he told me when I had trouble accepting his decision to end his Torah studies. I believe now that he meant that a great deal of who he was would for ever remain hidden. Were there landscapes inside him that he had glimpsed only fleetingly? That possibility grows more distinct as I age. And yet I would not wish to solve the mystery of him, since understanding his place in my life more fully might make him shine less brightly on the nights when he rises into my night-time sky to guide me.

7

After Yeshua and his disciples leave my home, hunger opens a furrow in my belly. With my obligations to hospitality fulfilled, I entreat my remaining guests to wish one another – and me – a *shalom* of parting so that I can rest in my room and have a proper meal.

My children and sisters remain at home with me, along with Marta's seventeen-year-old daughter Yehudit, who lives with her husband and baby boy in Yerushalayim.

I am gorging on a steaming patina stuffed with sow thistle and raisins when a delegation of local craftsmen and shopkeepers knocks on my front door. Mia and Marta escort the six men into my alcove. They wear their Sabbath shawls and address me with the deference of worshippers entering the Gate of Firstborns.

Saul ben David, who owns a fruit stall at the marketplace, hands me a basket of dried apricots and figs, and from his cousin Hector, an importer of ceramics, I receive a drinking cup from Crete decorated with a stupendously endowed Minotaur. Does he believe that my taking a few sips of barley beer from the creature's hands will increase my potency? Such odd ideas these Judaeans have about widowers and their needs!

What sets my teeth grinding is that they are certain to expect me – now that I have been obliged by my sisters to accept their gifts – to petition the Almighty on their behalf.

Once they are gone, Mia calms me by explaining that the men also had a more prosaic – and easier to fulfil – motive: they want me to steer future well-wishers and curiosity-seekers to their shops. In short, they are convinced I will create much the same inflow of visitors to Bethany as the two-headed cobra that was put on show in our marketplace the previous spring.

'I don't think I'd like to be kept in a cage,' I tell my sister.

'If you agree not to bite anyone, only a lead will be necessary,' she replies drily.

Though it is a comfort and relief to laugh with Mia again, the moment our voices cede to silence, death seems to shiver inside me.

My sisters live in a small old house across our shared courtyard, and, later that afternoon, when my alcove becomes too confining, I limp to Marta's workroom, since watching her weave may help me regain a measure of composure.

I sit by her side without interrupting. To see her skilful, darting fingers uniting strands of wool into white and black dolphins leaping out of a friendly blue sea is to know that she was truly made in the Creator's image.

As she moves her shuttle between the warps, I realize I have a secret motive for coming to her. But I cannot tell her. And I see that in another, easier world I would not have to ask her to embrace me.

It baffles me now how all the time I'd been in my tomb the sun had continued to rise and the moon to set.

Yeshua had preached in Pella and neighbouring towns.

Gephen had hunted for mice.

And Marta had added a hundred new rows to the rug she is making.

Yet I had not been aware of any of these things.

No one who has died knows that he is dead. I keep repeating that truth to myself, but it does not seem to fit inside my head. So, once I am back in my room, I face west, towards the Temple, and chant the first six verses of the Torah, since six is the number of cardinal directions when added to *up* and *down*. In this way, I am hoping to find a map leading back to myself in scripture.

As though to make me suffer further for my heretical thoughts, Melech ben Aaron, the ancient wheelwright who lives next door, decides to visit. He has become a mop-haired skeleton and prankster since his wife's death, and his bulbous, pock-marked nose starts twitching like an Egyptian hound as he moves downwind of the supper I've just eaten. Despite our own meagre resources, Mia hasn't the heart to turn the hungry man away, and she fries him an egg with onion and summons him into our courtyard to eat it. All too soon, however, he shuffles into to my room. While he is licking the last traces of his meal from his knobby fingers, he drops down beside me, places a cushion on his lap – as though intending to stay for hours – and whispers in my ear, 'Eli, my boy, so who's this enemy you've made?'

His calid, pungent breath makes me lean away. 'What kind of enemy?' I ask.

He slaps my leg. 'A witch or sorcerer – some filthy night-hag who might've put a spell on you! Or who slipped a viper's egg in yer food.'

I sometimes believe I can hear what people would most wish to confide to me if they dared, and here is what Melech's mischievous, too-eager glance now tells me: *My wife prevented me from doing what I most wanted to do, which was why I greeted her death with dancing, and it is to make my friends and neighbours as disgruntled as I am, and I accomplish it by reminding them not to trust anyone, not even their families, and, though it is thankless work, I do it with an invigorating sense of purpose.*

To consider the hidden matters raised by Melech would only draw me into morbid territories where I would not wish to walk with him. 'For the last five months,' I tell him, 'I've worked from dawn to dusk laying mosaics in Lucius ben David's villa. I don't have time to turn anyone against me.'

After Mia manages to lure Melech out of the house with a handful of dried figs, the possibility of my having been cursed sets in motion a cascade of conjectures that leads me back to my original doubts about the story I've been told.

We have all heard of powerful potions that can bind a person in an inert state of dormancy, and I begin to consider it possible that the decoction of vetch and willow bark that I drank slowed all my bodily workings to imperceptible levels and that its effect on me might have begun to wear off just prior to Yeshua's visit to my tomb. Laying his hands on my chest might have been enough to rouse me.

I'd have no memory of any afterlife because I was never actually dead!

Relief makes me laugh aloud, but, when I summon Marta to me, she swears that she tested my breathing twice and on both occasions detected nothing.

'How much time did you wait between the first and second time you checked?' I ask.

'Eli, I don't appreciate you talking to me as if I were a fool.'

'Marta, please just answer my question.'

'I checked you twice – maybe a quarter of an hour apart.'

When I summon Mia to me, she confirms Marta's estimate.

To my great disappointment, both my sisters confess that they did not enquire of the physician from Persia what effect his elixir would have on me.

Guessing at my thoughts, Mia says, 'I placed my ear to your chest when I first felt your soul leave your body. There was no beating. And Marta checked your breath a second time, as she just told you.'

'This Persian who treated me . . . Kurush. Was he a Zarathustrian?'

'We didn't ask,' Mia replies, and Marta adds, 'Lykos, the Baal Nephesh's assistant, said he was a friend, and we didn't think we needed to ask anything more.'

'Lykos *said* he was a friend or *claimed* it?' I question in a hectoring voice.

Marta makes an irritated, guttural sound and looks to Mia to reply for them both. *He's your problem now,* she is saying in their sisterly language. At such times, it seems that it has always been two against one in my family.

'If you're asking if we believed Lykos,' Mia tells me, 'then the answer is yes.'

'Did you see the ingredients he used?'

'That's it – I have work to do!' Marta announces, and she flees the room with her hands over her ears.

After she is gone, Mia drops down next to me, and we listen to women's voices coming from the street, discussing where to purchase the best lambs for sacrifice.

'It's hard to believe that it's nearly Passover again,' she tells me.

'God blinks and a year goes by,' I reply.

She takes my hand. 'I know what you're thinking,' she says, frowning, 'but do you really think the Persian wished to imprison you in a trance? Why would anyone want you to appear dead?'

8

After I call Yirmi to me and ask him to return to Lykos – our physician's assistant – to find out all he can about Kurush of Persia, Mia sits with me again in my room, leans back against the wall and squeezes her eyes closed as if she has no plans to open them any time soon.

A few minutes later, however, when she notices me studying her, she takes my hands in hers and swings them between us until they become – for the children inside us – an ark of polished cedar, exactly three hundred cubits in length and fifty cubits high. 'Two of every kind shall come to you,' she says in a sing-song voice.

'I am sorry, Mia, but I don't want to play right now,' I tell her.

'If Mama were here . . .'

My sister says that because we used to play this game with our mother after every Sabbath supper.

'Mama died long ago,' I say.

'Two of every kind,' she repeats, squeezing my hands.

'Later.'

'The sacred ibises and finches,' she continues, and the ruthlessness in her squint makes it plain that I have no choice but to cede to her wishes.

'And the butterflies and bats,' I say, obeying the formula we have known nearly all our lives.

'And the cats and mice,' she replies.

'And the jackals and lions.'

'And the snakes and crocodiles.'

We end with our voices joined, as it must be: 'And the two of us as well.'

Having transported a pair of each of God's creatures to safety, we unlock our fingers. A moment later, I catch a glimpse of the pale and isolated life I'd have had if Mia had not tugged me out of my gloom following our father's death, which had ended any chance I had once had for a life of study and travel.

'I'll be right back,' she tells me as she gets to her feet.

Soon she returns with her jars of fragrant oils, and she informs me – no dissent permitted! – that she can wait no longer to cleanse me. 'I'll try to be gentle,' she says, and then, inexplicably, cupping a hand over her mouth, she succumbs to girlish giggles.

'What's so funny?' I ask.

'Boaz said the same words to me on our wedding night,' she says, adding amidst her laughter, and in a confidential whisper, 'Except that the hairy little beast wasn't gentle at all!'

Despite their divorce, Mia is still in love with Boaz, though she has never admitted that to anyone but me. He took up with a young Judaean courtesan a few years earlier and lives with her and her children near the salt mines beyond Qumran.

This time, my skin welcomes Mia's sponges and strigil without pain or protest, and in less than an hour she has removed the fetid layers of sweat and tomb-dust from me. To my itchy scalp she applies a mixture of ash and sulphur water. It's the same wash that we use to take off the tainted patches of skin from Grandfather Shimon's diseased face and back.

And so – glistening and perfumed, with my hair combed back over my ears – I once again resemble the man I was before my illness and burial.

'You know, from a certain angle,' Mia says, tilting her head far to the side and showing me an astonished expression, 'I might even mistake you for a handsome man!'

I test my feeble legs in different ways over the next hour, hoping they will soon relearn the secret of keeping me upright without my having to lean against walls and grasp on to furniture. Mia turns away the friends and acquaintances who come to my door, explaining that I am still too weak for conversation. All this newfound interest in me seems harmless enough until a youth I have never seen before pushes open the shutters on the window by my front door. He leans his head inside and holds out a silver coin. 'I'll give you a shekel for a thread from your shroud,' he says.

His skin and eyes are yellowish – as if he has been poisoned with weld. He looks no older than sixteen or seventeen.

'To tell you the truth, I . . . I don't know where it is,' I stutter.

'Maybe you could find it for me,' he says. 'It's important, and I'd be very grateful.'

His beseeching expression moves me, and I manage to locate my shroud in my clothes chest. I pull away a thread for him, and when I hand it to him, he bursts into tears and kisses my hands.

A number of other strangers soon come to my door, imploring me to relieve their ailments and afflictions, but Mia permits no one inside. Just before supper, my family and I are conversing in my room about our plans for Passover when the noise of feet scrabbling across my roof makes us gaze up fearfully at the ceiling. Two barefoot boys dressed in rags soon drop down into the courtyard. Mia manages to catch the younger of them – a grubby-looking waif with filthy feet – and shoves him back out into the street. The second – with frenetic, terrified eyes – shows my grandfather a nasty-looking blade, however, so I tell Shimon to let the boy steal whatever he wishes. The little thief yanks Mia's spare robe from the cord strung across our courtyard, makes his way to the front door – his knife held high – and races away.

While I calm my daughter, who has begun to cry, my sister locks my door again. Binyamin, her fifteen-year-old son – and the only one of her children who still lives with her – goes off to bolt all the doors and windows in their home.

And so I await Yeshua, wondering how long this siege will continue.

Unfortunately, we are unable to refuse entrance to two subsequent visitors because we must remain in their good graces. The first is Lucius ben David, the wealthy *garum* importer who has commissioned me to decorate his home and garden with mosaics. He lives in an opulent villa in Yerushalayim's Upper Town, and, as he is in fierce competition with his patrician neighbours, he is adamant that my designs must be the most colourful and complex in Judaea. He has also obliged me give my word to have all my work finished by early summer, since the Roman branch of his family will then be visiting for the fairs that follow Ludi Apollinares. In short, I have been labouring like an Egyptian pack-mule since the autumn so that he can strut about Yerushalayim while wearing the crown of the most ostentatious Jew in Judaea.

Lucius is a heavyset, round-faced man – somewhere near sixty years of age, by my reckoning. His thinning hair has been curled and dyed black and permitted to drape over his ears like a floral ornamentation.

He enters my alcove ahead of his bejewelled young wife, whom I have never met before. His bodyguard – a blond-haired behemoth with sand-coloured eyelashes and a caterpillar of whiskers on his upper lip – deposits a small amphora of kosher *garum* on my floor as a present.

My nephew Binyamin carries in two folding chairs for Lucius and his wife, who appears to be no older than sixteen and who displays an affecting faun-like hesitance whenever I set my glance upon her.

After I kiss Lucius' hands and speak the traditional Greek formulae of hospitality, he holds the yellow rose he has been carrying to his nose.

'I'm sorry if my scent is still less than pleasing,' I tell him.

'It doesn't matter – you smell only a bit more earthy than you always do,' he replies.

Does he mean to offend me, or is that simply one more indication of how the Roman Jews despise their cousins from the Land of Zion?

Lucius keeps his rose by his nose the entire time we converse. We speak in Greek, since my Latin is halting and his Aramaic – even after seven years in Yerushalayim – is hesitant and error-filled.

Mia and Marta serve palm wine in our amethyst-coloured glasses, which we generally reserve for Hanukkah and other celebrations.

Once we are settled, Lucius makes several jests about the odd and archaic customs of Judaean Jews, possibly because he knows that, as a Galilean, I have often been maligned and derided by the long-time inhabitants of Yerushalayim. What he says may very well be amusing in Latin, but in his Greek translations these attempts at wit fall between us like dead seagulls. Perhaps my ordeal of death and revival has dulled my powers of deduction, for it takes me some time to understand that this tidal wave of false mirth is down to Lucius' discomfort at being in my home; though I studied the Torah of Mosheh and the epics of Homer throughout my youth and though my Greek is more fluent than his – owing to my apprenticeship in Alexandria – he considers me a common craftsman, and the Latinized Jews, like their Roman masters, regard men who earn a living with their hands as only one small step above brigands and bandits.

As we converse, neighbours and pilgrims keep coming to my front door to receive my blessings. Others bang on my shutters. One half-made man, who identifies himself as a rug-maker from Tzor, stands outside my closed window calls out a list of his ailments to me. To my astonishment and that of my guests, he does not seem to mind all of those in the vicinity knowing that he has dropsy, bleeding haemorrhoids and an infestation of Persian lice.

We do not ask him to leave us be; Marta and Mia decide that silence is our best strategy.

Blessed be the Lord who bestows patience upon the weary . . . After Marta serves Lucius and his wife a plate of dried figs and apricots, my guest finally speaks of his reason for visiting me. 'We lost a week while you were ill,' he tells me in an injured voice. 'I'll expect you back at work tomorrow.'

To emphasize the unfairness of his demand – and even perhaps win from him some admiration for my wit – I apologize for dying at an inconvenient moment, but he is either too Roman or slow-witted to catch my irony.

'Apology noted,' he says. 'And delays like this one', he adds, fixing me with a withering look, 'are why I've urged you to hire an apprentice. He might have been making progress while you've been . . . been . . . '

He glances away and searches for a euphemism for *dead and in your tomb*.

'Absent,' I suggest.

'Exactly.'

His young wife chooses that moment to reposition her legs and sigh; her dull eyes tell me that she is far away in her thoughts – and that she finds her husband as tiresome as I do. *I don't blame him for his protruding belly and ridiculous hair,* I imagine her telling me, *for time disfigures us all. But if he lives much longer, I will die of boredom.*

Once our business is settled, I expect Lucius to leave, but he embarks instead on a serpentine story of a friend of his who died after an illness drawn to him by the noxious humidity of Nicaea. At length, I realize that he wishes to *take the lyre from my locked chest,* as we say in the Galilee – to convince me to share my thoughts with him about a private matter without his actually having to ask for them. As best I can guess, he would like an answer to the following delicate query: where exactly did my soul go after my death – to the afterlifes envisaged by those who worship the Greek and Roman gods or to the rather more vague and undefined Eden of the Jews?

I am trying to steal the lyre from *his* locked chest – to find out which of these futures he would prefer – when I am rescued by the unlikeliest of saviours, Annas ben Seth, our former high priest. Short and frail, with an impressive grey beard that reduces his lips to a judgemental slit, he is clothed in a white linen robe belted with a wide purple sash. He hobbles into my alcove ahead of his daughter, Sara, wife of the current high priest, Yosef Caiaphas. By then, twilight has given way to nightfall.

Marta flees across the courtyard to her workroom just after ushering Annas into my alcove. She cannot abide the Temple priests and refers to them – when we are alone – as our *palace eunuchs*, though she saves her sharpest barbs for Caiaphas, whom she delights in calling *Kakiaphas,* which is Greek for what is evil or to be avoided. Why such nastiness? Seventeen years earlier, when she was unable to give her husband David a child, Caiaphas instructed him to choose another woman to receive his seed. David selected their Nabataean servant, and a baby girl was born to her eight and a half months later, and he named her Yehudit after his grandmother. Though Marta raised her as her own, whenever she looks at her daughter – to this day – she feels the barren hollow in her belly that lost her the loyal affection of her husband and rendered her useless in the eyes of her own family.

Annas requests that I refrain from kissing his hands or touching him, for I have been in a tomb and must not, therefore, have any contact with a priest. Lucius offers him his armchair and sits on a bench that Binyamin carries to him. A few moments later, Mia brings in two more glasses of palm wine.

As I watch my sister's deft and deferential movements, it amuses me to think that if my life were a Greek farce she would have handed Annas my Cretan cup decorated with the impressively endowed Minotaur, and my sisters and I would find ourselves accused of idol-worship and hauled off to prison.

Lucius' constricted voice brings me back to myself. 'I'm very sorry,' he tells us sadly, 'but I must be going. A father with young children is never truly free to socialize.'

Young children? The sons he has by his first wife are already married, and his new bride – according to the gossip I have heard – has had difficulty becoming pregnant.

At the front door, Lucius dangles his hand before me so that I might kiss it again and reminds me I have given him my word to start work again the next day.

'Honourable Annas, if you'll permit me a question, to what do I owe the unexpected pleasure of your visit to my home?' I say on returning to my alcove.

'I've heard tell that you've undergone an exciting transformation today,' he replies.

His pursed smile and mocking tone set my feet itching. 'I'm afraid I did not witness what happened,' I reply.

'No?'

'They tell me I was dead, but I was not aware of anything. When I awoke, it seemed I had been with fever just a moment earlier.'

'What awakened you?'

My mouth is suddenly as dry as the desert. 'I am not sure,' I say, taking a rushed drink of water. 'I did not hear any voices or stirring. I apologize for my ignorance.'

As though making a first move at senet, he says cagily, 'I understand that Yeshua ben Yosef entered your tomb.'

'He was there when I awoke – that is true,' I reply.

'Are you in the habit of consorting with heretics?' Annas raises his eyebrows challengingly. The sagely kindness in his demeanour has vanished.

'I do not regard Yeshua as a heretic,' I tell him.

'But I do!'

Then I would strongly suggest that you refrain from befriending him, is the reply that I would make if I did not fear his wrath.

He gets to his feet with the unsteady effort of his age and eyes me scornfully down the line of his nose.

Such loathing is for far more than just me and Yeshua, I think.

'Are you aware of whom you're talking to?' he demands.

'The blessed and honourable Annas ben Seth, former high priest. To whom I now apologize if I have given offence.'

'I ask you now,' Annas says, as though drawing a line beyond which I may not cross, 'what sort of evil magic did Yeshua use to summon you back from the arms of death?'

I have dealt with such accusations of sorcery against Yeshua before and give him my carefully worded answer: 'You have been misinformed, honourable Annas, for Yeshua has never resorted to necromancy, devilry or bewitchment to heal those who come to him.' I then raise my hand palm out to warn him that, although he may steer this conversation where he likes, there are betrayals he will not be able to force on me. 'The Lord has conferred on him his special abilities, and I shall never say otherwise.'

He fixes me with another bemused look – to let me know, most likely, that he cherishes this undeclared war between us. Does he feel the blood of a hunter flowing through his veins? From the way he smooths his hand across the waistline of his robe and shifts his prayer shawl, it seems that the stiffness of his youth may be returning to him.

'That isn't what I've been told, Eliezer ben Natan,' he tells me. 'Apparently your friend chanted an incantation over your body: "From the depths of the earth, you will again bring me up."'

Fear beats its wings by my ears; a traitor amongst those who grieved over me must have visited Annas and told him the exact verse of the Torah spoken by Yeshua.

'My teachers always gave me to understand that no man of honest faith could confuse the words of the Lord for a mere incantation,' I say. 'And in any case, as I've now told you twice before, I did not observe my own resurrection. I heard nothing that Yeshua may have said to me.'

He sucks in an exasperated breath. 'Men do not return from death of their own accord.'

'Please, dear Annas, take your chair again. I fear you are uncomfortable standing.'

'I shall sit again when I'm ready! Now tell me who awakened you?'

'The Lord must have wished for me to live again,' I reply, and, to fend him off, I reach for a shield of Torah: '"I and I alone am God; no other god is real. I take life and I give it."'

Annas flinches; my knowledge of scripture has astonished him. And it is the shock in his eyes that convinces me that I have discovered how I shall defend myself.

'Do you claim to speak for *Elohim?*' he asks angrily.

'No, I'm just an ignorant mosaic-maker. But I do know this: if the Lord wished me dead, I would be.' Closing my eyes for reverential emphasis, I raise my shield again: '"Trust in the Almighty with all your heart and lean not on your own understanding."'

Dismissing my solemn tone with a displeased grunt, he says, 'I begin to suspect that you are no God-fearing man but only a fool who *sounds* like one!'

'"Blessed is the man who fears the Lord and delights in his commandments,"' I quote from the Psalms.

Annas reaches for a dried fig and pops it in his mouth, pleased with himself for a reason that eludes me. Perhaps he is convinced that, no matter how apt my quotations from Mosheh, he will leave me bloodied and battered in the end. Is he aware, however, that he chews his fig not like a lion but from side to side like a ewe – and that I have discovered that I am no longer afraid of him?

'You can't really want a war with Rome,' he says, sounding conciliatory, though we both know that he is merely changing his tactics.

'No, I've seen what Caesar can do,' I say.

'Have you?' he asks, and he sits back down. 'When was that?'

'We lived briefly in Sepphoris when I was a young man, and it was still in ruins.'

He leans back in his chair. 'The sons of Esau will do the same to the Temple and to all of Yerushalayim if Yeshua provokes them too far.'

'Believe me when I tell you, honourable Annas, that I've long wished for more . . . influence over my friend, but, in truth, I have little.'

Annas joins his crooked hands in his lap, preparing for a new round of sparring with me. 'Tell me about the journey of your soul after your death,' he says mildly, pretending to be motivated by mere curiosity, but I sense his sly grin hidden under the word *nefesh* – soul.

If I say I glimpsed even the tiniest shadow of the Almighty or one of the seraphim, Annas will accuse me of heresy for presuming to be the equal of Mosheh. Yet if I admit the truth – that I recall nothing – he may rightfully condemn me for denying the existence the Lord.

'I beheld a stone,' I finally say, though I do not know why. And yet after the word is spoken, it forms the image in my mind of a blue gemstone, and it is sitting in my hand, waiting for me to describe its purpose.

Do any of us know from which hidden corner of our mind such spontaneous replies come? Unless . . . It occurs to me now that Yeshua might have been observing me from the *Hekhal ha-Melekh* – the Palace of the King – and drawn it from me.

'A stone? What are you talking about?' Annas questions.

'A sapphire,' I reply, and, a second later, I am jolted by the certainty that my long practice at word games has at last become useful. 'It was sitting in the palm of my hand – shining with the light of creation,' I continue. 'Yet, after a few moments, it changed and became something . . . much more valuable. You see, it was no longer a sapphire but a Torah scroll. The *sappir* was, in truth, a *sefer*.'

'My goodness, man, do you expect me to be awe-struck by this semantic trick of yours?' he asks with a sneer.

'All I know, honourable Annas, is that during the brief time that my soul dwelt in the Palace of the Lord, He graced me with an insight – that the greatest and most valuable jewel of all is Torah!'

The priest's daughter thrusts her hands over her mouth and speaks a blessing for having received a revelation. Given this small triumph, I permit myself to imagine that our conversation will now shift to a safer road. Instead, Annas glares at his daughter. 'Child, I would warn you not to embarrass your father again!'

The priest shows me his mocking smile and says in a sarcastic tone, 'The constellations have favoured you, Eliezer! Your story has impressed a woman. But I'm growing weary of you. Now, as you know, rumours of miracles spread fast amongst the rabble. Though I'm powerless to prevent that, I can do this . . .' Stepping forward, he holds his shrivelled hand over my head. 'In the name of the Lord our God,' he says, 'I forbid you to speak a word of what took place in your tomb this day. And if you disobey me, Eliezer ben Natan, your soul shall be chained to a rock in the wilderness, and the night wind will take away your voice, and the sun will blind you, and . . .'

While Annas threatens me, I chant the Shema to myself to form a battlement in my mind.

'. . . And no sorcerer from the Galilee or Judaea or any other land, no matter how well versed in the curious arts, no matter whether he is under the guidance of David and Shelomoh or Lilith and Asmodeus, will be able to rescue you,' he ends. As he lowers his hand, he says, 'Are we clear, Eliezer?'

'Perfectly,' I reply. 'And I swear that I shall not . . .'

Before I can finish my oath, Annas spreads apart two of the panels of my curtains and limps through the opening. Mia meets him at my front door and tries to assuage his fury by offering him more wine. A mistake; cursing all women as *reka* – empty-headed – he knocks the cup out of her hands, splashing her tunic.

How is it that my fury can overtake me so swiftly and completely, even when I know that voicing it might be a fatal mistake?

'*Reka* is the guest who disrespects a woman in her own home!' I remind him gruffly.

Mia shows me a fearful look and shakes her head, meaning, *Don't say another word!* Annas replies with a disbelieving stare that soon turns deadly. And that is when I hear him tell me in my mind what he has refused to admit: *I should have been granted a miracle, not Yeshua!*

Why did it take me so long to grasp that his hate is born of envy?

'I want you to tell your heretical companion something for me,' he says, seething so bitterly that his words come out with spittle. 'Should he speak of this false miracle at his gatherings, my son-in-law will have him dragged away in chains to Machaerus – like that filthy old friend of yours, Yohanon ben Zebediah.' He traces a fingertip across his neck with slow delight to indicate the fate that awaited our mentor. 'I should not be surprised if Yeshua also ends up with his head fed to the palace mastiffs as their afternoon snack,' he says, grinning at what must pass for wit in the inner courts of the Temple. As he turns the handle on the front door, he thinks of a parting gift for me. Smiling so broadly that I can see the brown stumps he has for teeth, he recites, '"And that dreamer of dreams shall be put to death, because he has spoken in such a way as to turn you away from the Lord your God."'

9

Dearest Yaphiel, before you read any further, the time has come to tell you of the most important lesson that Yeshua ever taught me and his disciples. To do so, I must write briefly of the event that turned my fealty to Temple priests to ash.

After you read it, I think you will understand more fully why I was about to take risks with myself and my children that most other men would have avoided at all costs.

Yeshua and I were then twenty-six years of age. It was the Eighteenth of Tishri.

Several days earlier, my sisters and I had constructed our tabernacle for the festival of Sukkot in the modest plot of land we rent outside Bethany. For the previous two days, Yeshua and I had remained under its palm-leaf roof, fasting, chanting and weeping – and often deep in *derash ha-Torah*.

Spirit dreaming that it is matter . . .

That was what I imagined myself to be as I walked with Leah and Yeshua through the bustling streets of Yerushalayim. And perhaps there are truths so timid that they will only show themselves to us after we have withdrawn from our usual existence and spent a day or two in contemplation, for every surface I could see – every rooftop and wall and paving stone – was glowing with a subtle and mysterious radiance.

I carried my sleeping son in my arms, and, as we descended from the Upper Town, I was the first to see a bedraggled and bleeding young woman being led by bailiffs down the Temple steps. She was barefoot, and three silver anklets circled her right leg. Her hair – shoulder-length – was ragged and soiled. Her robe was ripped at her hip.

We were a hundred paces away from her, but I could already see that she was probably no more than eighteen years old, which was my wife's age at the time. Her wrists were bound, and a small elderly bailiff kept jerking her forward – and with such spiteful impatience that she soon stumbled and fell, bruising her arm.

She comes from the southern desert, I told myself, because her skeletal brown arms spoke of years of hunger and hardship lived beneath a burning sun, though my guess would later prove incorrect. In fact, I was soon able to discover that her mother was a Judaean and her father a Nabataean and that she lived in the warren of gloom-darkened streets behind Yerushalayim's hippodrome.

'She must be an adulteress,' Leah whispered to me.

I reached out for her hand and gave it a squeeze. 'Probably so,' I replied.

'And that must her husband beside her.'

The man had a brawny chest and arms and short bristly hair.

Behind him walked a young man who reminded me of a locust – he was loose-limbed and slender, with bushy hair and fleshy lips. He leaned far forward as he walked, as though burdened by a leaden weight around his neck.

He and the young woman were both hollow-cheeked and unusually tall, which led me to believe that they were very likely brother and sister.

Three priests, dressed in white robes and turbans, walked behind the prisoner and the bailiffs. The eldest amongst them shuffled ahead with his hands joined together over his ample belly and his lips pressed tightly together, as though on a sacred mission. I later learned that his name was Eitan ben Itzhak and that he was a cousin of Yosef Caiaphas.

The woman moaned now and again as she was led towards the Eastern Huldah Gate and the place of stoning outside the city. Her laboured, limping gait made me believe that she might have been so badly brutalized that she was not completely aware of what was happening to her. Or was that simply my most fervent hope at that moment?

When the young woman set her dazed and perplexed eyes on me, here is what I heard her tell me: *My husband never wanted me, and he hurt me whenever possible, and he always told me I belonged to him, and, without knowing the risk I was taking, I sought affection from a man whom I have known since we were children and whom I had wished to marry, though my parents would not hear of it. He was good and kind to me, as I had hoped, though he was also ashamed of our conduct, since he, too, is married. And yet I do not regret having gone to him for solace, though I wish I had not been caught, because my children will now be shunned by one and all, and they will grow up hearing that I was a Jezebel who betrayed their father. To you who wonder why I did what I did, I ask this: what laws and customs would you break to prove you belonged to no one but yourself?*

When Yeshua began rushing towards her, Leah and I followed behind him.

I soon noticed that the back of young woman's hair was matted with mud and her right cheek badly bruised. Blood was smeared from her mouth to her chin, and her nose was twisted at an angle that made me wince. Flies were swarming over her bloody lips.

After I handed my son to Leah, I took Yeshua's arm. 'You'd best not try to save her,' I whispered.

'If an angel had not come to Isaac's rescue, the boy would have perished,' he told me.

'But you're a mortal man – and the priests can have you arrested.'

'All who do the Lord's bidding are His angels.'

Yeshua stopped before the lead bailiff and held up both his hands. *You shall not pass this way while I have the strength to stop you,* was the message he conveyed.

Did the tiny rancorous bailiff jerk hard on his rope at that moment to show Yeshua that he was in control here?

Women's laughter cackled behind me when she fell to the ground and again when she tried and failed to raise herself up. I saw then that a large crowd had gathered.

Yeshua went to the woman and reached for her arm to help her to her feet, but she slapped at his face with taut, outraged hands and caught him on his cheek with so fierce a blow that his eyes teared up.

Was it while wiping away his tears that Yeshua gave up all hope that the priesthood could be reformed? I cannot say for sure, but I do know that he never again spoke to me of how he would rebuild the Temple as a sanctuary of *racham* – tender compassion.

'You have shamed the God of Mercy!' Yeshua shouted at the lead bailiff after stopping the procession.

As I felt for the vine-knife I nearly always keep in my pouch, the head priest, Eitan ben Itzhak, ordered Yeshua to let justice be served, but my friend replied that he had a right to know the nature of the woman's crime.

'Who are you to ask?' ben Itzhak demanded.

'I'm a traveller who knows where he came from and where he's going. But I appear to be addressing a man who has lost his way.'

'What I've lost is all interest in you self-righteous young fools!' the priest snarled, and, with a cutting gesture of his hand, he ordered Yeshua to let them pass.

'Do you intend to end this woman's life?' my old friend demanded.

Her husband stepped forward. 'I'll stone her myself if I have to!'

Yeshua stepped up to the young woman, took hold of her hands and asked her name.

She shook her head and moaned as if his kindness were only deepening her misery.

'My name is Yeshua ben Yosef,' he told her.

She yanked her hands free of his and shouted, 'Leave me be!'

He reached to her lips and with the fresh blood that came off on his fingertip, he traced the word חֶמְלַת on his brow. He turned then in a slow circle to show all of us that he had created *mercy* from her wounds.

A host of onlookers gasped, but others shouted that she was a whore who deserved to be stoned.

Eitan ben Itzhak – speaking with the authority of an elder – told Yeshua that the time for mercy and *a great deal else,* as he put it, had passed. His abrupt tone made it evident that his patience was coming to an end.

'Please tell me your name,' Yeshua again urged the woman.

She mouthed her answer to him; perhaps she believed she had forfeited the right to speak it aloud.

'Rachel, we are all of us broken and blemished,' he told her.

Eitan ben Itzhak ordered bailiffs to start off again. 'And if this young sinner tries to stop you,' he told them, 'slice him in two!'

'Two witnesses are needed to condemn this woman to death,' Yeshua called out. 'One is clearly her husband. We have the right to know who the other is.'

'The Lord already knows who the witness is!' the priest shouted back.

'Then He will not mind my knowing as well.'

Many in the throng laughed at Yeshua's witticism, but others hooted their disapproval and aimed insults at him. With renewed resolve, he strode up to the loose-limbed youth, who was nearly two palms taller than him. 'What is your relation to Rachel?' he demanded.

The boy – was he any older than seventeen? – looked at ben Itzhak for permission to speak.

Yeshua gripped his arm. 'Forget the priest. Answer for yourself, young man!'

'I'm her brother,' he replied.

'Tell me your name.'

'David ben Reuben,' he said, gazing down as if he wished for a hole to open in the street and swallow him.

'Did you truly witness your sister's crime?' Yeshua asked him.

The youth held tight to what seemed to me a silence born of guilt. Yeshua kneeled down, took his knife out of his pack and made a quick cut in his left thumb. With his blood, he wrote on a flagstone. I stepped closer. The sign he had scripted looked to be a letter *yod* inside a circle.

I assumed that it was a symbol meant to defend Rachel and keep her safe. Later that day, when I asked Yeshua what it meant, he told me cryptically that it was the written form of the cry he needed to make in order to bring the warrior-angel Raphael to us. I believe now that his design of a *yod* – the first letter of his name – probably alluded to the meaning of *yeshua* in Aramaic: *a cry for help*.

'Yeshua ben Yosef, I'm asking you one last time to step out of the way,' Eitan ben Itzhak said gruffly.

At the time, I was so upset and infuriated that I was unable to understand that the old priest evinced admirable patience that day, for he might have already had Yeshua arrested and lashed.

My old friend raised his bleeding thumb high above his head and faced the multitude. 'Let he who is without blemish or who has never lost his way cast the first stone!'

'I've heard enough!' the woman's husband announced. He rushed at Yeshua while his back was turned and pushed him so hard that he fell forward on to the dusty street and skinned both his hands.

I ran up to the lout with my knife in my fist. He was standing over Yeshua, taunting him. I was trembling with rage. 'If you lay a hand on him again,' I shouted, 'I'll kill you!'

Very likely Rachel's husband sensed that he was facing a man who had lost all fear of either heavenly or earth-bound judgement, since after hurling a quick insult at me – to save face – he backed off.

A bailiff came forward at the same moment, his sword drawn, and ordered me to put down my blade.

Yeshua took my knife from me and tossed it to the ground. He stepped then to the woman's brother and pressed his bleeding thumb to his brow, leaving a red shadow behind. All those present surely knew that this was a way of creating a bond between them, but I had an inkling that it was something more – a way of drawing grace or courage to the boy.

Might it have been a second attempt to bring Raphael to us? Unless – is it possible? – the angel had already joined us.

I had squatted on my heels to catch my breath, and, when I next looked up at Yeshua, the sun was directly behind him. Light-shafts – striated and dazzling – were issuing from his head and chest towards Rachel, and, as I turned in a slow circle, I understood – I know not how – that my old friend had confronted the bailiffs not only to rescue the adulteress but also to save her brother David and the rest of us – because, if she were stoned, everyone gathered here on this day would all be complicit in that crime.

Was I seeing the primordial light that had connected us all since the sixth day? Did Yeshua see it all the time?

The moment he placed his hand on the brother's chest, the radiance faded. 'If you do not judge, you shall not be judged,' he told the young man. 'And if you do not condemn, you shall not be condemned. And if you forgive, dearest David – if you forgive – then you shall be forgiven.'

The boy's eyes gushed with tears.

Very rarely do we recognize a turning point in our lives as it is happening, but I believe that he saw clearly that he was standing before the Gate of Righteousness, and he had been brought there by a man greater than any he had met before, and that this chance for redemption and justice would never come again.

'I did not see her commit any crime,' David said to Yeshua, and, when my old friend asked him to tell that to the priests, he faced them and repeated his words.

It took considerable bravery for him to speak this confession, since he might have been arrested as a false witness, though, in the end, he and his sister were both set free.

We shall never know if what David ben Reuben, brother of Rachel, said that day was true, but we shall always know that his voice prevented a grievous affront to all of creation, and that is all I need to know.

Yaphiel, all who have ever heard this story believe they know the lesson that Yeshua wished to teach us. It is contained in these words: 'Let he who is without blemish or who has never lost his way cast the first stone.'

But, while that is an important lesson, it is only the one we see at first glance, written across the polished surface of his actions.

If you gaze below this level of meaning, dear boy, you may glimpse the second – and, some would say, more life-changing – lesson that Yeshua intended for us that day, and it is this: *The only hands and eyes that the Lord has to right injustice in our world are our own.*

10

'"And that dreamer of dreams shall be put to death, because he has spoken in such a way as to turn you away from the Lord your God."'

Annas makes that thinly veiled threat against me just before leaving my home. I sit in my workroom and listen to his words again, over and over, as though they are the blows of a hammer against the roof of the secure edifice I have tried to build for myself and my family.

Nahara lies asleep in her bed, but Yirmi is not home yet. It was hours ago that I asked him to find out about Kurush, the Persian who treated my tertian fever with decoctions. I know he is a clever boy, with a detailed map of Yerushalayim in his feet, but, if any evil should befall him while on my errand, I could never live out the rest of my life.

At length, a bard playing the lute begins entertaining the pilgrims bedded down on my street with the tale of Daniel, Bel and the Dragon: 'The beast was a horned serpent, a colossus the height of Nebuchadnezzar's palace, with the feet of a lion and golden wings. He had only one weakness, though only the Lord of Heaven knew what it was . . .'

Is our storyteller an old man? His singing voice is simple and affecting, though it belies a certain weariness of the flesh when he is forced to intone a long phrase on a single breath. His repetitive melodies make me think of a dry wind blowing over sunbaked stones, but it is how he trembles on the high notes that makes me lean my head against the shutters so that I might hear him more clearly.

I know I ought to surrender to my drowsiness of spirit and join Nahara and Gephen on her mat, where they have curled into a single knot of slumber, but I want to wait up for Yeshua. Also, my apprehension about Yirmi's whereabouts has begun chasing its tail just below my need for rest, around and around and around, without any end in sight, and I know from experience that I shall not be able to find sleep until he has returned to me.

Through the cracks in my shutters, I see pilgrims seated around their campfires, listening with rapt faces to the bard, and, although I would like to join them, some of them would surely recognize me as the man who was resurrected. I limp instead into the courtyard and build a nest for myself beside the mosaic peacocks with which I long ago decorated the floor.

A little while later, Grandfather Shimon eases down beside me and rests his arm on my leg and talks to me of what he calls 'the patterned beauty of a star-filled sky'.

From my grandfather's powerful and callused hands I have always drawn poetry and faraway dreams, just as I have always drawn loyalty and laughter from Mia's.

Out of habit, Shimon enters our courtyard only after dark, and he never dares leave our home during the day because people often mistake his skin rashes for leprosy and chase after him, throwing stones and sticks. Many of our neighbours still refer to him behind our backs as Shimon the Leper.

On Shimon's shoulder stands Ayin, our little Greek owl, whose name means *eye* in Aramaic. We called him that because his otherworldly golden stare has been known to cause trembling in even the bravest visitors. Mia discovered him several years earlier, drawn by his heartrending screeching to an imposing villa in the Upper Town, where the poor creature had been nailed through his wings to the wooden door. Unfortunately, that is the torture the Romans and Latinized Jews inflict on any bird that ventures accidentally into their homes, as a way, they claim, of chasing away the ill fortune that they are said to carry inside.

The wind changes direction as Shimon points out the constellations to me. A chorus of crickets has begun singing of their hopes for the spring.

Youth and old age are two separate kingdoms. That is what I think as Shimon raises his arm to point out the stars in Argo to me. And why, too, I embrace him, breathing in deeply on the yeasty scent of him – of more than sixty years of sweat-soaked struggle.

Some time later, Yirmi nudges me awake. We are alone in the courtyard; Grandfather Shimon must have gone back to bed.

'Blessed be the Lord for returning you to me!' I tell my son.

'I'm sorry, Father. It took longer than I thought.'

As he helps me sit up, I ask what he found out about Kurush.

'The Baal Nefesh confirmed that he's an old friend. And you were right; he's a magus of the Zarathustrian faith.'

I wish I could receive this as good news, but, if Kurush did not seal me inside a trance, then I was indeed dead – and I encountered no afterlife waiting for me.

The panic rising inside me seems to be a living thing – greedy and unyielding and eager to possess me, which is why I reach out for my son. When the throbbing in my chest subsides, I ask him if the Baal Nefesh told him where Kurush has been staying.

'At an inn near the Roman theatre,' he replies. 'But when I went there, the innkeeper told me he'd left on the day you . . . you no longer . . . When your breathing stopped.'

There are good silences and bad ones, of course, and the silence that follows his words soon becomes one of lost hope. *I have been changed for ever,* I think. *Nothing now will be as it was.*

'Did the innkeeper know where Kurush went?' I ask.

'No, so I asked all the guests I could find. I had to wait many hours for two of them to return to the inn. That's why I was gone so long. But neither of them knew anything.'

Once I have assured him that he did well, Yirmi tells me about a guest he questioned who was from distant Cochin. 'He spoke such a strange form of Aramaic that I had to puzzle out every word. And, Papa, you should have seen his clothes! He wore pointed slippers and a hat decorated with embroidered lotus flowers. Do you know how the Hindus call the *neshamah?*'

'No, I've no idea,' I tell him.

'*Atman,*' he announces. 'They say we all have a spark of God inside us. And do you know the name they have for Elohim?'

I shake my head and laugh. *Your youthful zeal is balm to your father,* I tell him in my mind.

'Brahma!' he exclaims. 'And he swore to me that wool does not grow on animals there, or even on trees like Herodotus says, but on spindly little plants!'

My son's voice is filled with his eagerness to see faraway lands. *If only I may see this eager traveller of mine safely to the dawn of adulthood,* I think.

Who is the traitor who told Annas what Yeshua said in my tomb?

When I stir in the night, this question lies in wait for me inside the chilly darkness. Invaded by a solitude so wide and deep that it holds everything I have ever lost, most especially my wife, I give in again to tears.

I did not know I was dead. No one ever does. Such simple words they are, and yet they prove too cumbersome to fit inside my head once again.

I curl my arm over my eyes. *Odysseus drifted nine days on the ocean, clinging to a fragment of his ship*, I think. *For how long shall I, too, be awash in this deep, grey, limitless abyss into which I have fallen?*

A little while later, a stirring behind me makes me let out a high-pitched yelp that might be comic under other circumstances.

A caped figure is seated with his back to the far wall, his knees up. He raises two of his fingers – a signal that he and I agreed upon years before. It is his way of telling me that, although he is visiting distant worlds inside himself, all is under control.

'How did you get in?' I ask.

'I tapped on Mia's shutters and she was kind enough to open them.'

'She must have thought you were Gephen.'

'So that's why she seemed so disappointed!' he says, laughing.

Yeshua crosses the room and drapes his cloak over my shoulders. Only then do I realize I have been shivering.

He sits behind me, circles his arm around my chest and pulls me close. The slow rise and fall of his chest becomes the protection we have always given each other. Tears come again; they seem to have their own desires and needs at the moment.

At length, we lay back together on my mat – into the togetherness of who we are and have always been.

My own flesh shall be my comfort, I think.

Yeshua's scent of barley and wood smoke soon becomes a trail leading me back to our childhood in Natzeret.

'What are you thinking?' he whispers. His breath is scented with wine.

I say nothing; how can I tell him that death has taught me that he and I shall one day be dust – that we shall lose everything we once loved, even our childhood?

He pulls me closer. His woodworkers' hands are strong and coarse. How could I not feel pride in a friend who has never tried to hide his years of labour, even when the Pharisees, Sadducees and priests have ridiculed him for it?

'The people trust you because you are one of them,' I whisper.

'I shall be who I shall be,' he replies.

Do you understand his word-play, Yaphiel? *I Shall Be Who I Shall Be* is, of course, one of our names for God.

'And yet I'm no longer who I was,' I tell him. 'I've been overcome by doubts.'

The fragile sound of my voice makes me cringe. I sit up, out of his embrace, feeling unworthy of him.

'Death has taught you that you're now a different man?' he asks.

'I'm not sure.'

As though reading a verse of Torah, he says, 'The sea would tell you that the separateness of islands is an illusion.'

I grip his hand as if it were a protective talisman, for my reply is not one that he will like. 'Unless the sea itself is an illusion.' I fear his anger, so I rush to add, 'I'm not like you,

Yeshua – I'm unable to journey to the remote realms you visit. I know almost nothing of God's hidden life.'

I release his hand so that he can flee from me if he so chooses, though I know I am also testing his loyalty, which chills me because it means that my resurrection may end up provoking me to ask too much of him.

He sits up and spreads his right hand on top of my head, as if to gather in my thoughts. After he blesses me in the name of the Lord, we listen to the footsteps passing outside my window. An elderly neighbour – Weathervane, we call him – is complaining to his hound, Moonstone, about the pains in his back and hip. We say nothing as they pass us by, as if we were two mischievous boys pretending to be asleep. It occurs to me that our years of shared plotting – against our brothers and sisters, our parents, the world – is something that I would not want to have missed.

'Lazar, the Nabataeans of the high desert never see the sea,' he tells me, 'but they know it exists.'

'Because they trust those who have seen great waters,' I reply, implying with my tone that such confidence is no longer mine.

'You sat on the Throne of Glory for two days. And then you separated from the Lord – one became two. So you feel you've been abandoned. And you wonder how you can live this way – separate from the source of life.'

'I can't live with all these doubts. I need . . . need my faith.'

'Knock and the door shall be opened to you.'

'But what if I no longer believe there is any door?'

'This is my fault,' he says with a moan. Turning away from me, he holds his head in his hands.

I kneel next to him, angry at myself for speaking of my troubles. 'You could not have foreseen all the consequences of your miracle,' I tell him.

'I should have. Perhaps I ought not to have come to you in your tomb.'

His glassy eyes remind me that being unique can be a curse. Imagine having such porous borders around your heart that the afflictions of others become your own.

'You gave life where there was none,' I tell him. 'That could not be wrong. You saved my children from becoming orphans – for which I'll never be able to repay you. But perhaps all miracles come with a price. Yeshua, I saw nothing of God or of any life everlasting.'

He gazes down and rubs his hand back and forth across his hair, as he does when he is perplexed. I fetch him my water jug in order to give him a moment to consider what I've told him without my scrutiny; he has been observed and studied since he first started his lessons in Torah, and there are times – such as now – when he cannot bear to have anyone's glance upon him.

Once he has slaked his thirst, he gazes beyond me, as if he has spotted a figure on a distant horizon. I say nothing; to be loved by someone far greater than myself is so overwhelming an experience at times that it keeps me silent when I would otherwise wish to speak.

'I shouldn't have delayed my return to you,' he says. 'I'm sorry.'

'You don't need to apologize.'

At length, he begins to talk of our first encounter.

Dear Yaphiel, Yeshua and I met when we were eight years old. One spring morning, he simply stepped up to me in the marketplace in Natzeret and asked me to tell him my dream of the Lord as an eagle. It was my sister Marta – eager to stir up trouble – who had revealed it to him, disobeying in that way my father's injunction to keep it a secret.

Now, Yeshua does not explain why he returns to the past, but I hear in his speech-rhythm – hesitant and slow, as though he were climbing up a steep hill – that this is important to him.

After he finishes his story of our first encounter, he says, 'And now, after twenty-eight years, I have left you standing alone outside the Gate of Life.' Leaning close to me, he whispers, 'I see the impressions that the grasp of the Angel of Death has left in your flesh. I understand how it feels.'

The conspiratorial urgency in his tone brings gooseflesh to my arms. Was he, too, embraced by Death during his time in the wilderness, as I've always suspected? Who – or what – descended upon him in the Syrian desert?

He stands up and goes to my window. Cold air rushes into the room when he opens the shutters, and he peers into the courtyard. When he turns to me, he says, 'I know the way back through the Gate of Life, and I shall guide you.'

*

Yeshua and I chant hymns for a time, but I am unable to find the right rhythms, and trying to join my voice to his only proves to me that the rituals of faith that once came so easily to me no longer do. Will he guide me home through prayer? He does not say.

My friend's devotion to me soon allows me to talk of other matters that have been troubling me, however. 'Annas ben Seth paid me a visit this evening,' I tell him, using a tone of warning.

'Marta told me that after Mia opened the door to me. She blames me for his visit.'

'She blames you for everything!' I say with a grin.

Yeshua shrugs disappointedly. 'Maybe she's got a point.'

'She's just irritated by all the attention I've received of late.' When Yeshua gazes out the window again, I say, 'Apparently Caiaphas was too cowardly to come himself.'

He makes the hand gesture of a Greek puppeteer tugging a string. It is his way of saying that our Temple priests are controlled by Caesar.

'Listen, Yeshua, I've realized something alarming about what took place in my tomb. Someone in my family or one of your disciples memorized the exact words you used when you raised me from the dead and repeated them to Annas. You'll have to watch even your closest friends carefully.'

He shrugs as if it is of no import, which gives me the idea that he knows who the traitor is. When I ask, he whispers that he suspects Yehudah of Kerioth, one of our oldest and dearest friends.

'But why would Yehudah betray you?' I ask.

'I'm sorry, Lazar, but I don't want to speak about him. Annas may question you again, and the less you know about his betrayals the less you can reveal.'

I join him at the window. 'I don't want you staying in Yerushalayim because you're worried about what's happened to me. You can guide me from afar.'

'I am not staying because of you.'

I suspect he's lying, so I hold up my oil lamp between us to read his expression, but he hides his truth under a resentful frown.

'Return to Perea – or go to the Galilee,' I say, lowering my lamp. 'I'll sleep better knowing you are with our friends at home.'

'No, I want to walk amongst the Passover pilgrims,' he replies. 'The time has come for me to proclaim His name aloud to them and everyone else.'

At the time, I interpret his words symbolically; it does not occur to me that he has already planned a very public entry into Jerusalem.

'If you suspect Yehudah,' I say, 'then you have to find an excuse to send him away.'

'No. His betrayal is not without its usefulness.' When I press him to explain, he says, 'Twice now I have given him false confidences, and twice he has passed them on to Caiaphas.'

'That would seem a dangerous game.'

He kneels down to remove his sandals. 'In the end,' he says, 'it makes little difference what Yehudah says and does. Pilatus can arrest me any time he likes.'

'Then why doesn't he?'

When Yeshua is barefoot, he stands back up. 'Because my work has gone well in the Galilee. I have thousands more followers now, and Pilatus and his friends in Rome fear that an uprising would begin there if anything should happen to me. They're also aware that, with some help from well-placed allies, we can cause troubles here in Judaea.'

'In that case, Annas may prove a more intractable enemy.'

'I'm not sure. He's known for years that I aim to end the privileges of the priesthood, and yet he has made no serious moves against me.'

'But now he has another reason to loathe you.'

'And what's that?'

'He envies you!'

Yeshua shows me a doubtful look.

'It's true. While he and I were conversing, I realized what's motivated his rage. You've a mastery of spirit and matter that goes far beyond his capabilities. When you raised me from the dead, within sight of Jerusalem –'

'*El Shaddai* raised you from the dead,' Yeshua cuts in.

'But you summoned Him. I'm convinced that Annas took that as a personal affront.'

Yeshua shakes his head disappointedly. 'The priests profess to have entered the Gate of Knowledge, but they haven't the courage or the grace to do so – and they hide the keys from the rest of us.' He places an imaginary crown on his head. 'They strut around in their embroidered robes as if they were royalty. Yaaqov told me that Annas attended a funeral last week with his *tzitzit* dangling for all to see?' He points a finger of warning at me. 'Beware of men who display their prayer shawl in public. They represent a great danger to you in particular.'

'Why to me?'

'You try to hide your contempt for them, but you nearly always fail.'

'Annas told me I must never speak of what happened today,' I say.

'Yes, I agree – that would be far safer for you.'

After drawing a deep breath Yeshua reaches out to the window frame to steady himself and lowers his chin to his chest, as though to doze off while standing up, which I have seen him do on a number occasions, after hours of preaching and healing. How did I fail to see that his candle flame is nearly extinguished?

I sit him down on my mat, and he leans back against the wall with a grateful sigh. When I believe he is asleep, I lay down beside him.

Gazing at Yeshua, whose eyes are closed and who is breathing gently, I see that he has succeeded where I have failed; he has the life that was meant for him. *I shall never become a teacher or travel far beyond the borders of Zion*, I think.

And yet I feel neither sorrow nor envy. Is it my affection for him that saves me from useless and unwanted emotions?

I can live with my disappointment if I have him and my children, I think.

When I stand, Yeshua asks me where I'm going. 'To check on Yirmi and Nahara,' I whisper. 'Now go back to sleep.'

'No. Wait for me a moment and I'll come with you.'

As I give him my consent, I think, *Yes, of course – on this night we shall all be together, Yeshua and my children and me, even if for just a few moments,* and I offer my thanks to the Lord.

Yeshua sits up and wipes his hand down across his face and neck. I expect him to yawn or smile, but instead he shows me a troubled look.

'What's wrong?' I question.

'There are things I must tell you about our past together. And I dare not let them wait any longer, for they have been crying out to be heard for far too long already.'

II

Yaphiel, I fear that I have not made an important point clear to you: it is possible for a sage or prophet to confer with the Lord at the same time as he converses with a friend or preaches to a crowd. In short, and contrary to what you may have been led to believe, a man can be in two places at the same time. In fact, if what Yeshua told me on a number of occasions is correct, then we are always and inevitably in two places at once – in this world, where we are travellers, and in our true home.

Our Torah teacher, Rabbi Baruch ben Enoch, was the first to apprehend that Yeshua could explore the *Hekhal ha-Melekh* at the same time as he studied with us.

If you do not accept this as possible, then we can be certain that you have never met anyone like Yeshua, and I am sorry for that, for I believe we should all have a chance to benefit from the company of someone magical – a *gaon* who can put wings on our assumptions and certainties and encourage them to fly from us. Need I say that such a companion makes us more aware of the infinite possibilities that remain hidden from us most of the time – of the nearly imperceptible filaments of light connecting everything we perceive to everything we do not.

If you believe in this supernal radiance – or have been fortunate enough to catch a glimpse of it – then you also know that all we say and do can have a profound effect not only on our earthly realm but also on the Kingdom of Heaven.

Remember this: the same laws that rule over the motions of the planets and stars also govern the shape of the human body and the flow of thoughts in our minds. All that we see and hear and touch has taken part in creation, and everything – without exception – speaks the same holy language, which is another way of saying that everything grows and develops according to fixed and definite patterns.

It is this correspondence between our realm and God's – their material and spiritual closeness – that makes it possible for us to influence both worlds at the same time.

Yaphiel, I am certain that Yeshua would be heartened to learn that I am writing of him to you, just as I am convinced that he would be relieved to discover that you and your mother are well. Unless . . . Unless he did not put her in my path, as I have always believed. Did I find her accidentally? Is there even such a thing as *pure chance*?

12

Gephen returns from his night-time prowling as Yeshua begins to tell me about what in our past has been crying out to be heard. The exhausted little creature has soiled and matted fur and the dried blood of some unfortunate victim streaked across the pink triangle of his nose. When I pick him up, he looks at me with those scintillating topaz eyes of his as though he can't quite remember my name or his relation to me. *Would you remind me who you are?*

I sit back down with him, and after he yawns – eyes closed and fangs flaring – he rubs an itch out of his forehead against my hip, climbs up on to my belly and goes to sleep.

Yeshua sits opposite me with his legs crossed. Now, years later, as I listen again to our conversation, all our words seem filtered through the soft warm pressure of Gephen's chest against my flesh and the low, seductive gravel-sound of his purring. Indeed, his feathery white softness reminds me of all I once had in Zion and all that I shall never see again – my sister Mia most of all.

'Sometimes I am certain that I summoned you to me,' Yeshua begins.

'Which means exactly what?' I ask.

'I imagined you before you appeared in my life.'

Fear that I may disbelieve or criticize him makes him gaze down and recite the first words of the Shema.

'No matter what you reveal to me, I won't be angry,' I say.

'It was Marta who told me your dream of the Lord as an eagle – despite your father telling her to keep it a secret,' he reminds me.

'No, you don't understand – it was precisely because he ordered us to keep it a secret that she told it to you!' I exclaim, laughing with admiration at the way my sister has flouted the most sacred of rules since she was a little girl.

Yeshua closes his eyes and takes two quick breaths, then a longer third.

'You've been fasting, haven't you?' I ask on a hunch.

'Yes, but just for a day.'

'Before you leave me, I'll serve you a proper meal.'

He waves a dismissive hand in the air between us, but we both know that I shall win this battle, since he is in my home and cannot refuse my hospitality.

'As Marta was telling me about your dream,' he continues, 'a verse from the Book of Names started repeating inside my head – and I knew that Elohim was summoning me on a new path.'

'Which verse did He speak to you?'

'"This thing is too heavy for you – you are not able to perform it alone."'

I repeat the previous words from the Book of Names so that he knows I shall follow him into the Torah of Mosheh wherever he wishes to go: '"You will surely exhaust yourself and the people who are with you."'

'On the day that Elohim spoke to me,' he continues, 'I tracked you down in the marketplace, and I made you describe your dream. As soon as you finished, I realized I had a difficult decision to make – to remain alone or bring you with me.'

'You've lost me.'

He taps my foot with his. 'Do you remember that my parents took me to the Temple when I was seven years old? The priests had heard that I could quote much of the Torah from memory and wanted to hear me for themselves.'

'You told me that they were extremely impressed.'

'Yes, they mistook my memory tricks for knowledge. I cannot blame them; it was what I wanted them to think.' He shakes his head as though astonished that he had once performed tricks that set the eyes of a dozen elders ablaze. 'On returning to Natzeret,' he continues, 'the local rabbis, who'd been informed that I was a precocious young man, convinced my parents to give me to them for a routine of daily study. Of course, I'd have preferred to have my father teach me how to polish a table top or plane a door – I was only seven, after all – but he wouldn't hear of it. So I found myself yoked to those old scholars four days a week, from sun to sun. They were good men, most of them – and intelligent and wise. But their scowls of displeasure when I didn't understand a reference or failed to discover the vowel in a word that was new to me . . . At first, their criticisms felt like brands in my flesh and made me cry. Worst of all, I hadn't anyone my age to keep me company. I was Yaaqov at Peniel – embracing and wrestling with the spirit of my solitude. So, a few months after I started studying, I told the rabbis of your dream of the Lord as an eagle. I requested that they speak to your parents about having you study with me. That's what I've needed to confess to you all these years.'

'I'm not sure I understand,' I say. 'Why exactly did you tell them my dream?'

'Because of the *peshar* I gave it,' he replies, using the word for *interpretation* that occurs in the Book of Daniel. 'It meant that God the Father chose you to free me – and that we would become lifelong companions.'

'Why?'

'If that wasn't His intent, why would He have spoken to me of lessening my burden? Lazar, do you remember the way you described your dream?'

'No. Did I do a very bad job?'

'Not at all. You told it well, and I was very excited to hear a boy my age speak so articulately and with so much emotion. And why? Because I realized you could join me in my captivity. The rabbis might scowl at you on occasion instead of me!' He kneels before me and puts his hands in mine. 'I'm sorry. Sometimes I think that the right thing to do was turn away from you and never speak to you again.'

My heart tumbles inside my chest. 'I wouldn't want to live a world in which we did not meet.'

'But I altered the course of your life without a single thought to your needs.'

'Our studies opened many doors to me. I'd be an illiterate stonemason were it not for you.'

'Still, what I did was wrong.'

He wants me to censure him, but the only fault I can find in him is of a different order. 'Wouldn't you have travelled lighter if you'd confessed all this to me years ago?'

'Yes, but when we were boys I was afraid you'd hate me, and later, after we grew into men, there seemed no need. Except . . . except that lately, since your resurrection, my thoughtlessness has caught up with me.' With renewed enthusiasm, he says, 'Do you know what struck me most about your dream?'

'No.'

'You'll think I read too much into it.'

'I might – but we'll never know unless you tell me.'

'What's the meaning of my name?' he asks invitingly.

'*Yeshua* is a cry for rescue, of course.'

'And that's how I can be sure that the Lord chose me for you.'

'I don't understand.'

'Don't you see? In your dream, you were surrounded by an ocean of fire. The sky was glowing red and was about to collapse. So you made *a cry for help* to God – a *yeshua!*'

I cannot stop myself from scoffing. 'I'm sorry, but we both know that Aramaic is a very easy language in which to find such correspondences,' I point out. 'Every name means something.' Lifting up Gephen's forepaw, I say, 'Every time I see a grape vine, God does not necessarily wish me to think of my cat. Or to believe that holding him in my arms will make me drunk.'

He waves off my criticism. 'Tell me what happened next in your dream,' he says in a challenging voice.

'A man called my name behind me and said, "I am the gate you seek." And he pushed me through the ocean of flames to safety.'

'Through the Gate of Fire. And you were reborn as Ziz, the Lord of Hosts in the form of a griffin, soaring in defence of the Galilee. As I recall, you were unable to identify the man's voice back then – the man who shoved you. But I think you must have figured out whose it was by now.'

The mysterious tone he uses makes me realize he is going to claim the voice was his. 'But you were only eight years old at the time,' I say. 'You didn't have a man's voice!'

'But I do now.' He whispers a verse from the Psalms in triumph: '"For You have been my help, and in the shadow of Your wings I sing for joy!"'

'So I dreamed of the voice you would have twenty-eight years into the future? Is that what you're saying?'

'Yes, though I can see you don't believe it. In any case, what I'm sure of is that I'm the Gate of Fire in your dream.'

'You're asking me to believe something that seems . . . unlikely.'

He stands up and reaches down for my hand, then bends to kiss it. 'Blessed is he who existed before he came into being.'

13

At my insistence, Yeshua eats a bowl of barley gruel and a roundel of bread topped with *charoset*. We share several cups of posca and honey as well, since it will keep him alert. Just before he heads back to Yerushalayim, while he is finishing his meal, I take a peek at my crooked little street – only a hand's-breadth wider than a donkey cart – and discover a carpet of pilgrims bedded down for the night. Those few who remain awake are huddled under blankets and conversing in whispers.

At the south end of the street, near the old well, a pregnant woman who will soon give birth stands with her husband. He is pointing up, and she is bending backwards, squinting at the sky. Is he reading the date of their child's birth in the heavens?

When she covers her husband's mouth with her hand and laughs, I hear her speak her thoughts in my mind: *Tell me no more divinations. All I want is for the baby to be born with ten toes and fingers and a nose and eyes and everything else in its proper place.*

I bring four roundels of matzoh to Yeshua for his blessing, since I'd like to offer some sustenance to the pilgrims who recognize him as he walks through Bethany. After all, many are a long way from home and beset by hunger.

'Lazar, I have come to Yerushalayim to offer much more than crumbs,' he tells me, frowning, but he blesses the bread all the same, and I slice it into morsels with my vine-knife.

'When can you visit me again?' I ask him at my door.

'I'll try to return tomorrow at sundown.' He pats my shoulder. 'So you aren't angry with me?'

'No, of course not. You know, when we were small, I told your mother that I wished we'd been born in the same nest, and I haven't changed my mind.' I suggest that he come for supper if he can. 'Bring Maryam and Yohanon or anyone else you want.'

At the door, he leans towards me and rubs the stubble of his cheek against mine. It has long been his way of confirming that we have both reached manhood. You see, Yaphiel, for many years, he and his parents feared that he would die young.

When we embrace, I think, *To hold this man in my arms is to have within my grasp all that still surprises me about the way my life has gone.*

Outside my door, moonlight has turned the edges of our rooftops to burnished silver, but we have no time to study them; a woman stands up and shouts to her friends, 'It's him – the man who came back to life!'

Pilgrims soon crowd around me, and, when Yeshua is recognized by a Galilean, everyone starts to demand our blessings.

While he is laying hands on a gnarled old grandmother who tells us she walked for seven days from Beroea to Yerushalayim to offer a lamb to God, a giant carrying a sword at his belt takes hold of my arm and starts to tell me a story of misery in halting, heavily accented Aramaic, beginning with his ill-fated birth: 'It is forty years in the past I am born in a flax field, and it . . .'

How shall Yeshua and I free ourselves from all those who want our attention?

The moment he finishes comforting the old woman, I extricate myself from Goliath by blessing him and reminding him in a firm voice that there are others awaiting my help. I intend to tell Yeshua that I shall attend to each and every suppliant so that he can return to his inn, but a young mother with tangled hair offers him her newborn baby, folded inside a linen coverlet, before I can finish my offer.

Yeshua cradles the child. On pressing his lips to its brow, however, he flinches.

And then something unexpected: the mother drops to her knees and holds up a small cup she had hidden in her robe, asking for Yeshua's tears.

'They will raise him from the dead!' she exclaims.

Yeshua kisses the lifeless infant again and hands him back to his mother, but she pushes the child away. 'I redeemed him with two doves at the Temple, exactly as the priests told me to do.'

Her unasked question is one that plagues all parents who outlive their children: *Why did the Lord take him from me so soon?*

Yeshua kneels and lays the baby next to her. 'Have you no kin in Yerushalayim who can help you?' he asks, but she has begun to weep and does not answer.

'Do you have any friends who live near by?' I ask.

She looks between me and Yeshua. 'Would you have me leave my child in the valley of Ge Hinnom for the jackals to feed on?'

By way of an answer, Yeshua places his hand on her head and presses his whispered prayers for her as deeply into her as he can. I can see from the way she shakes her head, however, that his gesture is not nearly enough. In years hence, will she think of Yeshua with bitter resentment – of the day he failed to raise her son from the dead and restore justice to the world?

Yeshua stands and calls out to the crowd. 'You may all come to the Father through me. I shall bless you all.' He puts his hand on my shoulder. 'But I would ask you to let this dear friend of mine go back inside his home. A great mystery has changed his life this day, and he needs to be by himself for a time.'

Goliath is now telling the story of his miserable childhood to Yeshua, but my friend interrupts him with a blessing and tells him to go in peace.

'Return to your room,' he tells me.

'I can't leave you,' I reply.

'It's the life I've chosen,' he says, though his resigned smile tells me that he, too, sometimes walks beside other men whom he might have become. Is there a Yeshua who remained an unknown woodworker in some hidden and cherished corner of his mind?

There is so much that even he will never be able to mend.

He makes his way slowly down my street, praying over everyone whom he passes. He stops only once, to hug a boy with stumps for legs, dressed in rags, sitting in a basket being dragged along by an older brother. Just before turning the corner of our central street – the one that will take him back to Yerushalayim – he looks back at me and raises two fingers of his right hand, so that I shall be certain he is all right. I join my hands together above my head to show that we are together in spirit.

Back behind my locked door, I whisper a prayer of my own authorship that I have said to myself since the day I left him for my apprenticeship in Alexandria: 'Turn Yeshua's soul to light so that he may always see the dangers before him even though they be made of darkness.'

I awake in the morning dry-mouthed and bleary eyed, as though I have been asleep for ages. Loneliness sits heavy in my gut.

After eating some bread soaked in olive oil and a handful of dried apricots, I make ready to work, though my right leg is still frail and wooden. Marta often gives voice to what I dare not say – as though she is the part of me that can never be stifled – and she tells me I am still too death-weakened to work. When I reply that I have no choice, she says that she forbids me from limping off to Yerushalayim 'like a wounded tortoise', as she puts it, which makes me laugh and kiss her hands.

'Make light of it if you want,' she tells me in a haughty voice, 'but, if you must go, then take Yirmi to help you up the hills.'

It seems sound advice, and, when I summon my son to me, he assures me that Rabbi Elad will not scold him if he arrives a little late to his studies. Mia accompanies the two of us as far as Bethany's dungheap, since she is part of a group of local women who have made it their job to search every morning for the unwanted infants often left amongst the refuse.

Although I bless everyone who has been waiting for me, three meddlesome strangers – two men and a woman carrying a hen ready for cooking – find that insufficient and insist on questioning me about my revival as we make our way through Bethany's crowded streets. In exchange for the incantations that they presume to have brought about my revival, they offer me copper and silver coinage. When that fails to work, one of the men tempts me with a tiny bronze amulet of Sobek, the crocodile-headed Egyptian god, and the woman tries to hand me her hen.

My exasperation prompts me to shout a lie that finally chases them away: 'The illness that took my life has not yet been cured, and Yeshua ben Yosef told me that it is highly contagious.'

Just after my son and I pass Bethany's small synagogue, I spot the Goliath who told me a bit about his ill-fated childhood ducking behind the trunk of a broad sycamore. I give no indication that I have spotted him, and – happily – he does not follow us.

To demarcate the northern edge of the town – where the roads east and west out of Bethany converge – our elders long ago placed a cracked old millstone etched with protective invocations, and my son and I find the youngest son of our blacksmith sitting on it. His name is Alexandros, and he is twelve years old. He has a sun-darkened face and hands, wild brown hair and tiny black eyes that roll back in his head from time to time. He is here nearly every day from dawn to dusk, rocking back and forth, jabbering and humming in a language he alone understands.

As always, I ease my hand towards his cheek, but he leans away from me, flails his arms and shrieks. After I apologize, I leave a marble tessera on the rim of the millstone. Although I have never seen him pick up one of these tiny gifts of mine, the stone is always gone by the time I return in the late afternoon, so I expect that he has a pile of them at home.

'Why do you keep trying?' my son asks as we get on our way again.

'Because one day he may let me touch him,' I say. 'And, on that day, Alexandros will know that he is not alone.'

14

As Yirmi and I make our way to Lucius' villa in Yerushalayim's Upper Town, five besotted youths wearing rumpled and stained togas spill out the door of the brothel just ahead of us. Have they been cavorting with Venus and Bacchus all night long? My skin begins to tingle with the dread that only those born in a land ruled by a foreign sword can grasp. Three of the young men are fledglings with downy cheeks, and the other two cannot be more than twenty. Such a number of silly names for their members that they use in their shouted jests – *radix, rutabulum, caulis, cauda,* root, rake, stem, tail – that a score of passers-by stop to gape at them.

Though I speak Latin only haltingly, I understand a little of their sexual banter from having read the graffiti on the walls of the bordello that I visit after my children are safely tucked in bed.

The two eldest youths are wearing garlands around their necks woven of purple lilac and orange wildflowers. Are they truly bridegrooms or are they satirizing the practice of wearing blossoms for some purpose beyond my imagination?

'Say nothing to them or me until we are inside Yerushalayim's gates,' I whisper to Yirmi, though he already knows that it is safest to make himself appear as puny as possible in front of those who have colonized Zion. I lead my son between a scruffy goatherd and his foul-smelling trip so that we can cross over the nearby stepping stones to the other side of the street.

'You, the labourer with the boy!' one of the youths calls out to me, but I do not turn around.

'Hey, Mosheh,' another one says, 'come over here and talk to us!'

I continue to lead Yirmi forward. As we pass a dove-seller sitting by his wooden cages, one of the younger boys yells something about my manhood that makes his friends burst into insolent laughter, and, when I glance over at him, he wriggles his little finger in the air to mock me. The Romans are always amused and astonished by the covenant of circumcision we make with the Almighty.

At such moments, I know I shall never fully escape the despair bequeathed to me by my father's early death, for I am suddenly dripping with sweat and short of breath. In a furtive whisper, I remind my son not to let himself be provoked. 'We do not want to give the youths an excuse to strip us,' I tell him. *Peeling a Jew,* our conquerors call that particular indignity.

The two young men wearing garlands dash across the street to us, mischief burning in their eyes. I recognize the shorter one as Servius, the second son of the Imperial Theatre manager. Though I decorated the courtyard of his family home two years earlier with a mosaic of Pan, he does not seem to recognize me. He asks in a voice made gritty by drink if my son and I would like to sample the pleasures of the bordello girls and boys whose *ripe fruit* they have just *plucked,* as he puts it.

Are such stock phrases meant to be witty?

Servius then speaks to me so quickly that I am unable to decipher his Latin. When I entreat him to address me more slowly, he mocks my Aramaic accent. 'If your son is a virgin,' he adds in a mixture of Latin and Greek, 'I'll pay you to watch him do some pounding! Or be pounded, if that's what he'd like!'

It is best to play the ignorant labourer at such times, so I bow subserviently and apologize for being but a poor Jew unable to speak the language of the Empire: *Paenitet. Iudaeus pauper. Non dicere linguam Imperii.*

I add that we have work to do and must get on our way, but, as I take Yirmi's hand, Servius closes on me and pushes me in the chest. 'You're going to be late for work today, Mosheh,' he says menacingly.

In his deep-set black eyes there is no empathy that I can find. Could my son and I make it safely to the tanners' synagogue just inside the Fountain Gate?

Across the street, a crowd has gathered to watch us. The only person I recognize is Goliath, who must have decided to track me after all. With the beating in my chest swaying me from side to side, I stammer an appeal to Servius for mercy, but, before I get very far, a big-bellied Roman gentleman with the bald head of an Egyptian priest strides up to me and barks an order for me to keep my *Jewish mouth* quiet.

'And you, stop this nonsense!' he commands the youths.

'*Somnias!*' Servius replies, meaning, I suppose, *You must be dreaming!* In a more serious tone, the young man uses a well-known idiom to tell his elder that I am only pretending not to speak the language of Rome: *in Iudaea etiam arbores Latine loquuntur* – in Judaea even the trees speak Latin.

My fear of the violence I sense in the youth makes me reach into my pouch to check for my knife. By now, the three younger boys have joined us. One of them – no more than fourteen or fifteen – clears his throat and spits at me, hitting me in the neck and cheek.

How could a boy spit at an elder? It seems so impossible to me at the time that I can find no reply equal to my astonishment.

Across the street is a fair-haired woman carrying her baby on her back, in the Greek fashion. I know I will always remember her because she has seen my shock and humiliation and begun to weep.

While wiping the spittle from my face, my need to teach Servius and his cohorts a lesson makes my hands tremble. I decide it best to make an appeal to the higher nature of a big-bellied aristocrat, however, and I tell him that I am a simple craftsman who wishes only to avoid trouble. I add that I am in the employ of Lucius ben David, since my being in the service of an important Jewish *Philoromaios* – admirer of Rome – ought to win my son and me some protection.

As soon as I mention Lucius, however, Servius charges forward and bulls up into me. I find myself lying in the street with a badly scraped knee and hand, and fighting for air. Yirmi rushes to me, tears in his eyes.

While I am getting my breath back, I notice Goliath watching me from a few paces behind Servius. He looks disappointed. Would he prefer for me to use my fists and end up with a knife in my gut?

'*Porci!*' Servius growls at me and my son; it is the most common epithet the Romans use to try to provoke us, since they know that we are not permitted to eat pork.

Did he attack me because he suddenly recognized me and feared that I would speak of my having worked for his father in front of his friends?

Now that I am wounded, the boys let us get on our way with a few final jests. While Yirmi brushes the dust from my tunic, the Roman gentleman, from whom I expect a few words of solidarity, looks me up and down as though I am covered with manure and curses me.

Infuriating? On the contrary, it is the perfect reminder that we must never count on men who believe that honest labour is a misfortune and poverty a contagious disease!

One of Lucius' house slaves opens his garden gate to me and my son. I hope to avoid discussing my debasement with Yirmi and start to tell him of the work I have in mind for him, pretending enthusiasm, but he refuses to look me in the eyes.

'I'm sorry you had to go through that,' I finally confess, and, to cheer his mood, I tell him that he can add a design of his own choosing to the mosaic on which I am currently working, but he makes his lips into a slit of forced silence, exactly as he does when he wishes me to know that I have punished him unjustly. I realize then – falling into gloom – that he is likely hiding a secret no boy wishes to have: that he is ashamed of his father.

My own guilt is no less cumbersome, of course. And I, too, am hiding a secret – one that proves the near uselessness of the strategy of servility I adopted with our foes: Servius seems to have badly bruised – perhaps even fractured – one of my ribs.

'Fear is a remarkably useful emotion,' I tell my son.

He looks up at me with a hard, accusatory expression, and I see then that it may take some time for so young a boy to forgive the frailties of his father – and his limitations.

'It's God's way of making sure you seek protection,' I add. 'Why were we not stripped and further humiliated – or beaten? Because we listened closely to the Lord speaking inside us. Though I would not blame you for wishing that we could've taught those drunken imbeciles a lesson.'

When he shows me a judgemental frown, I tell him then how I learned to pay close attention to my fear when a Roman aristocrat named Felix Marcus Octavianus – may even his shadow be erased from history! – paid for my father to be murdered in order to avoid having to pay us what he owed us for the stonework we had completed on his villa in Sepphoris, where we were then living. Yirmi has never before heard my version of his grandfather's murder, and, when I tell him how I discovered my father's blood-soaked body in his bed, the boy's judgemental coldness breaks and he sits close by me. I must be in a confessional mood because I tell him that we never learned the identity of the spy who informed Octavianus that his assassin would find my father at home with a high fever and not at work. I mention, as well, that my mother permitted the Roman to pay a condolence call on us after the funeral and that when I asked her how she could permit such a criminal inside our house she replied, 'Because I still have a son and two daughters, and I plan to do everything I can to make sure that they outlive me by many years.'

There is a great deal more I would like to tell Yirmi about how to survive in a Roman colony, but tears gush in his eyes when I tell him that my father's funeral was the worst day of my life, and he presses into me as though he had withheld his love from me for weeks.

As I console him, he says, 'Papa, your hand is still bleeding.'

'It'll stop soon,' I say, tousling his hair. 'And it doesn't hurt.'

When our shared intimacy grows too much for my son, he steps to the red granite fountain at the centre of the garden, leans over the rim and studies the playful fishes – their skin turned to gold by the sunlight – who, improbably, live out their entire lives inside a circle of stone. Two hoopoes are preening on the walkway leading to the grape arbour, fanning out their black-tipped crown feathers as if to reveal their hidden majesty.

Unfortunately, the beautiful birds take wing the moment I point them out to my son.

The delicate and mysterious vibration of life hiding in the trees and bushes, and in the air itself . . . It is all around us – and inside us as well. Could that not be enough for me? Perhaps it is too much to ask to be certain that God is watching over us.

My son looks at me while swirling his hand in fountain, and I see that he wants to remain with me all day, but he does not wish to risk angering me by asking my permission.

'Listen, Yirmi,' I say when I go to him, 'would you mind if I kept you with me today and put you to work? It would be good to have your help.'

'Of course I'll stay with you. But what about my lessons?'

'We ought all to permit ourselves one day each week when we ignore what other people think of our behaviour. And today shall be ours!'

His smile is what I picture in my mind all that morning to keep the pain stabbing into my chest from making me abandon my work. But if the rib is indeed fractured, I do not know how I shall continue earning a living for my family. Might this bad fortune be my punishment for doubting God's existence?

My son and I start work on the base of the blue menorah that I have designed for the floor of Lucius' swimming pool. The candelabra is four paces of a man in height and seven in width, and I have placed it as an exuberant crown on the head of Ziz, the mighty griffin whom the Creator chose as King of the Birds. Above him I have depicted the winged chariot of Yechezkel soaring through an amber-coloured sky. The griffin's hooked beak is open because he is speaking to the first woman and man, Havvah and Adam, who are huddling together beneath three date palms at the bottom left. I have made the outlines of the first man and woman with tesserae of polished obsidian as a reference to the glassy protection with which the Lord originally covered their bodies before it was reduced – at the time of their exile from Eden – to the nails on their fingers and toes.

I have used tesserae of lapis lazuli for the stem and six branches of the menorah. The candle flames are black and made of onyx.

When Lucius first studied my sketches, he thought it was inappropriate to place a menorah under water. 'Absurd and foolish!' was his pompous proclamation, and he ordered me to remove Ziz and substitute Leviathan and a school of friendly bream, as is the standard for pools and fountains amongst the Roman Jews. I won our dispute only when his regal elder sister Eliana assured him that my mosaic's originality and daring would impress their family and friends far more than what she called the *usual fishy mess*. As to why I truly designed a menorah burning under water, I was not at first sure, since the idea came to me in a fleeting vision, but Yeshua later told me that he believed it was the Lord's way of reminding us both that even an ocean cannot put out the flame of *tsedeq* – justice – once it has been lit.

As Yirmi and I work, the dry, sharp, metallic clink of my son's hammer against our slab of lapis lazuli makes me think of all the years of patience and effort it has taken me and my sisters to create our modest life – and of how easily it might be destroyed by Annas. Before the spring sun of Judaea can singe our winter-pale skin, I unfurl the canvas awning over the pool. A few hours later, when the bell for our midday meal is rung, we climb to the surface and wash the stone dust off our faces and hands in the channel of icy water that irrigates the garden. Affection for Lucius comes to me as I refresh myself. I realize that this quiet enclave of trees, flowers and birds is a child's dream given form, and that he – some fifty years earlier – must have been that dreaming child.

My son and I are served lunch by an elderly Idumaean house-slave named Siron. We sit under the marble colonnade at a wooden table painted with seven insatiable satyrs and an equal number of ravished nymphs. Yirmi studies their urgent and acrobatic coupling whenever he is certain I am looking the other way, pressing down hard on his own desires. Ought I to take him to my preferred brothel one day soon or wait until he asks to come along with me?

As a treat, I permit my son to take a few hearty sips from my wine cup, which makes him as drowsy as Noach, just as I had hoped; he has laboured enough for one day.

While we are eating our almond cakes, Lucius' young wife appears in an upstairs window of the villa, watching me with curious eyes, which turns me into the eighth satyr at our table – and the only one lacking a consort. Blessed be Dionysos, for he soon sets my son snoring with his head on our table, which allows me to return to the bottom of the swimming pool under the concealment of the awning.

Pity the solitary widower who is travelling alone towards old age; as soon as my virile fantasies reach their climax, my fear of my own mortality takes hold of my mind and spirit. Will visitors to this pool a hundred years from now know that my life was as real to me as theirs is to them?

I am reworking Havvah's light-filled eyes – making them Leah's – when a drowsy Yirmi starts down the ladder to me.

As I put down my hammer, a revelation opens inside me: we need the Lord because He alone has no yesterday, today or tomorrow. Our only chance to dwell in a perpetual present is to cleave to Him.

15

Will men and women ever live out their lives without coming to recognize the scent of burning human flesh?

While walking home to Bethany, Yirmi and I encounter an unruly crowd of several hundred that has gathered below Methuselah's Hill. Above us, on the summit, where the grand old patriarch's tomb is said to have been before the Great Flood carried it away, three naked men have been bound to crosses.

A fourth victim, tied to a pole, has become a smouldering mass of melted flesh and bone. The sulphurous stink of the flaming pitch the executioners poured on him forces me to breathe only through my mouth, and I advise Yirmi to do the same. A fifth victim has been nailed to a cross that is taller than the others, and he is just a boy, fair-haired, slender and long-legged. Blood from the scourging he has been given is splattered over his shoulders and hips.

I suspect the Romans have chosen today for such a spectacle because of the impact it will have on the thousands of pilgrims already in Yerushalayim; these visitors will return to their towns and villages in lands as far away as Lusitania and Persia with word of how useless it is to defy the Emperor.

The crucified men plead for the clemency that they will never receive, for the very concept of mercy connotes weakness in the benighted language of Caesar. The force and tenacity of their shrieks mean that they were bound to their crosses but a short time earlier and are still many hours from death. I hear the boy's despair-filled cries most piercingly of all. Need you ask why? Do you not see my son beside me?

Know this, Yaphiel: one hears one's own greatest fears above all else, even if they come in a whisper.

As we walk on, I keep my son ahead of me where I can watch over him.

If I could make judgement cede to compassion, I think, *then the nails through the men's heels would come loose out of respect for their flesh, and their bindings would fall free, and the crosses themselves would shiver with gratitude for having been freed from their evil purpose.*

The crucified boy begs the Lord of Hosts for forgiveness, though for what he does not say. After a time, he uses the intimate name for God we rarely speak: Yahweh.

An incense-seller I approach tells me that the boy is named Aron ben Yaaqov. He is from a fishing village called Kaphar. So, although my son and I are too far away to see him clearly, I am fairly certain that his hands have been coarsened by fishing ropes and nets, and that he hears the breaking of waves before sleep on nearly every night.

If Yahweh grants young Aron mercy, then the salt air of the seashore will fill his lungs before death, and he will see himself aboard a sailing ship on a perfect spring night, skimming along the reflection of the moon towards home.

A woman from whom I purchase a cup of water flavoured with mint tells me that the boy and his father killed two Roman sentries. For what reason she does not know. Apparently his father escaped capture. Would the boy prefer that he had been caught so that he did not have to meet the Angel of Death alone? God forgive me, I fear that that is what I'd wish for in his place.

I ask you this, Yaphiel; even if this youth committed capital offences against the Empire, could not our governor, Pontius Pilatus, have simply exiled him to the island of Sardinia, where our brethren from Rome were banished by Tiberius, or some other far-off nowhere land? So powerful and well guarded a man as Pilatus could not possibly fear a beardless youth, which causes me to wonder what his secret motive might be. Does he murder our children to take away our future? Perhaps that is the symbolic meaning behind the death of Aron ben Yaaqov, and why – even today, so many years later – he still pleads to have his life returned to him in my dreams.

'I have done nothing!' Aron ben Yaaqov protests as my son and I do our best to make our way around the multitude.

The boy's words help me identify his age by a scale other than years, for he is plainly old enough to reason logically but too young to have learned that innocence is not a valid defence under the Roman system of justice – at least, not for Jews.

Legionaries guard the place of execution. Do you see them? No? Well, the rest of us do, and they are heavily armed, which is why even the most courageous amongst us do not rise up and free our brethren.

A noisy marketplace has grown up at the far end of the crowd. Stalls thatched with palm fronds have been erected, and musicians, dancers, fire-eaters and a troupe of dark-skinned Nubian acrobats are performing there. An overly friendly barber nibbling on a knot of cheese offers to shave my stubble for half the going rate, since he has cousins in Bethany and recognizes me as the man revived by Yeshua ben Yosef.

Yirmi and I refrain from speaking of the crucifixions as we make our way home. If you find that strange, then so much the better for you, because you have not been forced to learn that a public execution stifles nearly all speech. It is my experience, in fact, that the vast majority of those living through a long slow war rarely mention the conflict.

As we descend an escarpment on to which we've detoured and rejoin the road home, I ask Yirmi to say nothing to his aunts about what we have just witnessed – unless they make it clear that they already know. 'And please do not mention those young imbeciles who ridiculed us this morning,' I add as an afterthought.

Alexandros is rocking back and forth on the cracked millstone that marks the entrance to our town, but the tessera I left him is gone. I detect the faint odour of grilled onions as I approach him. His midday meal? I wave, but he is lost to our world.

Our crippled, hard-of-hearing old neighbour Weathervane hails us from the side garden of his scruffy little house, where he is busy weeding. His wife and daughters gave him that nickname many years before, after he mounted a wooden hand on his roof.

Next to greet me is one of Nahara's playmates, Akiva. He is seven years old and small for his age – dark-skinned with beautiful green cat-like eyes. He runs to me just before my son and I reach our street and, with his hands reaching up to my chest, entreats me – as he always does – to hold him upside down by his ankles and spin him in a circle. When I do, he shrieks with joy, and afterwards he walks around in a dizzy arc, as though glutted with drink, and falls in a heap. Who can say why he delights in losing his balance, but I'm glad he does, since it gives Yirmi and me a chance to laugh with him.

A ragged, bare-chested Samaritan approaches me as I am helping Akiva get to his feet. A bucket of water hangs from each end of a pole balanced over his shoulders. His wife and two children trail after him. The tiny boy and girl cling to their mother. They are barefoot and filthy, and they have immense, deeply shadowed, mud-coloured eyes.

The Samaritan's hair and eyebrows have become a warren for lice. I press two copper coins into his hand and suggest the barber I met a little while earlier, for his head will need to be shaved and oiled if he is to rid himself of this plague.

Yaphiel, my father once told me a brief story that I'd like you to consider before I reach home and the pleasant surprise awaiting me there. For the simple reason that it was the first time that I considered – in that vague, ticklish way that insights come to children – that life sometimes gives us no favourable options and that we must choose the path of least suffering for ourselves and the people we love.

When he was a boy in Yerushalayim, my father witnessed a team of horses dragging the bloody carcass of a bull into the square outside the governor's palace. Sewn inside the great creature's belly were a bearded man and a girl who looked to be seven or eight years old. Their heads poked out of two gaps in the creature's tightly stitched skin.

My father was told that the man was a Roman who had poisoned his father in order to inherit his wealth. As to why the little girl was sentenced to this torture along with her father, no one seemed to know.

The bull's carcass was left in the blazing sun from early morning until mid-afternoon, when it was dragged off to the Imperial Theatre, where four starving bears were released from their cages. As was to be expected, the crowd exulted in the man's shrieks as the lumbering brown beasts tore into him, but even the sight of his head ripped from his shoulders did not make up for their disappointment when they realized that the girl had not uttered a single shriek or plea for mercy. You see, she must have already been dead when the bull was hauled into the theatre, though everyone could see that her eyes had been open – bulging, in fact – when the bears bounded out of their cages towards their meal.

Apparently her father had managed to strangle her before reaching the theatre, my father told me. When I asked how he could know that, he replied that people who are choked to death end up with bulging eyes. Kneeling down and gripping my shoulders, he added, 'But I can be sure that's what the man did because that's how I'd have killed you, my son.'

16

When my son and I turn the final corner into our street, we are stunned to find Mia and my cousin Ion waiting for us. My sister is wearing a frown. 'Your fame has spread,' she tells me.

A hundred or so paces beyond her, in front of my house, a throng has blocked the street all the way down to the southern perimeter of Bethany and what is left of its ancient town
walls.

'I have nothing to give them – no words of wisdom,' I say.

'I have been speaking to a few of them,' Ion tells me in Greek, 'and they are good souls – respectable citizens.' He grips my arm as though to convince me. And his use of the expression *respectable citizens* – so typical of the Alexandrian Jews – gladdens me. 'If you bless them, they will disperse,' he assures me.

As we head home, Mia notices the dried blood on my skinned hand. I tell her that I had a terrific battle with the canvas awning over the swimming pool. 'And I lost,' I tell her with what I hope is a charming grin.

She stops me and studies my palm as though the scrapes will reveal my future.

'See if you can discover what we're having for supper,' I suggest, but my effort at humour proves a failure, and she returns my hand to me with a withering look.

'Tell me what really happened,' she says menacingly.

'I slipped in the street.'

'Do I look like an idiot?' she asks.

'Mia, I'm too tired to quarrel.'

'Did you get into a scuffle with someone?'

'No, of course not.'

She turns to Yirmi and gives him the imperious squint she learned from our mother.

'Dad tripped,' he agrees.

'You make a fine pair of liars,' she tells us, 'but just tell me if this injury has anything to do with Annas.'

'No,' I say. 'Look, Mia, it was just some drunken Roman young men. They were eager to ruin someone's day, and for some reason they chose me.'

I do not have the heart to deny each person who seeks my benediction or healing an opportunity to speak to me for a short while about their tribulations, and they plainly value this chance to be heard by a man who has passed a second time through the Gate of Birth, so it takes me well over an hour to finish with them. Whenever they question me about my resurrection, however, I steer our conversation back towards their ailments, since it is likely that one or more of them are spies sent by Annas to test the oath of silence that he forced on me. Hearing of the events that shattered the lives of so many strong-looking men and women reminds me that we never know what sorrows other people carry inside their hearts.

Once I am safely inside my locked front door, Cousin Ariston sits me down in my alcove and brings me a bowl of bread sopped in warm milk and honey, and Binyamin, my nephew, carries in a basin of hot water tempered with vinegar so that he can wipe the dirt from my bruised knee and hand.

With my family watching over me, I permit myself to close my eyes and drift away. I only awaken when my grandfather enters. He puts Ayin down on my clothes chest, his perch in the late afternoon, since from there he can observe the progress of sunset from my window.

Shimon sits beside me and takes my hand. He tells me that I shall always be his beloved little grandson and asks after my health. After that, we do not speak; along with Ayin, we watch the evening sky shed the blue of wisdom and dress in the pink and gold of mercy and kingship.

Shimon embraces me before returning to his room, and the pressure against my ribs makes me moan. 'Are you really all right, son?' he asks.

'Just exhausted,' I lie.

From out of nowhere, Nahara comes running towards me, but I grab her before she can crash into me.

'Dad, what's a *mashal?*' she asks.

It is while I am explaining the concept of a parable to her that Marta steps in from the courtyard, arm in arm with Yeshua's mother. I have not seen Maryam for more than two years, since the wedding of her youngest daughter, Sarah. Her hair has greyed over her temples, but she looks vigorous and happy.

I release my daughter's hand and get to my feet. I do not know what Maryam makes of the unshaved and barefoot labourer that I have become, but I see a woman who has nursed, bathed and fed five children to adulthood and buried four others and who has been kind enough to share Yeshua with me since I was eight years old.

When she spots me, she thrusts her hands over her mouth as though I am a gift she had no right to expect, which makes me shiver; it seems too great a responsibility to have such a central place in her life.

'*Dodee,*' she says, reaching out to me.

Her touch brings me back to the warm evenings of Natzeret, when we would eat our suppers in her courtyard. I smile at the memory, but she does not, because holding the boy-turned-man who saved her twelve-year-old son from drowning always means too much at first.

Maryam was the first adult outside my family who took the time to see me not as the son of my parents or a friend of her son but as a person in my own right. In truth, she did not much care for me at first, and so she also taught me that our initial impressions of others can change, though I later learned that it often takes a terrible trauma to make us do so.

As always, Yeshua seems to be standing beside us when she and I separate. Two individuals of different ages who are joined for ever by their fondness for a third person is a form of love that has no name I am aware of in either Hebrew, Aramaic or Greek, but perhaps there is a language in some far corner of our world with greater awareness of the human heart. Indeed, I hope there is, because what Yeshua's mother and I share has grown dearer to me with each passing year.

Maryam holds me away from her and leans her head back to study me, and this ought to be a moment of solidarity between us, but instead – absurdly – it merely reminds me of how much taller than her I have become. Do we ever grow used to the true height of the adults who ruled over our childhood?

She must be thinking much the same thing, because she gives way to easy laughter, which allows me to do the same.

She and I sit side by side at supper. When she addresses me, she takes my hand – a habit she had with Yosef and her children for as long as I can remember. I notice a throbbing in her jaw whenever there is a pause in our conversation, however. I begin to suspect that Yeshua has sent her with a message for me that she will deliver only when she and I are alone.

We are twelve at supper: Maryam, Yirmi, Nahara, Mia, Marta, my cousins Ion and Ariston, Grandfather Shimon, my nephew Binyamin and my niece Yehudit and her husband Rafael. Gephen, who would paw and whine for scraps if we permitted him to stay with us, has been banished to the courtyard.

We eat *patinas* stuffed with leeks, carrots and coriander. Marta and Mia have prepared two different styles, the first with a healthy dose of the kosher *garum* that Lucius gave me as a gift, the second without, because I am of the opinion that the fermented juices of fish would better be used as fertilizer.

A number of strangers and neighbours come to our door over the course of the meal, soliciting my blessing, but Marta tells them that I am already asleep. Even to those who are adamant and tactless she does not raise her voice, since we have an honoured guest with us.

No one talks of the executions that have taken place. Or of my death and revival. I know from experience that these two subjects will, as a result, wait for me in my bed.

My sisters talk with Maryam of the old friends we had in Sepphoris. Her husband Yosef and my father – along with thousands of other woodworkers, bricklayers and stonemasons – restored life to that city after the Romans crushed an uprising in the Galilee and turned nearly every street to rubble.

After Maryam takes a final almond biscuit, she leans close to me and asks in a whisper that I escort her back to her niece's house. And so, finally, we are to be alone.

Even at this late hour, the streets are filled with pilgrims conversing in animated voices and eating little treats. The gleaming lanterns everywhere give our town an atmosphere of celebration. I bless all those who approach me and, as is my habit, hand out our leftover bread to those who are hungry.

Maryam and I take a circuitous route to Yerushalayim to avoid the crucified men on Methuselah's Hill. When we pass the small bridge and dry riverbed where Mia found her first abandoned baby eight years before, I tell Maryam how my sister rushed the cold and listless child to a wet nurse she knew in Yerushalayim. 'It was when the little girl opened her eyes and reached out a straining hand', I say in triumph, 'that Mia discovered her life's work.'

After praising the way my sister has grown into such an industrious and good-hearted woman, Maryam looks across the ancient hills of Judaea as though she is searching for what she has little hope of finding. She removes her headscarf and shakes the tight weave out of her hair. I wish to ask what is bothering her, but, at the moment, our age difference seems to make that impossible.

An evening marketplace has grown up on the far side of the riverbed, and a Galilean wine-seller has decorated his stall with lanterns glowing red, blue and yellow through fabrics of different colours. I reason that Maryam might tell me her troubling thoughts if she takes a drink with me. I buy a cup for the two of us, and we sit on my cape under a plane tree turned into a dark many-armed giant by the moonlight.

Sharing our wine – drinking from one cup – becomes our unspoken oath, certifying that, although we have not spoken in two years, we are still – and shall for ever be – family.

'I am working for a wealthy Roman Jew in the Upper Town,' I tell Maryam, hoping that some light conversation will put her at ease. 'I've made a ferocious-looking Ziz at the bottom of his swimming pool, and I've put a menorah on his head, like a crown.'

'You and your birds!' she says, laughing girlishly. 'You used to drag Yeshua off to the most outlandish places to watch them.' She wags a finger of rebuke at me. 'I used to worry that you two would be swallowed by quicksand. Or eaten by crocodiles!'

Would I like her to believe I've changed hardly a whit from the boy I was? Leaning towards her, I whisper, 'It would have been thrilling to have to escape a hungry crocodile on occasion!'

After we share another laugh, she falls silent. Perhaps a secret of mine will prompt her to reveal her concerns to me. 'I'll tell you something no one knows,' I say. 'Adam and Havvah are talking with Ziz in my mosaic. I've given the first man my face and the first woman Leah's.'

'I know what my Yeshua would say about that,' she says confidently.

'What would he say?' I ask.

'We are all of us Adam and all of us Havvah, for the moment we realize we are alive – and separate from God – we become exiled from Eden.' She takes a quick sip of wine, licks her lips and hands the cup back to me.

'I had a more . . . selfish reason for choosing my own face,' I reply while waving away the bothersome mosquitoes that have just found us.

'What reason is that?'

'I want something of me to remain after I'm gone.' As I speak, I notice how my Galilean accent grows more prominent when I converse with Maryam.

'And yet stone is a poor . . . vessel for carrying who you are into the future,' she says.

'But what if it's my only option?'

Maryam looks up to the firmament and places a motherly hand at the back of my neck. 'All the stars and the smell of this spring night . . . Nothing can take them from us. We are here now, and there is so much beauty everywhere.'

'But is that beauty enough?'

'Oh, Lazar,' she says, 'now that I've buried my husband and lived through more than half a century of winters, it seems a luxury even to ask that question.' As she gazes past me – towards Yosef, I believe – tears sprout in her eyes.

'I'm sorry if I've upset you,' I tell her.

She squeezes my hand and fights to smile, and it's her effort to appear more resilient than she is that makes panic beat inside my ears. 'Is there something wrong with Yeshua?' I ask.

Her lips tremble. I feel as if I am standing on a needle point and about to tumble off – and the needle is made of all the terrible things that might take her son from the two of us.

'I'm worried that he is in danger,' she says.

The night darkens around us. 'Why?' I whisper.

She dries her eyes. 'Can we keep walking? Sitting still like this . . . It's no good for me.'

As we start to walk, she says, 'I suspect that my son has remained in Yerushalayim for an important reason, but he won't tell me what it is.'

'You've asked him?'

'Yes, two days ago.'

'What did he say?'

'He said that it was better for me not to know – safer for both of us. But I was too worried to talk of anything else. I haven't felt like this in many years – since he was small, when we all feared he would die young. Do you remember?'

'Yes, of course.'

'I never told you or him that, shortly after he was born, an oracle from Cyrene told me that Yeshua would always be in danger, because great good attracts great evil.'

As I study her worried face, I realize that I have begun to think of Annas and Yeshua as opponents in a war that extends all the way up into the Throne World. Perhaps Yeshua was destined from birth to become the enemy of tyrants and despots.

'Do you think what the oracle told you is true?' I ask.

'Yes, through my son – unfortunately – I've learned it is.' She slaps at a mosquito that had landed on her arm. 'When I insisted that Yeshua tell me of his plans,' she continues, 'he told me that it would be better if he had no mother or father. He said that this was why he'd never remarried.'

'I don't follow you,' I say.

'He began to weep when he told me he wanted no parents,' Maryam says, as though excusing him. When I tried to comfort him, he pushed me away and ran off. It took me until this afternoon to understand. I knew then that I had to see you.'

'What did you understand?'

'If he considers my feelings, he won't be able to carry out his plans. He must try to live as if he has no mother – as if there is no one who would suffer for the rest of her life if anything bad were to happen to him.'

So he is about to put himself in grave peril.

It is not necessary for me to say that; that is what our tense silence along the rest of the way to her niece's house confirms all too well.

17

When I saw Yeshua carried away by the River Jordan, the surge of fear in me left no room for thought. I was in the frigid water without knowing how I'd come to be there. The current was relentless, and I fought it at first, but when I looked ahead at Yeshua, who was struggling to keep his head above water, I let my arms and legs go limp.

We were both then twelve years old.

I do not know how I knew that if I restrained the urge to fight against the current – if I surrendered to its will – it might carry me towards him much faster.

My father had taught me how to swim when I was nine, having predicted – correctly – that I would often wade into marshes, streams and lakes in order to observe birds more closely.

Yeshua was gulping for breath and straining to reach back to me.

I found myself being driven closer him, as I had hoped. Had he fought his way into a gentler channel? It seemed likely at that time, but in truth he had been slowed by his feet scraping against the stony riverbed; later we would discover his painful cuts.

The true wonder of it all was that, when his head went under the surface of the water and I lunged for him, I caught hold of his tunic on my first try. My feet soon found purchase against a large boulder, and I hooked my arms under his shoulders, and my next memory is of dragging him on to a sandbar and from there up on to the riverbank. Pulling him out of the water required only the decision to do so; my strength seemed to have doubled or even tripled.

After I dragged Yeshua through the rushes fringing the river into a clearing, he pressed a hand of thanks to my chest, too weak to speak. His long hair was slicked to his neck and brow, and he was crying with relief. His eyes shone with an otherworldly light, as though his near-death was a sign of God's glory.

Yeshua's eyes were dark brown but rimmed in black, like his father's.

It never occurred to me at the time that he might have been testing me. Or trying to alter his mother's feelings towards his study partner and friend. I only began to consider those possibilities more than twenty years later, after fleeing Bethany and going into exile. And yet, whenever I remember his tearful gratitude towards me, and our hands locked together, and the weight of his soaked flesh as I hauled him on to the riverbank, I am certain that this near-catastrophe came about just as he had told me: he had been lost in fervent prayer one moment and the next was being carried downstream.

Yosef had heard his son's cries for help and came dashing down the pathway from our encampment soon after we reached safety. A few moments later, Maryam ran to us as well, barefoot, holding her shawl in her white-knuckled fist, panting for breath. I tried to tell them what had happened, but everything had taken place so quickly – and still seemed so confused in my mind – that my words trailed off after just a few sentences. 'In any case, we're both all right now,' I concluded.

Yeshua told his parents all that he considered essential – that I had jumped into the water and rescued him.

Yosef embraced me so hard that even then I realized that he was not just holding me but also the future that the waters had nearly stolen from him.

'Your courage has saved my family,' he whispered.

While he ministered to the cuts on Yeshua's feet and legs, Maryam cupped my chin in her hand and looked at me as though she were seeing me for the first time. 'Bless you, beloved Lazar,' she said. 'I'll never forget you in my prayers.'

It was the first time she had ever called me *dodee* – beloved. Very soon Yeshua and I would adopt this form of greeting as well.

'It wasn't courage,' I admitted to her and Yosef, and I explained how fear had taken hold of me and determined all I had done. 'Even pulling Yeshua out of the water and on to the bank was done before I'd even thought of it. The strangest thing of all is that I never felt so powerful.'

'The River Jordan turned you into Shimshon!' Yeshua told me, laughing in the wild and exultant way of those who can still feel the terror of death in their gut.

'It's true!' I said, awed by the potent magic inside my body.

Maryam laughed with us, then apologized to me; for what I didn't then know, and I didn't ask, because she had begun to sob.

It was the first time a woman had ever cried in my arms, and I was overwhelmed with her compact fragility – and my own failure to know how to help her.

That evening, I wove together clues out of the hundreds of times Maryam and I had spoken, and I realized that she must have apologized to me because she had never trusted me or even particularly liked me.

As Yeshua watched me trying to comfort his mother, his eyes continued to shine with their stark, mysterious light, and he smiled at me in that way that made him seem much older than he was. At such moments, it seemed that he might not be the young man we knew him to be, that he might, in fact, be what we never dared say: a prophet.

18

After bidding Maryam goodnight at the door to her niece's house, I head to the modest inn near the Woodworker's Synagogue where Yeshua usually lodges in Yerushalayim, vowing not to start a quarrel with him even if he had deliberately put himself in serious danger.

If you gave birth to a boy who could make visible what is hidden, would you not always fear that he would reveal what those in power would prefer to conceal?

A thousand sleepless nights Maryam must have endured while thinking of her son, and yet I am certain that she would not give up a single one of them – not even if the Lord asked her.

Because I would not.

On entering the inn, I discover that Hozai, the owner, is away. A new assistant – sweaty and unkempt, and reeking of the barnyard creatures with whom he must share his home – tells me that my old friend and his followers have not been there for weeks.

'But . . . but he always stays here,' I stutter. 'He would have told me if he was staying anywhere else.'

'Apparently he forgot to tell you.'

'That seems impossible.'

'Are you listening to anything I say? He wasn't here!' The man takes out a knife from behind his desk, faces away from me and starts cleaning his fingernails.

How do I explain to him that such indifference is a luxury no Jew can afford? 'I saw a boy crucified today,' I tell him. 'He couldn't have been more than thirteen.'

He swings around to me with an indignant curl to his lips. 'What's that got to do with me?'

'Terrible things can happen at any moment. We need to help each other. And I need to know if you have seen Yeshua ben Yosef – even if he asked you not to say so. We're old friends, and I . . .'

'Like I said, I haven't seen him in weeks,' he interrupts in a surly voice.

Back on the street, I come to the only reasonable conclusion: Yeshua led me to believe he was staying at his usual inn – and did not share the truth with me – because he feared I might be compelled to give up his whereabouts to Annas or another of our enemies.

Nikodemos ben Gurion is the only good friend of Yeshua's who lives all year round in Yerushalayim. Although we have known each other for the better part of a decade, our friendship began in earnest only after I started work on a mosaic in his villa six months before. It took me nearly seven weeks to complete his extensive and eminent family tree – sprouting from King David! – and it adorns the entire western wall of his atrium.

We are extremely fortunate to have Nikodemos as an ally, since he is a well-respected and powerful Pharisee serving on our ruling council, the Sanhedrin; his authoritative voice has saved Yeshua from charges of blasphemy on a handful of occasions and, at least once, from allegations of heresy.

If the truth be told, I have never been entirely comfortable in his presence, however, for his manners are so refined that I grow embarrassed by my own rough ways. Does he notice how I hide my callused hands behind my back when we are together? I am also secretly envious of his collection of ancient scrolls; at least two of them are so rare that their knowledge would probably be lost to us if his copies were destroyed. One of them is a *Book of the Just* that is more than five centuries old, and the other, scripted by the renowned Petros of Alexandria, is *The Story of Iddo the Seer*.

Nikodemos' personal slave Anekletos answers my knocks with the traditional Judaean formulae of welcome and sends his young son to tell their master of my arrival. On receiving word that Nikodemos will receive me, Anekletos escorts me to the *triclinium*, where his master is reading by the light of a standing menorah and munching on small round biscuits. 'Eli, there you are!' he says with an affectionate smile. Sensing that it is more than just the uphill walk to his home that has left me out of breath, he rushes to me and takes my hands. 'What's wrong? Is it your leg, my boy? I've heard it's been giving you difficulties.'

'No, I'm fine. I just don't have all my strength back yet. And I'm worried about Yeshua.'

With his hand steadying me at my back, he escorts me to the red silk couch where he has been reading. I accept a cup of mulled wine from Anekletos to avoid giving offence.

'Start at the beginning,' Nikodemos tells me, sensing my apprehension.

After I speak of Maryam's concerns, I make him vow not to let Yeshua know that she came to see me; I would not wish to risk creating a deeper rift between mother and son. I do not mention Yeshua's suspicions of Yehudah of Kerioth, since I do not know what Nikodemos has been told. When I mention that our old friend has not been staying at his usual inn and that I don't know where he might be, my host pulls his head back like a hen and puffs out his lips with irritation. 'But he told me he'd be with you!'

'He visited me, but he's staying somewhere else,' I reply.

'Of late, Yeshua has become as unpredictable as an eclipse,' Nikodemos says, shrugging as if to say that we have no choice but to resign ourselves to his whims.

'What do you think he's planning?' I ask.

Nikodemos considers my question as Anekletos refills his master's cup. 'For some time, I've sensed him moving towards an important moment in his life, though he seems to be sneaking up on it, so to speak – as if to draw no attention to himself.'

'Have you any idea what it might be?'

'No, he hasn't told me.'

'And do you know where he is right now?'

'No, but Loukas and Yohanon told me today that he'll be leaving with them for the Galilee at first light. They said he'd be preaching the day after tomorrow in Capernaum.'

And yet he told me he would try to return to me in the evening, I think, which means that he wants to keep Nikodemos and me guessing – and probably most of his other friends as well.

My host reads the continued concern in my countenance. In cautious voices, we discuss possible reasons for Yeshua's deception and conclude that he must have predicted that my resurrection would deepen the conflict between him and our priests.

Nikodemos puts his arm over my shoulder and assures me – nodding in his kindly, authoritative way – that Yeshua knows how to protect himself. 'With God's blessing, you and Yeshua will both have long and fulfilled lives,' he adds. 'And don't forget, I'm expecting another mosaic from you after you finish at Lucius' villa!'

Is it odd that a friend twenty-two years my senior can ease my preoccupations by using only his voice and hands? Perhaps this is how those of us who have lost a father too young become aware of the nature and depth of the void inside us.

After I have wiped away my tears, a candle in a window at the far end of the room catches my attention. Its halo – like the diffuse glow around the polestar – seems to have a mysterious purpose. I step to it as though compelled by a dream. And beyond its light, in the darkness of the firmament, I see Annas watching me from far away, through sorcery.

I am with a friend, and I deserve a moment of peace, and I won't permit you to intrude on us, I tell him, and here, in this room, my powers must be greater than his, because his hostile gaze vanishes from my mind.

The windows in Nikodemos' dining room are made of highly polished mica. We mosaicists call this astonishing material by its Roman name, *lapis specularis*. It is a stone mined and cut in distant Hispania Tarraconensis, far in the west, and I sometimes use papyrus-thin slices of it in my work to add resplendence to the eyes of my figures. But its transparence is always imperfect, and now, as I move left and right, forward and back, the lanterns and lamps in the night-time city waver and ripple in strange and elusive ways. For a moment, I also catch my own ghostly reflection, which chills me, for I seem to be imprisoned in a place where no one but Yeshua can help me – on a bridge between death and life.

A man standing by a window overlooking a city that has always seemed too crowded for him thinks of how Yehoshua commanded the moon and sun to stop still in their paths. He wishes that he, too, had that mastery over all the stars and planets, and all the people of the earth. *Then there would be no death,* he thinks.

Extending his hand over a candle flame, he is grateful for its sting because it makes him realize that he is being moved about the streets of Yerushalayim and Bethany by forces he senses only vaguely. He has lost control.

I understand almost nothing about what is happening to me, he thinks. *I shall have to look for signs in everything I see and hear.*

The Temple stands in the distance, silent and imposing under the moonlight. Nikodemos comes up behind me so silently that I start when he places his hand on my back.

After apologizing, he asks for my thoughts. When I tell him, he quotes the prophet Yirmihayu in a whisper. "'All your adversaries, every one of them, will enter captivity.'"

It would be rude to challenge the faith of my host, so I do not say, *But what if our adversaries may be more formidable than we ever imagined?*

After I leave Nikodemos, I head off to my usual brothel, sensing that only in the arms of a courtesan shall I be able to free myself from the feeling of dread in my belly. But so many pilgrims have been led there by Eros, and they are in such an impatient mood, that I am unable to talk my way past them to the owner, who has long valued my loyalty and who would surely escort me inside without delay. Street prostitutes frequent the rotting alleyways near the tanneries – mostly Judaean and Galilean young women and men, but Nubians with polished black skin have started appearing amongst them of late, and their statuesque, otherworldly grace seems the cure for what ails me, so I make my way there.

Unfortunately, the Lord of Creation abandons me when the Nubian young woman I have chosen kneels before me, and she and I are unable to entice him to return.

*

As though sensing my despair, Gephen steals into bed with me that night. He curls into my belly and purrs consolingly, as if to remind me that, at the very least, Yeshua is far away and safe.

When I wake in the night, I tiptoe to my children's room. I watch them sleep, for it is by their side that I am still able to believe that I can choose the future I want.

I cannot say how, but observing the two of them also graces me with a revelation: Annas would have ordered at least one spy to watch my every movement and make certain that I have been keeping silent about my resurrection. The man would have been told to plunge his dagger into my heart if I were to slip up even once.

Goliath . . .

Being dead for two days must have slowed down the workings of my mind, for I ought to have understood much sooner who he was and why he has been trailing me.

19

Yirmi and I step outside into the chilly dawn shortly after cock-crow, intending to visit Yeshua's mother and then head to Lucius' villa. But a large group of people are waiting for my blessings outside my door, including an ancient widow with so crooked a back that she resembles the Hebrew letter *dalet*.

My blessing is not enough for her, and she begs me for a charm that will permit her to stand up straight. At a loss to know what to do, I give her one of the tesserae I always keep in my scrip. She tucks it under her tongue and assures me – tears rolling down her cheeks – that she will tell her children and her children's children about the *mitzvah* I did for her this day – and never take my gift from her mouth.

Will the hope I've given her only deepen her despair when no miracle takes the bend from her back? And will the others I soon bless return for vengeance when they find that their ills have not disappeared?

Yirmi and I find Maryam still asleep, so we leave word with her niece, Helena, that Nikodemos has assured me that Yeshua is returning this morning to the safety of the Galilee.

On our walk to work, I look behind us whenever we turn a corner, but I do not spot Goliath. In all likelihood he has grown more cautious. Or, if good fortune is with me, then Annas has realized by now that I shall keep my vow to him and has withdrawn his henchman.

A sense of embarking on a journey – of escaping forced isolation – eases my heart as we reach the Upper Town. There, the swallows of Yerushalayim – who are the most wild-hearted and talkative in Zion – dart around us as though guiding us to treasure. A woolly-looking carob tree peers at us over the disintegrating wall of an old villa, greeting us with its shimmering brown pods. I face the sunrise and breathe in on its crimson-and-rose radiance, and, when my son and I overhear morning prayers coming through the open window of a house near by, we repeat them to ourselves, hand in hand, eager to embrace the community of words that we have inherited from Mosheh.

My bruised rib voices few complaints this morning, which is a solemn relief. But the continuing pains in my right leg make it difficult for me to climb uphill. Still, I refuse my son's assistance and deny any discomfort, since I do not want him to worry about me. When I am forced to pause on one occasion, I tell him that I want to admire the exuberant purple wildflowers growing out of the ancient roof tiles of a house just ahead – and it does indeed seem worth reminding ourselves of the colourful affection of plants for the sun.

We no longer see the glories of God that have become familiar, I think when I finally turn my eyes from the blossoms.

'What's wrong?' Yirmi asks a few moments later, because, without realizing it, I have begun staring at him.

'Nothing,' I tell him, though I catch myself wondering what I fail to see in his face because we are together every day. Did he always have my mother's delicate lips, and is it fair of me to be sure from the suspicious way he looks at me that he will grow to share her love of secrecy?'

Blue.

I see now that that is the colour of my love for him, because it is the colour of the sky and the sea, and of their union at the horizon, which, in the language of Torah, is also the home of all those who love honestly and fully.

When I tell my son this, he says, 'Father, you don't speak like anyone else I know.'

In case I might interpret his comment as an insult, he grimaces comically and sticks out his tongue. Leah used to call it his frog face.

It fills me with hope to know that he is again at ease with me after the humiliations of the previous day.

Soon after we set off again, I recall that the Gate of Sabbath will open today at sundown. My sisters and I shall then join hands with our children and with Grandfather Shimon, and – together with Gephen and Ayin – we shall board our Ark and continue our pilgrimage to the centre of God's creation, as we always have.

What I most love about the Sabbath are the sacred prayers we speak, which are soft and honeyed in my mouth, as though created by God to feed the first man and woman and all their children.

Yirmi and I work all day on my mosaic at the bottom of Lucius' swimming pool, and it is a relief to inhabit my hands. In the late morning, my employer visits us. From the rim at the pool, he surveys our latest improvements with a hopeful face. At length, he nods to himself – satisfied with what he has seen – and asks how much longer the mosaic will take.

This is a question to which he already knows the answer, but he asks me every few days all the same.

'I'm still uncertain,' I answer, wiping the sweat from my brow with my hand.

'But seriously, Eli, a week, two weeks . . . What do you think?'

'A month if you keep me talking!'

Despite his ugly frown and grumbling retreat, Lucius reveals how pleased he is with my progress by serving my son and me his best Anatolian wine with our midday meal.

Late that afternoon, as we are making ready to leave, he leads an elderly Roman guest to the pool. The visitor has grey whiskers on his cheeks and stunning sky-blue eyes, and his languid, gracious, feminine hand gestures make me think of Aphroditos, the bearded Aphrodite worshipped in Cyprus.

After we exchange greetings, the elderly gentleman, whose name is Paullus, gestures towards Yirmi. 'And is this your son?' he asks.

'Yes, his name is Yirmiyahu, though we call him Yirmi.'

I summon the boy to come to me and put my hands on his shoulders, since he looks as if he is searching his mind for an incantation that will render him invisible.

'Do you understand me when I speak Greek, Yirmi?' Paullus asks.

'Naí, olígin ti,' he replies, meaning only a little.

'I'm afraid my son is being modest,' I interject. 'He takes lessons from a learned master of Greek and is fast becoming fluent.'

'My teacher, Rabbi Elad, was born in Elis,' Yirmi explains.

'I've been two Elis on two occasions!' Paullus tells us, smiling brightly in order to encourage my son, which wins me to him straight away.

'Then you've seen . . . seen the statue of Zeus . . . in Olympia?' Yirmi stammers excitedly.

'Indeed I have, young man.'

'Is he really covered in gold and ivory? And as gigantic as Rabbi Elad says? Will I be able to go right up to him and touch him if I visit?'

Paullus laughs good-naturedly at my son's enthusiasm. 'The statue of Zeus of which you speak is ten times the height of the tallest man,' he replies. 'And the shine of the dawn sun off his golden robes is blinding. But what is truly astonishing about him is that he always seems ready to stand and speak. His hands, his sandalled feet, his lips . . . every part of him seems ready to come to life, which is why it is said that the sculptor, Phidias, must also have been a masterful sorcerer.' Paullus raises his hands in the way Romans do to signify obedience to Olympus. 'So many visitors from distant ports have fainted from God-terror while approaching Zeus that the residents recommend that one always worship him accompanied by a local. They call the condition Olympian Vertigo.'

He uses the word *sunkope* to indicate the onset of dizziness and loss of strength that overwhelms worshippers; it is a beautiful, wedge-shaped word that I had somehow forgotten.

Lucius nibbles on a small roundel of cheese as we converse. He explains that he has an important business deal with a mining developer pending and that he has been told by his personal augur to eat only that one food until it is concluded, since the Latin word for cheese – *caseus* – has a similar sound to the word golden, *aureus*.

The four of us talk more of the marvels of the Greek world, but our conversation soon reaches the impasse of those whose differing social positions will always prevent them from embarking on true friendship. Paullus puts us at ease, however, with his generous-hearted smile and tells me he has two questions for me. 'If you will permit me, that is.'

'Of course,' I reply.

'Why are the flames black in your menorah?'

To encourage my son to participate in our conversation, I ask him to reply for me.

'Because they symbolize the letters of the Torah,' he says, gazing down as if I might reprimand him for not giving the reply that I would have given; to be thirteen years old is truly to be a prisoner of all one's misgivings.

'Tell me more, young man!' Paullus says, bemused twinkling in his eyes.

Yirmi turns to me and gives me a pleading look, so I say, 'The letters of the Torah are generally written in black against the white background of vellum or papyrus.'

'But why do you symbolize them as flames?'

'Under the right circumstances, each letter of the Torah may catch fire.'

'What circumstances are those?'

'When the person chanting scripture seeks the hidden life of the God who dwells deep below the letters. And when the Holy One wishes to be found. The flames serve as torches, lighting the way of those who receive His grace.'

'Are these flames real?' he asks.

I have been asked that question before and offer Paullus my practised reply. 'Are the numbers that you use to do calculations in your head – one, two, three and so on . . . Are they real?'

He takes a sharp inhale of breath. 'I . . . I've never considered that question.'

'If they were merely an illusion, would you be able to add them together?' I continue.

'Ah, I see what you mean,' he says, though his voice is unsure. He furrows his brow, then laughs, amused by his own confusion – a sure sign of a curious and intelligent mind. 'And have you ever found any of your gods this way?' he asks.

'We only have one God,' I remind him. 'And I have never seen Him. But I have a close companion from childhood who has been so blessed.'

'I would very much like to meet this man.'

'I will tell him of your desire,' I say.

At the time, I am certain that I am merely being polite and that I shall never try to bring Paullus together with Yeshua, but I am wrong.

'And now my second question,' he continues. 'Who are the two figures in the great bird's eyes?'

'Ah, that is just a bit of silliness,' I say with a dismissive laugh, in order to hide my true sentiments.

'What kind of silliness?'

'A visual pun.'

What I tell him is true enough, but I do not mention the deeper meaning in my design, since I would never reveal any of the greater mysteries to any man or woman who has not been initiated.

'You see,' I continue, 'the name of the bird is Ziz, who is mentioned in the Psalms. He is the king of the birds, just as Leviathan is king of the fish. In his right eye, I have placed a woman because Greek word *kore* means both beloved daughter and pupil of the eye.'

'So who is the *kore* in the bird's *kore*?' he asks.

'All girls and women,' I tell him. 'Symbolically speaking, of course.'

'And in Ziz's left eye?'

'That would be you and all other men.'

His eyes brighten as though I have performed an astounding magic trick just for him. When he and Lucius look at each other, they smile with fond complicity. Paullus takes his friend's hand and holds it over his heart. Looking closely at their locked eyes, I understand that the old gentleman once played an important role in Lucius' life. And perhaps still does.

'I'd like all your guests to see themselves in the mosaic,' I say to Paullus when he turns to me again. 'If they look closely enough, that is.'

'And if they don't look closely?'

'This may sound rude, but I don't make my mosaics for those who refuse to observe the world and themselves closely. And I try to surround myself with people who do not run from riddles and paradoxes. "And their eyes were opened, and they knew that they were naked,"' I quote from the Torah.

'Eliezer has given us some wisdom from our holy book, which was written by an ancient prophet named Mosheh,' Lucius tells his friend.

'The people whose eyes were opened were the first man and woman,' I add.

I point to Adam and Havvah in my mosaic. Paullus kneels down at the rim of the pool for a closer look, and, when he looks back at me, he shows me a mischievous grin. Is he reacting to anatomical accuracy I have given my figures or something greater he has glimpsed in them?

20

Is it death that has made me forgetful?

That evening, it is my niece Yehudit who makes ready to light the Sabbath lamps, so I ask Mia why she has delegated this holy duty to Marta's daughter.

'But, Eli,' she says, stunned, 'I touched you while you were in your tomb. I'm ritually unclean.'

According to the laws of Mosheh, all who come in direct contact with the dead remain tainted for seven days. But what about the dead themselves?

The panic rising in my chest overflows my limits and spills out – unfairly, I realize – as rage. 'How many days must the corpse himself wait to regain his purity?' I demand.

Mia winces at my use of the word *corpse,* then stutters an apology.

Grandfather Shimon – our family elder – pats at the air to indicate our need for calm and asks me to keep anger out of my voice. But no one in the room ventures a reply to my question; none of us can recall any verse from the Torah that might prove of guidance.

'For now, we'll conduct the ceremony as we always have,' Marta rushes to say, doing her best to rescue the evening. She asks me with her eyes not to make any trouble, and I would do as she requests, but she then makes a proposal that I consider a veiled attack. 'If you want,' she says, 'Mia and I can go to the Temple tomorrow to ask what to do. Maybe we were wrong to assume we were unclean.'

'Have you lost your mind?' I shout. 'I'd never put my life in the hands of Caiaphas and the other priests! What if they tell me I'm forbidden from embracing my children ever again?'

'Eli, don't raise your voice to me!' Marta warns.

'I'll talk to you however I like – this is my life, not yours!'

My expression must reveal an enmity that goes beyond this time and this place – all the way back to our childhood – because Mia, who is seated on the floor between us, bursts into tears. Nahara is sitting on her lap, and at her age she is a sponge for the emotions of adults, so she starts to cry as well.

What kind of man does not go to his daughter when she is weeping?

The kind I am, apparently, since I rush to my front door and go out to the street without another word, and I do not return even when Yirmi calls to me.

Over the next half-hour, the fury inside me becomes a hyena circling around me. And yet a path to freedom soon presents itself . . .

This time, there is no tumult at the door, and I appear to be the only Jew who has slackened in his duties to the Sabbath; a Lydian trader and Egyptian silversmith are the only men sitting in the highly perfumed waiting room when I enter. I choose a slender Etruscan girl who is new to Judaea, and she teaches me the words in her language that I most want to learn by touching my tingling fingertips to her breasts and lips and bottom.

We sip palm wine from the same cup and play our pleasant form of dictionary until we come to the Etruscan word for the moist cleft between her legs, and she tells me the term commonly used in her homeland is *vagina*, meaning sheath, and it is a word that the Romans have apparently adopted, for I have seen it in graffiti. She asks me – giggling – for its translation into Greek, and, while she is perfecting her pronunciation of *myche*, I enter her from behind.

Do I grow unruly from too much drink? All I recall is the girl shoving me away when I ask her to tell me about her childhood and a burly man tugging me out into the street.

I stumble home and tell the new group of hopeful visitors waiting for me at my door that the blessings of a cadaver will only diminish their chances for a fruitful life. I fall into a drugged sleep in the courtyard. Some time during what must be the third watch of night, I burst awake. Runnels of cold sweat are sliding down my arms and back, and my hair stuck to my neck, as though I have been fleeing desert seraphs. I check on my sleeping children and sit vigil over them, apologizing for the offences I have given them, praying to become the attentive father and pious Jew I was only a few days before.

Why do so many hopeless tears continue to fall from my eyes?

I place my head between my legs – as the prophet Eliyahu did on Mount Carmel – and chant the secret names of God I have been entrusted so that He might grant my wish and allow me entrance to the Gate of Mercy. *Be gracious to me,* I tell Him, *for my soul seeks refuge, and in the shadow of your wings I wish to stay until the destruction passes.*

The only scroll I own is an ancient copy of the first book of the Torah, which we refer to as *In the Beginning*. Its graceful Hebrew letters are complemented by tiny illustrations in the margins, and I read it by the flickering light of an ancient lantern, moving my fingertip over the figures of men and women, animals and trees and rivers, wishing I could disappear into a story that is not my own.

To escape another wave of despair, I climb up to the roof, and Ayin is there waiting for me, and, when I reach out to him, he nuzzles his head into my hand to give me his consent, so I lift him on to my shoulder. Together we search the darkness in all directions, and, though we cannot find Goliath, I sense he is sitting on my street amongst the pilgrims.

Gephen is waiting for us back inside my home. He curls around my ankle, eager for companionship, and he accompanies Ayin and me out my door and down the street. By Bethany's new well, however, he seems to change his mind about joining us. Standing on its stone rim, he gazes out into the fields east of town, summing advantages and disadvantages, then jumps down and trots off towards home.

I need the freedom of the night air and stars, however, and soon I am standing on the barren hill just beyond the plot of land we rent, gazing at the towers of Yerushalayim, which have been polished silver by the moonlight. To remain there and never go home again seems a worthy protest against all the events I cannot control.

And yet I spend most of my time on that abandoned hilltop berating everyone who has ever wounded or wronged me, starting with Marta, who has excluded me from her heart since we were children, and ending with the Lord Himself.

Is it progress to confess all my grudges to a God who may not exist?

I walk east for a time along the road to Yeriho, towards the stream where I go to admire the sacred ibises that gather there in the early morning. For the first time in my life, I have no fear of brigands or bandits; even the most ruthless amongst them would surely keep his distance from me on learning that I am a living corpse. And even if they were to overcome their dread of contagion, what more could they take from me? I have spent all the silver I kept in my pouch on my generous-hearted Etruscan dictionary, and my clothes are worthless. To be left naked and shivering might even prove a blessing, for I would then be obliged to start over without even sandals to weigh me down.

If you want to enter the Kingdom, you must give away everything, even the identity you have always had.

It seems that only now – at the age of thirty-six – am I finally beginning to live out the most difficult parts of Yeshua's teachings.

Just before reaching the stream, I hear men's voices coming from an encampment of pilgrims, and, as I would not want to converse with them, I tiptoe off the road and walk slowly forward along the raised border between a barley field and a grove of date palms. In spite of my caution, one of the men soon detects my presence. As Ayin and I take cover behind one of the palms, his squat, moonlit figure approaches, holding a dagger in his fist.

I call out *tamê* – unclean! – so that he will take me for a leper.

'We have nothing of value, so stay away from us!' he shouts, and he slashes his blade through the darkness, back and forth.

Perhaps being an outcast – with only a night-bird for companion – makes me more sensitive to what all of nature would have me understand; a short time later, after the man has returned to his companions, I wade into the stream, and its waters whisper that the journey through life is always arduous, no matter who we are.

You did not have any right to expect that your way forward would be free of obstacles, it tells me, and when I look up into the firmament, questioning a thousand stars about what the afterlife looks like, they tell me, *Even Aietos the Eagle will one day tumble out of the sky and leave us.*

Is that a moment of clairvoyance? It will seem so for a number of years, but, now that I am older, I see that a sanctum of dreams and visions has shaped all my most important decisions, so it seems only natural that it would also supply me with the strategy that I would come to use to try to save Yeshua.

Why is the entirety of nature willing to address me on this night? If I am truthful, Yaphiel, I think it is because while standing in a stream beyond the borders of Yerushalayim and Bethany, free of expectations, I can be candid with myself.

When my eyes are drawn skywards again, and they rest upon Vega, and for the first time since my youth, perhaps, I recall the new star that appeared within its halo when I was four years old and Grandfather Shimon carrying me on his shoulders up a hill to see it. Dozens of our neighbours from Natzeret were around us, braving the frigid gusts of wind, and everyone was whispering together. At the time, I did not suspect that they were speculating about whether an anointed king – a *Mashiah* – had been born amongst us. After a time, Grandmother Rut sat me on her lap and bundled me up, so that my memories of that icy, adventure-filled night are filtered through the reassuring weight of her woollen mantle.

Why does that particular memory occur to me and not any of a hundred others?

When I close my eyes to ask the 'I' who resides inside my darkness, it is Leah who gives me the answer by kissing my cheek.

She does not need to say, *The loneliness you're now feeling also unites you to Yeshua,* for I am well aware – and have been so for many years – that every time he takes my hand or even just smiles at me he poses a question that I try never to answer: can you love me without possessing me?

An hour or so later, in Bethany, I spot a caped figure sitting by the old well, bent over himself, seemingly asleep. I am unable to see his face because he is wearing the wide-brimmed *petasus* typical of the Greeks of Alexandria. Might he be another of our Egyptian cousins? I excuse myself from the insistent pilgrims whom I have been blessing at my door and start towards him.

When I am half a dozen paces from him, he thrusts out his staff. 'Don't move!'

I jump back and tell him that I come in peace.

Then, recognizing me, he lowers his weapon and laughs.

I study his face in the moonlight, and everything that has taken place over these past few days seems a dream leading directly to this one moment, since the smiling man is Yosef, Yeshua's father. And yet he has been dead for nearly a decade.

I am living now in a dream of the Lord's, I think.

'No, I'm not a night-demon,' Yosef tells me in an amused tone, misunderstanding my trepidation.

His voice gives away his true identity. 'You scared me!' I whisper-scream.

Yeshua takes off his hat and pats down his long hair to show me he is without horns, since we Galileans say that *Mastema* – the angel of lies – resembles a goat.

'Without your beard you look just like your father,' I tell him. 'I'd forgotten.'

'The best disguise is sometimes no disguise at all!' he says, too pleased with himself for my liking.

He starts towards me with open arms, but I thrust up my hands again to have him keep his distance; not only am I ritually unclean, but I must use my irritation if I am to have any hope of convincing him to flee Yerushalayim and find safety in the Galilee.

The moonlight is too frail for me to see the radiant depth in Yeshua's eyes, or I would know that the deepest part of his soul has ascended and that he is intoning hymns even as we speak.

'You're supposed to be in the Galilee,' I tell him in a disapproving voice.

'Who told you that?'

'Nikodemos.'

'So you've been checking up on me!' he says in a gleeful voice, as though he has caught me enquiring into his private affairs.

'Would you prefer for me to forget about you?' I ask challengingly.

He holds out his hands palm up – a sign of apology in our personal language. I would like to take them in mine, but his touch might dissuade me from insisting that he leave Yerushalayim.

'We ought to go inside,' I say.

'First give me your hands,' he replies.

'I'm unclean. I was a corpse. I shall be pure again only after my resurrection is seven days in the past. And, even then, I don't know . . . Perhaps the priests will have to cleanse me with the ashes of a sacrificed beast.'

He shakes his head as if I have misunderstood everything. 'Would I have embraced you had your soul been defiled by death?'

'How do you know it wasn't?'

He glares at me. 'Lazar, if I tell you of earthly things and you do not believe me, then how will you believe me if I tell you of the heavenly things?'

I give him my hands, as he has requested, and he covers his eyes with them, as though seeking shelter inside a darkness that only I can grant him. It is a moment that tugs me far out of myself, and I see us both as though from high above: two men standing at the shore of a deep ocean into whose limitless, life-giving depths only one of them can see.

With my hands pressed to Yeshua's closed eyes, I chant the Shema, over and over, and a latch opens inside me, and what enters me is his trust so freely given that the borders between us begin to fade. His voice – when it speaks my name – sounds inside me, and being united with him changes the direction of all my thoughts, and I am rising towards a hope so full that it overflows my mind and appears to my inner eye as a shimmering black sun lifting into sky.

You will enter the Kingdom when you make two into one, he has always told me. And yet we are too easily called away, and, in only the time it takes to hear his words spoken aloud to me once more, I return to myself, and the sun loses its dark fire, and he and I are separate once more.

Lifting my hands away from his face, he kisses them, then gives them back to me. His movements – overly precise, as though he is fearful he may make a mistake – confirm to me that the breath-part of his soul – his *neshamah* – is still communing with the Lord and far from us.

'I decided to remain in Yerushalayim,' he tells me. 'Though I have played a small trick on the Pharisees and their Roman masters.'

'What kind of trick?'

'They're certain I have left for Capernaum.'

'How did you convince them of that?'

'I told Yehudah of Kerioth and several others that I would be going there.'

I make no reference to the dangers that may accrue from trying to manipulate a traitor, but my expression must reveal my thoughts.

'Lazar, I need to be here in Yerushalayim,' he tells me, 'where Elohim has set the thrones of judgement.'

'And where's Yehudah?'

'I sent him to Capernaum yesterday and told him to wait for me.'

'He'll be angry with you when you fail to join him there.'

'Let him be angry! If he stays in the Galilee, he won't be obliged to betray me and his people.'

'Let's go inside,' I say, taking his arm. 'A man has been following me of late. He might be observing us even now.'

'What man?'

'A giant, with dark hair and eyes. Annas must've sent him to follow me – to make sure I say nothing about how you revived me.'

'This man won't harm you.'

'How can you be sure?'

Yeshua's answers with a pledge from the Book of Zechariah. '"Never again will an oppressor overrun my people, for now I am keeping watch."'

It does not occur to me until later that he quotes this particular verse to prepare me for what he will soon ask of me.

I do sense, however, the he wants me to respond with a verse of Torah so that we might build a high protective wall out of our words; it is a practice we adopted as boys when we felt pressured by others.

'"In peace I will lie down and sleep,"' I say, '"for you alone, Lord, make me dwell in safety."'

'"The children drink their fill of the abundance of Your house, and You give them . . ."' Yeshua continues.

As we renew the defensive battlements around us, I am reminded of what I have known since we were twelve years old:

> Yeshua is the word and the sign, the vowel never written,
>   the twenty-third letter.
> He is the uptake of breath and exhale after each prayer.
> He is the seer and the seen, the speaker and the spoken,
>   the lover and the beloved.
> He is the Torah into which God has breathed life.

I lead him down the street to my home, my hand around his wrist, because he is often only vaguely aware of his steps when he has divided himself between the land of his birth and the   *Hekhal ha-Melekh.*

Once my front door is closed behind us, I put Ayin on my windowsill where the obscure sounds of the night will reassure him that he is where he is meant to be. When I turn around, Yeshua embraces me and rests his head on my shoulder. And there it is once more, the scent I have known all my adult life – of the fertile earth of the Galilee and the hundreds of miles of forgotten roads he has walked over the past months.

Through Yeshua, I embrace the hidden beings who dwell inside him and give him their strength when his is depleted, and, though I am unlikely to ever even catch a glimpse of them, I beseech them to watch over him with all their care.

If I could be envious of his power, would it seem less alluring to me?

As I sit him down, the fear that he will sense my ongoing doubts about the afterlife closes in around me. He reads my discomfort in my manner and reaches up to caress my cheek. 'There will be no death for those who come to the Lord of Heaven through me,' he says.

'I . . . I am not the man I was,' I stutter.

'You've heard me say many times that I've come for the sinners and heretics and for those who are troubled in spirit. Did you think I was lying?'

'Of course not.'

'For now, I would ask you to put your fears and troubles aside for me if not for yourself. I need you to stay up with me tonight and remain alert.'

Once we are seated across from each other, he shuts his eyes and chants as quickly as he can, reordering the letters of the secret names of God that Rabbi Baruch taught us when we reached adulthood. Soon his voice grows silent, and his breathing slows and deepens, and as he raises his hands . . .

Here I must cleave to silence, for I am forbidden from speaking of the mysteries that Yeshua uses to untie his knots of mind and allow the Holy Spirit to enter him. I shall tell you, however, that he invokes the name of one angel aloud – Jahoel, the heavenly scribe.

When he struggles to remove his cape, I lift it off of him. He sits with his legs crossed, and after I prop a cushion behind his back, he reaches urgently for my hand, and I know from experience to fetch him a cup of water, which I lift to his lips.

To help him at such times seems the sacred duty for which I was born.

His whispered prayers carry him off to the Lord, and the heat of his spiritual journey is such that steam-wisps begin to dance across his shoulders and hair. I brush his brow with a moist towel, then drip water from my cupped hand on top of his head. Beads of water run down his neck and back.

What is it like to walk with God? Before Yeshua discovered the dangers of speaking of the Kingdom to the uninitiated, he used to occasionally scribble observations about his experiences, and I once discovered a parchment in his pouch where he had written a few fragments of poetry. Amongst them was a verse that he gave me permission to repeat: *I am clothed in light, burning with radiance, in a world without shadows.*

I carry in two oil lamps from our storage cabinet and place one on each side of him for when he returns to this time and place; demons and shades are only too eager to take on human form, and the flames will deter them from stealing into our world when the Gate of Return opens.

Once I neglected to perform this duty properly, and a foul-smelling demon in service to Asmodeus took up residence in my home for two days, and it was only by painting a menacing talisman of Tobit on all the doorways and ordering the evil wraith to leave us that Yeshua and I were able to send him back to his benighted realm.

As I take a sip of water for myself, Gephen jumps on to my windowsill and sniffs at Ayin. The owl bats him away with his wing, and the cat tumbles, twisting, into the room, landing – astonishingly – on all four feet.

Gephen looks from me to Yeshua as though awaiting our praise, so I whisper that he is an acrobat of the highest order. I also ask him to return outside, flapping at him with my hands so there can be no error of interpretation, but he disregards me with regal indifference and patters over to Yeshua, climbing on to his thigh. I would chase him off, but Yeshua remains unperturbed and deep in trance, which frees me once again to become a man whose sole purpose is to watch over his friend. And yet I prove on this occasion a poor guard; some time later, I awaken to Yeshua cupping my chin.

'The Lord has sent me to open the prisons this Passover and take all our captives to the Promised Land,' he tells me.

His hand is still burning with the heat of the Palace. I scent Gephen on his fingers.

I sit up, but my mind is still drugged by slumber. I look around the room, but the cat is gone.

'I sent him back to the courtyard,' Yeshua says.

'I must have fallen asleep,' I say, as if that were not obvious.

'It makes no difference.'

'And you're all right?'

'Yes.' His eyes glisten in the lamplight, and he gazes at me for a long time, as he does when he is astonished to see that so little has changed while he was away. 'I have prepared an important place for you on the morning following the Sabbath,' he tells me.

'Where will you need me to be?' I ask.

'Many hundreds of my followers are coming from the Galilee. I'll ride into the city of the Lord and trace its entire circumference, and you'll be with me. Together we'll enter the house and throw open its doors to one and all. "I shall take the battle chariot from Ephraim and the warhorse from Yerushalayim, and I shall destroy the arrows of war."'

I recognize his words as those of Zechariah, of course.

To test if I understand him correctly, I reply with the next verse: '"See, your king comes to you, righteous and victorious, lowly and riding on a donkey."'

'Exactly,' he says, and he explains that he has already picked out a he-ass belonging to a friend, which means that he intends to fulfil scripture – and risk revealing himself as the Living Torah to those who have vision enough to see the truth.

'I'll walk with you,' I tell him, 'but I won't speak to the crowds of my miracle. I've been sworn to silence by Annas, and to break that vow would put me in danger. I can't risk making my children orphans.'

'The people know that you've returned from the dead, and they'll see you with me. And, seeing death and life together, they'll know what I can do – and they'll know, too, that the time has come for God to take back what is His.'

So many matters I intended to broach with him before his appearance this evening – the crucifixions I witnessed, and his mother's concerns, and my own revelations – but I sense that he is still far away, receiving counsel from Zechariah and others who have come before him. Though I do not believe he will be able to remain focused on our conversation or heed any advice I might venture to give him, I risk a single plea for caution. 'I may not be near enough to you the next time you are swept away by the River Jordan.'

He nods his understanding and thanks me with his smile.

After I fetch a cushion for his head, he lies next to me on my mat and clasps my hand in his, as when we were boys. He must sense my continuing apprehension, because he tells me, 'Tomorrow will worry for itself.' Paraphrasing the words of Mosheh from *In the Beginning,* he adds, 'I am with you and shall watch over you wherever you go in your dreams, and I shall bring you safely home.'

When I awaken in the night, I draw our covers up over him more fully, and, though he stirs, he remains asleep, and I turn on my side, away from him, so that my thoughts are less likely to brush against him and awaken him, and I listen again to our conversation from a few hours earlier. When I hear him tell me of his plans to enter Yerushalayim, a startling discovery tugs me to my feet: he intends to construct a spiritual *eruv* around the city!

It never occurred to me before that such a feat was possible. Yet the Lord must have assured him that by tracing his way around the perimeter of Yerushalayim he would limit the power of the priests and Romans over him.

Yes, of course, this is how you must start! I think, gazing at him as if this strategy were an inevitability we ought both to have predicted years ago. *Together we shall turn the entire city – every alleyway and square and house – into sacred space.*

Overwhelmed by the boldness and immensity of what he is about to do, I sit at my open window, exulting in the breezes blowing against my face, for they are telling me in their cool and delicate language that we are about to enter history.

After a time it seems only fair that I have come to understand what he has not told me, because tonight we can lie beside each other until dawn and appreciate our quiet intimacy. But I do not return to my mat just yet. I squat on my heels by his side and move my palm over him – a finger's width distant – so that I might feel my ache of longing for him as a deep and essential part of me before I let it go.

21

Mia was the first child born to our parents, and, from what she has told me, our father began teaching her to read on her seventh birthday. Every Sabbath afternoon, they would sit side by side in his workroom and study the scroll of *In the Beginning* that had been passed down in our family for generations. Marta, nearly four years younger than Mia, would sit next to her elder sister, forbidden from speaking but gleaning what she could from their lessons.

Marta . . . Picture a slim, dark girl with her curly brown hair tied at the nape of her neck with a woven ribbon, leaning on her elbows over the table, chin cupped in her hands, coming to learn the challenging, rewarding, mouse-like art of being curious and silent at the same time.

A little less than a year after Mia's studies began, I was born, and Father never again gave his daughter another reading lesson. He left it to his wife to explain to Mia that the birth of a boy made her education unnecessary.

To our mother's surprise and relief, the girl received the news without tears; Mia would later tell me that she had already realized that the Gate of Words, once it had been opened to her, could never be shut again. Over the next few years, she would also learn how to write, under the clandestine tutelage of our Aunt Zilpah, my mother's half-sister, who was raised in the

Roman colony of Caesarea and who had come to regard the education of women as a birthright.

For Marta, however, the end of her elder sister's lessons came with the purposeless and tormenting finality of a stillbirth. She could not have put her feelings into neatly ordered words, but she regarded it as a profound betrayal; she had behaved exactly as our parents had asked and had nothing to show for it.

When she was twelve, she told me once – and with matter-of-fact certainty – that she felt only loathing for our father, since he had done all he could to ruin her childhood.

And you, little brother, are responsible as well.

She never actually said that to me, but it was implied by her vicious cruelty to me over the coming months.

When I was eleven and she was fifteen, I came to her when I heard her crying in the night and offered to give her secret reading and writing lessons.

'Are you really so dim-witted to believe that I could ever accept any charity from you?' she demanded before pushing me away.

I have long suspected that Marta has never forgiven me for being born. Even so, I might have ended up winning her grudging affection were it not for one more tragedy.

When she was seventeen and about to be married, she refused to proceed with the wedding, announcing that the man to whom she was betrothed – a stonemason, like my father – was unworthy of her. My father took up his rule measuring two Roman feet in length and summoned Marta into the bedroom she shared with Mia. He gave strict orders that my mother, my eldest sister and I were not to enter, no matter what we heard.

Marta's shrieks for help made neighbours assemble around our house, and my mother turned so pale that Mia and I had to help her into bed. When Father finally opened the door, his hands were stained with his daughter's blood. I did not see Marta that night; he expressly forbade me from comforting her.

By the time Marta shuffled out of her room the next morning her face had swollen into a mass of bread dough. Somewhere under all that bruising was her right eye. We didn't know it at the time, but the hearing in her left ear was damaged permanently.

She was married a month later.

It may sound impossible, but the beating she received might easily have been worse. I believe, in fact, that my father would have taken her life or sold her into slavery if she had told him the truth – that she was in love with Yeshua. He was just thirteen at the time and the son of a poor woodworker.

Marta never told Yeshua that she would accept only him, but he knew it. As did I.

Boys grow up more slowly than girls, and I understood nothing of love when I was thirteen. I am ashamed to say that I ridiculed her behind her back for what was, to her, a lonely and desperate wish to marry the boy she loved.

Yeshua and I went to visit her at her new home in the stoneworker's district of Yerushalayim, but she was always so short-tempered with us that we stopped visiting. I can see now that conversing with Yeshua was a reminder that she would be for ever trapped in a life she could not bear.

About a year after her marriage, when she was pregnant with her daughter Salome – who would not survive her first year – Marta told me that Yeshua had failed her at her most difficult time. She stunned me by ordering me to give him up as a friend, and, when I refused, she told me – tears of rage sliding down her cheeks – that I would one day come to regret having chosen him over her.

I am reminded of this cruel history the following dawn, shortly after I see Yeshua off on the road to Yerushalayim. While I am sitting on my mat, drinking my barley broth, Marta comes to me and says, 'You ought not to allow him into your home, you know.'

'Marta, I'm thirty-six years old. I'll do what I want.'

'He didn't even return in time to save you,' she tells me resentfully.

'Because I'd provoked a bad quarrel with him. And he was busy preaching.'

'Eli, when will you learn that he uses you, just like he uses everyone?'

I have noticed Marta generally jabs at me in the morning, when I am least prepared to defend myself. 'I'm sorry, Marta,' I tell her, 'but at such an early hour, I find there is nothing I want to argue about – not with you or anyone else.'

'The truth must not be made to wait!' she says in a haughty voice, as though she has become – overnight – our family philosopher.

'Marta, if you keep pushing me, I'm certain to say something we'll both regret.' I speak slowly and precisely, so she cannot later deny that I did not warn her.

'You ought to hear what people say about the two of you!' she says, sneering.

So it is that I learn that her hate is spilling over into places where it will stain even the small comforts and pleasantries that remain to us.

I stand up so that she can see I am a man now. And since I would not want my children to have to listen to mean-spirited condemnations of their father, I warn her to never voice her criticisms of Yeshua and me in front of Yirmi or Nahara. 'And when I say *never,*' I add, 'that's exactly what I mean!'

Is revealing my anger a mistake?

'Listen closely,' she hisses at me. 'If anything happens to you because of what you are planning with Yeshua, don't count on me to raise your children or help them in any way. They will be dead to me!'

To put some distance between Marta and me, I take Nahara and Yirmi outside Bethany late that morning, to the plot of land we rent. I spread out our tattered old rug under a mammoth carob tree, but the tiny brown ants of Judaea prove so envious of our bounty that we are forced to move twice while eating our modest lunch and end up hiding from them in an orchard of plum trees.

After Yirmi joins some boys playing in a nearby field that has been left fallow – and when I am certain that my daughter and I are not being watched – I have Nahara practise reading some simple Aramaic phrases that I have scripted on a sheet of papyrus. I know I shall always remember that day because of the delighted laughter we share when she misreads *chesed* for *chasidah*, turning the sentence 'The Lord's kindness saved me' into the glorious 'The Lord's stork saved me!'

As we work, my thoughts return to Marta, and I am reminded again of those difficult words from the Book of Names that have helped me understand her: 'I, the Lord your God, am a jealous God, punishing the children for the sin of the parents to the third and fourth generation of those who hate me.'

Dearest Yaphiel, this may be the most misunderstood verse in all of the Torah, and I believe I can adjudge the discernment of any man or woman by the depth of their interpretation of it. Know this, my child: the true meaning of these words is not – as most people believe – that God holds us accountable for the actions of our forefathers. No, the Lord of Gifts is giving us a far more subtle and insightful teaching: that we are formed by the deeds and desires of our parents and grandparents, and our punishment for failing to make peace with all they have given us – both good and bad – and for not assuming responsibility for our own path in life is that we shall be for ever forced to repeat their mistakes.

Yeshua arrives at my home shortly after my children and I get back that afternoon. Yohanon and Maryam of Magdala have accompanied him, and, as a gift, they bring us a basket of plump and pimply citrons and two bunches of wild asparagus.

The citrons give me an opportunity to perform an old comedy conceit of mine for my Nahara and our guests as a prelude to our meal; I juggle three of them high in the air but always fumble one and make sure it hits me square on the head. It is just a bit of silliness, but my daughter squeals with laughter, over and over, and her unbridled glee gives me hope that our lives are regaining at least some of their usual tranquil contours.

Yeshua soon takes to my little stage in the courtyard, taps lightly on Nahara's head and pulls an asparagus spear from her ear.

'Do it again!' she shrieks, clapping her hands.

He next pulls a spear from her bottom.

When the girl looks back at me for an explanation, I tell her that Yeshua can do many things that other people can't, which makes her squat on her heels and look up at him as if he were a mountain she is preparing to climb.

As his final trick, Yeshua shows my daughter that he is concealing nothing in his hands, then taps his own head twice and opens his mouth to reveal a citron. As he hands it to her, he says, 'Keep knocking, dear Nahara, and the door will open!'

The girl looks back and forth between the fruit and Yeshua with astonished eyes. 'How did he do that?' she asks me.

'I have no idea,' I say truthfully, for, though it is possible that Yeshua put the citron in his mouth before stepping into my home, he could not then have spoken to me and my daughter without mangling his words.

To my questioning looks, my friend shakes his finger at me. 'You have to knock on your own door, not mine!' he says with a hearty laugh.

While Yeshua gives Nahara a ride around the courtyard on his shoulders, Marta plays our family matron. It is as she is filling Maryam's cup with wine that I take note of the delicate, fawn-like grace of her movements. Do our guests, remarking her mournful eyes, feel the turn of a sympathetic wheel inside them?

Mia sees me eyeing Marta suspiciously and seats me far from her at supper. And, to give her no cause for jealousy, she has Grandfather Shimon and Cousin Ariston sit between Yeshua and me.

Perhaps the absurdity of worrying about our seating arrangements has set Marta thinking about forging a truce; after we have finished our sweets, she comes around to me and whispers excitedly, 'Come and see the progress I've made on my rug!'

'Now?'

'Please, Eli – for me.'

She leads me across our courtyard to her workroom. I see that she has added a large, four-pointed star below the final row of both black and white dolphins. After I compliment her talents, she tells me that she mixed madder and indigo to make its stunning shade of violet. 'You know, Eli, the star is meant to represent you – your central place in all our lives,' she says.

The movement inside me is that of a younger brother turning away to find safety, for I suspect that her sudden affection is a tactic meant to win my continued allegiance. To hide my doubts about her sincerity, however, I squeeze her hand. 'I'm sorry I caused you to worry,' I say.

She caresses my cheek, and her hand is so like my mother's that it chills me. 'Eli, I say malicious things to you because I know you won't give up on me – it's simply not in your nature,' she says. 'But I know I went too far today. I'm sorry. If ever your children are in need of my help, they'll have it. I pledge that to you. Though I'd understand it if you wanted to keep them far from me.'

I would like to confess to her that the hostilities between us exhaust me, but I have heard apologies from her too many times in the past to entirely believe this one. I limit myself to assuring her that I shall always seek out her help with my children. Is she disappointed? Undoubtedly, but what she shows me is a grateful smile. As I've discovered, one reveals very little during an undeclared war.

After Grandfather Shimon makes his way up to bed, Yeshua and I are left alone with Maryam and Yohanon. He tells his disciples that he will spend another night with me and meet them just after dawn at Bethany's western boundary.

For *dawn*, he uses the word *shepharphar*. It is a spiralling, exuberant word, and it reminds me of how the Aramaic language has shaped and coloured my inner landscape.

As we watch Maryam and Yohanon walking away down my street, Yeshua tells me that he recently healed a seventy-year-old Nabataean woman who was so afraid of butterflies getting tangled in her hair or fluttering into her mouth that she had not left home since she was a girl.

If the lightest and most delicate of the Lord's creatures can become our enemy, I think, *then is there any hope of ever ending our miseries?*

When Yeshua notices my disquiet, he whispers a verse of Psalm, '"Because the poor are plundered and the needy groan, I shall now arise."'

So it is that he begins to tell me of his plans to bring justice to Zion. We sit opposite each other in my room, and he tells me in an excited voice – as though striding towards a triumph just ahead – that he will lead his followers through Yerushalayim the next morning and address them at the Synagogue of the Woodworkers.

'And I need you there with me,' he says.

'I promised you I'd be with you and I shall,' I reply. *I'll bring my knife and keep my eyes on you,* I do not add.

A small comfort . . . When I ask if Yehudah of Kerioth will accompany us, Yeshua tells me that he received word before supper that he has remained in Capernaum. 'May the Lord show him favour there,' he says. 'And may he be wise for the rest of his days.

When I awaken in the night, I find Yeshua in my courtyard, naked and shimmering in the moonlight, walking in a slow and careful circle, as if around a sleeping child. He is whispering the Passover prayer, the aim of which is to make us understand that the Exodus is a call to freedom that sounds in us at every moment: *Bivhilu yatzanu mimitzrayim, halahma anya b'nei horin. In haste we went out of Egypt with our bread of affliction, and now we are free.*

The papyrus ribbon on which I have written the incantation meant to heal my leg has come loose, so I retie it around my ankle before standing up.

I squat on my heels inside the circle he is walking and join my chanting to his, and this time my voice is secure and confident, and, even though my leg begins to cry out in pain, I do not pause, since I shall never make him walk alone.

It would do you well to remember, Yaphiel, that in any battle of wills, it is sometimes difficult to know who is the cat and who the mouse . . .

Early the next morning, while Yeshua, Yirmi and I are passing the stalls of our marketplace, we spot some two hundred followers of my old friend already gathered at the western boundary stone of our town, and Yehudah of Kerioth is one of them. He carries his pack over his shoulder and shades his eyes from the just-risen sun. He stands between Andreas and Yeshua's younger brother Yaaqov.

Yeshua does not pause in his step, but I do.

Yirmi comes to me and asks if I'm all right. 'I'm fine,' I reply. 'Now go to Lucius like we agreed and tell him that I'll be late to work today, and then head straight to Rabbi Elad's home. And listen, if Lucius replies angrily, just apologize and do your

best to look contrite. If you can summon tears, then do so –
he'll be very pleased to think that he's ruined your day.'

My small witticism earns me a bursting laugh from my son,
which makes saying goodbye to him a little easier. Yeshua is
twenty paces ahead of me by then, so I start after him,
preparing the smile with which I shall greet Yehudah.

22

Anyone familiar with the story of Ezra the Scribe knows that he led several thousand of our brethren back from exile in Babylon to Judaea, at a time when all of Zion was under Persian rule. Will the men and women of future days have a chance to read of Yeshua and those of us who followed him from our long exile of spirit into Yerushalayim on this bright morning in Nissan, in the ninety-fifth year of the Roman conquest?

My old friend strides out of Bethany beside Yehudah, Loukas and Mattiyahu. I walk several paces behind them, my watchful shadow at their heels. I lag behind because I discovered long ago that I wish to be Yeshua's refuge and not his disciple.

Do you see that figure near the southern horizon, standing at the top of a lookout tower rising from a great and populous city where there is neither hunger nor poverty and from which all tyrants have been banished? That figure is me, for when I consider the true destination to which we are all walking, I journey in my thoughts to a time when we shall finally be able to live the lives we were meant to have.

A quarter of a mile beyond Bethany, Philippus – another of Yeshua's followers – comes walking towards us from a side road, accompanied by a sturdy brown donkey with long splayed ears, a sagging belly and what seems to be an expression of satisfied humour in his eyes. Is he a well-fed old sage transformed into a beast? When Maryam of Magdala whispers that speculation to me, our nervousness gives way to complicit laughter.

Maryam's excitement about our mission makes her sensitive dark eyes seem to sparkle, and, as we speculate about the words with which Yeshua will address us at the Synagogue of the Woodworkers, I come to understand that she has finally begun to trust me. I was with Yeshua seven years earlier when he pulled a ruthless demon from her, and because I had seen her naked, bloody and tormented – and heard her brethren repudiate her with curses – she has nearly always limited herself to shameful silence in my presence.

Yeshua uses his cape as his saddle. He turns for me once he is settled on his mount, anxious to make sure I have not lagged too far behind, and I join my hands above my head to show him that I shall stay with him as long as he needs me.

His eyes linger on me, and they are grateful, but I sense a question in him as well, and here is what I hear him tell me in my mind: *Do you wish to know if I have envisaged this moment since we were eight years old? If I were to say* yes, *you would believe that we're more different than we are, but I can tell you this . . . If I weren't listening to the Lord at this very moment, my mind would also be racing to that tower above your perfect city of justice and compassion. But you have made one error, Lazar, for the world to come is here with us now, and even this forgotten Judaean byway we walk on – like all the roads you and I follow – leads to the Lighthouse and Library of your ideal Alexandria, as surely as it leads to the Temple, so do not let yourself fall any further behind me!*

Here is the prayer I whisper to myself as we start off again towards Yerushalayim:

Let all of us find freedom this Passover – Yeshua, Mia and
Marta,
   Nahara and Yirmi, even Yehudah and our other enemies. Let
no
   one remain in slavery.
No sinners or orphans.
No paupers, lepers or heretics.
No Samaritan, Greek, Nabataean, Egyptian, Phoenician or
Essene.
No Pharisee or Sadducee.
No priest or scribe.
And no Roman.

Are you surprised that I would ask the Lord of the Armies of Zion to grant the Romans freedom? No, my hatred of the torments they inflict on us and their bellicose ways has not diminished one iota, but there is a lesson of Yeshua's that I struggle with every day – to love and respect my enemies – and it would be miserly of me to forget it on the day we shall cross to the Promised Land.

Know this: when the Passover of Passovers descends in the west, the angels will glow red and gold and white, which are the colours of divine mercy and justice, and their radiance will enable the Romans to see with fresh eyes, and the illusions that have misted their minds will be burned away, and it will be as obvious to them as their own reflection in the waters of memory that we are all of us made in God's image, and that there that can be no conqueror above the conquered, and they will know that we are – and have always been – but one people.

Two young men are assigned to watch over me that morning, and they permit only one person at a time to come to me for blessings.

The older of the boys guarding me is so proud of his first beard that he reaches up to stroke it whenever he talks to me, which brings back memories of my own laughable vanity at his age. His name is Shaul, and he is from Natzeret, which was undoubtedly why he was chosen to watch over me. His great-uncle is the surgeon Hanoch ben Levi, who performed my circumcision.

The younger boy who keeps watch over me – doe-eyed and slender, with a dusting of whiskers on his upper lip – is a Samaritan by birth by the name of Uriyah ben Avram. His tunic is too long and large for him, and I conclude that it must be an inheritance from his father or an elder brother, but I shall soon learn that I am wrong.

This handsome Samaritan youth is a ferocious nail-biter, so I try to ease his mind with conversation. After I bless a moribund old woman carried to me in her son's arms, I toss him harmless questions about the landmarks of his homeland. Unfortunately, they only serve to make him withdraw under a mantle of shame.

Perhaps a secret confided by an elder will lead him out of himself, I think, and I whisper to him that I once prayed on Mount Gerizim.

He shows me a disbelieving look – as I expected – since the Jews regard the mountaintop, home to the Samaritan temple, as a place of sin.

'To the Holy Spirit', I assure him, 'one gateway to the Palace is as good as another.'

He gazes away from me. Does he think I am a madman? Taking him aside, I whisper, 'On Mount Gerizim, Yeshua and

I kneeled at the spot where a guardian angel appeared to Avraham and saved Isaac from certain death. The Lord spoke to Yeshua there.'

What did He say?

Uriyah keeps his lips sealed to silence but asks that question with his eyes.

'The Lord told him, "Remember the greatness of He who also preserved your life and the lives of everyone you know!"'

The boy arches his eyebrows, plainly confused, so I pat his shoulder encouragingly. 'You see, Uriyah, the angel who saved Isaac drew an end to the age of human sacrifice. He changed the world for ever!'

The boy looks at me as if I were an enigma, and I sense that my scholarly tone has made me seem pompous – or perhaps even sinister.

'I apologize if I have made you uncomfortable,' I tell him. 'All I mean to say is that if you look underneath the surface of the stories in the Torah, you may come upon a guide who has waited all your life to meet you.'

He smiles weakly, clearly wishing that the old fool whom he has been forced to guard will allow him to return to the sanctity of his own thoughts. And it is a wish I grant him, of course.

I name Yeshua's donkey Iason, the leader of the Argonauts. Is it an odd choice? Very likely. But he is about to turn Yeshua into the fulfilment of Zechariah's prophecy, and he deserves a name that we shall all remember.

In the Book of Numbers we read, 'A star will come out of Yaaqov, and a sceptre will rise out of Israel.'

Today, Yeshua is our star and sceptre. Just as we, his friends and followers, are the rivers of Paradise – every stream, tributary and rivulet – for we are flowing onwards with a single purpose. Our names are Euphrates, Pison, Gihon and Hiddekel.

I remember that it was through a cloudless morning that we flowed behind Yeshua and Iason. A grey haze hovered over the eastern horizon, however, and it was a red sun – coloured by desert sands drawn skywards – that kept watch over us.

I remember, too, that after taking a misstep on the road, the grinding pains in my leg grew worse, and I was forced to limp.

Do other men and women taste the bitter absence of friends in every small happiness? I keep telling myself that Yeshua's mentor, Yohanon ben Zechariah, ought to be with us. For it was he who first imagined how we would one day become a river and how our hopes would flow into the future. It was he who baptized Yeshua and me in the knowledge of where to find the sea that is our eternal home.

Halfway to Yerushalayim, where the road bends south, is an apricot orchard belonging to my distant cousins Eliav and Levi. Yeshua chooses to turn Iason around by one of the pink-blossomed trees and reaches up to a particularly resplendent branch as though grasping a staff of kingship. He calls out to the five hundred or more now following him with a rephrasing of words once spoken by Mosheh: 'How shall we be able to know we have found grace in the sight of the Lord unless you walk with me?'

He means this question to be a reminder, I think, that our destiny is not fixed – and that all who hear him must decide for themselves where they stand this day.

A young woman is the first to reply to Yeshua's question. 'We are with you!' she shouts exultantly.

Other voices join hers, but when a group of youths calls for death to the Romans, violent voices surge amongst the crowd, describing the tortures and indignities we ought to inflict on our conquerors.

Yeshua dismounts from Iason and runs to an elderly one-legged man balancing on crutches who has called for the blood of our conquerors to water all of the Promised Land. 'We shall meet our enemies with open arms,' he tells the man, then all of us.

The cripple glares at him. 'And when they come at us with swords?' he asks.

'We'll turn their swords to staffs. And we'll walk together towards El Elyon and the light that never ceases.'

'You're a fool!' the old man shouts, and he shoves Yeshua away.

My old friend whispers to him, and the cripple replies with a shake of his head and a frown – as though declining an offer. Yeshua takes his shoulder and confides something in his ear that makes his eyes grow moist.

Come with me, I beseech you, for the Lord's eyes, hands and feet are yours, was what he first whispered. And then, *I would ask you to walk with me today, even if you are certain I am wrong, for I shall not leave this spot until you are with me. You see, I intend to leave no one behind – not even those who take me for a fool.*

This, I will later learn, was what he told the angry cripple, and, although the man still refused to walk behind us, he hobbled along from the side of the road the rest of the way to Yerushalayim, his eyes fixed on Yeshua as if he were trying to fathom a great mystery.

Twelve men come forward as we start off again and gather around Yeshua and those nearest him. I have positioned myself just to the right of Iason – a hand's width beyond his whisking tail – and find myself inside their protective enclosure. My face must reveal my astonishment, for Maryam of Magdala takes my arm and says, 'All this has been planned, Eli. Don't worry.'

Yehudah of Kerioth starts to walk on the other side of Iason from me. Has Annas asked him to do so? I watch him furtively, but there is nothing in his expression that reveals consternation or conflict. He has beautiful lynx-like eyes – tender and aware – and, when he gazes over at me, I see that in another time or place, he might be leading us. *The priests must have also recognized that he was a special soul,* I think. *And they turned him against us because they feared him.*

Yehudah, my old friend, I remember that you told me that you once had a vision of rain falling out of a perfectly blue sky, and, when you awoke to yourself, you realized – laughing – that the impossible happens all the time. 'Everything is a miracle,' you said to me, picking up a blade of grass and holding it between us, and for a few moments, seeing the radiance in your eyes illuminate that tiny filament of creation, I understood you were right.

You may think it silly, but here is what I most valued in you: how you would become so caught up in your interpretations of Torah that your hands would begin to dance.

I never met anyone with more expressive hands or who spoke more articulately.

Now, when he catches me staring at him, he smiles at me with complicity, as though to say, *It gratifies me that you have never forgotten what I told you about the rain.*

If such a steadfast and trustworthy man as Yehudah can be made to betray his closest friends, then who amongst us is safe?

Just before we reach the gates of Yerushalayim, Uriyah, my callow Samaritan guardian, tells me that he saw Yeshua perform miracles in a long-abandoned field near his home. A young man's courage to finally address an elder must not be wasted, so I ask him which town he is from.

'Shalem,' he replies.

'Wasn't that where Yaaqov, son of Isaac and Rebekah, once camped?'

I ask my question because I know it will please him that I know of the significance of his home town.

'Have . . . have you been to Shalem?' he asks excitedly.

If I were speaking to him in Greek, I might risk telling him that the smile he is now showing me is that of a flower overcoming its timidity and greeting the day, but in Aramaic such poetry seems so forced that it always makes me cringe.

'No, but perhaps some day you will show me around, and we shall pray together on Mount Gerizim,' I tell him.

His eyes show astonishment. He must not have believed me when I told him that I had prayed with Yeshua on his holy mountain.

After I minister to the requests of several people who have been waiting for my words of healing, I turn again to Uriyah. 'I'd be interested in knowing what miracles Yeshua performed in that abandoned field near your town.'

'You . . . you really want to know?'

'Of course.'

'First, the Most Honourable Rabbi Yeshua banished a night-demon who'd possessed a wretched old woman. And then he gave back a voice to a man whose neck . . . it had been stepped on by an old mule. And then . . . one other thing,' he adds, his black eyes shining with so ardent an admiration that he has trouble putting his words together, 'but I . . . I must ask you . . . to keep it a secret.'

'You have my word,' I assure him.

'Rabbi Yeshua removed the iron anklets from a runaway slave.'

'Did he pull them apart with his hands alone?' I ask, for once, in a village an hour's walk from Natzeret, I saw him do just that.

'No, he used a hammer and a chisel,' Uriyah replies.

'Then I am afraid it was something less than a miracle,' I say, laughing.

'No, you've missed the point!' he whispers conspiratorially. 'The miracle was that he removed the anklets even though he was not supposed to.'

'Not supposed to? What does that mean?'

'The slave asked him not to remove them.'

'But why would he want to remain in fetters?'

'Because he'd had them on since he was five years old. He said that taking them off was like removing his feet.'

That reply hits me like a punch in the gut. *This boy is sensitive and well spoken,* I think, and I surprise myself by wondering if he might be skilful with his hands as well. 'Tell me what you are trained to do?' I ask.

'Bricklaying.'

'And are you good at it?'

'My master never told me otherwise,' he says proudly. 'But why do you want to hear of my work?' he asks, and I see in his expression that I have become an enigma once again.

I tell him that I am a mosaicist. 'And I've long been in need of an apprentice,' I confess. 'Though I've no idea if such work would interest you.'

'You would consider me for an apprenticeship?' he asks in disbelief.

I show him my hands. 'Yes, but I warn you – you'll end up with these unsightly beasts as companions if you start work with me.'

He turns over his right hand, which has a deep scar across its back. 'Made by my last employer,' he tells me.

'I'd never hurt you. You have my word on that.'

He fights to smile, but I can see that, once again, he does not believe me. *If this boy joins me in my work, I'll have to vanquish the ghosts who have scarred and wounded him,* I think.

A great swell of shouting turns us both towards Yerushalayim, where a jostling crowd awaits Yeshua inside the high arch of the Eastern Huldah Gate. Uriyah and I have no chance to talk further. And who could ever have predicted that I would soon regret the few words I'd already addressed to him?

23

Iason swats at the persistent flies of Judaea with his tail and veers to the right whenever he drops one of his grassy turds to the ground, as though his desires at that delicate moment are curved. Will anyone remember that he was real a hundred years from now – that he had a past and future?

If you who hold this scroll in your hands have received it from Yaphiel or one of his descendants, I want you to know that my today was as real to me as yours is to you and that what Yeshua did for me is what made me memorable, perhaps, but is not who I am.

A familiar Phrygian melody starts up behind us – intoned by distant voices – and then seems to catch up, like a wave yearning for the shore.

Blessed be he who comes in the name of the Lord. That is the start of the Psalm that the faithful offer to the sky and earth and everything in between.

Love's voice will accompany us today, I think, and, after I sing a first verse, I hold my breath as if I am about to submerge into frigid waters. *Remember the shiver of truth that shook you,* I tell myself, *for you will one day need to tell others what it was like to have been here on the day that everything changed.*

Thousands have been waiting for us inside the walls of our capital. A surprising number of them carry palm leaves and citrons, as if this were Sukkoth. Perhaps they wish to remind us that, although the Passover will free us from Pharaoh, we still might be forced to wander in a Roman desert for many years to come.

From rooftops and windows well-wishers call out praises and prayers to Yeshua. Dozens cluster around me for healing, and Shaul and Uriyah are no longer able to keep them from jostling and bickering. An ancient rebel with a knife scar across his cheek and livid red sores disfiguring his face causes me to stumble when he grabs my collar in his fist. He begs me to grant him a quick death, adding in a voice choked by emotion that his life has been a worthy adventure but that he is suffering too greatly to continue. And so, in the prayer I speak over his bent head, I ask the Lord of Mercy to call him home.

Many of those who come to me reveal their poor understanding of our mission by referring to Yeshua as our *melekh* – king – but it is easy to forgive them, for in their acclaim is their longing for a ruler who has come from their midst and whose crown will not glisten with the gold of earthly riches but shine instead with the crimson of divine justice.

After Yeshua pulls on the reins and brings Iason to a halt, he turns around to measure the length and breadth of the crowd with his eyes, and his gaze passes over me, and, for a tense, throbbing moment, I feel his thoughts brush over mine, and what he is thinking is this: *I must find a way to show them the path to a place they have never been before and the existence of which they may doubt.*

Over the next two hours, he leads his donkey and the five thousand men and women who have anointed him with their hopes through the streets, alleyways and squares of the city, on a route that follows its ancient walls, and even those who are not familiar with the concept of an *eruv* sense – in the very soles of their feet, most probably – that there is a higher purpose to the perimeter he traces.

Twenty-four Roman foot soldiers do not suspect his arcane and invisible purpose, however, and they keep vigil over what they likely regard as a degenerate mob. They march by our side in the broader streets and ahead of us through the narrower passageways. Youths on rooftops taunt them with insults about their masculinity.

I would venture to say that most of the faithful are able to forget that the Romans are observing us; we Jews have become adept at looking above and around what we would prefer not to see.

Once we have walked the perimeter of the capital, Yeshua leads us to the Synagogue of the Woodworkers. Annas, Caiaphas and seven other priests await us there, alerted by Yehudah, perhaps, as to the place where the troublesome preacher from the Galilee will address his friends and supporters. Do they understand that he will also consecrate it as the centre of the holy territory he has created – of his divine *eruv*? They stand with several score supporters, including a number of influential Pharisees well known to Yeshua and me. A large retinue of guards cordons them off from the people.

Caiaphas is dressed in his ceremonial robes. The golden seal on his turban reflects the sun, and, as he turns towards an assistant, a nymph of light races across the square, climbs up Iason and perches on one of the houses opposite.

I know the secret purpose behind his formal attire, but Shaul – the boy from Natzeret guarding me – does not. 'How could any of us trust a man who dresses like a peacock to receive a crowd of pilgrims and labourers?' he asks me with a snarl in his voice.

Apotropaios? Would he understand my Greek? I doubt it. And I do not dare speak to him of matters that would pose a danger to him. 'Remember how Aaron ended the plague' is all I tell him.

'What do you mean?' he asks.

Maryam has overheard our conversation and gives Shaul information that I would have preferred to withhold. 'His priestly robes are not merely a covering for the body, just as his breastpiece is not a decoration. He dresses that way to safeguard himself from all he cannot see or hear or even conceive and that would compromise his power – and from Yeshua's magic, most of all.'

After we stop walking, Yeshua brushes the dust from his tunic and sandals. His awkward gestures tell me he did not expect to be met by Caiaphas. With dread in my heart – like blood spilling – I wonder what his next move will be.

Is it our decades of training in scriptural interpretation that leads his thoughts to the third book of the Torah? Here is the verse he must have already recited to himself: 'When anyone amongst you brings an offering to the Lord, bring as your offering an animal from either the herd or the flock.'

Just after he sets off towards the rickety stalls of the marketplace opposite the synagogue, a naked little boy breaks though the line of guards brought by the priests and runs to him as if dashing towards a gift of which he has long dreamed. The child's hair is a tangled mop and his feet are filthy.

My old friend lifts him high into the air and says something that prompts the boy to giggle. Has he asked for the tyke's blessings? The boy presses both his hands on to Yeshua's head and shouts the prayer we use before eating bread, which sets the faithful laughing and cheering.

Has this moment of grace been planned?

I am about to conclude that it has when his mother – taut anger twisting her face – rushes up to Yeshua and grabs back her son, slapping him hard on his bottom, which sets him shrieking and wailing.

When I turn back to Yeshua, I spot Goliath standing twenty paces behind him, to the side of a stall belonging to a rug-seller. His eyes are fixed on Yeshua, who has started walking towards an elderly bird-seller.

The frantic beating in my chest tells me that there is a tether stretched between Goliath, Yeshua and me, and I slip my knife from my pouch. If he takes even one step forward, I intend to rush out to him, but he does not move; he watches Yeshua step up to the haggard-looking bird-seller, who shows him a pinched, suspicious face. *Go away – I want no trouble,* she tells him with her resentful eyes.

After he takes a coin from his scrip and hands it to her, she stands and goes to a large cane-work basket overstuffed with doves.

Goliath continues to observe, his head above all others. I hold my mother's amber necklace in my hand and pass the beads through my fingers, but even their smooth and generous roundness – the shape of thirty years of a mother's apprehension – is unable to keep me from picturing him charging Yeshua with murder on his mind.

The bird-seller wears two silver anklets on her right leg and a heavy carnelian charm around her neck. Her robe is a patchwork of remnants and rags sewn hastily together. The two birds that she withdraws are slender and grey, with a thin band – a graceful calligraphic stroke of black – around their necks. They are bound with twine.

Yeshua and the bird-seller speak for a time, but prayers and pleas shouted around the square cover their words. After she cuts the twine with her knife, she hands the doves to him, and he takes a bird in each hand.

Yeshua walks to the priests, intending, it would seem, to pay his respects by offering the doves for sacrifice. He speaks to Caiaphas with his head slightly bowed, and yet his message must be defiant; the High Priest ornaments his replies with frowns and abrupt hand gestures that would seem to indicate that he believes he has been insulted.

Goliath, still just watching, begins to bite his lips.

When Caiaphas turns his back on Yeshua and steps away, the golden bells sewn into the hem of his robe sound in my ears like a signal of attack, and an upsurge of fear sets me rushing forward until one of our bodyguards grabs my arm in his fist.

'My orders are to keep you with us!' he says gruffly.

'Let me go! Something very bad is about to happen,' I tell him.

But I am soon proved wrong; neither the priest's guards nor Goliath advance on Yeshua.

My old friend still holds his doves. Has Caiaphas refused his offering?

Yeshua starts back towards his followers but then halts abruptly at the centre of the square, as if he has just remembered an important duty. He holds out his doves out to us.

His gestures seem spontaneous, but it occurs to me that this moment might have been planned for years – in a place where he has longed ventured alone.

In the High Priest's outraged countenance, I read a single thought: *If I do not win this battle, this insolent Galilean will turn me out of my Temple, and I shall become as wretched as he is.*

Yeshua faces east, towards the sun. From the Book of Enoch, he shouts, '"For the chosen there will be light and joy and peace, and they will inherit the earth."'

He repeats the quotation three more times, facing north, south and west, and, when his eyes close, he chants an incantation from Yeshayahu: '"Yerushalayim, you shall be a crown of beauty in the hand of the Lord and a royal diadem in the open hand of your God."'

He then brings the two doves together, slowly and purposefully. Later, I will realize that he sealed the ends of his *eruv* together the moment they touched.

Have his actions summoned a visitor?

Yeshua scans the horizon, and when he spots who – or what – he is looking for, his eyes open wide with awe and he holds the birds high over his head.

'It's not sacrifice I seek but mercy and *racham!*' he calls out.

Yeshua turns in a slow circle, still holding the doves over his head, and he repeats his invocation to mercy and compassion three more times.

The same angel who saved Isaac has come to witness this moment.

I do not know how I know that, but I do.

And his message? *The Lord wishes no more sacrifices, not even of doves.*

And if that is the case, then I know that Yeshua is in for the battle of his life; without our rituals and rites of bloodletting, the Temple will cease to function as the centre of our lives, and the priests will no longer rule over us.

'"Ask now of the wild animals and they will teach you,"' Yeshua calls out to us, citing the Book of Job. '"Or speak to the Earth, for she will guide you."' He kneels, and the worshipful voice that comes from him is one that I seem to have known all my life. 'All the birds of the air will also tell it to you.'

He tosses the doves skywards.

It is time for their own flight to freedom – their own Passover – and those sleek, strong, graceful birds flap around the square in two rising circles.

Freedom is what they are announcing with each wingbeat.

It is a shock, of course, to see how easily Yeshua has released two creatures whose blood would have redeemed us before the Lord, and some in the crowd have prostrated themselves to ask forgiveness of the ruthless tyrant that they know from the Book of Job. Yet it makes me laugh in spirit to watch how the doves defy their terror – and all the limitations that men and women might impose on them.

Nothing can tie us to the earth when we lose our fear, I think.

One behind the other, the doves disappear over the rooftops, heading east, towards the birthplace of the sun.

When I look down again for Yeshua, he is threading his way through the crowd to my left.

An elderly shepherd with a white beard makes him pause by handing him his wooden goad. 'I've had this for forty years, and I am never without it, but I want you to have it now,' the man says.

Yeshua thanks him with a kiss but hands it back. 'Blessings to you who came into being before being born,' he says, which

I take to mean that the man's generosity and goodwill are far more important than the gift itself.

Perhaps the shepherd and I have made the same interpretation; he smiles excitedly and lays his tattered, fur-lined cape on the ground before my old friend. 'Our king has come at last!' he cheers.

24

Lucius is nowhere to be seen when I arrive at his villa, which is a blessing, since he gives me long, hectoring lectures on those occasions when I come late to work. While I prepare my tools, I endeavour to keep my thoughts earthbound, but they keep slipping free of me. They carry me high above my perfect Alexandria, to the crown of the lighthouse, where perching cormorants and cranes tell me of the wonders of Siracusa and Epidauros and all the other glorious places they have visited.

In comparison with these colourful fantasies, my mosaic comes to seem a static thing – servile, devoid of dignity. To smash all the tesserae to powder would seem my best option. And yet I do not take my hammer to them; I have learned there is a message worth reading in every failure, though finding it is not always an easy task.

Lying on my back and gazing up at the canvas awning that blocks the merciless sun from me, I consider what my mosaics would reveal about myself and the world if I had the courage to defy all expectations – if I could free what has been marked for sacrifice in my own self. Because that is, after all, Yeshua's message, even if only a handful of us have heard it.

After my midday meal, Lucius comes to see me at the bottom of his swimming pool. His brow is ribbed with worry, and his toga has been draped in a hasty manner by his personal slave. Without a word of greeting, he tells me in an outraged voice that he just received news that I accompanied Yeshua ben Yosef on his entry into Yerushalayim, which he calls a shameful display of *moria,* meaning stupidity or foolishness.

'Please, let's not quarrel,' I tell him, and, getting to my feet, I add, 'I've got a great deal of work I need to do today if I'm not going to fall behind schedule.'

'He offended Caiaphas!'

'Did he?'

'You know he did!'

'I didn't hear a word they said to each other. I was too far away.'

'So you admit you were there!'

'Of course I was there. I've never tried to hide from you that I've been friends with Yeshua since we were boys. But all I saw was him releasing two doves.'

He rolls his eyes. 'I know you're not a halfwit, Eli, but I must say that you're doing a perfect imitation of one at the moment!'

The amused pride he takes in his jest prompts me to laugh.

'Eli, Eli, Eli,' he says with a long sigh, as though calling for a truce, 'we all know the point he was making to the rabble.' He throws up his hands. 'The way they all follow that emaciated Galilean everywhere, as if he were draped in a golden fleece . . . It never ceases to amaze me.'

Lucius uses the word *ochlos* for rabble. His guttural pronunciation makes it sound as if he is speaking of peasants who ought to be cast into the nearest dungheap.

I take my time sitting back down, hoping to keep the terse, angry reply that is hiding under my tongue from coming out and losing me my back wages.

'Did you really think I'd be pleased with your behaviour?' he asks.

I open my hands and show him a questioning look that means, *Can you take the truth?*

'Go ahead,' he tells me.

'My companions and I were not part of any *rabble*,' I say.

'What word would you have me use?'

I take a marble tessera in my hand and squeeze it, considering how honest I can be. Looking him the eye, I risk the truth. 'I would say *citizens*.'

'Citizens!' he shouts back at me, then bursts out laughing.

Lucius becomes a little boy when he is bemused. While he is giggling with his hand over his mouth, I toss my tessera at the wall of the swimming pool, and it skitters back across my mosaic as if it, too, has been unable to find the exit out of this quarrel.

'I'm sorry,' he tells me after he has regained his composure.

'No, I'm pleased that I keep you in high spirits. Though I believe I deserve an additional payment for improving your mood.'

He dismisses that suggestion with a snort. 'Listen, Eli, your dear friend Yeshua told these *citizens* of yours that the priests and their sacrifices are of no importance.'

It's my turn to sigh. 'I just want to get on with my work, Lucius. Is that too much to ask?'

'Yes, Eli, it is. Because an acquaintance of mine who saw you with Yeshua just accused me of hiring a *lestes* to decorate my home!'

I hold up my callused and powdery hands. 'Do I look like a *lestes?*'

'As you well know, rebels come in a multiplicity of guises.'

'As do citizens!' I snap.

'Well played!' says Lucius, and he does his best to loosen the pinched fit of the toga over his hip while he thinks of an adequate reply.

More and more I have come to understand that Lucius respects only those who push him back. To block his next move, I say, 'The last thing I want is bloodshed.'

'Can you say the same for the Emperor in Rome?' he asks, lifting his brow.

'I try never to speak for Tiberius,' I tell him, 'especially since I am a very poor ventriloquist.'

As he laughs again, the rancour between us withdraws a few paces. He flashes me a fearful look and says in a hushed, tension-filled voice, 'I've been warned that they may be looking for an excuse to crush us again. And they will turn the Temple to rubble this time! You're too young, Eli, but I remember only too well when two thousand of our young men were crucified.' Spitting behind him, he says, 'Their stench still spoils far too many of my dreams.'

Lucius' reference is to the brief struggle for independence that took place around the time of my birth, after the death of the King of Judaea, Herod I. Varus, the Roman general who crushed the rebellion, decided to celebrate his victory – and give thanks to Mars – by decorating the hillsides around Yerushalayim with crucified Jewish warriors.

'Who told you the Romans want more blood?' I ask.

He stands back up and moans while pressing his hand into his lower back. 'Eli, you would do well to convince that Galilean sorcerer of yours to mix you a youth potion before you reach my age!' he says.

'I'll see what I can do. So who told you what the Romans want?'

'It makes no difference who it was. All you need to know is that I wouldn't like to see you, shall we say, *compromised* by ill-advised friendships. I aim to help you protect those artistic gifts of yours – with or without your assistance!'

Since neither of us is a fool – as we have already established – he does not need to add, *At least until you have finished my mosaics!*

In the middle of the afternoon, I hear Mia and Yirmi calling to me over the wall of Lucius' garden. After I open the gate, my sister rushes into my arms. Her eyes are ringed red, and the scent of her distress makes me shudder.

I hold her so tightly that she knows not to speak, for I need a few moments to prepare for the terrible news I expect her to give me; I am certain that it concerns Yeshua.

When I ease my grip on her, she says in a clenched whisper, 'The body of a young man . . . it was left at your door.'

Relief flows through me, since she has not spoken Yeshua's name. 'Which young man?' I ask.

'I don't know, but neighbours saw you walking with him this morning.'

An unruly crowd has assembled in front of my house, and Ion and Ariston are having no luck dispersing them, so we cross to the next street and make our way to Mia's home. In our common courtyard lies the young man about whom she has spoken.

'But I was just with him,' I say; the eternal protest of those who cannot forgive death for failing to announce a date and time.

Uriyah has been dumped so roughly that his right arm is pinned behind his back at a painful angle. His mouth hangs open, and his throat has been cut from ear to ear. A dark crust of blood circles his neck. The collar and right sleeve of his tunic have been soaked with blood.

To look at a boy whose lithe and perfect body has been so cruelly defiled means only one thing to me at that moment: there are men amongst us who cannot permit beauty to live.

I ask Yirmi to return to his room and wait for me there, then sit with my back against the wall and hide my grief behind my hands. The Torah of Mosheh teaches that we are each of us a universe, which means there are no longer mountains, rivers and forests in Uriyah – and no star-filled firmament to guide him.

And I am the reason why.

Mia questions me about who the boy is, but I intend to sit at the very bottom of my guilt for a time before climbing up again to speak of it. I owe that, at least, to the good-natured youth who spent his morning protecting me.

Some time later, footsteps I recognize cross the floor towards me.

Just turn around and leave! I exhort her in my mind, but she does not hear me.

'Eli, this silence of yours is selfish and absurd!' Marta snarls from directly above me.

I dare not look up at the outraged face she must be making.

Mia sits with me and whispers that she will support and defend me no matter what errors I have committed, and the tense hesitation in her voice tells me what she is imagining about the nature of my relationship with the young man. *Would that it were true,* I think, *for at least then I would have the taste of his youth in my mouth and feel of his timid grace in my hands.* Not for the first time in my adult life do I think that my life would have been easier if I had stayed in Alexandria.

At length, the wish to punish myself – to inform my sisters of my fatal mistake – coaxes me out of silence. 'I ought not to have walked with Yeshua this morning,' I confess. Marta will extract the perverse nectar she feeds on from my self-loathing, so, looking at her, I add, 'If I had gone to work at Lucius' villa this morning, this boy would be alive.'

'Eli, what are you talking about?' she demands.

'His name is Uriyah. We walked together behind Yeshua. He and another young man protected me. He's a Samaritan. And I realize now that –'

'A Samaritan?' Marta exclaims. 'No wonder this has happened!' Frowning viciously, she says, 'Eli, I want this creature out of our courtyard now!'

'Marta, please, this is no time for orders,' Mia tells her. 'We have to find out if he has family in Judaea.'

Marta grips the silver talisman of the Angel Rafael that she keeps around her neck, locks her panicked eyes on Uriyah and chants, 'From this foreigner's land come plagues, storms, demons and disasters, but my Lord shall protect me!'

Her incantation makes me understand that whoever killed Uriyah probably chose him – rather than the other boy who guarded me – because Samaritans are regarded as filth.

'Did anyone see who dropped him at my door?' I ask.

'A rag-picker with a donkey cart,' Mia says. 'He told me that a pilgrim came to him just outside the Dung Gate and paid him to carry the boy's body to your home.'

'Did this rag-picker know the pilgrim's name?'

'No.'

'Did he tell you anything about how the boy was murdered?'

'No, nothing. He said he asked no questions of the pilgrim.'

While gazing at Uriyah, I hear him say: *I couldn't have known any better – I am just a boy. But you ought to have predicted that this might happen and protected me!*

When I agree, he replies – gentler now, as though to acknowledge that I did not harbour any ill will towards him – *If I could return to this morning, I would refuse to walk beside you. I would be alive, and you would be spared this grief.*

His regret seems proof that destiny separates into a thousand different directions from every moment, but only one of them comes to pass, and none of us will ever know why that one was chosen, not even the dead.

'We must see that his body is buried early tomorrow morning,' I tell my sisters, and I kneel down to close his mouth, but Marta grabs my wrist. 'Don't touch him, Eli. He'll bring you bad fortune!'

I twist my arm free. 'Don't you understand? He shielded me from harm.'

While Marta glares at me, I close the boy's mouth with my hand, then free his twisted arm from behind his back. It is stiff and cold, which means he has been dead at least a few hours.

'Eli, you never seem to care how you put us in danger!' Marta says in an exasperated tone. 'You're selfish, exactly like our father, and you –'

'Damn you, Marta, leave me be!' I roar, and I kick the wooden stool that Mia keeps by her cooking tripod towards her. The dry thud of it crashing into the wall reminds me of how easily she turns me into a confused child. In a careful voice – warning her that a vial of poison is concealed behind each of my words – I say, 'You've paid me back a hundred times or more for having been beaten by our father all those years ago – and for my cowardice at not coming to help you. It's enough!

Either you give up your need for revenge – here, right now – or we cannot remain brother and sister.'

Why do I choose that instant to draw a border she dares not cross? I believe now that it is because I returned from death knowing that we have far less time than we think.

'Oh dear, I hadn't noticed until now what a bully you've become!' Marta says in a superior tone.

She swings around to Mia. 'Well, what do you have to say?' she demands, which is her way of trying to turn this into a two-against-one combat.

'Maybe it would be best if you returned to your weaving,' Mia tells her.

Marta thrusts her hand over her heart, looking – probably even to herself – like a mime who is trying way too hard to be convincing. 'Have you, too, come to hate me, dear sister?' she asks, and, though her voice seems genuine, the tears caught in her lashes are a strategy covered in twenty years of dust.

'Marta, please stop,' Mia replies, 'I can't think with you sniffling like that.'

Perhaps Mia's words have some special meaning to Marta that I do not know about; her eyes bulge and her face reddens. She extends both her hands palm up towards Mia, inviting hidden life to descend into the room, and speaks a curse in a slow, venomous chant, in a mixture of Aramaic and Egyptian, hoping, perhaps, that we will be unable to defend ourselves against what we do not understand.

I catch the words *shed*, meaning devil or demon, and *tsalmaveth,* a deep, penetrating shadow, and twice she uses the verb *yaqad* – to set ablaze – which leads me to conclude that she has asked a night-spirit to turn Mia to ash.

Who would have ever suspected that when Marta finally gave voice to the full, lethal scope of her wrath that she would direct it at the one person who has always supported her?

Mia reaches stunned hands up to her cheeks. Without thinking, I jump up, raise my hands over her head and recite the Shema from back to front, as Rabbi Baruch taught me. 'I've deflected her evil,' I whisper to Mia.

Is the sound of Marta's footsteps leaving the room the end of our lives together?

'This has become impossible,' I say. 'I'll ask Ion and Ariston to come up with a suitable reason for insisting that Marta join them when they return to Alexandria. We need to get her far away from us while we think of a permanent solution.'

Mia is sick in her stomach and unable to reply, so I fetch our basin.

At such times I perceive that no one can make me suffer like Marta; she knows that I shall worry far more about Mia than myself. Like a trained hunter, she can always find the part of me that is most dependent and fragile – the little brother in me.

I pray and chant over the lifeless husk that once gave home to all that was Uriyah, then walk seven times around him, enjoining his soul to find its path to the Lord without delay, since a sudden and violent death can make it adhere so tightly to our world that it remains amongst us as an *ibbur*. 'There is nothing left for you here,' I say aloud, and I adapt the words of Mosheh from the Book of Words to help his soul find its way: 'Climb ever higher, and do not look back at Balak and Balaam, and lift your eyes to the west and north and south and east, and gaze out over all the earth, and then cross the waters of the Jordan.'

I do not add that I wish I could revive him; if he is still with me, then he hears that unmistakably in my voice.

When Mia joins me, she kneels by Uriyah. 'What a waste death makes of youth!' she tells me with a reproving expression, and she begins to examine his hands. 'His fingers are stained by soot of some sort,' she tells me. 'But I'll clean them well – don't worry.'

While she removes his sandals, I cut away his blood-soaked tunic and discover the Greek letter *theta* etched into his right shoulder. It is engraved inside a crude circle.

'What could it mean?' I ask my sister, pointing, but she ventures no guess.

Scars that look like worms burrowing under the skin cover his back, a sign of repeated scourging. They extend up to the base of his neck and down to his buttocks.

Unspeakable things happened to me, Uriyah tells me as I study his face.

Mia takes the signet ring from the index finger of his right hand and inspects the inside of the band. 'For Avraham,' she reads, 'on his twentieth birthday.'

'Probably an inheritance from his father,' I suggest.

'Maybe his mother is still alive and we can find her,' Mia says with hopeful eyes.

I take a long look at her, and it seems that I have failed to see my sister as she is for many months – perhaps even years.

Mia, whose protruding, rabbit-like teeth and pointy face make her ugly to others.

Who gifted me young with the knowledge that only the beauty that love permits us to see can withstand the passage of time.

Who sometimes, even today, says her Sabbath prayers with her eyes open, keeping watch on her mischievous younger brother.

Mia waves at me irritatedly because my gaze has become too probing, then stares off beyond me – into the past, I soon learn. 'When you were born,' she tells me, 'your fingers were so tiny, and yet each one was so . . . perfect. When I held you for the first time, I began to understand some things that had eluded me until then.'

'Like what?'

She looks at Uriyah regretfully. 'I understood that the Lord made us too fragile. I wanted each moment of your life to involve a great deal more than just breathing and sleeping. I wanted every instant to be incredibly complex.'

'Why?'

'So that it would be harder for you to die.' She lowers her head as if to make a confession. 'I understood, too, that your life was an extraordinary gift, which meant that mine was, too.'

In the downward tone of her voice, I hear a final confession: *But I wasted so many years on things that didn't matter – most of all, on trying to please a husband who no longer loved me and a sister who wished to draw evil to me.*

She suddenly taps me playfully on the head. 'You know, Eli, when I get up in the morning, I feel the sunlight tugging me out into the world, but I want to stay in the darkness. I find I want to be alone more and more.' She raises her hands to her mouth and laughs. 'My goodness, I sound so morose. But the truth is, the world seems more beautiful to me today than it did when I was young.'

As she carries the basin into the corner, the sound of a baby crying reaches us.

'What's that?' I ask.

'I found a newborn exposed on the dungheap in Bethany this afternoon. She'd been burned badly by the sun. I'd better check on her.'

A few minutes later, the crying subsides. When Mia returns to me, she says, 'You haven't told me yet why Uriyah was murdered and dropped in front of your house.'

'It was a warning from Annas and Caiaphas.'

'What kind of warning?'

I take both her hands because I am about to frighten her. 'If I am seen again with Yeshua in public, I'll be next.'

25

The Jews of Alexandria say that sorrowful tidings fly more swiftly even than Raziel, and, that evening, as though to prove them right, an agitated crowd assembles outside my house and overflows the street into the dusty square surrounding Bethany's abandoned well. Still, my sisters and I allow no one – neither friends nor relatives – to come inside. We dare not, lest some malicious-minded guest spit on Uriyah or express his enmity for Samaritans in some equally odious way. Few understand why we are so keen to protect his body, however, and, since gazing at a dead youth will make them feel their good fortune more acutely, a number of them bargain with us for a peek at him.

Does our cobbler neighbour Aron ben Socrates really believe that I would grant him entrance to my courtyard in exchange for a pair of smelly old sandals?

I remain patient with all such infuriating proposals I hear until Mia lets our cousin Hannah and her husband Theodoros into my home. Hannah is tiny, feisty and built like a miniature bull, and she long ago crowned herself queen of her own small kingdom. In fact, she never looks up when she is speaking to the rest of us – her subjects – so that if you want to meet her glance you must lean down to her level. At the moment, she is standing just inside our door, talking to Mia while panting hard; it seems she has run all the way from her home in the bakers' quarter of Yerushalayim for a look at the body. Her eyes are painted with so much blue eyeshadow that they resemble peacock feathers. Without so much as a greeting, she peers around me as though I am a palm growing in the wrong place and points to the courtyard. 'Is he in there, Eli?'

The covetousness in her voice – implying that Uriyah belongs to her now – frees me from constraints I've so long held that I would have thought them part of me. I take my knife in my fist and tell her that she has to leave.

Mia presses my wrist back down. 'Eli, please stay calm,' she says.

Theodoros is an olive-oil importer and the son of rough-mannered nomads from Egypt, and he sizes me up with the sneer he reserves for townsmen that he considers overly educated. 'Talk to my wife properly!' he snarls.

'Theo, I hear your mother calling you,' I say. 'And she wants you home without delay.'

'Eli, what's got into you?' Hannah asks me.

At that moment, I realize I am being tested again – by the world itself if not by God. 'The greedy eyes of strangers shall not defile him,' I tell her.

'Strangers?' my cousin questions. 'Don't be absurd! You and I have known each other since we were tiny!'

'My point is, you didn't know the murdered boy.'

'Oh, please,' she scoffs. 'As it stands, he couldn't tell the difference between a crust of matzoh and the Megillah,' she adds in an authoritative tone.

I clutch my outrage to me as my shield. 'You wish me to accompany you into the wilderness, but I am staying here with Uriyah.'

'Good God, man!' Theo exclaims with a groan. 'You talk like you're reading scripture!'

'I'm not reading scripture, I *am* scripture!' I assure him, since that will scandalize him.

'You've always got to prove you're better than us,' he says resentfully, and, while he sweeps his hairy, monkey-like hand at me, Hannah shows me a fearful look and forms a protective symbol with her fingers.

'If I were a demon,' I tell her, 'I wouldn't bother speaking to you. I'd simply cast you straight into the Underworld.'

'Eli, please – let's keep this conversation friendly,' Mia requests.

In this context, *friendly* means *we must cede to their wishes, since they are family,* which is why I say, 'I have no intention of being friendly!'

Maybe it is true that my wits have forsaken me, for Hannah and Theo seem to me at that moment no more important than two wasps who have crossed the threshold of my doorway unbidden. Hannah is surprisingly gullible, and so, to rid myself of her, I ask to be permitted to tell her a story. 'It will prove I'm right,' I tell her.

'Right about what?'

'About you having to leave.'

'I doubt you'll prove anything but your own rudeness, but go ahead,' she says with regal courtesy.

I then adapt a story that our Torah master, Rabbi Baruch, once told me. 'When I was a boy of nine and living in Natzeret,' I begin, 'a nasty-looking viper followed me home on Yom Kippur. Yeshua used a powerful spell to force the creature to tell us why it was pursuing me, and it opened its mouth as though to attack us, but, instead, the soul of a man rose out of it, and it was a dark and red-glowing thing, like a burning shadow, and he confessed that he had been a tailor I'd once met with my father, and, when he recognized me passing in the street, he followed me, for he wished to confess his sins to someone he'd known in life. The tailor –'

'Is this the truth?' Hannah cuts in, running an uneasy hand down her neck.

'Why would I lie?' I ask her, and I continue my story before Mia can contradict me. 'The tailor explained to us that, after he was murdered two months earlier, he possessed the body of a snake so he might avenge himself upon his wife. He told us that he still slithered into her bed every night and forced her to couple with him. And do you know why he wanted vengeance, dear Hannah? Because she'd dishonoured him after his death by permitting his murderer inside their home so that he might gloat over his body!'

Hannah's eyes cloud with tears. 'That's a horrible story!' she tells me.

'Eli, was that really necessary?' Mia asks me disappointedly.

Sensing a defeat going far beyond this time and place – a test failed – I am about to ask Hannah to please simply grant my request and leave, but, as I begin to speak, she makes an error of judgement. 'Everyone knows how kind I am', she interrupts, 'and that I'd never do anything to hurt anyone. So I don't know why you are so eager to make me leave.'

'Hannah, how can you not be embarrassed to speak so highly of yourself?' I ask. 'And why can't you understand that the dead deserve our respect?'

My cousin removes her headscarf, which means she plans to continue this argument for as long as it takes to get her way. 'Mia, please tell Eli how I helped your dear mother after your father died,' she says. 'He must have been too young to remember.'

Speaking of those desperate days to my sister is another error; she will not lie about our mother's suffering simply to be kind to a visitor. 'Helped my mother?' she exclaims in disbelief. 'In all those desolate months, during our worst moments of despair and poverty, you came to see us all of once!'

'That's not true! I remember I brought you barley soup the first time, and then, there was another time, after your mother got ill –'

'Enough, Hannah! If you want the truth, our mother always hated having you in our home.'

'Eli, are you under the illusion that returning from the dead has made you into an important man?' she asks scornfully, and her husband adds, 'To us, you'll always be just a pathetic little labourer who has memorized too much scripture!'

A moment later, Hannah thrusts her royal spear into me as far as she can. 'You're an embarrassment to your family!' she says with a sneer. 'And you always will be!'

I smile then, because that particular insult will permit me to voice a sentiment I've been meaning to express to a great many neighbours and relatives since I came of age. 'Causing embarrassment to you and all the other sanctimonious simpletons in my life is the Lord's way of telling me that I'm on the absolute right path.'

She is so stunned by my words that it takes her a few moments to locate the shreds of her righteousness, and by the time she does I have turned away from her and passed into the courtyard. 'We shall pray for you, Eli!' Hannah calls after me.

If I go back to her I shall strike her, so I keep walking.

After Hannah has vented her continued outrage on poor Mia, she finally departs. I ask our cousin Ion to guard the front door and instruct him to let no one enter except Yeshua or his followers. I very likely ought to realize that I have terrified Mia with my outburst, but I am aware of little beyond my own nervous discomfort at that moment.

A short while later, as I anoint Uriyah with Mia's oils, my exhaustion is replaced by the comforts of ritual. *We all share the same needs* is what the movements of my hands mean, and, even if it isn't true, I am, for the moment, part of a community that includes every being that has lived and died.

While I prepare Uriyah for burial the next morning, I spot Yirmi stealing timorous glances at me from Mia's bedroom. I summon him to me and tell him of the obligations we have to the dead. From the way he shivers in my arms, I can sense that he is standing in the shadow of his own mortality, so I cut short my explanations and tell him all that a boy his age needs to understand: 'Everyone deserves an honourable burial, just as all of us deserve a good and fruitful life. And if he hasn't any kin to perform this *mitzvah*, we must.'

'But why aren't you afraid of touching his body?' Yirmi whispers to me.

'Because the dead wish us well if they wish anything at all.'

'How can you be certain?'

If Hannah had not insisted so vehemently on seeing Uriyah, would I have known what to reply? I caress my son's cheek so that he will remember the lesson my cousin has just taught me. 'What I am sure of is that it's the living who fail to show compassion and common sense at times of grief, and who all too often cherish the misfortune of others.'

Flies have begun gorging on the wound across Uriyah's throat, so I cover it with a linen cloth, which I fix in place with the beach-stones that I brought back years ago from Alexandria. Soon afterwards, Maryam of Magdala and Yohanon come to visit. They have already heard what has happened to Uriyah, and I speak to them of my certainty that his murder was meant as a warning for me – and that because of this I cannot permit myself to be seen with Yeshua or any of his disciples.

Maryam tells me that an undertaker has accompanied them to my home and is waiting outside with his donkey cart. I hand her the ring that Mia took from Uriyah's finger.

The undertaker has long curly hair and smells of sesame paste. He grips Uriyah under his arms and lifts him into his barrow. The scars on the boy's back catch my attention again.

'A letter *theta* has been etched into his right shoulder,' I point out.

'The mark of his master,' Yohanon says.

'Uriyah was a slave?' I ask.

'Yes.'

'He didn't mention that.' While wondering what else Uriyah failed to tell me, I ask if he was truly a Samaritan.

Maryam confirms to me that Uriyah was from Shalem and that it was there that they first met him. 'The little mischief-maker robbed us!' she adds, and her eyes shine with amused admiration. It is a look that reminds me that there is a great deal in Maryam I would like to know.

'Robbed you how?' I ask.

'He slipped into our camp as silent as a scorpion and took away two of our packs.'

'When we awakened,' Yohanon says, 'we tracked his footsteps to a stream, and we found him standing on the bank, devouring one of our fish.' Yohanon grimaces. 'Eli, he was eating it raw! I don't even think he'd removed the scales.'

'Around his feet were iron anklets,' Maryam tells me in an outraged voice. 'He told us later that his uncle had first put chains on him when he was only five years old. Can you imagine? Later, when he was twelve, his uncle sold him to a wealthy Roman builder. When we met him, he'd escaped and was being hunted by slave-catchers.'

Without my asking, the rest of the story of how Uriyah came to follow Yeshua spills out of her, as if it had been consuming all her deepest emotions for far too long. I have the impression that Uriyah meant something to her that she doesn't entirely understand and hopes to learn by speaking to me of him.

Here is what she tells me.

When Uriyah spotted us approaching him, he didn't flee. Maybe he'd decided to stop running and fight. He'd broken the chain between his legs, but he had been unable to remove his iron anklets. At least, that's what we'd thought. Yeshua walked towards him with his arms open in greeting, but the boy grabbed his axe and shouted, 'I'll chop off your head if you come any closer! I won't be taken back!'

Yeshua lifted off his tunic and threw it ahead. 'It's too big for you,' he said, 'but you still have some growing in you, and it will fit you within a year.' He then removed his sandals and tossed them to the boy as well.

'Why would you give me your clothing?' Uriyah asked suspiciously.

'Because it's mine to give.'

'But now you'll be naked.'

Yeshua laughed and replied, 'Naked we came from our mother's womb and naked we shall return.'

'How did you find me?' the boy asked.

'The others followed your footsteps, but I heard your cry for help.'

Uriyah kneeled down then to pick up Yeshua's tunic, but, on touching it, he drew back his hand as though from a fire. 'Have you put a curse into your tunic?' he asked.

'Why would I wish to curse you?' Yeshua replied.

'I saw you healing the people of a village once, years ago, so I know that you have great powers. How do I know you haven't turned to evil?'

'Because I always try to be worthy of the lilies of the field and lift my face towards the truth,' Yeshua replied. 'Now, what's your name, young man?' he asked.

'Uriyah ben Avram.'

'Come to me, Uriyah, for I mean you no harm and you need help, and my companions may soon lose their patience and ask me to leave without you, and I fear that if we abandon you, you'll soon be caught.'

As the boy reached him, Yeshua took his hands, which were soiled and scarred. He bent to kiss them, but Uriyah pulled them back. 'No!' he protested.

'I was once a slave, too,' Yeshua told him. 'So we meet as equals.'

'When were you a slave?'

'We were all of us slaves to Pharaoh at the time of Mosheh. I walked behind him then, just as I walk behind him now. Every sunrise, in my morning prayers, he and I journey together to the Promised Land.'

'The way you speak, it isn't how . . .' The boy shrugged to end his sentence, unwilling to risk offending Yeshua, who embraced him and told him he need not fear any of us.

Yeshua then helped Uriyah put on his tunic. Later that morning, we went to see an old friend, a blacksmith, and Yeshua borrowed a chisel and a hammer. 'Now we shall remove those anklets of yours,' he told the boy.

Uriyah nodded his agreement, but, as Yeshua was working, he burst into tears. 'Please stop!' he pleaded.

'But why?'

'I've had them on so long . . . It feels like you're removing my feet!'

Maryam's voice caves in as she finishes her story. When I go to her, she whispers something to me that still makes me come to a halt in the street on occasion. 'Uriyah told me when we were alone that he would never take Yeshua's tunic off, because it had been worn by the *Melekh ha-Mashiah*.'

It is not the first time I have heard Yeshua called our Anointed King, but the way Maryam covers her mouth when she speaks the words makes my spirit tremble.

Secrets confided to friends sometimes summon others, and I tell Yohanon and Maryam that Uriyah gave me to understand that it was a miracle that Yeshua was able to remove his fetters.

'No, nothing of the sort,' Yohanon replies dismissively. 'The chisel was sharp and the hammer sturdy. Yeshua has long known how to use such tools.'

Yohanon keeps a list of Yeshua's miracles, and he regards it a sacred duty, so I am loath to challenge his verdict. And yet this seems an exceptional case. 'Uriyah told me that the freedom Yeshua gave him was a miracle,' I say. 'And surely the scars of slavery that he carried in his flesh since he was five years old made him understand what took place between him and Yeshua far better than any of us.'

A fraction of an hour later, as the undertaker's donkey cart turns the corner at the end of my street, I am struck by how easily friends and acquaintances enter and exit the tiny stage I inhabit. Is it so with everyone? It is surely a great and important failing that we do not know how to keep our loved ones with us for ever.

Inside the cart, the tunic that once belonged to the *Melekh ha-Mashiah* again covers Uriyah's nakedness, as he would have wanted. I performed that *mitzvah* myself.

And here is what I think now, so many years later: how strange it is that we have so little control over who will converse with us only briefly, like Uriyah, and who will remain with us for ten or twenty years or more; and even more peculiar that a young bricklayer who walked with me on my journey for no more than a couple of hours has never faded from my memory. Indeed, he appears in my mind more worthy of the good and long life he never had than on the day he decided to hide his greatest truth from me.

26

Marta makes a noisy exit from her house as Mia and Yehudit are preparing supper, complete with the mutterings and repetitive coughing she indulges in when she wishes to draw attention to her suffering. A little while later, I discover that she has left with the sunburned baby girl that Mia rescued from a dungheap.

'She must be taking her to the orphanage,' Mia says, but there is doubt in her voice, and she runs her hand back through her hair as though assaulted by intolerable terrors.

That she and I can imagine Marta capable of infanticide – as revenge against us – is something we acknowledge as our eyes meet. Mia stops me at the door. 'You're worn out, Eli,' she whispers, 'and in any case, you won't be able to catch her. She knows the labyrinth of Yerushalayim's streets as well as you do.'

A half-hour later, the women at the orphanage confirm our worst fears; they have not seen Marta for at least a week.

During supper, Mia and I picture the crime our sister may have already committed. Inside our glum silence, it becomes evident to me that we are unable to predict how our actions will hurt others – even those, like the baby Mia rescued, to whom we are tied by only the slenderest of filaments.

I discover then what I would like for others to say of me after I am gone: *Lazarus ben Natan, who did as little damage as he could.*

Pity the father whose preoccupations make him unaware of the mysteries and miseries of an adolescent son; Yirmi bursts into tears as the rest of us admire the platter of almond biscuits that Mia carries to us. In a resentful voice, he refuses to tell me what is troubling him. Once we are behind his closed door, however, he starts to weep. I gather him in my arms and apologize for being so negligent of late. To press his slender chest to my own is to feel the oddness of our separate bodies.

After all these years together, Yirmiyahu ben Eliezer, do you know that I am still not sure where you end and I begin?

I sit him down opposite me on his mat. He catches his breath and dries his eyes with his fists, exactly as he has done since he was an infant.

'Lean forward,' he tells me, and he pinches a crumb out of the whiskers that I have allowed to grow of late on my chin. I take advantage of our closeness to brush his silken hair out of his eyes.

Strange are the deliberations of a man who knows that he has lost both control of his life and the will to counsel his children. It occurs to me that if the Almighty were to take pity on us and transform Yirmi and me into the sleek and beautiful animals – Galilean foxes, for instance – instead of a fearful father and his tacit son, he and I would get past this impasse by continuing to groom each other. I would lick the tangles out of his thick red fur, and he would sniff at my neck with his twitchy black nose and gnaw on my leg to see how far he could provoke me before I would tap him with a parental paw, and, when we'd had enough of tasting and testing each other, we'd trot off side by side in our confident, stiff-legged way, certain right up to the tufted tips of our ears that we'd understood all we'd ever need to understand about each other.

But we have been born as children of Adam, which is why I shake my head at my own awkwardness.

'What are you thinking?' Yirmi asks.

Dare I reveal my peculiar thoughts to my son? 'If you could become any animal you wanted, which would you chose?' I ask.

'A tiger,' he replies confidently.

'Why a tiger?'

He bares his teeth and growls.

'Do we need a fearsome beast in our lives?' I ask.

'You do.'

'Ah, I see. My need for protection is what has upset you?'

When he nods, I say, 'Listen closely, Yirmi. Whoever is behind Uriyah's death won't risk incensing the crowds who follow Yeshua by hurting me. No harm will come to me or any of us as long as I'm careful. And I intend to be *very* careful from now on.'

'I don't want you leaving the house,' he says.

'I have to go every morning to Lucius' villa. Otherwise, I shall not earn enough silver to keep us fed, and you and your sister and Aunt Mia will have to make do with berries and herbs foraged along the hillsides.'

'I wouldn't mind, if it would keep you safe.'

'Nahara might.'

As though I have misunderstood everything about him and his sister, he says in a voice ceding to despair, 'Nahara would do far more than that to keep you with us. She would do anything for you!'

Tears appear again in his eyes, which inevitably summon my own. So hesitant am I to give him any counsel, however, that I realize once again what a poor substitute I am for his mother. How many times have I learned and forgotten that this son of mine tends to spot trouble everywhere he looks? Rabbi Elad, who tutors him in Greek, says that Yirmi's soul was born in the River Kokytos, whose waters are the sum of all our tears, but the truth is that he was scarred too soon and too deeply by his mother's death. Still, perhaps there is a way I can turn this oversight to my advantage.

'You and I will make a deal,' I tell him.

'What kind of deal?'

'If I give you my word that I shall not meet with Yeshua or any of his disciples or friends in public, you must stop being so concerned about me.'

'Can you stop worrying whenever you want?' he asks with a frown.

'No, but you can try to let me do all the worrying for the two of us.'

'Very well, but I also want to go with you every day to Lucius' villa.' He senses that I am about to refuse his request and quickly adds, 'At least until the end of Passover.'

Only when everything is as it was shall my son and I find peace.

That thought seems like the very earth below my feet. 'No, we need to go back to the way things were,' I tell my son. 'I'll take you to your studies with Rabbi Elad every morning and then go on alone to work.'

'May I at least come with Aunt Mia to escort you home in the afternoon?'

'Yes. Anything else?'

'No, that's all,' he replies, but then, with a cagey smile, he adds, 'For now anyway!'

The pleasure of bargaining with my son is new to me and so gratifying that it makes me take him in my arms again.

I go to bed with Grandfather Shimon's old sword by my side, but every footfall on the street makes me picture Goliath and other assassins waiting for me, and it soon becomes clear that, if I am ever to sleep again, I shall have to assure myself that Annas no longer considers me even a minor nuisance, so I light my lamp and fetch my calamus. All my ink is dry, so I drizzle honey into my mortar and mix in a handful of charcoal, and I work this amalgam into a black liquid with my pestle.

Unless I have your permission, I write, *I shall never appear in any square or street or building in Judaea with Yeshua. If you have any doubts, then send for me. I implore you not to hurt anyone else.*

I end my adjuration with a Proverb of Shelomoh: 'Let not mercy and truth forsake you; bind them about your neck and write them upon the table of your heart.'

A lesson that writing this note teaches me: courage is a luxury that I shall not be able to afford again until both my son and daughter are grown, with families of their own.

In bed that night, I listen over and over to all I said to Uriyah as if needing to find a password to redemption. I awaken early the next morning to knocking on my front door. I jump up, but Mia beats me there. 'Who is it?' she asks suspiciously.

'A friend of Yeshua's.'

My sister and I look at each other curiously because our visitor has a child's voice.

The small boy on my doorstep has brown hair cut in a perfect line across his brow – like a young Caesar – and his eyes are obsidian beads. He carries a linden leaf in his hand, and on it is a ladybird.

'Are you Lazarus?' he asks me, and, as I tell him I am, the ladybird takes wing. 'They never stay where they're supposed to,' he says, but without any resentment, and he tosses his leaf to the street.

'Yeshua wants to speak to you,' he tells me.

The boy looks familiar. 'Do we know each other?' I ask.

He folds his lips inside his mouth as if the wrong answer might earn him a scolding. Mia leads him inside. I close the door, place a protective hand on his head and ask him if Yeshua told him anything else.

'He said he can't risk coming here because . . . because . . .' The boy grimaces.

'What's your name?' Mia asks him.

'Yonah.'

'Well, my little dove,' she says, playing on the meaning of his name, 'I suggest that you go back to the beginning of what you were instructed to tell us. And go slowly. That's always best when you're not sure where you're headed.'

The boy gives us a big nod. 'He said he can't risk coming here because he is certain that . . . that . . . your house is being watched!' Yonah smiles in triumph. 'He asks for you to meet him where you used to look for the Guardians of Mosheh.'

Mia turns to me for an explanation.

'Mosheh summoned ibises to kill the winged serpents that attacked him as he crossed an Ethiopian swamp,' I tell her, and to our young guest, I say, 'I'll meet Yeshua there, but he has to be certain he is not being followed. If he has any doubts, then he must not join me. Do you understand? Will you tell him that?'

After Yonah memorizes my message, Mia sends him on his way with an almond biscuit, which he sniffs, then eases into his pouch with admirable care.

'Do you want me to come to see Yeshua with you?' Mia asks as I dress.

'Is Marta back?'

'No.'

'Then you better stay for when she returns.'

'All right,' she says, 'but listen close, Eli . . .' Mia raises a finger to her forehead and taps it twice, which is our childhood signal for *don't take any chances*.

To confound Goliath and any other spies sent by Annas, I climb up to the roof and make my way across the adjoining dwellings, bent low to the roof tiles, and drop down to the cross street at the end of our row of houses. Even at this early hour, Alexandros is already seated on his millstone. As I pass him, an old friend, Onesimos the jeweller, hails me from the road west. He runs across a field of onions to me and tells me that he has been off procuring medicines from a herb-gatherer. He pleads with me to come with him to his home some time that day and bless his daughter, Ninah, who has a tooth abscess and high fever. I promise to visit as soon as I complete my errand and ask him to tell no one he has seen me, then hurry towards the pink-and-gold cavern of sunrise in the east. I take a circuitous route, cutting across two small farms belonging to acquaintances. Stabbing pains – the worst I have ever experienced – shoot up into my hip when I climb over the low wall separating the properties, and for a time I am forced to lie on my back against the dry earth.

By the village of Barsoum, a shepherd with the blood of birthing on his hands and tunic allows me to drink from his bucket. He tells me of the lambs he has bred for the Passover sacrifice and of a ewe that died in his arms at dawn just after giving birth.

Do I remember his affectionate and tender eyes as he carried the orphaned lamb to me because everything from that fatal time has taken on the glow of ancient myth? Perhaps I am looking for a sign of the flood that was soon to take my home from me.

Malakhi. That was the shepherd's name. He was twenty-two years old and had a red birthmark on his brow. Does he still live in Barsoum, and would he remember the hobbling Galilean who asked to hold the orphaned ewe in his arms?

*

Around a bend in the stream that is isolated by massive limestone boulders, in what has long been my preferred spot for observing herons and egrets, stands the gaunt, olive-skinned creature I seek. He is up to his knees in the glistening water, naked except for his Greek traveller's hat.

His goat-like ribs make me draw shallow breaths. Shall I bother him by mentioning that he must take more sustenance if he is to lead us into unknown territories?

When he turns to me, he flaps invisible wings, which in our private language means he needs me to watch over his body while he is with the Lord in the *Hekhal ha-Melekh*. This makes my heart contract in my chest, for it is a reminder that I am needed to safeguard his well-being. And yet I shall have to tell him that I cannot be seen with him over the coming weeks. Despite the smile I offer him, does he read my despair?

He steps out of the water, kneels down and searches amongst the stones on the stream bank, and, when he finds the one he wants, encloses it in his fist. As he walks to me, he touches it to his forehead. When he is twenty paces away, he stops and tosses it to me. I catch it effortlessly, for my hands remember the high, challenging arcs of our boyhood games. The stone is smooth and brown, with a white line near its centre – a horizon of grace and benevolence between sea and sky. I hold it to my brow to complete the circle he has begun and then cast it into the stream.

The trilling of birds turns Yeshua around. He spots them halfway up a nearby terebinth tree and points them out to me: three bee-eaters hiding behind showy red flower clusters, unwilling to reveal themselves to the featherless creatures who trap them in nets and sell them in their marketplaces.

The iridescent blue and green of their chests and comforting brown of their backs withhold nothing – and remind me that only men and women are condemned to learn the word *modesty*.

I turn in a circle because I sense the future tugging at me, and I want to see the exact shape of the world as it is now before I leave it behind.

A gust of wind suddenly thrusts up its hands and sets the branches of the terebinth shaking, and the bee-eaters begin to sing again, and their strange, discordant warbling seems to have a purpose just for me, but I do not yet know what it is, and they take wing as I start towards Yeshua, as if to keep me guessing. The vibrating energy I discover inside his arms means that he is chanting hymns in his mind. He leads me into a rocky clearing, and we sit together.

'You told no one, I hope, that you were meeting me,' I say.

'Only Yaaqov, my brother.'

I remember then who little Yonah was – Yaaqov's youngest son.

We speak of the boy and of his father as a way of easing into deeper matters. Or so I believe. At the first Gate of Silence that meets us, however, Yeshua stands and walks back to the stream. He splashes his face and arms with water and seats himself by an ancient olive tree that we have known for years and that must have belonged to a farm that was once here. He prays aloud while keeping his eyes on me.

I've misunderstood his needs, I think. *He is having trouble returning to our world from the* Hekhal ha-Melekh *and is using me to light his pathway home.*

Yeshua locks eyes with me while chanting a hymn to the Lord of Hosts. Neither of us looks away, even for a moment. And when he comes to me this time, his steps are more secure; he has returned in body and spirit to our world. He sits opposite me, and, as we speak of his entry into Yerushalayim and of the thousands who followed him, his eyes open wide with excitement. I tell him that I felt our future take flight towards the Promised Land when he released his two doves.

'We shall finally obey Shelomoh's instructions,' he says, referring to the Proverb, *To do what is right and just is more acceptable to the Lord than sacrifice.*

Our conversation turns then to Uriyah, and he tells me, fighting tears, that, when he removed the boy's anklets, he discovered that his bones had been stunted and deformed by his fetters.

He uses the word *qalat* for deformed, adding that he removed the curse of bondage from Uriyah – his *qelalah* – while anointing his legs and feet.

Qalat and *qelalah* . . . Does Yeshua mean to remind me of their likeness because he has realized that there is always a deformity of the soul where there is slavery?

After he tells me of the hopes he had for Uriyah, I sense that the time has come for me to speak to him of my decision. 'I'm convinced that Annas had the young man murdered to send me a message,' I begin.

'Which makes it a message for me as well,' he says. 'Lazar, Maryam and Yohanon told me what you've decided,' he adds, which saves me the difficulty of speaking aloud of the choice I was forced to make.

'Are you angry with me?' I ask.

'Angry? No. How could I be angry with you?'

'I can't take risks with the lives of my children. If Leah were alive, I would proclaim my allegiance to you from the steps of the Temple. But without her my children . . . they have only me, which means that the way to you is blocked to me right now.'

The finality in the words, *the way to you is blocked,* has too much meaning for me, and when he squeezes my hand – to convey his acceptance of my decision – I must look away from him. 'I'm sorry about all these tears,' I tell him. 'I don't know what's wrong with me of late.'

'I asked you to come here so that I can help you,' he says.

With our hands joined, I become what is most generous in me, so I speak of how proud I am of him and that I am filled with hope. 'Is now the time?' I ask, meaning, *Will justice finally come to Zion?*

'I can do nothing on my own but only what the Lord asks me to do,' he says.

His vague reply is an indication that he wishes once again to withhold his plans from me. Still, I question him about how he intends to use the *eruv* he constructed. He speaks of the archons he has stationed at Yerushalayim's gates and of the angelic language with which he sealed the borders of his *garden,* which is how he calls his *eruv,* and of other matters that are beyond the frontiers of my knowledge. Does he believe I am wider and deeper than I am? It occurs to me then that he is still watching me from somewhere above, and, from that perspective, my borders must flow and mingle into his own, like dyes running into each other.

Does he see my keen fondness for him as easily as I see the scars on his feet? What shape and colour does my love have in the Throne World?

'You must be lonely at times,' I tell him, because I am thinking that there is much he cannot discuss with anyone.

Adapting the words of Yehoshua to this moment, he shrugs and says, 'I am lonely only when I forget that the Lord my God is in every letter and word.'

Is that as close as he will ever come to admitting that there are times when he wishes a companion might ascend on the Chariot with him?

My bad leg is throbbing, so I stand up and stretch at the edge of the stream, and from there, with my feet tingling from the chill of the water, I question him about what he told Caiaphas before releasing his doves. He tells me that he reminded the High Priest that we have brothers and sisters who are living in misery and hunger and whom we leave behind each Passover, but that this year – a few days hence, when we leave Pharaoh behind and cross over to the Promised Land – he will ask the meekest amongst us to join him before any others. 'I shall feed the poor and dress their wounds, just as you ought to do,' I told Caiaphas.

'Now I know why he turned away from you with such an angry expression!'

Yeshua replies with a bemused smile and comes to me in the water. He helps me take off my tunic and leads me into a deep cold pool, where we talk of trifles for a time. Only when we are back on land and drying off does he tell me that he sees the Angel of Death beside me at all times.

'He is standing between you and me even now,' he tells me.

'And until I know where we go when we die, I fear he'll remain with me,' I reply.

Yeshua speaks to me again of when we first met, and the affection in his voice and hands and eyes assures me that I am exactly where I need to be and that it does not matter if I shall one day vanish, because we are together now.

Is that one of my old friend's most astounding gifts – the ability to assure whoever he is talking to that death is of no importance?

He blesses me and asks me to join him at the edge of the stream. When he begins to pour water over me with his cupped hands, I understand why he summoned me.

After my hair and shoulders are soaked, and while I am on my knees and shivering, he summons the Holy Spirit to us by chanting a *chayot* hymn that Yohanon ben Zechariah taught us. Then, on his request, we exchange places, and I drip water over his head while reciting the same verses.

After he stands, he comes around behind me, puts his coarse hands on my shoulders and presses down. Twice he orders the Angel of Death to leave me, shouting, *'Malak Malach!'* The third time, he whispers that same command in my ear, and his breath, warm, seems to scatter my thoughts away from me and up through the top of my head.

I am gone for a time. And I dream that a hand is covering my eyes, and its fragrance is sweet and pungent – something like the thyme sprigs that Mia chars as incense.

When the hand comes away, I find myself in my bedroom, seated on my mat, though that seems impossible. I wish to speak, but I do not wish to disturb the silence, since it seems holy. Yeshua is seated opposite me. *You are always with me,* he tells me inside my mind, and he smiles with bemused affection.

And then a sense of rapid descent – of free fall – makes me call out to him for help, and I awaken for real, and Yeshua removes his hand from my eyes, and I see that I am sitting under the terebinth tree where we spotted the bee-eaters.

'You are the resurrection,' he whispers, 'and I am the life.'

Yeshua and I put our tunics back on, and I am at ease with myself – at home in my flesh – for the first time since my revival. He sees the change in me and shows me a relieved smile, so I risk telling him that his mother came to me.

'I know,' he says. 'Friends told me.'

'So now you're the one spying on me!' I say, doing my best to look outraged.

I expect him to grin, but his eyes close again as if he has heard a summons from far away. 'Let's go back a different way,' he tells me, and, when we come to a split in our trail, we walk south instead of west, which will take us to the villages east of Bethany, and, as we make our way across a small farm, four women appear from behind a copse of oaks a hundred paces ahead, wearing tattered robes, three of them barefoot, dark mantles concealing their heads and shoulders. They cry out *tamê* in anguished voices and hold their hands over their faces in case we throw stones at them.

Did Yeshua see them on his way to the stream and wish to comfort them? Very probably, but I understand now that he was also anxious to teach me a final lesson that I might not otherwise have ever learned.

A breeze sends their putrid smell of decay to us, and I cup my hand over my nose. Still, Yeshua leads us closer, and, after he assures them that we shall do them no harm, they beseech us for food.

I remain thirty paces away. The tightness at the back of my throat is the physical form of my cowardice and shame, but I dare not go to them, for, if their affliction were to adhere to me, I would never be able to hold my children again.

Yeshua embraces each of the leper-women and gives them bread from his pouch. They lead him by the hand to an elderly man seated in the shade of the broadest of the oaks, unable to walk. Yeshua kneels and lays his hands on the sores along his skeletal legs, speaking prayers, pressing his healing into the ruined flesh. When the man removes his hood, the other lepers turn away. Yeshua takes his shoulders and presses his lips to his crusted forehead, then to each of his blinded eyes.

'Are you not frightened of them?' I ask my friend as we get on our way again.

'I'm frightened only of how they suffer.'

'How do you find the will to . . . to touch them?'

He stops walking. 'Embrace me!' he says angrily.

Terror pounds in my head, for he has touched five lepers and may spread their misfortune to me. Yet when he repeats his request, I take him in my arms and kiss his lips.

'How did you overcome your fear of me?' he asks as we separate.

'My affection and respect for you would not permit me to refuse you.'

'Exactly so.'

After the spires of Yerushalayim rise up at the western horizon, we reach the crossroads where we must separate, since Yeshua wishes to return to his disciples. 'Will you tell me what you'll do next,' I ask.

'I'll go to the Temple later today,' he says.

'To talk to the priests?'

'No, to tell them that God's blessings must not be bought and sold.' He holds up his hands when I question him further. 'I've already told you too much.'

'I've been told that the Romans are looking for an excuse to crush us,' I say.

'I've been careful not to provoke anyone since we were eight years old,' he says, meaning, *I can continue no longer.*

'Where are you staying in Yerushalayim?'

He replies that I can get word to him through his brother Yaaqov, then looks off towards Yerushalayim, and I can tell that he is eager to set sail from the island we make together. The fear that he will live the next months and years without me cleaves to my breathing, however.

'Stay with me.'

I do not know who speaks these words; they escape my mouth of their own accord, as though fleeing a collapsing city.

He gazes down, searching for an adequate reply, but I do not wish to make him find one. 'I'll walk you part of the way to Yerushalayim, then turn back for Bethany,' I tell him, and I lead him forward.

A short time later, I remember what Lucius told me about our conquerors. 'The Romans may destroy the Temple if you provoke them,' I say. 'What then?'

'Then,' he replies, choosing his words carefully, 'I shall build it back up before the next Sabbath.'

'How will you do that?'

'I'll build a Temple from the temporal.' He uses the word *zeman* for temporal. It can also mean to number, apportion or, by extension, to assign places to guests, so I conclude that he means to do away with the privileges of the priesthood and welcome all men and women to the Temple as equals. But that proves a misunderstanding; he explains that we no longer need a geographic centre. 'The Sabbath is the holy centre of our lives and always has been, though most of us have forgotten.'

'But your supporters will want a place of worship.'

Yeshua points to the broad sycamores and cedars along the side of the road.

'Many people will not understand that trees are enough,' I say. 'And the priests will lose all their power if there is no Temple.'

'You can't lose what was never yours,' he says, and he quotes Yeshayahu. '"Woe to those who call evil good and good evil, who confuse darkness for light and light for darkness."'

'Caiaphas will never give up his privileges without a fight.'

'Caiaphas is a *Philoromaios*. All his knowledge of the law has not made him wise.'

'He doesn't need to be wise. He has authority.'

'He has the authority Rome has given to him, nothing more. Very soon the sons of Esau will know they must put down their swords or leave.'

'How will you convince them of that?'

'I will make . . . life uncomfortable for them.'

'Still, while Rome rules, Caiaphas remains a formidable enemy.'

Yeshua scoffs and gets on his way again.

'Caiaphas has his robes,' I call after him, meaning *he has his magic.* 'He will fight you above and he will fight you below.'

My old friend returns to me. 'Lazar, the Lord is with me. I'll be victorious in this world because I shall be victorious in the world to come.'

'Your *eruv* was the start of your campaign?'

'It was a necessary . . . preparation.'

A group of pilgrims appears around a bend in the road and is coming our way. I do not wish to be seen by them. 'I have to go back to Bethany now,' I say. 'But, if you send for me, I'll come, even if it puts me at risk.'

He embraces me and says, 'I know what sacrifices you'd make for me. I've known it since we were boys. Don't think you've left anything unsaid between us.'

'If anything happens to me, then I would only ask you to visit Nahara and Yirmi from time to time. I wouldn't want them to miss the opportunity to know you.'

'Nothing will happen to you. You've been chosen by the Father.' He slips his hands from mine and thanks me with words he has never said before – 'for coming into my life' – which moves me out of myself. I am looking at us both from far away – miles and years – when he says, 'You'll be with me in all I do. For the dream you had so many years ago is about to come true for all of us – even for the Lord Himself.'

And then he walks on without me.

27

A man removes his sandals and steps heron-like through a field of leeks, craving the wholesome feel of the earth – of all that hidden life – beneath his feet. He sits on an outcrop of stone beside a field of saffron crocuses, his bad leg stretched before him, gazing to the north, towards Natzeret. Tears come for a time, and he does not know why.

To calm his mind, he plans a mosaic of Yeshua ben Yosef as the Living Torah. His old friend will stand in an ancient stream, and four bee-eaters will watch him.

Yes, there will be four, not three; they will be the earthly forms of Mikhael, Gabriel, Raphael and Uriel.

And this is what he tells himself: *I shall make my design in such a way that those who view it will see that they are an invisible presence in it – that its meaning depends on the depth of their vision. Those who have been chosen will see that Yeshua is the bridge between them and all that men and women might be. The others will see but a goat-ribbed man bathing in a modest stream. They will be certain I have wasted my time – and theirs.*

The bee-eaters will perch in a terebinth, the Tree of the Knowledge of Good and Evil, and they will speak to Yeshua in their language.

We shall give you our feathery cloaks, they will say. *So that your radiance does not blind your followers.*

And I will give you eternal life, he shall reply with an upraised hand.

He will hold eternity in his fingers – a polished grey stone with a white stripe down its centre that he has found in waters that are forever journeying to the sea.

The mystery is in you and me, and it is far deeper than we usually think. It is much of what forms us and sustains us, and it is the greatest part of the beauty we see in heaven and earth and every living thing.

That is what I would most like to convey. If I can find a way.

I shall give Yeshua his wide-brimmed Greek hat, but no priest, oracle or emperor will make me cover his nakedness, for we must not hide the beauty of creation if we are to fulfil our promise. Why build a better world for creatures who are afraid of what is best in them?

At home, Mia tells me that Marta returned with the baby girl shortly after I left to meet Yeshua. 'She was apologetic. She removed her curse from me and you. And she asked that –'

'Let me guess – she asked for our forgiveness,' I cut in with the sigh of a Sisyphus.

Mia nods and takes my arm, but I pull away, because I shall not be trapped so easily.

'The three of us are a family,' she says, meaning, *You must always forgive her.*

I keep my dissenting opinion to myself, since a quarrel would only ruin the rest of our day. I take a towel and scrub the road dust from my face and neck. 'Where did she go last night?' I ask.

'The baby girl was burning with fever, so she brought her to Rut.'

Rut is Marta's sister-in-law and a midwife. 'And where is Marta now?'

'She came home to change her robe. She told me she'll return to Rut's house this evening to check on the baby. She also gave me a talisman she made for Yeshua.'

Mia hands me a vellum square on a cord on which our sister has designed a muscular lion-headed man wielding an oversized sword. The figure is meant, I would guess, to be Maahes, the Egyptian lion-god who feeds on the guilty and defends the innocent.

The incantation she has written above the sword refers to the son of Yaaqov who was sold into slavery in Egypt: *Yosef is a fruitful bough, a fruitful bough by a spring.*

'Marta asks that you give it to Yeshua.'

'It's impossible. I can't allow myself to be seen with him.'

'Then I'll bring it to him.'

When I hand it to Mia, she presses her lips to the lion.

'Who scripted it for her?' I ask, since, to our knowledge, Marta still does not know how to write.

'She didn't say. Any guesses?'

'Someone who knows that the Jews of Alexandria regard Yosef is an earthly form of the Egyptian lion-god.'

'Still, it seems a peculiar verse to choose.'

'The descendants of Yosef are said to be immune to the evil eye,' I explain. I do not add, *And, whether he was aware of it or not, whoever wrote this is also warning Yeshua that he is in dire need of a lion's fierce protection.*

I need to take Yirmi to Rabbi Elad and start work at Lucius' villa, but there is a promise that I must first keep – and a message I must deliver.

The nine-year-old daughter of my neighbour Onesimos the jeweller has imbibed a decoction made with the seed-heads of poppy. In consequence, she has fallen into a twilight sleep. I find her curled into a ball on her parents' bed, murmuring in the universal language of fever. Her jaw is puffy and hot to the touch, and her breath is sour. Onesimos' wife tells me that this wickedness began as an abscess in a molar. Why was the tooth not pulled? She whispers that they have no money to pay a barber or surgeon. She and her husband fear that the girl will die if I do not help her, so I speak a verse from the Psalms over her: *He shall give his angels charge over you, and they shall raise you up in their hands, and no unseen evil shall have any power over you.*

Onesimos' poverty has made him lax with the Holy One's commandments on cleanliness; his daughter's face and neck are soiled, and dirt crescents her fingernails.

I tell her parents where Old Baltasar lives and that he will extract the tooth and give her a potion which will reduce her fever. 'Ask him to come to me for payment,' I add. 'And wash her before he comes here or he'll give you a vicious lecture.'

To thank me, Onesimos puts a snake-headed brass torc of his own creation around my right wrist. It is slender and crudely fashioned – a trinket for snake-worshippers and Passover pilgrims – but it is more than he can afford to give me, so I try to hand it back to him, but he refuses to accept it.

'Blessed are those who give too much,' he tells me.

On the road to Yerushalayim, I explain to Yirmi that I must pay a call on Annas ben Seth before I entrust him to his tutor. My son and I escape the throng of pilgrims following me only when a house slave gives us entry to the priest's home. The sumptuous waiting room is perfumed with frankincense and painted with frescoes of aristocratic men and women in the lifelike style favoured by the Romans. The slave tells me they are Annas' illustrious ancestors.

The priests in his family are pictured in ceremonial dress – with portentous countenances and poses – while the laymen all hold a scroll as a symbol of learning in one hand and a bunch of grapes – the fruit of the Tree of Wisdom – in the other. While I am examining the painter's technique, the house slave shuffles back into the room and tells me that Annas is unable to receive me. I entrust my papyrus to him and also speak the message aloud, so that there can be no misunderstanding: *Unless I have your permission, I shall never appear in any square or street or building in Judaea with Yeshua . . .*

It raises my spirits to hear my son reading the precisely measured prose of his hero, Herodotus, to Rabbi Elad: *The Egyptians were the first to discover the solar year and to portion out its course into twelve parts. They obtained this knowledge from . . .*

Already Yirmi recites Greek with such swift confidence – his cadences so apt and euphonic – that I know he will live out his dreams and journey far beyond the Erythraean Sea in the east and the Pillars of Hercules in the west.

Work cheers me as well, for I am a child at play when I choose my tesserae and ease them into place. At such times I am certain that by creating grand and allusive figures from tiny chinks of stone I am also fighting on the side of all that is small and easily overlooked.

Just before my midday meal, Lucius comes to the edge of the swimming pool. His eyes are puffy and red, and his bottom lip is bleeding. 'Make yourself ready!' he says in a hushed and pressing tone.

'Lucius, what's happened?' I reply, but he hurries away without answering.

A moment later, Annas comes limping across the garden towards my ladder, on the arm of bodyguard with a dark complexion and a tangled bramble of thick black hair. His expression is grave. Might my note have offended him in some way? 'Honourable Annas ben Seth,' I call out, 'you mustn't risk a fall. I'll come up.'

I make for the ladder, but he calls down, 'No, you shall not escape me. Stay where you are!'

My gaze slides behind me towards my hammer, which is within reach, but I dare not to pick it up; preparing a defence might only prompt an attack.

On Annas' command, the bodyguard jumps down into the pool with a casual bravado that seems to indicate a little too much wine at breakfast – a favourable sign for me – then climbs halfway way up the ladder so that he can guide his master's sandalled feet on to the highest rung. From above, Lucius secures the old man's shoulders.

Lucius calls the bodyguard by the name of Malchus.

The old priest is clothed in a white tunic decorated with embroidered pomegranates at the collar. His double-stranded necklace of lapis-lazuli beads is so heavy that he leans forward as he walks.

I offer him hearty greetings, but he waves them off and targets me with furious look. 'You've lied to me, Eliezer ben Natan!'

Sweat is suddenly pouring from my brow, and my scalp itches as if infested with lice.

'Your note indicated that you wouldn't see Yeshua again,' he continues, 'but you were with him this morning!'

How could he know that, unless . . . Could Yeshua's brother Yaaqov have betrayed us?

'Have you nothing to say in your defence?' Annas demands.

My thoughts shoot off in a dozen frenzied directions, but I am unable to locate a believable lie. 'I . . . I went to Yeshua to bid him farewell,' I begin. 'We were far from Yerushalayim, and we weren't seen by anyone. I've kept to my vow. I've told you the absolute truth.'

'Scorpions hide under such truths as those you give me,' he snarls. 'You shall confess to me exactly what Yeshua told you of his plans,' he commands.

'We spoke of our childhood.'

'What else?'

'Nothing else. Old companions speak of past times when they are forced to part.'

Annas makes a dismissive clicking sound with his tongue. 'You've disappointed me,' he says.

Disappointing a tyrant is a sacred duty is the reply I dare not make.

Who can say where the tactics of a cornered man come from? I hold the torc on my wrist up to Annas. 'Yeshua also gave me this as a parting gift. That's why he asked to meet me.'

The priest, eager to seize this advantage, summons his bodyguard to take it from me. To play my part, I fall to my knees and implore him to be permitted to keep it. When the brute grabs my arm, I struggle so vehemently – and believably – that he slaps me across the face, which is good fortune, because tears come of their own accord and make my pleading perfectly believable.

Annas examines the torc closely while I wipe my eyes. Objects worn for many years become extensions of our very selves, of course, and the priest's covetous expression makes it clear that he believes he can make magical use of this one to subjugate Yeshua.

Will he now permit me to take my midday meal?

Unfortunately, the priest's expression does not soften, as I had hoped. Instead, his attention shifts to my mosaic floor. He scans Ziz from crown to tail with a wrinkled, disquieted face and kneels to press his crooked hand over the thumb-sized figure looking out of Ziz's left eye, then hobbles across the arms in the menorah, careful not to step on any of the black flames.

I realize then that I have made a fatal error. The snake-headed torc – above all, my desperation to keep it – has given him the idea that I may know how to make use of its occult properties.

Has he recognized the flames of my mosaic menorah as entry points to the Palace? I am certain of it when he stops and stares at the central candle-holder, which is lit with the scintillating black sun I have often seen in visions.

After his eyes close, his breathing slows and his shoulders sag; he is considering what he has seen. The affecting grace in his gnarled old body and intelligence in his wizened face make me realize that my loathing for him has made me underestimate him.

When his eyes open, he grins at me. *I have unmasked you,* he is telling me.

I begin an appeal for mercy, but he waves away my effort and turns to Lucius.

'I know little about mosaics. Would you say this work is any good?'

'Are you . . . asking my opinion, honourable Annas?' Lucius asks in his trembling, heavily accented Aramaic.

'Yes.'

'First, I would say that Eliezer is quite gifted,' he tells the priest.

I thank Lucius with a nod, but he closes his eyes to me, which I take to mean *This is all the help I shall risk giving you.*

'And second?'

I am unable to follow what Lucius then says, since he speaks in Latin. Annas nods as if he is in agreement, however. He stops before Havvah and Adam. 'Tell me, Eliezer, how long ago were the first man and woman banished from Eden?'

Can he truly believe that I would admit to a foe that I make use of the mysteries in my work? 'I don't know – some time after the sixth day of creation,' I reply.

'I see,' he says, plainly aware that I am feigning ignorance of the higher meanings of the story. He gestures from Ziz to Adam. 'And where are you in all this nonsense?'

'I am standing right here before you.'

He frowns. 'Do you take me for an idiot?'

'I apologize if I have given offence or . . . violated any holy law, honourable Annas.'

'A great many people would think it silly of you to have a bird supporting a menorah. Or to imagine black flames under water.'

'Like all artists,' I reply, 'I've had to learn that what others make of my creations is beyond my control.'

The priest's lips twist into a sour grimace, and he points at the King of the Birds. 'Who do you mean this figure to be?'

'Ziz.'

'Yes, I know that! But who is it really?'

'I don't understand.'

'Might it not be a certain woodworker from the Galilee?'

'That was not my intention.'

His brow furrows – he is pretending to be shocked by my reply. 'So you don't regard Yeshua ben Yosef as your king?' he demands in a disbelieving voice.

'I want no sovereign but the Lord our God.'

'Then why put Ziz here in the first place?'

'Birds are able to fly. They reveal to us that much more is possible than we might think.'

'Would you like to fly?'

'Wouldn't everyone?'

He shakes his head. 'I'm perfectly content with the form that God has chosen for me.' He holds out his hands. 'Two arms, two hands, two legs . . . Are they not enough for you?'

Never trust a man who does not wish to fly, I think, and I realize as well – jolted by my certitude – that he is lying to me: his sagging flesh has become a burden to him, and he would gladly steal my vigour if he could.

Annas turns to my employer and asks in a voice of warning, 'Are these mosaics important to you, Lucius?'

'Important, no,' he answers in Aramaic. 'But they . . . amuse me.' In Latin, he adds what seems to be an apology for his having very bad taste.

He and the priest continue in Latin. I use my time to observe Annas. In the proud way he stands and in his dramatic hand gestures I see a flimsy and flaccid elder who grows hard again when he intimidates other men.

He suddenly targets me with a malignant squint. 'What if I were to have all this work of yours destroyed? And not just here but all of your mosaics in Yerushalayim.'

'It would sadden me,' I say.

'Sadden, nothing more?'

'Nothing more,' I lie.

'But what if I were to destroy two other creations of yours? Two small finely made figures.' He smiles with glee and fiddles with the fabric of his robe near his waist; he is growing evermore excited.

I make no reply because I am considering how I shall murder him without being caught.

'Eliezer, you best start telling me more about what your friend has planned!'

He believes he has conquered me, I think. *But he has chosen the wrong strategy.* 'We spoke only of our days in Natzeret,' I say

'Still you persist with lies!' he growls, and he limps closer to me, vibrating with rage. The urge to grab my hammer and end his assault forms my hands into fists.

'Does Yeshua ben Yosef intend to begin an uprising?' he asks.

'We both know that you don't need me to tell you what he intends.'

'I don't understand.'

'Someone close to Yeshua must have spoken to you or you wouldn't know about my meeting with him this morning. Whoever it was would also have told you of his plans.'

He laughs falsely. 'Can you really be such a perfect dolt?' He turns to Lucius. 'Is your mosaicist friend a simpleton after all?'

Lucius begins to stammer a reply, but Annas waves it off and turns back to me. 'If I already knew his plans, why would I have come to you?'

I gaze down into the only possible explanation: someone from outside Yeshua's inner circle found out about my encounter with Yeshua and went to Annas this morning.

'Who betrayed us?' I ask him.

He shakes his head in disbelief. 'You can't truly believe I'd tell you.' Then, in a beseeching tone, feigning sympathy, he adds, 'But I can see now that I may have overestimated your grasp of our political situation. Let me explain some truths to you.' He smiles at me as if I am a child in need of his wisdom. 'If a disturbance of any sort should disrupt the flow of goods in and out of Judaea, then the Emperor will fill the Great Sea with Jewish blood. Do you understand?'

'Yes.'

'And do you understand that many of your friends and family will die.'

'I didn't discuss Rome with Yeshua.'

'I know of your father's murder at the hands of a Roman. You can be sure that I wish to reclaim Judaea for the Lord as much as you do.'

'I haven't given you permission to speak of my father,' I warn him.

'Permission? It's not yours to give, I'm afraid.' Then, more softly, he says, 'Eliezer, can you possibly believe that I don't remember what Elohim asked of Yehoshua? I swear to you, when the Almighty permits it, we shall cleanse the Land of Zion of all idolaters! Not even one Roman child shall be left alive.'

A netting of dark foreboding spreads over me; the depth of his depravity exceeds even my worst speculations about him.

'What's wrong? Don't you yearn to see the Romans chased from our land?' he asks.

'It's not our land – it's the Lord's.'

'Yes, of course. But we are the sons of Yaakov, his chosen ones.'

'All those who recite the Shema in good faith are chosen.'

'So you are able to interpret the words of Mosheh better than a priest of the Temple?' he asks in disbelief.

'I understand the Torah that waits for me, just as you understand the Torah that waits for you.'

'You're a strange man, Eliezer ben Natan.'

'So I've been told on a countless occasions, Annas ben Seth.'

'And one prayer is enough to turn a Roman into a Jew?'

'I only know that if the Romans give up their swords I'll welcome them as brothers.'

'You're as mad as Nebuchadnezzar!'

'Am I? Have you forgotten the words of Mosheh: "You shall do no harm to the stranger who sojourns in your land."'

'"All who would make idols are nothing,"' he retorts, citing Yeshayahu. '"And the things they treasure are worthless."'

'Let the Romans worship Zeus and Hera, and let me worship the King of Kings.'

The crooked finger he points at me trembles. 'Is that what Yeshua preaches?'

'I never speak for him.'

'But you've known him since you were boys.'

'And all the many years we have had together has proved to me that I am nothing compared to him.' I repeat a conclusion I came to long ago. 'I dream dreams, but Yeshua dreams prophecy.'

He pulls his head back, horrified. 'You think he's a prophet?'

'That's a determination I leave to others. I only know that he is what he will be.'

'This Galilean *prophet* of yours cannot even see the most obvious truth – that Esau raises his sons only for conquest. Rome will never give up their empire. Its army will crush any rebellion he leads.'

'Our Father has told Yeshua that they'll give up their empire when they see that the Lord is One.'

He clears his throat and frowns as if he's preparing to spit on me. 'The God of Gods does not speak to woodworkers!' he yells.

'*El Roi* – the Lord Who Sees – speaks to all those who come to him to listen and to those who are granted grace.'

'Heresy!'

His shout seems to stun me into a state of greater awareness. Why? There are events that we have foreseen for many years, but, until they take place, we are not aware that we ever waited in expectation of them. It is as if we realize – in a lightning flash of clarity – that our dreams have been leading us by the hand all the time we thought we were making our journey without guidance. And so it is that I discover that I have known for years that a Temple priest would one day accuse me of heresy. And I know my reply as well; it is written on the scroll of everything I have ever done.

'In Greek, heresy is simply the right to choose one's own beliefs,' I tell him.

'But you aren't Greek! You're a Jew!'

'I'm both, honourable Annas – as are tens of thousands of our brethren. Have you never been to Alexandria?'

He points his finger of damnation at me again. 'You think you're clever! But tell me this – how does this prophet of yours intend to make the Emperor abandon his gods?'

'He prays for those who torment and persecute us. And he counsels all the hungry and poor of spirit who come to him – Romans, Greeks, Egyptians, Samaritans, Syrians –'

'Samaritans!' he interrupts. 'We've all seen what befalls these pious Samaritans who are silly enough to follow him!'

'Yes, I was stained by Uriyah's blood.'

'I'm glad you were,' he says, as if it is a lesson I had to learn.

And this is what his bitter face confesses to me then: *my heart is a tomb.*

'Why did Yeshua assemble his followers for his entry into Yerushalayim?' he asks.

'You know as well as I do!'

'What I know is that you're a man who tries never to speak plainly!'

'He came to . . . prepare the city.'

'So he'll strike against the Romans in Yerushalayim?'

'I don't know.'

With slow delight, he designs a crucifix in the air. 'The Emperor has a particular fondness for hangings. So tell your foolhardy and impertinent friend to go back to the Galilee and start his rebellion there, if he wants. He's obviously very dear to you. Don't you wish to safeguard him from harm?'

'My protection would not add even a finger's width to the height of the castellated walls that the Lord has erected around him.'

He turns to Lucius. 'This dunce has just admitted his life is of little use to him or Yeshua or anyone else. Can you tell me why he ought to be permitted to keep his head?'

Lucius proffers a hesitant reply in Latin that I am unable to understand. He looks at me as if to say, *Now would be an opportune time to plead for your life.* But I have just realized that Annas would have already had me arrested or executed if that was his plan.

With a certainty that seems to come from all that he implies but does not say, I realize that I must rush away now if I am ever to see my children and Yeshua again. I kneel down to put my hammer and my other tools inside my pack. The old priest shuffles to me and holds out the torc that I permitted him take from me and shakes it angrily.

'If you don't tell me exactly what his plans are,' he says, 'I shall remove your head and have it buried on the delta of the Nile, and the next Galilean sorcerer who wants to revive you will have to journey to Egypt and try to locate it first!'

He says the word *Galilean* with a sneer, as if we are filth, but I cannot permit myself to be provoked. I toss my pack over my shoulder and walk to the ladder.

I climb on to the first rung, then the second, and . . .

So tremendous a blow strikes me on my back that I fall to the floor of the pool, and the air is knocked from me. Has the Lord Himself cast me down?

When a gate opens in my chest, I pull the air into my chest in gulps. I soon see I am lying on my side on top of my mosaic, on the left wing of Ziz. Just to my right is Annas' bodyguard. As he sheaths his sword, his eyes show amusement.

Annas stands over me, his head high, as though posing for his portrait.

All along he wanted me like this – on the ground before him.

Trailing behind that thought is the hidden meaning of the composition he has created: *He wishes to be worshipped!*

'Are you in pain?' he asks, doubtless hoping I am.

I am silent, because I am aware – for the first time – of a damning truth: he and the other priests have transformed themselves into idols!

You have turned yourself into what you most despise! I tell Annas in my mind.

'Speak!' he commands.

'You don't regard anyone else as real, do you?'

'What are you babbling about now?'

'You believe that the Lord made Annas on the first day of creation, before anything else.'

My criticism is not bravado. At that moment, the priest and I are alone in the world, and my discomfort is nothing compared to understanding that the man before me cannot really see me or anyone else.

Lucius comes up behind Annas. His lips are but a fearful slit. He signals desperately with his hands for me to remain on the ground.

'Eliezer ben Natan,' the priest says sadly, 'I can pardon you for your wilful disrespect and your scheming and your want of honesty. And, because of my affection for Lucius, I can forgive your making these vulgar effigies in stone. But you have also forced me to treat you harshly, and that . . . that, Eliezer, I cannot forgive.'

I fight to sit up. 'What is it you *really* want?' I demand, since all the words we have exchanged prior to this moment now seem like a preamble.

'When will you next see Yeshua?'

'I've no intention of seeing him. Haven't you heard anything I've said?'

'What if he wishes to speak with you?'

'Then he'll send me a message – to which I won't reply.'

'No, no, no! I want you to meet with him.'

'Why?'

'Because you will come to me after you speak to him. But be forewarned – I'll know if what you tell me are lies. And those lies, dearest Eliezer, will make me even sadder than I am now, for they shall force me to have you chopped up and buried in pieces.'

28

A mosaic-maker from the Galilee lays himself down in the generous shade of a cedar tree and scans the ochre-coloured façade of the villa where he works, and the sunlight reflecting off the tile roof becomes tears on entering his eyes, and when he lowers his gaze he sees how the light folds around the columns of the portico, eager for the companionship of stone. He reaches out to the oleander bush beside him and pulls off a flower because its smooth pink scent has brought his childhood within grasp, and when a raucous cawing turns his head, he sees the frenzy of a black crow flapping out of reach of a small grey cat crouching on the wall near by, and the cat has a ring of soiled fur around his belly and is sniffing at the excitable gusts of warm wind, perhaps scenting its lost meal as clearly as he, the man, scents his own frailty and exhaustion.

I come to myself in Lucius' garden. I am lying on my belly, and in my hand – where I expect to find an oleander blossom – is a bloody tooth. My tongue finds a tender gap where my right canine used to be.

The agony in my back makes me fear that I shall never again be able to stand, but for the moment it is gratitude and not pain that keeps me from moving: despite my errant tactics, I have survived. And I know now why Yeshua has long regarded the

Temple priests as a peril equal to the Romans. Why didn't he simply tell me that Annas and Caiaphas had transformed themselves into idols?

Behind that question soon appears the answer: I would not have believed him.

Something hard brushes against my arm. I turn in time to see Lucius withdrawing his hand. I look up into troubled eyes. He is kneeling beside me.

'Can you stand?' he asks.

'I'd prefer to lie here a while longer before I find out.'

The heavy calm in me seems to reside in an endless space. Perhaps it is where our spirits find refuge when we do not even have the strength to panic.

Lucius' face shows weariness and concern. 'You said that Yeshua . . . that he is a prophet,' he says.

Lucius and I are speaking Greek, as we always do, and he employs the word *mantis* for prophet, which, when I whisper it aloud to myself, seems far more accurate than the Hebrew term *navi*. *Navi* would imply that Yeshua speaks for the Lord, but *mantis* describes an individual who lives in a state of holiness: God breathes in him and through him, which is why I tell Lucius, 'He is the Living Torah.'

'Which means what?'

'That he is the horizon between Man and God.'

Lucius sighs. 'Well, if that's anything close to the truth, then you'd think he could at least protect you from an old jackal like Annas.'

'The priest is my test, not his.'

'Do you know who betrayed you?'

'No.'

When I give the reply, it is the truth. But I realize a few moments later that the traitor may have been hiding from me in the most obvious place all along.

Lucius pinches my left foot. 'Can you feel this?'

'Yes,' I reply, but my thoughts are of Mia; I shall have to confirm with her that she told Marta I'd left the house to meet Yeshua – and learn, too, if she gave him the talisman of a lion-headed god that Marta made for him; in that case, he will need to be warned that it might be intended to bring misfortune and affliction upon him.

'It appears that luck is with you,' Lucius says. 'You still have sensation in your legs.'

'I'll try to stand in a little while.'

'Eli, you must have been mad to make for the ladder! How could you not have realized Annas would stop you from getting away? Didn't you see the way I was signalling for you to remain calm – and to do all he asked of you?'

'I saw, but I thought he wouldn't risk the revenge of Yeshua's followers by having me thrashed.'

I next remember Lucius rousing me by calling my name and offering me wine in a crystal cup. I drink it, hoping to dull the pain.

'Let's get you up,' he says.

He summons his personal slave Abibaal, who gently turns me on my side. The clinging of fabric against my back tells me that my drying blood has sealed my tunic to my flesh.

When Abibaal pulls me to a sitting position, I shudder, because it feels as though he is peeling the skin from my wound. His face pales when he looks at it.

The comic absurdity in being looked at with his grimace of horror makes me exhale a frail laugh.

'Abibaal, clean and dress the wound,' Lucius says.

'No, my sister will want to do all that,' I tell him.

'It cannot wait. You can apologize to your sister later.'

On my agreement, Abibaal helps me back on to my belly. His hand grips mine tightly, as though to keep me from falling, and in his eyes I see his affectionate caring for me, which comes as a surprise. After I thank him for helping, he rushes off to fetch towels and warm water.

'What did you mean about preparing Yerushalayim?' Lucius asks me in whisper.

'Yeshua will fight the Romans and the priests from above and below.'

'Above and below what?'

'It's best that we don't speak of these matters,' I say, since I cannot entirely trust him.

'Eli, I don't think you are aware of it, but you can be very irritating at times,' he says, and yet he smiles at me as though he cannot help but cede to his liking for me.

At that moment, his fondness seems proof that he has a deeper self that values loyalty and empathy more than he might believe. Though when I tell him that, he laughs and says, 'I'm sorry, Eli, but I have no deeper self! And, what's more, I wouldn't want one! Deeper selves are like live-in courtesans – they are good in theory but always end up spoiling our few moments of tranquillity and contentment.'

'Still, we're more alike than I first thought,' I say.

He lets out a quick burst of laughter. 'The pain has made you delirious!'

I reach out to take his hand. He frowns as if I am being silly, but he does not break our connection. He casts his glance towards the swimming pool. In profile, he looks depleted. 'Maybe it would be best if you stopped working here,' he whispers regretfully.

'I'll stop when I've finished all our mosaics,' I reply.

He gazes down at me and shakes his head as if we are both risking too much. A few moments later, he stands. He presses on his lower back and groans. 'Do you believe there is such a thing as empathetic pain? The spasms are like a snake coiling around me!' He sighs and shakes his head. 'Will you listen to me! You've been wounded badly, and I'm the one complaining!'

He laughs at his dramatic tendencies, which permits me to do the same.

Only later do I realize that the comedy we find in our behaviour is down to the euphoria of the body that comes after a near escape; in short, we are both a trifle drunk on having found our way – at least temporarily – out of a lethal trap.

'Did Annas order his bodyguard to strike me?' I ask. 'I didn't hear him speak.'

'He signalled with his hand. They must have already discussed his intentions.'

Lucius tells me that he will give orders for a donkey from his stables to be brought to his villa so that I can ride to Bethany. Abibaal has returned by then. He drips warm water mixed with vinegar on to my wound, which sets scorpions stinging my back.

And then, something odd: Abibaal begins to hum an ethereal melody to me. It gives me the impression that he has nursed wounded men many times before.

His admirable voice makes me gaze at him differently, and here is what his resigned smile tells me: *Yes, Lazarus, in another time and place I would have sung the great epics all over the known world, and the men and women listening to me would have told themselves that I had been born to be a poet and a singer.*

Abibaal ends his melody only when he has completed his dressing. I manage to stand with his help. Leaning on him, I watch the clouds make and unmake themselves. At first, all I espy in their slow and earnest transformations is my own gratitude in being alive, but soon I also see that I shall send my children to safety in another land.

Ester, my father's sister, lives in Alexandria and will be overjoyed to have them with her. Her sons, Ion and Ariston, will watch over my children on their journey.

And for the first time, Yaphiel, I begin to understand – as though hearing a voice that had been only the slightest of whispers before – that this Passover will be a test for all the world. *Shall we prove ourselves worthy of the Promised Land or, like Abibaal, remain in bondage?*

Lucius' bodyguard Germanus – the behemoth I'd met once before – helps me up on to a donkey that is as perfumed as an Egyptian courtesan. The beast shakes his head and hurls a magnificent sneeze the moment I am settled on his back. Am I the source of his discomfort? No, Abibaal is certain that the stable boys ought not to have smeared his muzzle and belly with myrrh before bringing him to the villa.

'You best keep quiet about the stable boys!' Germanus warns the slave.

When Abibaal catches my eye, he nods furtively in the direction of the bodyguard and shakes his bottom to indicate that he has loose morals. And so I learn that nearly being murdered in Lucius' garden has made me an honorary member of his household.

A dense and noisy crowd meets us on my street. Germanus unsheathes his sword and clears a path for us.

As I enter my house, Nahara hears me conversing with Abibaal and dashes in from the courtyard. Her right hand is concealed behind her back and her eyes are bright with mischief. 'Want to see a snake?' she asks, squirming with anticipation.

'I'm too exhausted for this,' I tell her as Abibaal eases me down on to my mat.

'No!' she shouts.

'Then give me a few moments before you show it to me.'

Nahara looks like my mother as she waits – her lips pursed, her free hand drumming absently against her belly.

I take a deep breath, since I am not yet prepared to re-enter my life. Nahara – playing my shadow – also breathes in hard.

'Is it a real snake?' I ask. 'Where is it?'

'It's here!' she shouts, and she shakes her wooden carving at me – green, with a black tail.

I shriek, which makes her jump up and down. Abibaal joins in our fun, grimacing and throwing up his hands.

My daughter and I have played this game before, and I have learned that what she loves most is in being able to predict exactly how I shall react. Children love knowing what is coming next, of course.

After Abibaal departs with my thanks, Nahara sits with me. Her slender shoulders and pulsing energy remind me of all that is too fragile to survive in this world of ours.

'Dad, you have a hole in your mouth,' she informs me with an overly serious look.

'I lost a tooth.'

'Where?'

'In Yerushalayim.'

'Want me to help you find it?'

'Later.'

'We should visit Romulo?'

Romulo is a cousin of Leah's and a renowned dowser. My daughter enjoys sitting on his shoulders while he uses a forked olive branch to find underground water.

'I'm too tired,' I tell her.

Nahara assures me that Romulo is sure to find my tooth if we ask him to look for it, and I praise her for that sound idea, but she hears the catch in my voice and wriggles around nervously to face me. My tears reduce her to stunned silence.

'I'm crying because I'm overjoyed to see you,' I tell her.

Mia comes in from the courtyard and swoops down for the girl, which sets Nahara squealing with glee. 'Gephen is in the courtyard looking for you,' Mia tells her.

My daughter whines that she would prefer to stay with me, so I promise to join her and Gephen in the courtyard after I've had a chance to converse with my sister.

'How did you manage to lose a tooth?' Mia asks as soon as Nahara is gone.

'Is the hole very visible?' I ask.

She nods, which sends a wave of despair through me.

'I had a small accident,' I say, since understatement is always an advisable policy when you have an overly protective eldest sister.

'What kind of accident?'

Mia is sure to spot the deep bruise on my back sooner or later, but I'd prefer to keep its cause to myself for now. My lie must not be too big or too small, however.

'The awning over the pool collapsed,' I say. 'It caught me on my back.'

'Let me see the wound.'

'It's nothing.'

'Take off your tunic!

'Mia, I'm a grown man,' I plead, as if that could convince her. 'Is Yirmi home yet?' I ask to change the subject.

'He must still be with Rabbi Elad. Turn over!'

She whistles appreciatively when she sees the line of blood and swollen skin. I am lying on my belly.

'Who dressed it?' she asked.

'Abibaal, Lucius' personal slave.'

'He did a good job.'

She helps me sit up, then drops down beside me.

'How did the awning fall?' she asks.

'Its support snapped.'

Mia accepts my explanation. Now would seem the right time to ease into delicate subjects, so I ask if she was able to give Marta's talisman to Yeshua.

'No, I had no time today. I'm sorry.'

When I request that she bring it to me, she asks why.

'I want to examine it.'

The moment Mia hands it to me, I tuck it under my mat. A mistake.

'And that was your examination?' she questions suspiciously.

'I'll study it when I am alone,' I reply. In fact, I intend to bury it under the floor of my storeroom, beneath one of the incantation bowls that protect my house. If I discover that Marta has betrayed us, I shall dig it up and set it aflame.

'You're behaving strangely,' Mia points out. 'Are you worried about Yeshua?'

'I'm nearly always worried about him.'

'So you haven't heard what he's done?' she asks in a shocked voice.

Only then do I remember that he said he would be going to the Temple. *My mind has been too long away from what is important,* I think reproachfully.

'What did he do?' I ask. 'Is he all right?'

'They say he's fine. But listen to this . . .' She curls her hair back over her ears as she does when she needs to put scattered thoughts in order. 'He chased all the money-changers out of the Court of the Gentiles!' she says in triumph.

'And he wasn't caught?'

'No, he was too quick! Imagine it!'

I have waited years to welcome this news, but, now that it has come, I find – to my surprise – that I would prefer to return to the safety of the day before.

'And you know what else he did?' Mia questions with a jubilant rise in her voice. 'He released all the doves from their cages. Imagine all those thousands of birds flapping away – fanning out into the sky! Then he and his friends freed the sheep and set them charging down the staircase into the square, and the animals got all confused, of course, and I was told that no one could enter the city at any of the nearby gates for more than two hours, and . . . and it was all a glorious mess!'

Mia, grinning, pauses for a well-deserved breath.

'Did the Temple priests not try to stop them?' I ask.

'How could they? Yeshua had dozens of men with him – many of them from our homeland. And he was quick about his work.' She jiggles her hand back and forth. 'He seems to have learned something from his grandmother, after all – he went in and out like a weaver's shuttle!'

Mia and I give thanks that he escaped injury. She gazes past me towards her hopes. 'Today, I remembered something Yeshua told us when we heard him preach last year in Natzeret. That it wasn't enough to understand the world – one must work each day to change it.' She drops down beside me again and clutches my hand excitedly.

Is it aberrant or fortuitous for a brother and sister to be united at such a moment by their devotion to the same man?

'If only he can change the way things are,' she tells me in a whisper.

For Mia, *the way things are* refers to a long list of injustices but most of all to the destiny of the young women who are forced by shame and poverty to give up their infant children.

'Listen, Mia,' I say, doing my best to keep alarm out of my voice, 'after little Yonah came here this morning to give me Yeshua's message, did you tell anyone where I was going?'

'No, no one.'

'Not even Marta?'

'Marta? Why?'

'Just tell me.'

'She asked where you'd gone, and I told her you'd left early for work. Given how mean-spirited she's been of late, I thought it best to lie about you going to meet Yeshua.'

'You did the right thing,' I tell her.

But if the traitor is not Marta, then who betrayed me?

That question must appear in my expression. Mia frowns. 'Eli, what's she done now?'

'Nothing, it seems I misjudged her.'

'Misjudged her how?'

'Annas ben Seth visited me at Lucius' villa. He knew I'd gone to see Yeshua. I thought Marta must have told him.'

She considers the significance of this new information. 'A spy must have followed you out of Bethany.'

'I don't think so. I was careful. And so was Yeshua. We were alone.'

'So what did Annas want?' she asks.

'He interrogated me about Yeshua's plans.'

Mia fiddles uncomfortably with the collar of her robe. 'I see,' she says in a dark tone. 'So it was Annas who sent the awning crashing down on you.'

'The awning didn't collapse. He ordered his bodyguard to strike me with his sword. Unfortunately, I was climbing up the ladder out of the pool when he struck me.'

Mia looks as if she has been made to swallow poison.

'Don't touch me!' she snaps as I reach out for her.

'What . . . what have I done?' I stutter.

'I'm your older sister – I ought to have warned you . . . protected you.' She pulls at her hair, creating wild tufts at the top. 'Ever since your revival, this world . . . Maybe I'm deaf to what it has always been trying to tell me. Is that it? Are we going to lose everything now? Is that it, Eli?'

'Please, Mia, nothing terrible has happened. I'm all right. And I'll be more careful now. We'll be safe. I've already told Yeshua that we cannot be seen together in public.' In rushed words – trying to calm her – I tell her then that of my belief that we're all of us being tested this Passover.

The shocked silence with which she receives my words chills me. When she knocks her fists against the top of her head and groans, I am reminded of the grief-stricken young woman she became after our parents' deaths – and of how she managed to salvage the little that remained to us. Ever since then, apparently, she has been waiting for a thief to come and carry away our modest but secure life.

'Listen, Mia,' I say in a whisper, in case Nahara is eavesdropping, 'I'm going to send my children to Aunt Ester after Passover.'

She dries her eyes. 'But why?'

'Annas threatened them.'

'What . . . what did he say?'

'That I'd force him to hurt them if I didn't follow his orders.'

Tears squeeze through her lashes. 'What are his orders?'

'To report to him on any conversations I have with Yeshua.'

'Will you do that?'

'No, which is why I shall ask Ion and Ariston to leave for Alexandria the day after our Seder, and I'll send my children in their care. Until then, I need you to promise me that you'll never leave Nahara alone outside the house. And that you won't say anything to Marta about where I am or what I'm doing when I'm not at home.'

'So you still think she betrayed you?'

'Yes, I can't get that feeling out of me. Though I don't know how she found out where I was going since you didn't tell her. Perhaps she has discovered some . . . occult way of hearing what isn't said in her presence.'

'Who will look after Yirmi until his departure?'

'I'll keep him with me.'

'Eli, I don't think you ought to show him the wound on your back or explain about Annas. I know your son – he won't agree to leave if he's worried about you.'

I nod my agreement.

'How long will he and Nahara have to stay in Alexandria?' she asks.

'I don't know. There are too many things beyond my control – just about everything, it sometimes seems.'

Mia covers her eyes with her hands and starts to shake, which convinces me that we must make one more sacrifice.

'I have something important to ask you to do for me,' I say, and I kneel next to her and start to comb the wild tufts in her hair back into place, but she pushes me away.

'I want you to go to Alexandria, too,' I say. 'And to take Yehudit and Binyamin with you – and maybe Marta, if you can bear travelling with her. It'll be safer for all of you in Egypt.' I manage an ironic laugh. 'And safer for me with Marta gone.'

'I can't leave you alone, Eli.'

'Grandfather Shimon will be here. And I'll rest easier knowing you're safe.'

'But who'll cook for you?'

'Oh, please,' I scoff. 'You know very well I can live on dried fruit and bread for months.'

'Yes, and a flagon of palm wine each night,' she says with a frown.

'Would you have me die of thirst?' I say with my little-brother grin.

Mia pulls the sleeves of her robe out to meet her hands – her long arms have always embarrassed her. She licks her tongue over her lips and nods at me, which means she has made a decision I shall not be able to alter. 'I'll send Binyamin with Ion and Ariston to Alexandria – and I'll speak to Yehudit and Marta – but I'm staying.'

'My children will want you with them,' I say.

Mia sits up straight and curls her hair behind her ears. 'After our parents died, I swore that I'd watch over you, and I won't break that vow now.'

'I was a boy then. I'm a man now. Mia, you're free of me.'

She takes both of my hands, forming that ark we make to carry all of Noach's animals to safety. 'Why in God's name would I want to be free of you?' she asks.

29

Marta returns home and steps into my alcove while Yirmi and I are discussing Herodotus. Her hunched hesitance and needy eyes give me to believe that her emotional resemblance to Mia is far deeper than I generally want to admit. She asks to speak to me alone, so I tell my son to check if his sister is still napping. Marta lowers my curtains, and, inside the saturnine gloom she and I make together, she dissolves into tearful shame. While struggling against her fear of judgement, stopping and starting, she tells me she is sorry to have cursed Mia and assures me – her hands raised in a position of prayer – that as soon as she realized her error she spoke a counter-spell seven times aloud while standing in Mia's room.

She looks pale and faint, so I summon her to sit with me. I had planned to tell her that she will be dead to me and my children if she ever tries to bring evil upon us again. Once we are together on my mat, however, I am assailed by misgivings. If she is conspiring against Yeshua and me, would I only be giving her an excuse to become more sly and secretive?

Tears slide down her cheeks as she awaits my reply. She raises her hand to take mine then pulls it back, fearing that I shall reject her. She bends over herself and sobs.

Either her emotions are real or she is giving the performance of her life.

When I squeeze her shoulder, she seems more compact and brittle than I remember. She looks up with lost eyes, cornered by fate.

'I have already forgiven you,' I say.

The words come from my mouth, though I did not decide to say them. *Who is this ever-accommodating man who speaks for me when I least expect it?* I wonder.

'I become so angry that I don't know what I'm saying,' she tells me as she cries. 'I hear my voice, and I can't believe it's me. But I'm unable to stop myself.' She catches my glance and holds her breath, as though she dares not hope for my renewed affection. She caresses her free hand down her neck and across her chest.

Even the most accomplished actors must have occasional difficulties distinguishing between the solid world and their own thoughts, and it seems to me that Marta may be certifying with her hands that she is absolutely real.

'Can you understand what I'm telling you, Eli?' she asks.

I say I do, but I don't. In fact, I realize that no matter how long I live I shall never fail to understand anyone else as completely as I have failed to understand Marta.

Such a storm of conflicting emotions must rage at times inside her. And yet, there are times when I think that if the Lord were to close his fingers around her he would find nothing.

Might Marta feel the injustice of the world more deeply than anyone I have ever met? Is that the key to understanding her?

And just like that I am rubbing her back and assuring that I shall not hold any grudge against her and that I know she has endured too much. When I ask her if her seething anger has ever taken her anywhere near where she wanted to go, she finds the honesty to admit that it has not, so I tell her that she must finally overcome it if we are to remain a family. And I mean what I say – at least for now. I know from experience that the encouragements I speak to her will fade and die over the course of a single day – like certain butterflies, I've been told – and tomorrow I shall not believe I ever said them.

Despite my protests, she kisses my hands. And then she returns to the life she keeps secret from me and I go back to the one I hide from her.

While I listen to the comforting sounds of Mia and Yehudit preparing supper, I consider what to tell Yeshua in the note I shall send to his brother Yaaqov. I must warn him, of course, that a traitor informed Annas of our meeting and that the priest interrogated me about his plans. I shall also tell him that under no circumstances is he to trust Marta, even if I have no proof against her. Finally, I shall say that I intend to send my children to Alexandria just after our Seder. And here is how I shall close the note: 'When my family is gone, we shall meet, and you shall tell me how I can be of use to you.'

How to send this message to Yaaqov proves a riddle, however; I dare not carry it myself, and I cannot ask Yirmi or Mia, since Annas' spies might be watching them. Only that evening, long after supper, does a solution come to me . . .

Onesimos' wife, Dinora, opens her door to my knocks and looks up at me with bruised eyes.

'Is Ninah any better?' I ask.

She shakes her head morosely. Yirmi and I step into Ninah's dimly lit chamber. The girl is lying on her belly, covered by a dark woollen mantle. Her eyes are closed tight, and she is moaning. Onesimos is seated beside her, a clay oil lamp cradled in both his hands. From the way he bends over the flame – protecting it – I know what he has sworn, for I kept vigil over my second-born son, Talmay, in the same position, nearly motionless, for two days and nights. When he finally stopped breathing, I did not feel any relief as I was told I would. Instead, I wanted to hurt myself for failing to save him – and in a way that could never be healed.

'You shall not have this girl!' is what I announce to the *memitim* who steal our children. 'In the name of all the blessed hosts,' I shout, 'I order you to abandon this place!'

Seven times I repeat my invocation while kneeling by Ninah. Then Onesimos and I converse outside the girl's door.

He tells me that Baltasar visited them but that he did not pull the tooth – and will not risk doing so until the swelling diminishes. He was able to lower Ninah's fever and put her to sleep with a mixture of henbane and valerian, but she has refused to drink another cup of the brew. 'It tastes and smells like vomit,' he whispers.

I sit by the girl. 'Ninah, it's your neighbour, Eliezer the mosaic-maker,' I say, and I hold her head between my hands as gently as I can – imitating what I have seen Yeshua do on countless occasions – and whisper a protective Psalm over her. As I finish, I sense a prayer shawl – a *tallit* – being spread across my shoulders. Has Yeshua put it there?

It is never easy to identify the significance of a gift from the Throne World, but in this case an unusual conjunction of words offers me a clue.

I remind Onesimos and his wife that the Lord of Righteousness has commanded us to dye the tassels on our prayer shawls *tekhelet* – turquoise.

'I don't understand,' Dinora says.

'*Tekhelet* does not only refer to a colour. It is also one of the names of the sky-coloured gemstone that Egyptians praise so highly and that your husband uses in his work.'

'What are you saying, Eli?'

'Ninah is the daughter of a jeweller. The Lord has given me a sign. To save her, I must cover her with the turquoise of a *tallit.*'

'But I don't own a prayer shawl,' Onesimos replies, grimacing.

I summon Yirmi and explain the errand I need from him.

Grandfather Shimon's shawl is frayed and worn but so much the better, since it has soaked up at least half a century of prayers. I drape it over the girl's shoulders and place one of the turquoise fringes over her swollen cheek. When I look back at Onesimos, I see from his sagging shoulders that he is too afraid to hope it will do her any good.

Yirmi and I accept his invitation to have some wine with him in his courtyard. We speak little at first. But a second cup lends me its courage, and I ask my favour of him, explaining first why I dare not take my message to Yaaqov myself or entrust it to Yirmi. 'You're under no obligation to do this for me,' I assure him. 'I'll do all I can for Ninah whatever you decide.'

'Won't Annas have my husband stopped and interrogated?' Dinora asks.

'It seems highly unlikely – by now he knows I've come here to help Ninah.'

'He knows that our daughter is ill?' Onesimos asks in disbelief.

'His spies follow me everywhere. I've seen one of them several times.'

'But why is he having you watched?' Dinora asks.

'He fears that I will use my notoriety to help Yeshua ben Yosef.'

'And will you?' she asks in an apprehensive voice.

'I would if I could, but at the moment I have to safeguard my family.'

'Have you written out the message you want me to carry?' Onesimos asks.

'No, not yet, but if you give me a few moments, I shall –'

'No, just tell it to me,' he cuts in. 'I'd rather not carry a note. I don't want anything that Annas and his men could take from me and use against us.'

So it is that I learn that Onesimos has already decided to help – and that he is far cleverer at this conspiratorial work than I am.

30

Just before supper, I summon Ion and Ariston to my room and explain what I need from them. I find it easier to address all matters of the heart in Greek, a language that respects my failures and frailties, and my cousins and I are able to settle matters quickly: Ion will take my children and nephew Binyamin to Alexandria, and Ariston will remain in Bethany for a time in order to conclude some delicate business negotiations. The travellers will make their way first to Caesarea and there book passage on an Alexandria-bound vessel. Although I have no savings to pay for my nephew's and children's expenses, I insist that Ion take what's left of my stock of lapis lazuli.

'It's also possible that Yehudit and Marta will go with you,' I add. 'I'll ask them for a decision soon.'

At bedtime, I tell Nahara and Yirmi of my plans.

I converse with my son in Greek, so that Nahara will not understand any doubts he might voice. When Yirmi hears he will soon disembark in the land of the pyramids, however, his eyes open as if he has glimpsed the future. *Something has finally happened in my life!* I can hear him exulting.

I tell him that I shall join them in just a few weeks. It is a lie, for I cannot predict how Yeshua's mission will go, but I do not wish to see my son's excitement fall prey to apprehension.

Nahara proves just as easy to persuade, though, in truth, she fails to grasp the nature of what I am proposing; she has no idea what journeying to so remote a land will entail.

'You'll be staying with Aunt Ester,' I tell her. 'Do you remember her?'

She curls her bottom lip out, which means *no*.

'You don't remember her because you were very small when she visited,' I say.

'How small was I?'

I hold out my hand a foot from the floor to show her height at the time. I do so with my palm facing up, because in the Galilee we believe that a hand facing down can block the growth of a child.

I pick up the wooden snake that Nahara has placed by her pillow and shake it. 'Aunt Ester frightens easily. You'll like her.'

King David has told us in one of his Psalms that if we are met at daybreak with love and mercy then we shall dance all day long. But what if we are welcomed instead by theft . . .

At cock-crow the next morning, when I reach for my mother's amber necklace I discover that it is missing. Neither my sisters nor my children have any idea where it might be. I have no time to hunt for it because Abibaal arrives at my home with Lucius' donkey while I am completing my morning prayers, and it would be rude to make him wait. Yirmi comes with us.

Shortly after my son and I start work on my mosaic, my employer hails me cheerfully from the rim of the pool. 'How's your back, Eli?'

'Better,' I say. 'Thank you for the donkey ride this morning.'

'My pleasure. Listen, a young friend of mine is here. I want him to see your design.'

'What's wrong with your back?' Yirmi asks me after Lucius is gone, since I did as Mia suggested and refrained telling him about my injury.

'I fell and grazed it,' I reply, 'but it's almost healed now.'

A few moments later, Lucius leads a slender man with a week's whiskers on his cheeks – perhaps thirty years old – down the ladder. I recognize him immediately. Indeed, how could I not, for I have known him since he was a toddler.

A raised flag of warning in my mind keeps me from waving or smiling, however: how could Lucius speak of Yeshua's younger brother as a friend? Unless . . . Unless Yaaqov is using a false identity, which means I must pretend that we have never met.

I soon learn, however, that I'm the one who has been deceived.

Yaaqov rushes to me with his hands out and eyes shining. 'Beloved Eli!' he calls ahead, and he embraces me as if gathering in all the memories we share.

'Does our host know who you are?' I whisper in his ear.

'Yes, don't worry.'

When I turn to Lucius, he grins at me mischievously. He fixes the drape of his toga over his arm and stands as tall as he can, as though posing for a statue. *He is cherishing this moment,* I think.

'Eli, all is *never* precisely what it seems,' he tells me, and in perfect Aramaic – with only the slightest trace of Roman accent.

'Lucius has been helping us,' Yaaqov tells me, and he goes to my son to give him a kiss.

'I don't understand,' I say.

Yaaqov tugs playfully on my arm, amused by my confusion. 'It's simple, Lazar. I received your message, and I wanted a chance to talk to you. So I came to see Lucius last night, knowing you would arrive in the morning. Don't worry – I took a circuitous route here to make sure no one followed me.'

'And you – what's going on?' I ask Lucius.

'What do you mean?' he replies, making the face of an innocent wrongly accused.

'For so long you gave me to believe that you disliked me! And that you thought it was foolish and dangerous of me to help Yeshua. I was certain you were our enemy!'

He hoots with laughter so hard and continuously that he begins to cry. 'Oh, it's just too perfect!' he tells me when he sees my confusion. Finally, pressing on a cramp in his side and taking a few deep breaths, he says, 'I had a role to play, Eli, and it was a very challenging one. I couldn't refuse it!'

'I could hardly understand your Aramaic! It was pitiful!'

'Don't feel bad. Annas ben Seth was fooled as well. I'm a devil with accents!' He scratches his chin thoughtfully. 'How would you like to hear a Galilean mosaicist speaking in the dialect of Corinth?' Without waiting for my reply, Lucius imitates my voice, declaiming a speech that he later tells me is from *The Birds*. '"What's the matter with you then, that you keep opening your beak? Would you have us fling ourselves headlong down on to these rocks . . ."'

I am certain that Lucius sounds nothing like me, but Yirmi starts to giggle. 'It's you, Dad!' he tells me excitedly.

'My first wife used to call me a parrot,' Lucius says. 'Though, to tell you the truth,' he adds, holding out his arm in the way Romans do to indicate an erection, 'she much preferred it when I imitated a cockerel!'

He erupts again into mirthful laughter, which means, at least, that his Latin sense of humour has not changed. Still, I shall have to create vastly new contours for the Lucius I keep in my mind – one with the boisterous, boyish laugh of a performer who delights in fooling his friends and who now smiles at me affectionately.

'But you . . . you lied to me!' I protest, unable to keep a cry of hurt out of my voice.

'I'm sorry, Eli, but such changes of identity are what I do best. You see, when I was a boy, my stepfather schemed to get me out of the way – he hated the competition for my mother's affection – and he apprenticed me to an itinerant acting troupe. Ionians, most of them – and talented. Not that I minded leaving my stepfather's home. He was a bully and a bore, and my Ionians – bless them! – were never tedious. In any case, my first big role was Hippolytus. In Euripides' tragedy, of course. To see all those rapt faces staring at me, hanging on my every word . . . I was hooked! My greatest early triumph, however, was in *The Banqueters*. Have you seen it?'

'No, never.'

'I was the froward and deceitful son. Wonderful role! For years, I specialized in brutal soldiers and devious satyrs and treacherous *hetaireukotes* and all the others we get such pleasure in despising. Though I have played sympathetic characters when I had no other choice.' He shakes his fist at me. 'I was Heracles battling Death in *Alcestis*.' His posture eases and he blows me a kiss. 'And once, in Mediolanum, I played the beautiful courtesan in *The Eunuch*, and I don't mind telling you I had a very . . . *stimulating* effect on a fair number of the men in the audience! One old murex manufacturer – so wealthy that his feet were purple from the dyed slippers he always wore – proposed marriage to me! I was sorely tempted to remain with him. I mean, how often to you get a marriage proposal from a sexagenarian with purple feet? And who hasn't much longer to live! But the climate of Mediolanum – have you been there?'

'No, I . . . I've never been anywhere near there,' I stammer, overwhelmed – and enormously impressed – by the fluency of his words and his passion.

'It's scalding in summer, with clouds of mosquitoes everywhere, and it's freezing in winter. Abominable place! In any case, I'm talking too much. I grow excited when I speak of the old days. Excuse me.'

'It's all right,' I say, still stunned by his good-natured vitality.

'I suppose that the point I'm trying to make, dearest Eli, is that acting is what I most enjoy. So when this role was offered to me . . .' He shrugs as if to say he had no other choice.

'You had me completely taken in,' I say. 'I am obviously no match for you.'

'If only you'd admitted that months ago, I might have gone easier on you!' he says, laughing again. 'But you dismissed me immediately as a rich buffoon. I could tell – you're not very good at hiding your unfavourable opinions of others.'

'I'm sorry. It was not my intention to offend you.'

'No, but I am afraid you must accept that you are a bit like *garum*, Eli – often sour-tempered and generally smelly and most definitely an acquired taste!'

When he grins, I realize I can no longer tell if he is expressing his real opinion or acting. As my only option, I bow to his genius.

31

Lucius leads us into his breakfast room and seats us around a circular wooden table. At the centre of its inlay design stands a bearded and fearsome Poseidon brandishing a menorah like a shield and riding towards a many-templed Greek city in a water-chariot drawn by seahorses.

I've seen his figures before, I realize with a jolt, though I have no idea where.

Yaphiel, does the future send us subtly coded messages that we usually mistake for past experiences?

A surprise draws my focus from Poseidon: Yeshua's disciple Yohanon appears in the doorway, barefoot, his face sweaty and soiled, wearing the shabby, threadbare robe of a mendicant. 'I apologize for arriving late,' he tells us, and he waves to me as though he were a little boy, a gesture that now seems a clue to the deepest workings of his mind.

You have always wondered why I am so fascinated by Yeshua's miracles, his eyes tell me as I cross the room to him. *Did you see the clue I just gave you? You see, to children, the world is a tower of wonderment and magic. We usually say that they see this tower because they are ingenuous and inexperienced, but ask yourself this: might they have a vision of the world based on intuition and imagination that is more accurate than our own?*

After Yohanon embraces us all, he takes off his robe and hangs it on one of the pegs by the door. At that moment, my fondness for him is greater than it ever has been, for I believe I have seen what he has previously hidden from me. Indeed, his register of miracles now seems an enquiry into the nature of the universe – and our place in it.

While I exchange jests with him – trying to turn his grave expression into a smile – Abibaal serves us posca in rock-crystal goblets and honey cakes dusted with pistachio powder. The slave also brings in a basin of perfumed water and washes Yohanon's fingers.

We are seated by then. My son is next to me. I take his hand under the table because he is uncomfortable in the presence of men he does not know well.

It is still hard to believe that I may speak freely with Yohanon and Yaaqov in Lucius' presence. As Yohanon tells me how Yeshua chased the money-changers, sheep-sellers and other merchants from the Temple, I sneak glances at our host now and again – to make sure, I suppose, that I have not made some fatal error of interpretation. On one occasion, he shows me a bemused but understanding expression, as though to say *it is equally strange for me to have taken down my mask.*

In answer to my queries about Yeshua, Yohanon tells me that he has been encouraged by the righteous commotion he caused in the Temple and is currently preaching outside Yerushalayim.

'He is extending his *eruv,*' I surmise.

Yohanon nods, but in the stern set of his lips I see a warning about broaching such matters outside the setting of a prayer room or synagogue. 'Yeshua wishes to know about your encounter with Annas ben Seth,' he tells me, and he spreads his hands far apart, which seems his way of assuring me that he will gather in all I have to say and report it to our old friend.

To keep my son from learning of plans best confided only to adults, Lucius summons Abibaal, who leads Yirmi off for a tour of the villa.

I then tell Yohanon, Yaaqov and Lucius all that I have written to you about my interrogation, dear Yaphiel. Lucius offers an occasional comment, and I am glad to have his interpretations of the priest's behaviour and motives, as they often reinforce my own. Yet he is convinced that one of my key findings is wrong – that, as long as I abide by our agreement, the priest will not risk having me hurt again because an angry crowd calling for his head would undoubtedly gather in front of his home if Yeshua were to ask for support.

'Annas would simply turn to the Roman governor for protection,' Lucius says, 'and fifty of his legionaries would be enough to chase off all but the fiercest of our supporters.'

On hearing that, Yohanon leans back and turns his goblet in his hand. 'Still, he did not kill Eli, and that means that Annas and Caiaphas are constrained by fear.'

'If they regard us as a true threat, then they will fight us all the more fiercely,' Lucius observes.

'And you know that because . . . ?'

Lucius takes a sip of his wine and sighs regretfully. 'Unfortunately, Yohanon, I've had ample experience with minor tyrants over the course of my life, and I've learned that they despise any sign of weakness in themselves.' He leans back confidently in his seat and crosses his arms. 'Annas will act without mercy to keep his own fear a secret from himself and others.'

I receive that observation with a mixture of trepidation and gratitude, since it reminds me that I must not waiver in my decision to send my children away. Yaaqov shows his youth, however, and proves unwilling to accept the logic of our host's reasoning or his expertise. 'Who exactly are these tyrants you've known?' he asks condescendingly.

'My stepfather for one.' He turns to me and says, 'He endeavoured to hide his cowardice under the blood of his victims – just like Creon.'

'Who is this Creon?' Yaaqov asks.

I rush to reply, so that Lucius will know that I value his judgement. 'A king in *Antigone,* a tragedy written by Euripides.'

'Lucius, do you really believe the theatre can give us an accurate picture of what we're up against?' Yaaqov asks in a sceptical voice.

'I had the great good fortune to play Creon's son Haemon for an entire spring,' Lucius replies with admirable restraint. 'I became familiar with how he thinks. And this may surprise you, Yaaqov . . . My knowledge of Creon's ruthless strategies saved my life. Were it not for my having played Haemon, it would never have occurred to me that my stepfather was having me slowly poisoned while I was on holiday in his home. I would not have believed that such unqualified cruelty was possible.' Lucius smiles affectionately. 'I know you doubt me, but it would be unwise for you to doubt Annas' resolve. If he feels threatened by Eli again, he will not hesitate to have him murdered.'

I reach out to Lucius arm and thank him, because he has risked ridicule in order to protect me.

Yaaqov is aware of his effort as well. He bows his head and smiles gratefully at our host. 'I apologize, Lucius – I can be foolish sometimes, especially when I'm the youngest man in the room and trying to prove myself. I vow to you that I'll tell Yeshua exactly what you've said.' He turns to me. 'Anything else we ought to know, Lazar?'

I have saved my most important observation about Annas for last, since I do not know how to express it. 'Despite what I first believed,' I begin, 'Annas is quite . . . intuitive, though that isn't the precise word I want.'

'Intuitive in what way?' Yohanon asks.

If he and Yaaqov were fluent in Greek, I would tell them that Annas was *gnostikos,* and they would understand me perfectly. Instead, I say, 'He provoked me in clever ways and outmanoeuvred me at least once. He's sharp-witted and relentless – like a skilful senet player. He recognized the gates I'd hidden in my mosaic almost immediately.'

Blessed be the angel Jahoel, who gave us the Hebrew language in its earthly form; as I watch Yaaqov down his posca, the perfect description of Annas' intelligence pierces the darkness in my mind. '*Sekel!*' I exclaim, meaning higher awareness or insight – or, in a negative sense, cunning. 'You have to understand that Annas is a man of *sekel!*' The word itself helps me now gather my thoughts and give them order. 'I believe that he has seen the world to come,' I say. 'He has understood that we'll no longer need priests guarding the Throne of Glory from us. In fact, he's aware of a good deal about Yeshua that is far from obvious – about *the hymns he sings in silence.* That was a shock to me.'

The hymns he sings in silence is a code I have long used for all that we dare not say about Yeshua's higher nature.

Yaaqov turns to look out of the window into the garden, searching, I believe, for the consequences of what I've just told him. In profile, his resemblance to his elder brother vanishes, since their kinship is in the singular depth of their eyes. That diminished physical affinity permits me to see him clearly, and I recognize his nervous exhaustion in the bend of his back and throbbing jaw. And this is what I hear him tell me when he turns to me: *I've known since I was five years old that I was the brother of an extraordinary being. It has been my test, and I'll never escape it. And my worst moments? When I fear that I'll make the wrong decision and that Yeshua will pay the price for my error.*

'I see now that we'll have to formulate a solid back-up plan,' Yaaqov tells Yohanon.

'Where will you strike?' Lucius asks.

'We've . . . we've yet to work that out,' Yaaqov stutters.

'So you still don't trust me yet?' our host asks resentfully.

'Your household is large.'

'You suspect a spy amongst my servants and slaves?'

'Annas and Caiaphas are having us watched. The Romans, too, in all likelihood. And we've come to learn that even our most trusted friends can be turned against us. There is no guarantee that . . .'

I hear no more of Yaaqov's explanation because a rising panic deafens me. *She cursed Yeshua when he entered my tomb!* I exclaim in my mind. *She told him she'd never forgive him.*

When I jump up, Yaaqov asks me what is wrong.

'I thought she was furious at him because he'd come too late – but it was for saving me,' I tell him.

'What are you talking about?'

'Marta – my sister. She cursed Yeshua because she knew he had the power to revive me. Maybe she'd even foreseen what he would do. She was glad that I'd died! She has wanted that since my birth!'

She told me that she'd never help my children if I were to die, I think, *but what if her true feelings are the opposite? What if she is desperate for the chance to raise them – to substitute for me in their lives?*

'Eli, what are you saying?' Yohanon asks, coming to me and taking my arm.

'Although I've no proof that Marta betrayed Yeshua and me, I see now that she has been my enemy for years,' I tell him. I turn to Yaaqov. 'You were only a boy, but maybe you remember that she was once in love with your brother.'

'I do remember.'

'I believe that her love must have changed into something else, and a long time ago – without my realizing it.'

'She's turned into Medea,' Lucius comments with a knowing nod.

'We'll have her followed,' Yohanon assures me.

'Good, but . . . but don't have her hurt if you discover she's a traitor. Send me word of what you've learned, and I'll deal with her.'

'Deal with her how?' Lucius asks.

Behind his words, I hear him ask me in a sceptical voice: *Do you really think you'll be able to kill your own sister if you find out she's betrayed you?*

'No, not if she has betrayed only me, but if she has put Yeshua's life at risk, I'll give her two choices – exile or death,' I reply, though my merciless voice seems to belong to someone else – a man I would prefer never to have met.

32

Just after Yirmi and I end work that afternoon, Lucius brings us a small sack of honey biscuits tied with a purple ribbon, since I have told him that today is my grandfather's seventieth birthday. At his garden gate, he apologizes for what he calls his 'shameful gabbling about the theatre', but I assure him that his observations helped me understand my motives and fears more fully. This earns me a solemn embrace, since, like all those educated in the Greek manner, he holds self-knowledge to be our most important goal. After I thank him for all his help, I confess in a comic voice that I used to perform in shadow-plays for my nieces and nephews when they were tiny, but that Mia and Marta would only give me minor roles, since they regarded me as the world's poorest actor.

'Is your father really so incompetent a performer?' Lucius asks Yirmi.

My son gives his laughing confirmation.

Lucius assures us that he has been forced to speak dialogue with actors no more expressive than Egyptian mummies, including – he notes with a horrified grimace – the *incomparable* Anaximander of Apollonia.

Did I fail to see that Lucius, too, is in need of an amusing conversation? Likely he has also envisaged Yeshua put in chains and Judaea turned to rubble by the Romans.

'Was Anaximander very bad?' I ask.

'Very bad? Is a python coiled around your neck *very bad*? Was the earthquake that reduced Ephesus to rubble *very bad*? My dear Eli, the little hairy weasel was forbidden by imperial decree from ever appearing in a Roman theatre!'

'What earned him a ban?'

'He always forgot his most important lines and invented the silliest improvisations – a summary of the day's weather, for example. But in truth, that wasn't the main reason. It was because he reeked worse than week-old squid. None of the other actors could sit or stand downwind of him for fear of passing out from the fumes! I once lay dying on the ground by his feet, but I couldn't play out my final demise because I was choking on his odour! I had to crawl to safety. The audience was in hysterics.'

Lucius paws at the air to show us how he saved himself.

Through my laughter I tell him he ought never to have given up the stage.

'Alas, at a low point in my fortunes, I discovered that my brother-in-law's *garum* was the goose that laid the golden egg.'

When I express my regrets for having fallen out of the habit of attending the theatre, his eyes brighten as though he has seen angels descending on Yaaqov's Ladder. 'Then you shall be my guest!' he declares. 'You and Yirmi both!'

'I wish we could,' I tell him.

'But why can't you, Eli?' he asks and then remembers what we both know – that he would be ostracized by his friends for inviting his mosaic-maker to join him at a public event.

'What an unjust world this is!' he says. He gazes at me as though failing in spirit. '"Return, O Holy One, to our city,"' he declaims.

'"Abide not far from us, you who quench our wrath. Strife and bitterness shall depart if you are with us. Madness and the sword's sharp edge shall flee from our doors."'

His words fix me in place, because I am certain he is speaking of Yeshua. I had not previously considered the depth of Lucius' devotion to him.

'You have awaited him for many years,' I say.

'I have awaited the better world he shall help us make,' he says. 'And there's something else – something I've just realized about us all . . . The despots of our world fear men who insist on telling their own stories. They want to control the words we speak and write. But we must not let them, Eli. Do you understand?'

'Yes, I do. And we shall all of us help Yeshua tell his own story.'

After Lucius reaches out for the handle of his gate, his mood becomes playful. 'Any guesses?' he asks, squinting at me like a tutor who has posed a trick question.

'Guesses about what?'

'The lines I spoke about the return of the Holy One – whose they are.'

'Euripides,' I try, since Lucius is plainly a devotee of the great dramatist.

'Yes, but which character speaks them?'

'I don't know . . . Andromeda?'

'It's Merope, from *Kresphontes*,' he says. 'It's her prayer for peace, and it has long been mine as well.'

At our birthday celebration for Grandfather Shimon, the shaggy old ram wears a crown of jasmine blossoms and leads us in the blessings over the meal, his sword by his side, as is only fitting for a rebel who has never given up his hopes for a Zion freed of the Roman yoke.

'May the Merciful One be as kind to you as He has been to me,' he tells us after we take our first sip of wine.

Generous words from a man who is known as *Shimon the Leper* to many in Bethany, and who – except to attend funerals – has not left our house during the daytime for the last seventeen years.

Mia sits next to him and cuts his onion-and-leek patina into tiny pieces, gazing at him with amused adoration, as if he were the oldest and brightest star in the sky.

During our meal, Marta is uncommonly gracious and tender with everyone. She grins at me now and again as if we share a wondrous secret, but what it is I dare not guess or ask. So that I might feel what it would be like to live without the ponderous weight of her inside my chest, I permit myself to believe that – despite all my suspicions – she has finally closed the doors of vengeance and retribution behind her.

Shimon empties our flagon of palm wine long before I have a chance to serve the honey-cakes that Lucius gave me. He grows misty-eyed and maudlin and clumsy of body. As I reach past him to remove the empty platters inside our circle, he grabs my wrist and tugs me so hard that I nearly fall. 'Eli, where's that selfish and silly wife of mine?' he asks with a moan.

'I only wish I knew!' I reply in a jesting tone, since I am aware that an honest reply will only give him an excuse to crawl deeper into drunken melancholy, but he shakes his head at me and frowns as if I am no help at all.

He asks my sisters the same question, and then poor Nahara, who huddles behind me and asks why *Pappas* is scaring her.

'Pappas misses his wife,' I explain to her.

'Where did she go?'

How ought a father to explain to his daughter where the dead go, especially when he has lost his faith? Thankfully, I am not given any time to answer because Shimon stands up and throws his bulky arm over my shoulder, drawing me into a fermented embrace. 'Why has that mean and odious woman abandoned me, son?'

'I know that these past eleven years have been difficult,' I tell him. 'I'm sorry.'

He heaves a sigh and tells me that he cannot keep saying *yes* to each new sunrise much longer, which seems so apt and poetic an expression that I place it in the special room in my house of memory that I reserve for Shimon's poetry.

He wishes to go to bed, so I help him to the ladder, but, even with me pushing and Yirmi pulling, he is unable to make it to the third rung. Irritated and dispirited, he tells me he wishes to be permitted to sit and cry by himself, and, since he will not take no for an answer, Yirmi and I help him to my mat. After he is safely seated, he reaches up to me with clumsy hands and implores me to bring Ayin to him, since he will not be able to sleep, he claims, without the owl guarding him. I bring Ayin down from the roof and stand him on the floor by my window, at a safe distance from Shimon, but straight away the old man crawls to the bird on all fours. 'What would I do without you?' he asks, and he presses his lips to the crown of Ayin's head. 'The featherless others never understand,' he says, and he begins to tell the bird the story of his marriage, starting with his wedding. 'Bityah wore a white dress with golden embroidery to receive me, and when I entered her father's home . . .' Yirmi grimaces and backs out of the room on tiptoe, but I am ever eager to learn more about Shimon's youth. A few moments later, he lies back against the floor and decides to address the cracks in the ceiling.

'I was shivering with fear that first night – I admit it. I'd already visited brothels, of course, and when I was sixteen my father and I fucked our way from the Galilee to Alexandria, but this was different.' He licks his lips. 'That sweet moist cleft between Bityah's legs . . . Oh, dear Lord!' He turns to me. 'My goodness, son, how happy a woman can make a man if she just agrees to bend over and stop talking for a little while!'

Shimon's delight in my grandmother makes me tingle, as if he has discovered what makes us holy. *The body that opens in jubilation is the Lord's greatest gift to us,* I think.

Soon, however, his voice fades and his eyes flutter closed.

I go off to fetch him a cup of water, and by the time I return he is snoring with his mouth open. An hour later, after I have put my children to bed, I sit again by him and study the wrinkles by his eyes and whiskered cheeks, and my thoughts return to when he was the benevolent emperor of my childhood.

'What is it the world wants from us?' I'd once asked him. I must have been eleven or twelve years old at the time.

'The world? It wants nothing from us, son,' he'd replied. 'After all, what could the mountains and seas possibly want from us that they don't already have?'

At the time, that reply made me shiver, since it seemed to signify that he and I and everyone else were of little worth, but it comforts me now to believe that the universe is not dependent on the ruthless and frivolous beings we are often proven to be.

I would like to lie beside Shimon, to feel the rise of his warrior's chest against mine, but I hold myself back and imagine his light going out – and his soul fleeing our realm – since the sharp pain of losing him for ever is the closest I shall ever come to isolating what it means to be the grandson of so beautiful a man.

I awaken in my children's room with Gephen lying across my shoulders, nibbling at my ear. I take him in my arms and remind him that I have no wish to be edible, but he is in one of his sullen moods and wriggles free from me with a serpent-like hiss.

My children's mats are empty. Dazzling light frames their window shutters.

A foul and bitter taste in my mouth prompts me to spit into my daughter's chamber pot, and it's then that I discover – dishearteningly – that my tunic is again stuck to the wound on my back, which must have bled during the night. As I stand, Gephen leaps on to one of Nahara's cushions and tests his claws, pricking at the fabric. I ask him to stop, since he will create a rip, but he continues his mischief. After I chase him from the room, the frigid edges of a dream fold around me: I am again at the night-time beach in Alexandria, and my father is with me. Blood covers his hands – from the blade wound in his chest. He pleads for my help, though I know in my heart that nothing I do will be able to prevent his death.

Now I close my eyes and still my breathing, as I have been taught, and I concentrate on my father – on his agonized countenance – and I extend my hand to him. I sense that he will reveal to me what I can do to ease his suffering in the Underworld if he takes it, but he does not.

In the courtyard, I discover that my family has already eaten breakfast. Shimon greets me with a hearty embrace, showing no ill effect from his overdrinking except for his stale breath.

'You're frozen,' he tells me, rubbing my hands in his.

'I had a bad dream,' I explain.

'About what?'

'I was on my way home at night, racing across Samaria, and I got lost,' I lie, though it seems as if what I tell him is also – in some sense – true.

I take my barley broth to my room because I can still feel my father dying inside me. I notice that my beach stones from Alexandria are gone from my shelf. I question Mia about them on returning my breakfast bowl to her, but she has no idea where they might be and has not yet had a chance to search for my mother's amber beads. *And don't rush me!* her expression warns.

Nahara reaches up to me and pleads to be lifted while Mia and I are conversing about the baby girl she rescued and who is now at the orphanage. My daughter buries her head in the curve of my neck as she does when she is upset. I suspect that she has finally grasped that she will be leaving for Egypt in just four days – on the morning after our Passover supper.

Mia notices the bloodstain on the back of my tunic as I am distracting my daughter with talk about Gephen. She tells me that she needs to clean the wound. 'Now!' she orders when I tell her that I am not yet fully awake.

A long and delicate operation ensues, involving warm water, ointments, a plentiful amount of blood and – when vinegar is applied – some healthy swearing on my part.

As Mia is coating me with her fragrant oils, Marta's daughter Yehudit escorts Onesimos the jeweller into my room. He carries Grandfather Shimon's *tallit*, folded into a perfect square. His walk is stooped and his eyes are sunken, which sets fear jumping through me, but I soon learn that I have misread his mood

'Eli, you did it – you saved Ninah,' he tells me in a hoarse whisper, and the tears in his lashes glisten, and he places Shimon's prayer shawl before me as though it were an offering to the Lord.

It is an astonishing thing to hold in your arms a father whose daughter has not died, to feel the ocean of gratitude in which he is drifting – and to be reminded again of the prodigious depth of feeling that is our heritage but that we hide from one another, as if it were shameful to admit that our spirit is made of compassion – *racham* – and love.

He reaches into his pouch and hands his daughter's blood-encrusted molar to me, and, while I turn the tiny four-horned bulb in my hand, he speaks my thoughts for me. 'It seems wrong that so small a thing could cause so much pain.' Gazing up at Mia, he says in a reverent voice, 'Your brother is a man of miracles.'

'It would seem so,' she agrees, which makes me gaze up at her, and we share a look that acknowledges that we would both like to return to how we lived before my death and revival but never shall.

Onesimos holds out a slender golden ring to me. 'For you,' he says.

'I already accepted one present from you. That was enough.'

'I swore to *Elohim* that I'd give this band to you if my daughter survived. It was my mother's. Ninah was named after her.'

With his ring in my palm, I calculate how many months of Yirmi's studies its gold would guarantee and arrive at nine. I make a fist around it, and it feels right in my hand, but I shall not steal from a friend. And, for once, I find the right words to express my thoughts. 'Give your mother's ring to Ninah,' I say, 'so that she may know that her life is special to her grandmother, even though she is not here to tell her so.'

After Onesimos departs, Yirmi and I make ready for work. Thankfully, Lucius has again sent us Abibaal and his donkey. As we make our way to the Upper Town, I offer benedictions to all those who beseech me, including a deaf Roman dwarf from Antioch who comes to have a prominent place in my heart because he teaches me the meaning of a verse from the Book of Names I'd never previously understood.

The dwarf's name is Maximus. A joke at his expense? Yes, he admits, his father intended the name as a humiliation. On leaving home at the age of twelve, he stopped concealing it from those he met for the first time, since he discovered that the name had become a sacred lantern that always revealed to him those he could trust and those – giggling at him and pointing – he could not.

Unfortunately, he has been deaf nearly from birth. His intelligent eyes gaze up at me out of a pale and shrivelled face, and he converses with me with graceful and intricate hand gestures that his son, who is of normal stature, translates into Latin. The young man's wife, a Judaean, translates his Latin into Aramaic.

While watching this time-consuming but captivating process, I understand the verse from the Book of Names where Mosheh tells us, 'The people saw the sounds', for I come to recognize – and hear inside my head – several of the words Maximus speaks with his hands!

The little man tells me that he lost his hearing as a five-year-old boy after a period of aching in both his ears. Watching him speak, I recall a visual prayer that Rabbi Elad taught me, and I sense that my recollection of it is no coincidence, so, after he finishes his explanation, I draw a circle in the air above him – representing creation – and picture the two of us at its centre. I compel the circle to expand inside my mind, and, when it surrounds Yerushalayim and Bethany and finally all of Zion, I ask Abibaal to take a drop of blood from my back on to his fingertip and trace it around each of the little man's ears. I then recite a prayer from Samuel that I heard Yeshua use to restore the hearing of a Galilean cobbler. '"In my distress, I called upon the Lord. And from his temple, He heard my voice. And my cry for help came into His ears."'

Although Maximus' hearing is not immediately restored, he thanks me with graceful, kind-hearted gestures. Abibaal watches me suspiciously while I am saying my farewells to him, as though he has just realized that I am not the simple artisan he has always taken me to be.

The elderly slave wears a handsome white turban today, and, as we enter Yerushalayim, he tells me it is because Lucius' right elbow has been aching, as it does whenever we are about to have rain. It's then that I notice that thick grey clouds have indeed rolled in from the east.

As I turn away from the sky, I sense the intimate connections between myself and the world as trembling in my chest. *Had I never been born*, I think, *I wouldn't have been able to learn from Maximus or help save Ninah's life. Everything would have been different, which means that the life or death of a single person may have consequences we cannot predict.*

Can you grasp what I am telling you, Yaphiel? You and I are connected to the men and women who lived a thousand years before us, as well as those who will be born a thousand years into our future.

How to express this truth?

At the time, I am unable to do so. Indeed, only many years later, after another flash of insight, would I hear Yeshua tell me again what he had said after I lost my faith: *the sea whispers that the separateness of islands is an illusion.*

33

As soon as we arrive at work, I realize that in my mosaic Ziz ought to be holding a royal staff in his claws. How is it that so important a detail escaped my notice until now?

I make his sceptre with exactly ninety red-granite tesserae, the numerical value of the word *melekh* – king – in Hebrew. I use the last of my Egyptian diorite – a sacred stone that is mottled black and white – to create a wheel of the zodiac at its tip, since even the king of the birds must be subject to the rules of time. Once I'm finished, I gaze down from the rim of the pool, and I realize – as though the future has just perched on my shoulder – that this was the last detail I needed to find. After Yirmi and I fill in the remaining gaps in the sky with white marble and lapis lazuli, the design will be what it is and what it shall evermore be.

'Completing the mosaic makes you sad, doesn't it?' Yirmi asks me when I tell him what I've discovered.

'Yes, a bit,' I tell him, 'but mostly I'm surprised.'

'Surprised?'

'By what it has become.'

'What do you mean?'

'I've found that my greatest challenge is to understand what the stones want to become – and to obey their desires as best I can.'

He shows me a puzzled countenance, so I take his shoulder and explain. 'Desire flows out of the stone – out of their shapes and colours – and enters me. The tesserae themselves determine how I come to alter my original plan.'

He shakes his head, still unsure of my meaning, so I tell him that all will become clear as he acquires more experience.

'What will we work on next?' he asks, with boyish eagerness lighting his eyes.

'The inner courtyard of the villa.'

'Do you have a plan?'

'Of course – I'll show it to you tonight.'

In the afternoon, the heavens open for a time, so Yirmi and I work on the sky above Ziz to the restful sound of rain drumming on our awning. In my daydreams, I watch Yeshua preaching to paupers assembled in the wilds of Judaea. The downpour leaves him soaked, but he sends away his followers who try to shield him with sackcloth, for he wishes to inhabit the rain, so that those who seek his help may become the fertile fields of Zion.

Only a small crowd waits for me when I return to Bethany in the afternoon. When Mia opens our door to my knocks, she is holding my mother's amber necklace in one hand and my beach stones in the other.

'You found them!' I exult.

She slips the necklace over my neck and hands me the stones. 'You need to talk to Nahara,' she says.

'Why?'

'They were concealed under her mat.'

'She stole them?'

'It seems so.'

'Did you ask her why?'

'No, but I already know why.'

'You do?'

'Eli, she doesn't want to go to Alexandria. The start of the Sabbath is only two evenings away, and after that . . .' Mia shakes her head gravely. 'A six-year-old girl has fears you can only guess at.'

'But why steal my things? How will that help?'

'She's confused. If I'm right, she thinks *you're* the one who is leaving. And she wants to make you stay with her by hiding what's precious to you.'

I find Nahara in Shimon's upstairs eyrie. She is seated opposite her great-grandfather, her legs crossed in imitation of him. They look as though they have been engaged in a deep philosophical debate, which gives me a good laugh. Shimon says he has been giving her lessons in arithmetic.

She laughs hard when I swoop down and lift her into my arms. 'Listen, Naha,' I say, 'my beach stones and my necklace went missing for a while. Do you know where Aunt Mia found them?'

She gazes away from me and makes no reply, so I assure her that I will not punish her. 'I understand you had a higher motive for your theft,' I say.

Still she says nothing. 'I'll join you in Alexandria as soon as I can,' I try, and I sense that she is about to reveal her fears to me, but, when I smile at her encouragingly, her face peels open to tears.

Shimon covers his ears with his hands; he has never been any good around sobbing children. With Nahara in my arms, I go down the ladder, and, once we are in my alcove, I sit my daughter on my lap and kiss her eyes and give the end of her foot a squeeze, so that everything I remember of my subsequent conversation with her is filtered through the salt taste of her tears and the feel of her tiny toes snuggling into my hand.

I do not know why, but I soon recall the ring offered me by Onesimos, and I know then how I shall help my daughter. 'Would you like to keep my mother's necklace as proof that we'll all soon be together again?' I ask.

Nahara looks up – a squirrel stirred by the sound of a falling acorn.

I hold out the necklace. 'It's pretty, isn't it?'

She nods warily, as if I have set a trap for her

'I have to warn you that the necklace is dear to me,' I say. 'I'd never give it to you unless I was certain that I would see it again very soon. Do you understand?'

'I can . . . can keep it?' she asks, sitting up as tall as she can, as though to see out over a field of hopes.

I put the amber beads around her neck. 'It's yours now,' I say.

'For ever and ever?' she asks, holding its curve in her tiny, joyful hands.

'Yes, for ever and ever.'

34

Blustery winds rattle the doors and roofs of Bethany that night as though searching every dwelling for a runaway slave. Or, more likely, for a man who has cheated death . . .

Who they find, however, is Akiva, the nimble little sprite who is always asking me to hold him up by the ankles and twirl him in crazy circles.

'No, God, no!' he wails over and over that night.

I lean my head against my shutters as against the Gate of Compassion and pray that his father, Alon the tailor, will not break his bones again.

God forgive me, I also pray for Alon's death.

I remember once Marta telling me that Akiva's beatings sounded far worse than they were, to which I replied, 'The human voice does not make the sounds of torture unless that is what is happening.'

About a year earlier, Alon even burned Akiva's feet over coals.

Does the little boy plead with me to twirl him upside down so that he can be sure there is at least one adult he can trust?

'"He who withholds the rod hates his son,"' Alon quoted to me when I saw the seared flesh on the boy's feet. I told him that I would raise Akiva if he did not want him, but he just laughed at me.

While the boy wails, I drape my cape over my head and chant Queen Ester's prayer, which we speak aloud only when all other options have been exhausted: '"My Lord, who is my only King, help Akiva, for he is in desolation, and he has no one else to whom he can turn."'

When the boy's shrieks finally end – has he passed out from the pain? – the silence that reproaches me for not rescuing him seems so deep that I know I would never reach its bottom if I were to fall inside.

Later that night, Gephen limps into my alcove and comes to me on my mat. He rubs his head against my leg, whimpering. His left forepaw is bleeding, and he smells of manure. *Has evil come to reign over all of Bethany?* I wonder.

I caress the cat's belly – trying to sooth him and, through him, all those in torment.

I fall asleep with Gephen in my arms and awaken in the morning as though spun out of a war-chariot, unsure of where I am. When I throw open my shutters, the bright-blue firmament startles me. I gaze out, holding tight to the lintel, very much like a lizard peering out from behind a rock after a stormy night.

I find a dead dog just outside my front door, already being fed on by flies, and it is then that I realize I have lived through what we in the Galilee call a Night of *Ophel*.

Ophel: a dense, destructive, bleeding darkness; the *darkness that can be felt* from the Book of Names.

Lack of sleep has left me weak of body, but it is a comfort to sit beside Yirmi at the bottom of Lucius' swimming pool and finish the sky in my mosaic, since it permits me to draw a line between my work day and the previous night.

When the composition is complete – every tessera in its final home – my son offers to prepare the grout for me, since my bad leg is stiff and painful. He lugs our sacks of quicklime and volcanic ash out of the shed by the garden gate and, under my guidance, pours their contents into an iron basin that Abibaal fetches for us. He mixes the resulting amalgam together with water.

Since Yirmi has never helped me finish a mosaic, I hand him my wooden paddle. 'The grout will be ready when it is eager for the feel of the wood but not so greedy that it refuses to let it go,' I tell him.

A short time later, when the mixture is perfect, I ladle a small portion of it into separate bucket and have Yirmi add the blue-black pigment I make from kohl and indigo. I shall apply this dark-grey grout in the slender gaps between the tesserae of the black flames so that their colour and their impact will be intensified.

I work alone because the grout tends to lick up every drop of moisture on one's hands, turning the skin to leather. My fingers and palms are, by now, a lesser form of cowhide, so they will not endure any further damage, but my son's tender flesh would suffer.

I do not pause for my midday meal, since I find this work so tedious that I might not return to it if I were to stop.

A pitiless sun has risen over Yerushalayim. Yirmi wipes my brow and towels off the grout I accidentally smear on my face and hair. He senses my waspish mood and cleaves to silence.

I finish shortly after the descent of the third hour, by my reckoning. I shall perform a few touch-ups the next day, as needed. After that, I shall do my best to let the mosaic go off without me and continue its journey alone, no longer burdened by its maker.

While Yirmi and I are resting in the shade of the cypress tree, Lucius comes to us. His eyes are tense and the set of his mouth is worried. 'I need to talk to you,' he says.

'Is everything all right?' I ask.

'Yes, but come see me in my villa when you get your energy back.'

Yirmi and I clean our hands and faces at the fountain. As we enter the *atrium*, Lucius stands up from beside the low table where he has been arranging golden wildflowers in a black vase.

'I'm grateful that you worked so long and hard today despite the heat,' he tells us.

'Thank you. Now why did you need to see me?'

'Yeshua needs to speak to you. He wants you to go to him. I just received a message from a courier.'

'Where does he want to meet me?'

'At the tavern his father used to frequent near the Woodworker's Synagogue. And he has asked for you to go to him right away.'

'If I see him I'll have to tell Annas.'

'I'm sure he'll invent something for you to tell the priest that will seem believable.'

Lucius leads us down two sets of stairs to the back entrance to the villa, which will leave us closer to our destination. 'Perhaps you ought to go to the Jewish bathhouse after you speak to Yeshua,' he suggests. 'You'll be my guest.'

'Has our hard work left us smelling that bad?'

He laughs. 'You always think the worst of me! No, I'm worried about the wounds on your back. I'll send Abibaal to the bathhouse to meet you – he'll wash the skin and apply his salves. And he's a magician with a strigil!'

'Lucius, thank you, but we can't go,' I say, before my son's expectations can soar too high.

'Why won't you let me do something nice for you? First you tell me that you can't go to the theatre with me. And now this.'

Maybe another time, I ought to lie but do not. Do I speak of matters best forgotten because of my excess of drink? Undoubtedly, but I see now that I was also hoping – in a small, neglected and never consulted part of my mind – that Lucius would plead my case to his aristocratic friends and win my family some justice. Though that was never a real possibility, of course.

'I once had an . . . altercation with a customer there,' I tell Lucius.

'What kind of altercation?'

'With my father's assassin.'

Yirmi has never heard this story and draws in a shocked breath. We are standing at that moment in the corridor that connects his villa to the private storage room for *garum* and olive oil where Lucius caters to his wealthiest customers. It is dark and dripping with damp, and our voices echo off the stone walls. The sense of being protected by a secretive space is what I remember now most clearly.

I told the story to Lucius and Yirmi quickly because I then believed that Yeshua was waiting for me. Yaphiel, I shall tell it to you now as a warning, since I have long been terrified that my wish to see my father's killer punished might one day draw him to you or one of my other grandchildren. Remember this, my child: should Julius ben Magnus ever cross your path, turn and run away as if he were in league with Asmodeus, for indeed he is.

After my mother discovered my father's blood-soaked body in his bed, Mia noticed that the amulet he always kept around his neck was gone. It was a solar serpent – the size of a large *dupondius*. The serpent's left eye was a yellow citrine and its right a pink tourmaline. The Egyptian symbol of eternal life – the ankh – was concealed cleverly amongst the etched lines of the serpent's hood.

More than a decade after my father's death – one cold winter afternoon – I decided to restore my flesh to vigour at the Jewish bathhouse. As I stepped into the *caldarium* – the hot room – I noticed a handsome, golden-haired slave cleansing the skin of a guest to the side of the bath. When I approached this youth for a closer look at his astonishing locks, I noticed that the man whose chest he was cleansing wore a familiar amulet around his neck. That this customer was a Jew was obvious, since he was wearing no towel and his covenant with the Lord was on show. He was lying on his back and his eyes were closed.

Why he had not left his amulet in the dressing room I cannot say. Perhaps he had had jewellery stolen at the bathhouse before. Or perhaps he feared being without its protection even for a moment.

On the excuse of questioning the slave about his handsome strigil, which had a handle made of mother-of-pearl, I stepped up to him. During our brief conversation, I managed a long look at the amulet. The serpent's eyes were of two different colours, yellow and pink, and the tiny silver *ankh*, though tarnished, was clearly visible.

The rage that surged up through me was like fire. In one swift and sure movement, I tore the amulet from the man's neck, breaking the silver chain. He was up and lunging for me before I had a chance to shout that he was a murderer. I remember the iron hardness of his hands around my neck more than anything else. We were separated by the other bathers or I would have died inside the grip of my father's murderer.

Blood was on my hands – my own, I would later discover, from a deep wound on my shoulder that he had made by biting my flesh.

He grinned at me. His brown hair was in a tangle, and he was dripping sweat from his brow, but I had done him no damage.

The amulet must have fallen out of my grip when I tried to pull his hands from my throat. It was now in his fist.

'You killed my father!' I shouted.

'You've mistaken me for someone else,' he replied with a sneer.

'That's his amulet!' I said, pointing.

'I bought it in Damascus. If it was your father's, he must have sold it there.'

Had I been mistaken? Was this man innocent?

Confused by emotions impossible to control, I permitted the manager of the bathhouse to lead me back to the street, where he warned me to never again approach the man I'd attacked since he was a killer for hire with powerful Roman friends. When I asked for the assassin's name, he hesitated a moment, then whispered it in my ear: Julius ben Magnus.

I learned all I could about him over the coming months and discovered that he had been born and raised in Joppa and had been employed for several years as a bodyguard for Felix

Marcus Octavianus, the Roman who had refused to pay his debts to my father. I discovered, too, that he had ended the lives of at least six other men. And I learned, as well, that my sisters and I had, in truth, been extraordinarily fortunate, for he enjoyed his work so much that in three of those cases he had also murdered the men's children.

35

Yirmi and I await Yeshua in the raucous tavern where the woodworkers of Yerushalayim and their companions drink away whatever portion of their silver and copper coinage that their wives have not yet managed to slip out of their satchels and stash away. We sit in a dark corner, at a small, square wooden table with misaligned legs, hoping that our hunched, defensive posture will keep strangers from joining us. I have almost no talent at the art of waiting, but Yirmi reads me the graffiti etched into the table's surface, and a few of them display an obscene wit that keeps us amused. One of them even makes us laugh aloud, although it is silly: *I was certain I'd fucked the ugliest woman in the world and then I met her mother.*

An impressive number of comments satirize our conquerors. Yirmi is at an age when bodily exhalations and excretions often seem hilarious, and this remark sets him giggling: *Every time the Emperor farts the Romans praise his genius.*

Surprisingly, one observation – freshly carved in Greek with a florid hand – sets me thinking of Leah: *My wife watches over me with her multi-coloured mind.*

Poikilophron – multi-coloured mind – has a twisting, somersaulting sound. But did the poet intend to write *thron,* meaning throne, instead of *phron?* That would make it a far more common term. In the end, it makes little difference, for a good deal of verse, as I was once told by a Galilean bard, is created by the trickster spirits – the *kesilim* – who jumble up letters and syllables on purpose so that all of us might have new words with which to play.

At length, a stick-thin, toothless old rogue opens the shutters on the window nearest us and starts to shriek profanities at the women passing by. Yirmi and I sip our posca, nibble our lupines and hope for a bolt of divine lightning to silence the churlish old idiot. While watching my son's face studying the girls who occasionally pass by our window, I realize why I have been feeling an intruder here: my father would have often taken the boy to taverns such as this. In my extravagant, long-defeated heart I know that Yirmi would have heard epic stories of the olden days – of war, hardship and sacrifice but also of miraculous love – that I shall never be able to tell him.

What could be keeping Yeshua?

Sunset soon creates clouds of carmine and sulphur above the houses across the square. I know we ought to make our way home, but, when the tavern manager sets his candle flame to the wick of the lantern on our table, he asks if my son and I can make room for another drink.

As I sip my palm wine, my son endeavours to engage me in conversation about the wonders awaiting him in Alexandria. 'Can one climb to the top of the lighthouse?' he asks. 'Shall I be able to take lessons in the Egyptian language? Are there trees and flowers that I have never . . .'

I fight through my apprehension to give the colourful replies he deserves.

By the time we leave, a dense netting of stars has spread across the firmament, and a frigid wind has swept in from the mountains in the east. I hold Yirmi close to me as we make our way to Yaaqov's home. He shivers in my arms but voices no complaint.

Sarah, Yaaqov's wife, confirms that her husband is with his older brother and tells me how to find their meeting place. I borrow an old camlet cloak from her and force Yirmi to put it on.

My son and I weave in and out of the labyrinth of streets behind the Imperial Theatre in order to confound any spies who may be observing us. Two armed guards admit us to the house where Yeshua is having supper. It belongs to a friend whose identity must remain a secret, since he still lives in Yerushalayim and might suffer reprisals if this scroll were to come into the hands of the Roman authorities. When I give the guards my name and purpose, the shorter of the two – a dark Galilean youth with hooded eyes – climbs up a ladder in the courtyard to the first storey.

The ceiling creaks with each of his steps. As I gaze up, the guard who has remained with us – elderly and lean, with the pointy profile of a hunting dog – reads my expression and says, 'The structural beams are secure.'

Two threadbare sleeping mats are rolled up in the corner beside a stack of logs and just-gathered pine cones that give the room the pleasant smell of a forest. On top of a flat-topped trunk against the wall is an old scroll discoloured by black mildew. I point to it. 'May I take a look?'

'Be my guest,' he says.

I discover a *ketubah* decorated with myrtle flowers, rue leaves and other floral motifs connected with matrimony. It was written more than forty years before. I read the first line aloud, then continue to the end in silence. What a pleasure even such bland and legalistic prose can be to a reader deprived of books!

Curiously, the contract stipulates the right of the bride – whose name is Margarite – to name all the couple's children.

'Women!' the guard sneers when I read that clause aloud, as if they are the origin of all misfortune and dishonour.

The smell of grilling fish steals in through the open door to the courtyard. Only then do I notice Andreas, one of Yeshua's young disciples, crouched over a cooking fire, a fisherman's hat pulled down over his brow. He waves to me as I observe him from the doorway, and I hail him back. When I breathe in on his oil-scented smoke, my stomach gurgles so loudly that the guard, my son and I have ourselves a good laugh.

Yeshua leads Yaaqov down the ladder into the courtyard only moments later. A wooden calliper hangs around his neck. Its graduated bow is made of yellowing bone, which identifies it as his father's. Has he been preaching about how we must measure even our enemies with compassion?

When we embrace, he brushes his cheek against mine to feel the prickly scratch of my whiskers. At such moments, I imagine us to be long-lost brothers in an ancient Greek epic, recognizing each other through the feel of their flesh – which may be why he now brings my hands to his lips.

'Do you laugh when you think of the future?' he asks me, paraphrasing a Proverb.

'I laugh so that your dearest father Yosef, who sits in the heavens, may also smile,' I reply, adapting a verse from the Psalms.

Yeshua and I each pick out one more quote from Mosheh to offer the other. It is our way of constructing our island. You see, Yaphiel, he and I spent too much time with our tutors when we were young, and we craved a territory over which we had absolute dominion.

A curiosity: Yeshua's eyes sometimes change colour in my dreams. Although he had the dark-brown eyes of his father, I have seen them as sky-blue and green and, on one occasion, silver – like the reflective gaze of Mosheh, whose soul was made from the light skimming off the waters of the rivers of Eden.

For a time, studying his face, the room and everything in it vanishes.

'There is only now,' he says, as though he has freed us from time. He opens his hands. 'There's no need to rush.'

Loneliness need not be my fate is what my quickened pulse is telling me. *This island we make is where I always live, even when I am not aware of it.*

Time starts up again when Yeshua kisses my son's brow and blesses him. He speaks with such tenderness that the strangest of all the strange thoughts that have occurred to me over my lifetime appears unbidden inside me: *If only we could have made a child together . . .*

Does my old friend read my mind, or have I failed to hear a previous comment from my son that would make his coming remark seem commonplace?

'We'll have to wait until the wheel turns once more,' Yeshua says. He uses the Greek word *kuklos* for wheel, and, since the concealed meanings of this term may only be revealed to the initiated, I can say nothing more about his intentions.

Did Yeshua speak aloud or only in my mind? I recall his lips moving, but maybe they did so only for me. Later, I shall have a chance to ask Yirmi if he heard Yeshua mention a wheel or speak the word *kuklos,* and he will reply that he heard nothing of the sort.

A vision is a higher truth that seeks entry to us through our eyes. But what ought we to call audible words spoken inside the mind of another person?

Over the years, Yohanon, Maryam of Magdala, Loukas and others have told me that they have heard Yeshua address them inside their minds, and his father once mentioned to me in passing that on four different occasions Yeshua called out to him over great distances, and each time he could hear his son as plainly as if they were standing together. On his deathbed, Yosef also told me that he heard his son speak a verse of Torah to him at the moment I saved him from drowning.

'Which verse?' I had asked him.

'"He reached down from on high and took hold of me,"' the old man replied.

Yosef and I were alone at that moment, and I asked him why he had never mentioned that to me before.

'I didn't want to make what had happened seem any more momentous than it already did,' he told me. 'Also, at the time, the verse seemed so unimportant compared to you saving his life. And, in any case,' he added, gripping my hand, 'we were all aware by then that my son's voice could carry over many miles.'

'Have you come to share our supper?' Yaaqov asks me now. 'Andreas has brought us fish from the Jordan, and you and your son are welcome to share our meal.'

'It's tempting,' I reply, 'but my sisters will worry about us if we don't go home very soon.'

Yeshua has closed his eyes by then. He breathes slowly, as if searching for slumber. I press my hand against his chest. 'Dodee, tell me why you sent word for me to come.'

Yeshua shows me a puzzled look. 'I didn't send for you.' He turns to his brother, who also says that he didn't summon me.

'Lucius said that a courier told him I was to join you at the tavern your father used to frequent,' I say. 'Yirmi and I waited there for you until long after sundown.'

'Who gave Lucius the message?' Yeshua asks.

'I don't know. I'll have to ask him. It seems odd. Unless . . .' Danger creeps up between Yeshua and me. 'Maybe someone wanted to separate me from Lucius,' I say. 'If Annas has learned that Lucius has been working on your behalf, then he might want to teach him a lesson – and without me and Yirmi as witnesses. I have to return to his villa.'

'No, it won't be necessary,' Yaaqov says. He summons the guard posted by the door and gives him instructions to check on Lucius – and to defend his life if needs be. While they are talking, Andreas climbs up the ladder to the upper floor balancing a platter of grilled fish in his hand.

After the guard departs, Yeshua takes his brother's wine cup and hands it to me.

He blesses the wine as I drink, then takes a sip for himself while I repeat the same benediction. When he requests that I sit with him in the courtyard, I ask my son to wait for me in the house.

Yaaqov reads the concern in my eyes. 'I'll take good care of Yirmi,' he says. He leans close to me and whispers, 'Be sure to see me before you go.'

Yeshua and I sit on our haunches facing each other. As his lips sculpt prayers, the wood fire crackles and sparks, and I remember being a boy with my father sitting with me in a Galilean meadow at sundown, and how he had told me the names of my ancestors going back seven generations and asked me to memorize them.

Yeshua brings me back to him when he points at my chest and asks what happened to my amber necklace.

'I realized that my mother wanted Nahara to have it, so I gave it to her. It's odd how it can take us years to understand the simplest requests that our parents make of us.'

He takes his calliper from around his neck and hands it to me. 'Take this in its place.'

'But it's part of your inheritance from your father.'

'Which is why I want you to have it.'

Once I have his calliper around my neck, he raises a hand of blessing over me. 'You came from the light and to the light you shall return.'

His words move me deep inside myself. 'And yet a bleak and ominous *ophel* descended upon me last night,' I tell him.

He spreads his arms far apart, as though gathering in all that the world would offer us as comfort. 'Trust in all you are,' he says, 'and you will see there is no death. There is only life.'

Those will be the words that I shall repeat to myself over and over on the day that my world comes undone, though they will offer me no solace.

The candlelight of the house slowly fades while we watch each other. Yeshua comes to me and brushes his hand over my eyes so that I will close them, then places his palm to my brow, as he does when he wishes to take me with him to places I could not otherwise go. He leads me in chant, and I listen to our voices, and, after a short while, they seem to be coming from out of the ground itself, and his hand grows hot, and I sense myself rising out of the top of my head, and I am tingling as though made of sparks, and somewhere below me is the man of physical shape and form I have left behind. An aura of blue-white light is emanating from his head and chest. When Yeshua smiles at me, I remember that we have both been here before, many times, and often in the dreams that follow our days of fasting, and where we are is not a place on any map, yet it is far more real, because it is not dependent on any invocation or charm or on any mood or desire, which is another way of saying that it can never be destroyed. After he gets to his feet, he takes my hand and lifts me ever higher, and he and I are climbing up a ladder towards a dazzling orb of light above us, and it glows brighter as it moves across the sky, and silver wings emerge from it, and I see that it is the divine eagle I dreamed of when I was a boy. It alights on my shoulder, and I speak the secret name of the Lord of Flight in greeting, and He blinks twice to greet me, and I am crying because He has come to me, but I soon grow frightened, for I have begun to feel the world tugging me back to earth and am certain I shall fall, so Yeshua holds something reflective out to me in his right hand, and I cannot see what it is because of my tears, but I take it from him because he will never fail me, and it is round and warm, and he calls my name as though I have been too long away from him, and I turn to him . . .

'Lazar!'

Yeshua stands before me, and I am back behind my eyes, and I am so secure and warm that I cannot imagine moving from this spot ever again, since I am at the very centre of all I have ever been.

In my right hand is his alabaster wine cup, and it is filled with wine.

'Take a sip,' he says, 'and repeat these words in your head: "No death, only life."'

I do as he says, and afterwards I return the cup to him, and he watches me as he drinks to be certain that I know he is closing a circle around us.

I am reminded of all the times he has shown me what I could not see myself, and I know I shall always be grateful.

'When you are sieged by doubt, hold that certainty in your mind as you would the hand of Yirmi or Nahara,' he tells me. 'And if you need me, I'll alight on your shoulder, just as I did a moment ago. I shall spread my wings over you and fly you to safety.'

'When I need you, will you always come to me no matter where you are?' I ask.

I know I am requesting too much of him and speaking like a small and desperate boy, but all of me is remembering the thousands of days we have spent together and longing for thousands more yet to come, and it seems reasonable for me to ask what I've never asked before.

'The one who seeks is also the one who reveals,' he says.

'I don't understand.'

'You've seen the truth. Walk inside yourself and follow the signs I've given you, and you'll find the ladder up to the Kingdom, where I'll always be waiting for you.' He raises his hands over me. 'Blessed is he who has helped teach me what I needed most to know.'

'What could *I* have ever taught you?' I ask.

'You taught me to ask for nothing in return.'

I would hold back my tears if I could, but I cannot.

With his hand on my shoulder, he closes his eyes, and he is gone for a time, breathing in and out fast at first, then slowing his rhythm and finally not breathing at all.

Would you ever leave us behind so that you could remain with the Lord for ever?

It is a question that I did not ask him when he opened his eyes, though I have wished for decades that I had.

Upstairs, I find Yeshua's disciples seated in a circle around a frayed old rug. Platters of fish, vegetables, nuts and dried fruit are spread before them. The tall Greek lanterns in the corners give a harsh yellow glow to all the contours of the room.

If I close my eyes, I can hear the jumble of congenial greetings and laughter that greeted me as I stepped in the room. In years since, many of those who never had the chance to meet Yeshua will ask me if I sensed any misgivings or apprehension amongst his companions that evening. *No,* I shall tell them, though, in truth, I might have failed to notice the worries of others because I had just returned from a journey with Yeshua that had created in me a giddiness of spirit.

To my shame, I had entirely forgotten my fears for Lucius' safety.

Only once do I hear apprehension in a friend's voice, after Maryam of Magdala insists that I take a few moments to sit with her. I notice that she has had her left palm painted in the knotted style that is common in the Galilee. After I confess that seeing it makes me homesick, she allows me to study its pattern, but she also whispers imploringly, 'Please, Eli, don't try to tell me my fortune, no matter what you see.'

I ask what is troubling her, and she speaks behind her upraised hand. 'If anything were to happen to Yeshua, then the demon would come for me again. I have lately seen him waiting for me.'

When Maryam puts her small cool hand in mine as though to show that she has grown to trust me, I remember that after Yeshua finally defeated the night-demon that invaded her and forced her to mutilate herself, she told us, 'For twelve years I wished to cry out for help, but, every time I tried, he took away my voice.'

How many of us never find a way to say the one thing we must?

'If you should ever wish to end your life again, come to me,' I tell her now. 'I'll always be ready to help you any way I can.'

She kisses my hand and then, with girlish laughter, puts some of the *charoset* she has made on a piece of matzoh and feeds it to me. My tongue curls around a sharp but sweet flavour that is new to me. Maryam says that it's produced by a powder made from the bark of a tree that grows in India. She calls it *kinnamomon*. 'I buy it at the spice market, though I can afford only a tiny amount,' she says, and she tells me which stall to go to in order to purchase it – and to use her name – since the owner keeps his rarities hidden.

Our relaxed and easy conversation makes it clearer than ever that we were born under the same sign, which pleases me. Even so, the room is too crowded – and our circle of friends too boisterous – for my solitary nature. I soon give my signal of departure to Yirmi, who has been talking with Yaaqov. As I stand, however, Yehudah of Kerioth approaches me with welcoming arms.

'Eli, will you be with us at the start of the Sabbath?' he asks. 'Our Seder promises to be very special this year.'

His smile is the generous one I have always known, which makes it more difficult to lie to him.

'Grandfather Shimon is not well,' I tell him. 'I need to stay with him.'

'I'm sorry. But Yeshua will want you with him. Maybe you can come late.'

It is evidently Yehudah's aim to bring us together, but for what purpose?

I decide that he is probably eager to have as grand a gathering as possible since he is unlikely ever to be invited again to eat Passover supper with us. It seems inconceivable today, but it does not occur to me at the time that he might be hoping for me to join the others so that I, too, can be trapped in his plot against Yeshua.

Blessed be the son who learns to recognize discomfort in his father. Yirmi takes my arm and reminds me that we must get on our way.

After I apologize to Yehudah, my son and I ease our way towards the ladder. Yeshua remains seated, in between Yohanon and Thoma. As I pass behind him, I kiss the top of his head. He twists around, and we wish each other a joyous Exodus in case we do not see each other before the start of Passover, which begins – like the Sabbath – tomorrow at sundown.

On reaching the ladder Maryam calls my name and makes a descending arc with her right hand. *Go slow!* she is telling me in the unspoken language of the Galilee. How easily I understand it still, especially when it is spoken by a friend.

Yaaqov comes to me and says that he will see me and my son to the door. Yirmi heads down the ladder first.

I turn back to look at Yeshua once my foot is safely on the first rung. A calyx decorated with dancing figures has been set before him, and he is about to wash his hands, so that he may recite the blessings before the meal. As Loukas places one of the tall lanterns in front of him, butterflies of light and dark flutter around the room. I picture one of them landing on my head, waiting, unsure of what to do next.

Yeshua senses my concerns and turns to me. So gaunt and frail he seems in the lantern light.

If we lived in a time of justice, you and I would leave this place, I hear him tell me. *We would travel far from the Land of the Gazelle and see all the wonders of the world and find the Indian tree that provides Maryam with her special spice and listen to the stories of all those we meet along the way.*

I lift two fingers to assure him I am well, which prompts him to wave to me.

How many rungs were on the ladder? And what did I say to my son as I joined him below? I cannot say. And not knowing even those small details seems unforgivable; surely we owe it to ourselves and our dead to know everything about the mistaken paths we take.

36

If I had been granted a moment of foresight and had learned that it was the last time that I would ever be able to speak to Yeshua, I would have returned to him and made him flee Yerushalayim with me. He would have told me that he could not turn away from his mission, but I'd have shaken him and shouted, *You owe it to me!*

He would have understood me without my having to say, *Because I saved your life when we were boys.* We would have walked east, crossing the Jordan River and the Syrian desert into Parthia and Persia.

The Zarathustrians would have welcomed Yeshua with roses, as they welcome all holy men, and we would have settled in the ancient and grand city of Persepolis.

And if all that had happened . . . If I had forced Yeshua to leave with me, nothing in the world would have come to pass as it has and I would not be writing this letter to you.

Sometimes in the early morning, before dawn, I am jolted awake in the night as though by his kiss, and I am certain I am back in Bethany, and that Passover will soon be upon us, and I jump up and rush to my door because there is still time to save him.

Perhaps one day the ink will dry on the sacred vellum where Raziel has recorded every one of Yeshua's words and actions that week, and not even the ophanim and seraphim will be able to change what came to pass, and I shall see that all hope is gone, and I shall no longer try to save him in my dreams. But I am an old man by now, and I no longer expect that to happen – or want it to.

Here is what I know and accept: every night of my life I shall crawl into my bed and find the man that Yeshua would have become waiting for me. I shall close my eyes so that I can see everything he now is and face him without shame, and when we embrace his breath will come warm on my cheek, and our hands will fit together as they always have, and he will smell of the fertile earth of our homeland, and we shall exchange greetings with quotes from the Torah, and I shall promise him that he will never again face the future alone, and I shall think, *Perhaps he will remain with me until morning this time if I desire it enough.*

37

As I reach the bottom of the ladder, I see that the guard has returned from Lucius' villa, and it is only then that I recall – shamed by my own forgetfulness – that Annas may have wished to separate me from him. The guard is conversing in hushed tones with Yaaqov and Yirmi.

'Lucius is safe!' my son tells me with a smile as I step to him.

'Did Annas pay him a visit?' I ask.

'No,' Yaaqov replies, and with a determined look he adds, 'which still leaves us with the mystery of why you were summoned away.'

I face the guard. 'Could Lucius have lied to you? Maybe Annas visited him, but he didn't want to tell us what transpired between them.'

'All I can say is that he hasn't been hurt in any way,' he replies.

'For the time being,' Yaaqov concludes, 'we'll have to live with this mystery.'

'In any case, I have to tell Annas immediately that I've been with Yeshua,' I say. 'What do you want me to tell him about our conversation?'

Yaaqov leads me out into the courtyard so that we can speak alone. 'Say that you came here because Yeshua wished to let you know that we shall strike again at the Temple three days from now.'

'Is that what you've told Yehudah of Kerioth? I whisper.

'Yes.'

'But you plan to strike sooner than that?' I whisper.

'I'm sorry, Lazar, but my brother told me that we mustn't risk your life.' He takes a steadying breath. 'Now I must talk to you about something disagreeable.'

'What is it?'

'It's about your sister.'

'What's Marta done now?'

'Not Marta, Mia.'

I sense my life turning around this moment. Perhaps Annas drew me away from her so that he could end her life. 'Has she been killed?' I ask.

'No, she's fine – but she went to see Annas this morning.'

'That's . . . that's impossible,' I stutter. 'Your spy mistook her for Marta. They look alike, and it's –'

'No, it was Mia,' Yaaqov cuts in. 'Our spy is a woman who knows both your sisters. And she learned that it was not the first time that Mia has gone to visit him.'

My legs start to tremble, so I drop down to the packed earth of the courtyard.

'Nothing Mia could have revealed to Annas would make any difference now,' Yaaqov says encouragingly, and he sits with me. 'Everything has been decided.'

I hold my head in my hands. *Why would Mia's deep fondness for me have turned to hate?*

'Maybe she thought she could help you by going to him,' Yaaqov says.

'If my sister spoke to Annas about Yeshua,' I snarl, 'she was not protecting me! How many times has she visited the priest?'

'Twice that we know of. The first time was while you were on your way to see my brother in the countryside.'

So she was responsible for my being struck down with a sword!

'Do you know anything of what she has told Annas?' I ask.

'No. As of yet, we don't have any spies amongst his household staff.'

In my head, I circle around my sister, trying to understand how she could have fooled me so thoroughly – and why.

Yaaqov calls my name again, but I do not look up, for I am trying to find some clue to Mia's betrayal that I might have spotted. When Yirmi comes to my side and puts his hand in mine, I tell him that I shall soon be myself again, though I can tell from the sickness in my gut that that is a lie.

*

'If you think you can't be duped by the people you most love, you're wrong!' I growl at Yirmi once we get on our way to Annas' home. 'Don't trust anyone!'

I realize I sound like an embittered drunk, but I cannot stop myself.

My son asks me what has changed my mood, but I dare not denounce his aunt to him until I have had a chance to confront her. I tell him instead that Yaaqov informed me of the death of a close childhood friend from Natzeret. 'Her name was Naamah, and she lived in the house next door to ours,' I add, since these details will convince my son I am telling the truth.

'Have I ever met her?' he asks.

'No, I haven't seen her in years.'

'And how did she dupe you?'

'She's been gravely ill, but in the messages she sent me, she always said that she was well. She never gave me the chance to say goodbye.'

As we head to the Upper Town, my lie comes to seems a disguised form of the truth, for, if Mia has put me and my son and daughter in danger, then she will indeed be dead to me.

Might Marta have also learned of Mia's treachery? I wonder. Perhaps that would explain her curse. If so, then I have blamed the wrong sister all along.

I plead with Yirmi to return to Bethany as we near our destination, but he refuses. God forgive me, I yell at him to leave me be.

'You're upset because your friend has died,' he says meekly.

'I'm upset because I have a wilful son who disobeys me!'

It's another lie, and this time we both know it, but I am unable to apologize. Over the rest of our walk, he trails several paces behind me, as though he were a stray dog.

A plan for learning the nature of my sister's betrayal comes to me at Annas' door; I shall find a way to introduce her name into our conversation and mention that I have always counted on her fierce loyalty. If I am in luck, the priest will laugh at me and – to humiliate me – reveal her betrayal.

His house slave informs me, however, that his master is unable to receive any guests this evening. Additionally, he tells me that the priest has included me on a list of those he shall only speak to after the Sabbath. As I had previously discovered, Annas is *sekel,* and he has likely realized that his silence will make me suffer more deeply.

Just after Yirmi and I enter Bethany, our neighbour Weathervane hails us from his window. His head is wrapped in a shaggy flea-bitten fleece, which gives him the appearance of the buffoon in a street performance. 'Go ahead and laugh,' he tells my son, even though Yirmi has not even smiled. 'Wait till you're my age and then see how enjoyable life is!'

His harsh words give me a chance to make up for my earlier rudeness, and I hold tight to Yirmi's hand.

Weathervane explains in a long-suffering voice that he has a painful ache in both his left ear and jaw. His wife is confined to bed with the same ailment, so he requests that my sisters bring them some soup and bread.

'I'll send food over later,' I assure him.

On hearing me and her brother enter the house, Nahara scurries down the ladder from Grandfather Shimon's eyrie, followed by the old man himself. Mia rushes in from the courtyard. 'You gave us a terrible scare!' she declares.

Did she believe her treachery had killed me?

When she embraces me, her familiar lavender scent makes me shudder. 'We had business to attend to with Lucius,' I tell her and our grandfather.

Nahara stands on her toes and reaches up to me until I lift her into my arms. She still wears my mother's necklace, which is a blessing, since it means that I have done at least one generous and good thing this week.

'Nothing else is wrong?' Mia asks.

I have decided to avoid confronting her until I have had time to consider the last few days in my mind – to search for clues to the war against me that she has been waging in secret.

'No, nothing,' I lie.

My room has been swept and straightened, since all evidence of leavening must be removed from our houses to celebrate Passover. After I thank Mia for performing this *mitzvah*, Yehudit brings me my supper in my room and agrees to take some barley soup and bread to Weathervane.

Guilt has clearly made Mia attentive to my needs, and she has prepared a favourite meal for me, our mother's recipe for *moretum*.

Marta sees me only briefly. She comes to me in my alcove to tell me she will be eating that night at the house of a friend. Might she be avoiding not me but Mia?

Mia dresses the wound on my back just before I go to sleep. I know I ought to send her away, but she would regard it as suspicious if I were to reject her. She tells me of her work at the orphanage and we discuss the mosaic I have just completed, but when she questions me about the sketches I've done for the inner courtyard of Lucius' villa I tell her I am too tired to converse, which is soon proven true.

I awake in darkness.

Nahara is asleep at my side, on her belly. Her head is underneath her cushion, as she prefers. Do other fathers always make sure their sleeping children are breathing before they do anything else? I cover her with my cape and stand up.

Will I have to kill Annas and Caiaphas to free myself?

That is the first of many impatient questions that crowd around me over the next hour.

Ayin hops to me when I join him on the roof. I stand him on my shoulder, and he surveys our town's last copse of ancient cedars, saved from the Roman shipbuilders by the stubbornness of their owner. I close my eyes and listen to the yelping of jackals in the distance, and there, in my inner darkness, the snowflakes of a particularly frigid winter evening begin to fall on to the intimate, moonlit streets of Natzeret, and I remember the moment I learned that my parents were mortal.

My father and I had been talking about how I had been made *b'tselem Elohim* – in the Lord's image – when he coughed into his sleeve, leaving behind flecks of blood. It was the way he studied them – like a hunter examining the tracks of his prey – that became a fist around my throat.

My father never mentioned the flecks – and neither did I – but I had glimpsed his fear of something far greater than his own blood.

Ayin and I walk to Yerushalayim and back, and the cool wind is comforting to us both.

On returning to my street, I spot three figures standing outside my home. One of them is Yirmi, but the other two . . . ? I must start or give Ayin another cause for apprehension; with a screech, he opens his wings and bats them against my cheek. 'Everything's all right,' I tell him, and I take him in my arms to calm him.

Yirmi comes running towards me. 'It's Yeshua!' he calls out in desperation. 'He's been arrested. Annas and Caiaphas have him.'

The sense of falling inside me makes me reach out to my son as soon as he reaches me. When I look past him, I see Yohanon and Maryam of Magdala rushing towards me, and I surprise myself by thinking, *My whole life has been a preparation for this moment – saving him from drowning, most of all.*

38

Do I pass Ayin to my son as Maryam and Yohanon rush towards us? I must have, but I am unable to recall. If I close my eyes, I can see Maryam's desolate face and her hands straining out for mine.

Leaves and dirt are stuck to the right side of her robe. Her hair is mussed. She begins to explain what happened to Yeshua – cautiously, gazing down, as though to avoid a snare – but a violent shudder soon overwhelms her. I sit her down by my front door. She hugs her knees and covers her head with her hands.

In the mosaic I have made of that day for my prayer room, Maryam is shipwrecked in a cove of despair. Each of the raindrops falling on the two of us is in the shape of a *yod,* which is the letter that unites the heavens to earth, since all that night and the next day I had the sensation that what was happening to us was taking place in the Kingdom of Heaven as well.

Pilgrims awakened by our conversation ask for us to still our voices, so we walk down my street to Bethany's old abandoned well. Maryam drops down at its base. I ask Yirmi to put his arm around her so that she will know that we shall safeguard her from all harm.

My conversation with Yohanon is bordered by the image of Maryam being comforted by my son and encircled by all that I should not have had to ask of so young a boy.

Here and there. Inside and outside. God and creation.

In between the words we speak, I see that Yeshua's arrest has joined together worlds that are usually separate. And I see now that my questions of Yohanon were also a kind of excavation; an effort to find the seam between the Throne World and my unimportant little street in Bethany.

Through troubled stops and starts, Yohanon tells me that, just after supper, Yeshua invited his friends to spend the night with him in the olive field at Gat Smane, in the Valley of Yehoshafat. There is no need for me to ask Yohanon why his mentor chose that spot, since it was there, twelve years earlier, during the dawn of Tu BiShvat, that he renewed his covenant with the Creator by planting a juniper, a cedar and a cypress.

On that cold but sunlit day, we had each taken turns digging holes for the spindly saplings in the rocky soil, ten paces apart. Yosef, Yeshua's father – blessed be his memory – had directed our work, since he had grown up on a farm near Natzeret and still possessed the wisdom of roots and branches in his callused hands. Yohanon was there, and Loukas, Mattiyahu and many other dear friends. When we had finished planting, Yeshua raised his cup and recited from the Book of Yeshayahu: '"The juniper, the cedar and the cypress are now together, and their beauty shall fill the sanctuary we shall make for Him."'

Yohanon tells me now that he and the other disciples sat before those same trees the night before and prayed for all of creation. 'Our voices were much as they were all those years ago,' he tells me, 'and yet the trees around us were so changed – so tall and strong! – that we all became aware, I think, of the forward movement of our lives. I can't speak for the others, but I was filled with hope – and so, I think, was Yeshua.'

As he speaks, I watch Yirmi lifting a damp strand of hair off Maryam's cheek and smoothing it back in place. It seems a very adult gesture for a boy. Perhaps this week – with all its trials – has brought him to the end of his childhood. Too soon, most likely.

'What a joy it was to chant under the moonlight!' Yohanon exults. 'But soon . . . soon everything came undone.' He makes and unmakes his fists. 'Yehudah of Kerioth was the first to hear the regiment of soldiers filing down the hillside from the Temple Mount. He called out a warning and then –'

'Roman soldiers came for Yeshua?' I interrupt.

'Yes. Annas trailed behind them with his bodyguards.'

My heart convulses, for I now see the cleverness of the priest's strategy: he convinced the Roman governor to help him and had the soldiers wait for Yeshua to leave the city – his *eruv* – before arresting him. Annas also thereby avoided the uproar – and perhaps even violent protests – that his followers inside Yerushalayim would have made.

Yohanon takes up his story again: 'Yehudah entreated us to flee the moment he saw them coming, but Yeshua said that he had no fear of the Kittim and that Passover was not yet upon us, so it was not yet time for us to make our way to the Promised Land. And then –'

'He used the word Kittim?' I interrupt.

'Yes, why? Do you see some special significance in that?'

As a designation for the Romans, *Kittim* is used only in the Book of Daniel, which is why I whisper to Yohanon, 'He has seen that he is Daniel's heir. That must be why he has been quoting from our scriptural writings about him so often of late.'

If true, this would mean that Yeshua envisaged – or was told by the Lord of Hosts – that he would be confined in the lion's den before being delivered from death, just as we read in the Torah: *For the Lord of Heaven sent his angel to seal the mouths of the lions set to devour Daniel . . . And the men who had accused Daniel*

*were cast into the den of lions – along with their children and their
wives. And the great beasts assumed mastery over them and broke
all their bones in pieces . . .*

'Some of our friends ran off straight away,' Maryam tells
me. 'Yeshua told Annas that he wouldn't make any trouble if
the Romans let them escape – and if they let the rest of us
remain free.'

'So no one else was taken captive?'

'No.'

Which means that he wished to face this trial alone, I think.

'But why did Yehudah warn Yeshua?' I ask.

'He may have had second thoughts about his betrayal,'
Yohanon answers.

'Yehudah of Kerioth is helping Annas?' Yirmi asks.

'That's what Yeshua told me.'

Maryam gets to her feet with my son's help. As she brushes
off the last of the leaves from her robe, I ask if anyone else was
hurt.

'Only one of the brutes guarding Annas,' Yohanon replies.
'A scuffle broke out because he tried to drag Maryam away
from Yeshua.'

'Thoma and Philippus and some of the others rushed
forward to help me,' she tells me, 'and Shimon struck the man
a blow on the side of the head. He was led away, bleeding badly
from his ear. The Romans –'

'Which bodyguard was it?' I cut in.

'We were told his name is Malchus.'

Those who plough iniquity and sow wickedness reap the same! I
think, and the justice in my mind seems a plough digging into
rich soil.

And then – who can say how? – an epiphany is born of that same fertile earth: *Yeshua has a secret friend working with Annas who will help him escape!*

To test my theory, I ask Yohanon and Maryam how Yeshua seemed on submitting to arrest.

'He was concerned only for the safety of the rest of us,' Maryam replies.

'He must have known that Annas would have him arrested,' Yohanon adds. 'I saw it in the expression on his face – in his ease of bearing and calm. He knew what was going to happen.'

Because he knows most things before they come to pass.

Yohanon does not need to tell us that; we have long known that he is convinced that Yeshua is able to foresee all that is important. But I know from Torah that even a prophet is not always privy to the Lord's intentions, and I have witnessed events that proved Yeshua's prescience both incomplete and fallible.

'What if he wanted to be arrested?' Maryam asks.

'But why?' I question.

'To force the people of Judaea to choose between him and the priests. The Father must have told him that the time has finally come for us to decide our future. We shall make our own Eden or not have it at all.'

Has Maryam grasped Yeshua's purpose more deeply than any of us?

In that case, the truth brings me precious little solace – then or now. For it invariably raises a question that only he himself might have answered:

Was there no other way?

39

Yohanon, Maryam and I rush to the farm belonging to an elderly friend where Yeshua's allies are meeting. We find five of them standing in the barn squabbling over tactics: Mattiyahu, Loukas, Bar-Talmai, Philippus and Nathaneal. Amongst those missing are Yehudah of Kerioth, who has vanished; Shimon, who is consulting with Nikodemos; Yaaqov, who is informing his family of his brother's arrest; and Andreas and Thoma, who are watching Annas' home in the event that Yeshua is either released or transferred.

In years to come, I shall see us as we would have looked and sounded to an outsider: a fellowship of ragged, hollow-cheeked Judaeans and Galileans, speaking in dazed and desperate voices, standing around the hay-strewn floor of a barn whose previous occupants – a flock of sheep, judging from stench of manure and fleece – have been led to the city for sacrifice earlier in the day. We could not see the profound affinity between all of us, but, even if we had, we would not have guessed – and would have been displeased to know – that it had been bequeathed to us by the Romans. We were, after all, a generation born in captivity and living under constraints so familiar to us that we were only vaguely aware that any other way of living was possible.

If you wish to understand Yeshua, then it would do you well to remember that he, too, was part of that same generation.

It soon becomes clear Mattiyahu and Loukas are counting on Nikodemos, who has long served on the Sanhedrin, to win Yeshua's release. They are convinced that he will bend the ruling council to his will if he lets it be known that for as long as Yeshua remains in prison we shall foment rebellions in every city and town in Zion.

No one hints at any spy that Yeshua may have in the priesthood or Annas' household. So if that is the case, he probably shared his plan with no one.

Yohanon argues that appealing to the Sanhedrin will do us no good and adjures that we plead our case directly to Pilatus, the Roman governor. 'Annas and Caiaphas have demonstrated absolute control over the Sanhedrin on numerous occasions,' he points out. 'What's more, since their livelihoods and status are at stake in this conflict, they're unlikely to be cowed by any threats. We shall lose precious time if we limit our efforts to the priesthood. It is urgent that we send a delegation of elders to petition the Roman authorities for clemency.'

His words ring in my ears like a hymn to reason, but Mattiyahu accuses Yohanon of wishing to endanger us all by inviting our conquerors to join what he calls 'an internal conflict'.

'But they're already involved!' Yohanon counters. 'Have you already forgotten that Roman soldiers took our brother prisoner?'

I have always admired Mattiyahu for his knowledge of scripture, and yet the strain we are under now draws him into a wilderness. After shouting down Yohanon, he points a damning finger at him. 'And I tell you this – if anything bad should befall Yeshua, his blood shall be on all the Jews!'

The Jews . . . ? He speaks as if he is not one of us.

Imagine you are guarding a room filled with devils and nightshades you must keep confined as long as you can, even though you know that they will escape and destroy you in the end. All that day I feel those forces of chaos – of ruthless and destructive impulses – clamouring deep inside me, and it is all I can do to keep from charging up to Mattiyahu and demanding that he apologize to Yohanon and the rest of us.

The question I dare not ask in this constrained atmosphere is this: *How can you not see that Pilatus will overrule the priests if he sees it is in his best interests to do so?*

Philippus and some of the others pick up on Mattiyahu's arguments and begin to assign blame to the differing political forces amongst the Judaeans, most of all to the Pharisees and Sadducees. Loukas must see the outrage and frustration in my eyes and takes me aside. 'All Mattiyahu means', he whispers pleadingly, 'is that we must reject those amongst us who are putting obstacles in our way.'

Is he implying that I shall be ostracized unless I agree with him? Perhaps he and Mattiyahu already have plans to found a secret fellowship or to merge with the Essenes.

I make no reply to Loukas, for I have broken out into the cold sweat of those who discover too late that they are headed in exactly the wrong direction.

Soon Andreas rushes in and announces that two bailiffs accompanied by Roman soldiers have taken Yeshua from Annas' house to the home of Caiaphas, where the members of the Sanhedrin are gathering. 'Yeshua's hands and feet were bound with rope!' he says with a groan.

Calls for vengeance cut through the air, and my long-suppressed mistrust for some of the men rises in me as they brandish their eagerness to start an armed rebellion against the Romans. I know that they are virtuous souls and courageous, but they seem to understand even less about our conquerors than I do.

Only years later does it occur to me that a part of me felt relieved to be given this chance to distance myself from them, since I always regarded myself as an outsider in their midst.

I lead my son out of the room, hoping no one will call me back. Yohanon runs to me outside the barn, however. 'I need you with me,' he tells me in a despairing voice.

'I can't go back in. I'm sorry,' I reply. 'I know you're right in what you've proposed, which means that every second I remain here is time I'm wasting.'

After Yohanon returns inside, I imagine Yeshua standing behind me – and about to tell me what to do – but when I turn around there is no one there.

'Are you all right?' my son asks.

'Yes. Give me a moment.'

In my thoughts, I ask Yeshua to show himself, but I do not see any sign at the tops of the pines, or in the stars, or on the trail leading to the road to Yerushalayim or anywhere else, so I close my eyes to look for him in the only place he might be.

An afterimage of the moon drifts through the darkness inside me, and it is blue and violet, the colours of kingship. I start to chant the Book of Names because Yeshua needs to know that I, too, shall be a prisoner for as long as he remains in captivity: *These are the names of Israel's sons who came to Egypt with Yaaqov . . .*

I recite as quickly as I can, as I have been taught, and after a time the blue-and-violet moon fades to darkness, dispelled by my cascade of words, and I dare not pause for breath now that I am moving deeper, but no vision or voice comes to me, so I shout a Psalm inside my mind in order to summon him, 'May those who wish to harm you be covered in scorn and disgrace', and I repeat this entreaty as quickly as I can, and the moment I lose myself in the cascade of words, I bring my breathing to a halt and I feel the ground giving way beneath me, and I reach for my son to keep from falling, but it is my father's hand who reaches out for me, and he lifts me up and smiles at me, and I am a small boy again, and he speaks a single word to me as if it is meant to save us both from years of suffering.

When I come to myself, I am seated on the ground outside the barn. Yirmi's hand eases on to my back as I draw the air deeply into my chest.

'How long was I away?' I ask.

'Long enough for me to get worried about you,' he replies.

'It seemed like just a few seconds.'

'No, it was much more than that. Will you tell me what happened?'

'My father came to me. And he spoke one word to me.'

'What was it?'

'Pharaoh.'

'Why did he speak of Pharaoh?'

'He meant, I believe, that my instincts are correct – I must seek an audience with the great tyrant's representative in Yerushalayim.'

'But we are no longer subjects of Pharaoh.'

'Indeed we are, though he goes by a different title today – and rules us from his palace in Rome.'

More and more, Yaphiel, I believe that we receive messages from beings deep inside ourselves, who speak in a language all their own – and what they tell me as Yirmi and I walk through the streets of Yerushalayim is that every dream I have had is still inside me and telling me which road to take, and everything I have ever done has taken me to this very spot, and that I must not fail or all I have learned will be for naught.

'Where are we going?' my son asks as we start up the stone staircase through the weavers' quarter towards the Upper Town.

'To wake a friend who has access to Pharaoh and his allies,' I tell him.

Abibaal comes to the door of his master's villa still in his sleeping robe. When I explain what has happened, he leaves us in the atrium and goes off to wake Lucius. My son and I pull two folding chairs up close to the hearth and its red-glowing embers.

'Will Yeshua . . . will he be all right?' he asks, and the break in his voice tells me that I must be careful not to reveal my fears to him.

'Yes, of course.' I pat his leg. 'Yeshua will soon be free, and we'll insist that he come tomorrow to our Seder!'

When I smile, he lays his head on my lap. I caress my fingers through his hair, and we say nothing more, because we both know that hope is a timid and hesitant guest in our thoughts at the moment and might be easily chased away.

Lucius rushes in behind two lantern-bearers, who light the candles in the tall, alabaster candelabra at the four corners of the room. He wears a dark sleeping cap and woollen robe.

My son and I jump up to greet him.

'Abibaal has given me the dreadful news,' he says, coming to us.

'For now, Yeshua is a prisoner in Caiaphas' home,' I reply.

After we embrace, I bend to kiss his hands, for I shall need him to risk his reputation for my old friend, but he lifts me up and leans close to my ear. 'Don't ask for my help,' he whispers, 'because I'll only have to refuse you.'

My heart seems to stop, and a moan issues forth from somewhere deep inside me. When we separate, I am unable to raise my eyes to look at him. And yet, as I turn towards the wall, a breeze – like an unseen hand – brushes across the back of my neck, raising gooseflesh and reminding me that there is much that I cannot see but that is real nevertheless – and that may be of help to me even now.

Has Yeshua touched me? Several times that night I sensed him sustaining me and summoning me forward. And yet he never showed himself or instructed me where to go for help.

Lucius, Yirmi and I sit at a low marble table in the family dining room. The air is soft and warm thanks to the hypocaust heating the floor. I have no appetite, but Lucius insists on feeding us. 'Dawn will soon be with us,' he says, 'and you'll need to eat.'

I request only barley broth. My son asks for the same.

I risk a furtive look at Lucius as he gives orders to Abibaal about how his eggs are to be prepared. Is it possible that his allegiance to Yeshua is but an actor's pretence?

I start to speak of what must be done to free Yeshua, but our host – showing me an expression of warning – jumps up and exclaims, 'Eli, for God's sake,' he snaps, 'give me a minute to wake up!'

I am terrified, his furtive looks tell me as he paces the room. *If I help you now, I may lose the villa and all I've worked for these past decades, and I'll become an outcast.*

'Lucius, I wish we had more time, but we don't,' I tell him. 'There may be . . .'

I cut myself short when a Nubian slavewoman carries in a platter of dried fruit, cheese and matzoh. Lucius sits again and reclines on his sofa, and his patrician pose seems his way of drawing a border between us – to convince me that he cannot reconsider his refusal to help.

And yet the moment the slavewoman leaves, he says, 'Eli, it's not what you think.' He shifts a plate of dried fruit closer to my son and smiles. 'Have some figs, Yirmi. Healthy bowels are a blessing.'

'Lucius, if you speak again of my son's bowels or anything else that's of no importance, I shall strangle you!' I warn.

He turns to me and takes a deep breath. 'Don't you see, Eli? I want to help, but, if I show my support for Yeshua in public, I'm finished. I lose all my usefulness to him.'

I nod my understanding, but I am not convinced. I take a long sip of my barley broth to prevent myself from saying something offensive again. Lucius nibbles on a knot of cheese and drinks his broth. With an ugly frown, he says, 'Eli, that look you're giving me . . . I can't bear it any longer. Tell me exactly what's transpired, and we'll think of a way I can help while standing backstage, so to speak.'

I hesitate to reply, since he seems to shift so easily – one moment he is terrified, the next inviting and avuncular. He might be any of a hundred men he has played.

At that moment, he also proves a capable mind-reader. 'You're just going to have to trust me even if you don't want to,' he says.

'Not necessarily,' I say defiantly.

'We both know that if there was anyone else you could've gone to you would have.'

I am reminded that he is a deeply intelligent man – though often far too eager to play an empty-headed patrician.

'Go ahead,' he says.

I speak first of Yeshua's arrest and move on to the meeting of his friends I attended.

Today, all these years later, when I recall my explanation to him, I imagine having fallen into a deep well. I see myself standing at the bottom and shouting up to the rim without ever knowing which of the many Luciuses I might be addressing.

I pause only when Abibaal brings our host his boiled eggs.

After I tell Lucius that I wish to plead our case to the Roman Prefect, and that I shall need his help to secure an audience with him, he wipes his mouth, gets to his feet and, after loosening the drape of his toga, begins a flowery speech in Greek, complete with quotations from Aristophanes and a handful of other renowned dramatists.

Lucius is a gifted orator. But down where I am, at the bottom of my small and circular world, surrounded by mossy walls and the ghosts of drowned men, I cannot grasp the point of all his complex rhetoric.

At length, I think, *If only he were speaking Aramaic,* for it is a language that values simplicity and modesty, and his grandiloquent speech – his delight in circumlocution – would seem laughable to us both.

'I'll go to Pilatus,' I interrupt, sensing that my only hope of detouring around his performance is to tell him my plan.

'What was that?' Lucius asks, scowling as if I have offended him.

'Either you help me or I'm going to have to leave. We're losing valuable time.'

'My God, man, have you heard nothing I've said?' he asks me in a furious voice. 'I've been trying to help you!'

'I've no time for philosophy.'

'Without philosophy to guide us, how do you plan on reaching a civilized end to this conflict?'

'Lucius, perhaps one day, if we are very fortunate, civilization will reach us here in Judaea. For now, I need a way out of the trap that's been laid for us.'

Lucius glowers as though I am the most impetuous pupil he has ever had. Still, he manages to stifle his rage and sit down on his sofa again. 'What I've been trying to explain to you, dear Eli, is why Pilatus will never permit you an audience.'

'Tell me why – and without flourishes!'

'The Romans have nothing but contempt for labourers and craftsmen. As for Galileans, they regard them as mules who have – through sorcery, perhaps – learned to balance on two feet, almost as if they were men.'

'I'll speak only Greek to him,' I reply.

'Eli, I'm sorry, but your chipped fingernails and calluses give your status away immediately. Even if I lent you my finest silken toga, Pilatus would refuse to sit in the same room with you.'

'A curse on the Romans!' I cry, and – on an impulse I can no longer control – I hurl my bowl of barley broth past Lucius' head.

It crashes into the wall. Ceramic shards scatter around the room, and one large, triangular piece slides across the floor to his feet. He picks it up with a grunt. 'I was wondering how long it would take for you to start breaking my expensive crockery,' he says sadly, but a moment later he grins at me as if we have shared a jest.

I do not smile back because my affection for him is flowering again, and I am not certain he deserves it.

'I swear to you that I'll find a way to see Pilatus,' I tell him, though I have no idea how. 'And I'll manage it with or without your help.'

'If you were to see him, what would you say?' he asks, and his forward-leaning posture indicates that I may have tempted him to choose another more helpful role.

'I'll tell Pilatus that trade in all of Zion will be disrupted if a rebellion breaks out. And I'll say that a rebellion is inevitable unless Yeshua is released.'

Lucius glares at me. 'If you tell him that, dearest Eli, he'll have you flogged and raised on a cross!'

Yirmi grabs my arm. 'Don't go to Pilatus! I won't let you!'

I hold him close. 'I'll proceed with caution. And you'll be with me every step of the way, so you can make sure I keep my word.' Then, without deciding to say any more, a truth I had not understood before enters my voice: 'You'll be my shield against evil.'

I do not know why, but I believe that my son has become a living talisman – that, for as long as he is at my side, no harm shall come to me.

'You're going to have to convince Pilatus some other way,' Lucius tells me, and I hear in his resigned sigh that I am losing him already.

As if I have entered one of those dreams where we do something impossible with the greatest of ease, I go to him and kneel before him.

One moment, we are the person we have always been, and the next all our designs for our own life are gone and we are someone new, and we wonder how we could have failed to remember that a part of our soul will always remain as wilful, cryptic and unpredictable as the Almighty.

'What do you think you're doing?' Lucius says, glowering, and he struggles to his feet.

'If you save Yeshua from years of confinement,' I tell him, 'I'll work for you for the rest of my life as your slave.'

I reach for his hands, but he pushes me away. 'Eli, you always say the silliest things at the worst possible times. Don't you understand that I have too many slaves already, and they are nothing but trouble!' To Yirmi, he says, 'Please summon your father back to you.'

'You know how the Romans think,' I rush to add, 'and I . . . I can't even put together a proper sentence in Latin. You're the only person who can help me!'

Lucius looks between me and Yirmi, fearing that he may have to lose face in front of a boy. In the way he gazes down, I sense he is searching his memory for a speech that will save him.

'No more quotes from eminent men!' I plead. And then, by chance, or through the intervention of an unseen guide, I manage to say the right thing. 'Don't you see? This is the part of a lifetime! You shall help a smelly two-footed mule convince a Roman despot to release a Jewish mage!'

Lucius squeezes his eyes shut and holds his head in his hands as though I am driving him mad. Where does he go in his thoughts? Later, he will tell me that he travelled back to the three occasions when he was permitted to remain in the presence of Pilatus.

Blessed be the remarkable memories of Roman-Jewish actors!

He opens his eyes and stands. 'There just may be a way,' he whispers. 'But this part of a lifetime . . . It will be for you, Eli, not me.'

40

Lucius bases the identity I am to assume on a cherished role he was once given in a Phlyax play written by Sopater of Paphos. I am to be an ascetic augur and oculomancer on a pilgrimage to Yerushalayim from the wilds of the Galilee. My austere existence at the fringes of society will explain my threadbare clothing and rough hands.

We give my alter ego a Galilean mother and an Ionian father, so that my knowledge of Torah, as well as the customs of the people of Zion – if revealed – shall seem wholly credible.

Although our conquerors tend to keep to themselves, we can take no chances on my face seeming familiar to any of the servants or slaves I might meet, so Abibaal clips my hair short and dyes it obsidian-black with the mix of kohl and charred frankincense he uses on his master. As he effects this transformation, Lucius tells me that the augur he played was a youthful ornithomancer who read fortunes from the flight of birds. He researched the part by consulting a blind and elderly haruspex living in the port city of Ostia, and he tells me what he still recalls of their extensive dialogues, which turns out to be a great deal. He can still name the different birds that are said to reveal the future by the direction and swiftness of their flight. This includes, he says, the blackbird, raven, crow and glede.

'And the owl?' I ask.

On receiving Lucius' eager affirmation, I sense that I have reached a crossroads where all the knowledge I have accumulated over the last three decades has come together. And, once again, it occurs to me that I have prepared all my life for this test, and I am certain now that I was right to come to Lucius. It even seems possible that, without being aware of it, I agreed to work for him months earlier precisely because this trial was in the offing.

I am exactly where the Lord – and Yeshua – want me to be, I think.

I ask Yirmi to run home to collect Ayin, for I shall use him to put the fear of Zeus into Pontius Pilatus.

I beheld a shooting star as my companion, and I spoke of you, I shall tell the Prefect. *And then I saw that it was no star, but instead . . .*

Lucius tells me that Pilatus' official astrologer and haruspex is named Augustus Sallustius and that I must, at all times, exhibit humble obeisance in front of him. 'He will treat you like an insect,' he says. 'If you accept that you have six legs and a proboscis, you'll get along with him. If you persist in asserting that you have two legs and that Galilean nose of yours, you're sure to quarrel.'

Lucius adds that Augustus Sallustius takes on superior airs with everyone but Pilatus because he is shamed by his family origins, which he has long kept a secret. What no one is supposed to know is that he is the youngest son of an illiterate Sardinian custodian at one of the gargantuan Roman apartment houses – an *insula* – near the Cloaca Maxima. 'Augustus Sallustius grew up on the eighth floor!' Lucius says with a hideous scowl, as if that is a fate fit only for a barbarian.

'How did you find that out?'

'We have a friend in common whose lips loosen when he drinks too much. But, make no mistake, Augustus Sallustius is much respected. As a boy, his astrological acumen was discovered by a wealthy patron who sent him for study at the famous school for augurs in Fiesole.'

Augustus Sallustius is well known to Lucius because he makes regular purchases of the highest-quality *garum*, which he adds to all he eats to maintain his potency. Rumours have it that he has a nearly insatiable sexual appetite, so Lucius has Abibaal fetch me a silver charm of a stupendously endowed satyr that I am to give to him as a gift at the start of our conversation.

'And, whatever you do, don't quote Torah to him!' he pleads. 'Like many of us, he's sure to find that tiresome.' With a sweep of his hand, he says, 'Tell him what you've come to say, then leave. Don't give him time to question you at length. As a good friend of mine says, "When talking to a Roman official, trust only your mistrust!"'

Lucius drops down next to me once Abibaal has finished combing my blackened hair and dressing me in an overly large tunic, yellowed by age, with fraying gold embroidery at its collar. The old actor praises his slave on a job well done and takes this opportunity – patting my back in a fatherly way – to assure me that our plan is a good one, for it is well known amongst the Roman colonists that Pilatus makes no personal or professional decisions without first asking his haruspex to *take the auspices,* as they call divination. 'The Romans jest that the Prefect neither pees nor shits without first having Augustus Sallustius consult his sacred hens!'

To further my chances of gaining an audience with Augustus Sallustius, Lucius has forged a letter of recommendation for me from the augur with whom he studied, Demosthenes of Chalcedon. In it, Lucius bestows upon me the Latin name of Lazarus Valerius Lenticulus. We have taken the risk of using my real name as my *praenomen*, since Lucius is certain I shall become a hive of nerves once I enter the palace, and, if I stumble on so obvious a detail, I am unlikely to ever leave the astrologer's chambers alive.

Yirmi returns with Ayin shortly after Lucius seals his letter of recommendation with his grandfather's signet, imprinting a lion-headed man deep into the pale-yellow wax. He has chosen this particular ring because Augustus Sallustius is rumoured to serve as a priest in a Mithraeum in the cellar of the palace and will, in that case, presume the ferocious beast to be a representation of the Mithras, the god he worships.

Before I leave for Herod's Palace, where Pilatus maintains his offices and living quarters, my host and I go over my story one last time, standing at his door, for I am desperate by then to get on my way. He corrects the two minor lapses I make in Greek syntax even though Lazarus Valerius Lenticulus – having lived for years in the Galilee – might also make an occasional error.

As he is explaining my errors, a pang of doubt strikes me; perhaps we have created too complex an artifice. Must I play a role so different from the man I am?

'Lucius, maybe I'd be better off asking for an audience as myself – simply appealing to his sense of justice?' I tell Lucius. I rub my hand back over my now-bristly hair. 'I'm likely to look ridiculous to him.'

Lucius rolls his eyes. 'Eli, have you not yet figured out that imperial officials have no sense of justice? And you look fine.'

'But I could be wrong about everything. Maybe Mattiyahu and Loukas are right – we need to pressure Caiaphas.'

'Roman soldiers arrested Yeshua, which means that he will be judged by Pilatus – or, more likely, by one of his staff – after the Temple priests are through with him. Trust me on this, Eli – I know how the Romans handle such matters.'

But that's just it. I can't trust you, I think. *For you may simply be playing a role, and this is my life!*

Just before my son and I get on our way, however, Lucius embraces me with the tears of an affectionate elder in his eyes, and it takes him a moment to find his voice. When he leans close to my ear, he whispers, 'I'll tell you a secret, Eli – you're far more powerful than you believe. You see and hear things that others don't, so I have no difficulty at all imagining you as a soothsayer. Don't you see? You won't fool him with a pretence – you'll convince him you are right because you are! You'll convince him that if he is cruel to Yeshua in any way his life will be in danger from forces that even he doesn't understand.'

41

When Yirmi and I reach the street outside Lucius' villa, we discover that a cavern of sunrise has opened over the eastern horizon, blazing with a searching light. I tell him that we must separate, since his being seen with me might give away my identity.

'You walk ahead of me,' I say. 'I'll keep twenty paces between us. Don't slow down when you reach the palace. Keep going past the bronze doorways and only turn around to look for me after you've counted to fifty in your head.' I take his hand to fix his attention. 'Now, listen closely. If I'm admitted to the palace, go home. I'll meet you there as soon as I can. And this is important – don't tell your aunts where I am.'

'But why?'

'Just do as I say,' I reply. 'We'll speak of why when we have more time.'

In my memories of that moment, I am forever brushing the hair out my boy's eyes and kissing his brow and praying that this will not be the last time I hold him in my arms.

Yirmi nods his agreement gravely, as if I am the master of everything that he does not yet understand. At such moments, it seems like the greatest generosity of all – but also a foolishness beyond measure – that children are convinced that their parents perceive so much more about life than they do.

While trailing him across the Upper Town, I divert my gaze from him only once that I can recall – at the ringing of a bell. I twist around and see a bard removing a lyre from its case. He is a stout man with pox-pitted cheeks, wearing the extravagant, saffron-coloured costume of the poets of Thira.

At any other time, I would stop and listen.

Ayin's eyes are shut tight, since slumber overpowers him in the daylight. Is it lunacy to believe that an owl with two broken wings is part of a grand plan stretching back to my birth? In any case, his soft motionless weight on my shoulder is a reminder that all the creatures of the Ark are with me on this mission. And that we shall not fail.

Yirmi proves a natural at this secretive work of ours; he pauses before turning on to each new street to make sure that I do not lose sight of him. At the last corner before our destination, he stops by a cluttered ceramics stall and feigns a careful examination of a large amphora painted with Perseus slicing off Medusa's head. As I turn past the same stall, the towers of the Citadel rise up.

You're nothing compared to the powerful men who rule over Zion is the message that those three marble giants bring down from the clouds that have blown in from the north.

The towers rise out of the sea of rooftops around me. If they had souls, would they even take notice of the men like me who live out their days so far below them?

One often sees vultures wheeling around the towers at this time of year, drawn by the charred odour of sacrificed lambs and the smoke from burning offal. But this morning belongs to swallows and swifts. What does Lazarus Valerius Lenticulus make of their precipitous dives and twittering arcs? If he is anything like me – and if he is a philosopher as well as an augur

– then he regards them as proof that the Creator values beauty and freedom far more than obedience.

Eight scarlet-caped Roman guards are standing before the colossal doors of Herod's Palace. I would like to stride towards them unburdened of my Galilean meekness, yet my bad leg refuses to cooperate.

The guards must regard the bedraggled Jew limping towards them – sweating like a swine and scratching his itchy scalp – as a figure of comedy, part of a near-endless flow of local labourers who seem to have been born just to keep them amused. Yet one of them, a young man with the stark blue eyes of a Gaul, watches me with a curiosity that seems to be an acknowledgment of kinship – perhaps even empathy.

I do not want to be here, his eyes tell me. *I was forced to join the army by my father. I wanted to remain at home and work on our farm in a country where the sun does not burn your skin, but he said that he could no longer feed me. I've been away from home for seven years, and I fear I shall die before ever seeing my mother or homeland again.*

Are the thoughts I ascribe to him close to the truth? No, it seems I am unable to read foreign faces, for he glares at me and growls in Latin when I tell him that I have come on business with Augustus Sallustius. I swallow hard on all I was about to tell him and ask if there is a Greek-speaker amongst his colleagues. With a wave, he summons a small, beardless youth – a courier, it would seem – who stands to the side of the palace doors. He comes to us with a light, prancing gait, lifting up the fringe of his toga. After the guard addresses him in a clipped voice, the boy turns to me. 'You may speak to me in Greek,' he says.

His pronunciation of certain vowels piques my curiosity. Is he a Galilean as well, or is that my deepest wish at this moment?

I repeat my request and mention my home as Natzeret, but, to my disappointment, he does not show any sign of complicity. When I offer him my scroll, he takes it in his marble-white, delicate fingers. 'Wait here,' he says.

After he enters the palace, I turn to look for my son. He stands at the end of the square, under the canvas awning of an elegant bread shop favoured by the Judaean elite, biting his nails. Somewhere amidst the odours of yeast and olive oil in the air must be the rich barley scent my boy has had since he was a baby, but I am not sensitive enough to detect it. Does he see my apprehension? He raises two fingers of his right hand to tell me he is well.

A tall man in a white toga soon strides out of the palace and tells me to follow him, which means that I am about to step on to the first of a number of bridges I must cross if I am to successfully ransom Yeshua from Pharaoh. Such is the frenetic state of my mind that all I know for certain about his face – all these many years later – is that he had the popping eyes of a fish.

'You cannot come inside with the owl,' he tells me as we reach the bronze doors.

'I have to. He's the reason I'm here to see Augustus Sallustius.'

He shakes his head. 'It's bad fortune for a bird to enter any dwelling.'

'This owl has been sent to me by the goddess Minerva. She has entrusted me with an important message for Pontius Pilatus and his augur. If you like, I'll tell Augustus Sallustius that you advised against admitting him to the palace but that I insisted.'

'No, I'll tell him myself,' he replies in a resentful tone.

I keep a list of things I do not like, he seems to be telling me with his glare, *and at the moment you are at the very top.*

We enter a long hallway lit by towering, intricately carved, alabaster candelabra and painted with a series of frescos depicting a bearded and robust Hercules subduing the Lernaean Hydra and other monsters. Impassive guards securing spears in their right hands stand at intervals of twenty paces. Two Romans in elegant dress approach us from down the corridor, each footstep producing a thudding echo. They converse with animated gestures, but I am unable to catch the sense of their quick-shuttling Latin. My escort says nothing to them as they pass, and I am careful to look away, since our conquerors tend to regard it as an affront when a Jew meets their gaze.

A slender pale-skinned youth – pimples on his forehead – comes dashing down the stone staircase at the end of the hallway. Does he seek the two men we passed? He calls out the name Manius on reaching the bottom step and runs past us. My attendant leads me up the staircase.

We emerge under a colonnade bordered by stone columns painted with blue-and-red geometric patterns. In front of us is a monumental courtyard some two hundred paces of a man in length and fifty in width. At its centre is a circular pool made of polished travertine. Inside its rim stand six rose-coloured flamingos, two of which are poised – miraculously – on a single needle-like leg.

I trail my host down the colonnade. My heart is racing so wildly that I fear I may pass out. We stop by double doors in sculpted bronze. To calm the chaos of emotions in me, I take a deep breath and ask if we have arrived at our destination.

'You're the augur. You tell me!' my attendant snaps back, a response that strikes me as both impertinent and admirably clever.

He has me sit on a carved wooden bench to the side of the doorway. To escape his expression of disdain, I go over in my mind the story I shall tell Augustus Sallustius.

After perhaps an hour, the doors open, and a fair-haired, foreign-looking gentleman in a purple cloak emerges. I expect now to be shown inside, but a guard closes the doors behind him. Before striding off down the colonnade, the aristocrat studies me from head to toe, plainly thinking that I am a question that he would rather not have answered.

A short while later, when the doors again open, my attendant orders me to follow him, and we enter a low-ceilinged, cluttered room with an open window giving out on to a patio with a feathery palm in the centre. A short, flat-faced man – perhaps forty years old – stands leaning on the sill, gazing out longingly.

He holds my scrolled letter of recommendation in his left hand. The seal has been broken. Ought I to bow before him? I would ask the servitor who led me here, but he is standing at attention behind me.

I presume that my host is Augustus Sallustius and address him as such, but he informs me that he is Appius Claudius Pomponius, secretary to the imperial astrologer. I take a calculated risk and offer my bow, but he shows no sign of caring. As he takes the seat behind his desk, he gazes again out of his window and asks – without facing me – why I would ever presume that Augustus Sallustius – 'A master of all that remains hidden to you and I' – would permit me an audience.

I tell him my story, using the standard formulae of self-abasement that Lucius has recommended, but I only manage to turn his head towards me when I speak of Ayin plummeting out of the sky and breaking his wings.

After he orders me to stand the owl on his desk, Appius grabs Ayin's head in a firm, sure grip, but he neglects the bird's talons, and my little friend strikes out so violently with them that Appius lets out a shriek and releases him. Ayin tumbles off the desk with a piercing call. Thankfully, he is more startled than hurt.

'Silence the wretched beast or I'll choke the life from him!' Appius shouts at me.

I soothe the owl with whispers and take him in my hands. He has gone limp with fear, and the drumming inside his chest is even more frantic than mine. When I am finally able to calm him down, Appius has me spread out his broken wings. Lucius and I took care to prick my finger and paint the old fractures with blood, and the dried brown stains fascinate my host. After sniffing at them, he rushes out of the room.

Unsure of what to do, I sit on the floor and offer soothing words to Ayin. When Appius finally returns, he barks an order in Latin at my attendant, who leads me out to the colonnade, his expression that of a pouting child. We walk back the way we came until we reach a set of wooden doors ornamented with colourful depictions of the Roman zodiac. He points to a gold-painted bench set to the side. 'Sit there and keep quiet!'

My desperation to save Yeshua does not permit me to remain seated very long. I pace back and forth, my hands curled into fists, and I pray to the Lord of Hosts for the patience to see my plan through to its end.

After close to an hour, the doors finally open. Inside, I find Augustus Sallustius sitting by a large window. He has shoulder-length grey hair that has been polished silver by the slanting sunlight.

The skeleton of a cat or small dog lies before him on his onyx desk, and its intricate architecture seems to express a great and hidden truth that most of us would prefer not to know. My host appears to have been weighing a leg bone on an iron balance, the pillar of which is an ivory figure of Thoth. Augustus' toga is white with scarlet stripes and a purple hem. I suspect that those colours indicate his office, for I have never seen them on another man.

The room is circular and some ten paces in diameter. The domed ceiling is painted with the Roman constellations. The floor is a mosaic senet-board pattern in black and white.

Hundreds of scrolls are lined up neatly on the wooden shelves that circle the room. *He has so many treasures that I shall never be able to read!* I think with envy.

My escort whispers in Latin to the astrologer and passes me on his way out. Following him with my eyes, I see that two stiff young soldiers with Roman daggers at their belts guard the door.

Augustus Sallustius picks up my scroll and summons me forward. I ease Ayin to the floor, approach my host and thank him for granting me an audience, though my voice – quavering – reveals my apprehension too clearly for my liking. When I am two paces from him, he holds up his hand.

If you do not speak like a man, then why would I heed what you have to say? he seems to be asking with his questioning eyes.

I begin to stutter further expressions of gratitude until he asks for silence in Greek.

I drop to my knees and press my brow to the floor for a count of eleven, which is the numerical value of the Hebrew word, *ga'ah,* to triumph. When I look up, the astrologer dangles his hand out for me to kiss. On his fingers I scent myrrh and some other sour-sweet fragrance I am unable to identify. Sumac? On his index finger he wears a golden band crowned by a cabochon sapphire the size of a cherry.

As I lean back from him, Augustus Sallustius' eyes glow darkly with amusement, as if in response to a silent jest. A part of my spirit steps backs and observes, while another part – surprising me with its courage – rises up to meet him.

He seems a cat-like creature – regal and aloof. Is he drugged with poppy or some other soporific? Throughout our conversation, he closes his eyes at the most surprising moments, as though plunging in his thoughts towards a well-deserved sleep.

Now that I am kneeling close to him, I see the vulturine folds of skin on his neck, which tell me that he might be a good deal older than I first thought – even as old as sixty-five or seventy.

He addresses me in Latin, which forces me to apologize for being an ignorant Ionian, unworthy of an audience with so formidable and influential an astrologer, but with an important tiding that I –

He cuts me short with a raised finger. 'I knew you'd come,' he says in Greek. 'I've seen you in dreams.'

'Great are the powers of Augustus Sallustius,' I say, and, for the first time in my life, I feel the tingling, perverse pleasure of what it must be like to worship a Pharaoh or king – the baseness of it, the ceding of all control, the acceptance of our own inadequacy.

Footsteps reach us from somewhere below the floor. I hear muffled speech as well. Augustus Sallustius closes his eyes and leans his head forward to listen. Or perhaps to send an order for silence through channels unseen to me, for the voices soon fade.

If I survive this day, how shall I explain the depth of my disorientation to Yeshua? I think. *I didn't know if I was meant to stand back up or remain kneeling,* I shall tell him, and together we shall ridicule the etiquette of tyrants.

Augustus Sallustius shuffles across the chamber, his hands joined behind his back. He sits on a throne of Egyptian design with a seat of shimmering scarlet, a golden back and arms inlaid with alternating stripes of lapis lazuli and turquoise.

He surrounds himself with colour, I think, *like a blind man who has only recently gained back his vision.*

Later, I shall speculate on whether his childhood of penury is the grey he is fleeing.

Here is what his cool and languid gaze tells me now: *I never need to look beyond myself. I am enough.*

When he squeezes his eyes closed, he speaks to himself in a language unfamiliar to me. I have been told that Mithras-worshippers make use of a personal spirit-guide, and perhaps Augustus Sallustius was then giving him orders.

While permitting myself a furtive look around the room, I realize – discomfited by my previous ignorance – that we are conversing in what is likely the top half of a sphere. In that case, the lower half would be below the floor. Might it be the Mithraeum?

The silence my host summons to the room soon closes in on me so tightly that I fear that he has uncovered my ruse through his mastery of the curious arts. Again I ask for Yeshua's help, and, as I speak to him in my mind, a strange calm comes over me, and I sense that my own voice is the way forward and that it will see me to safety, so I start to tell my story to Augustus Sallustius, cautiously at first, and, since he does not interrupt, I allow it to tumble out of me with what I hope is a convincing urgency.

As I tell him of how I left for Yerushalayim four days before, his eyes open and he steps to the statue behind his desk – an emerald-eyed Apollo subduing the serpent who guards Delphi. He takes hold of the quiver fastened to the god's back, which seems an indirect way of telling me something he cannot say with words, but, at the time, I do not know what it could be. All I notice is that Apollo's face looks oddly familiar.

Am I too nervous to see his connection to Augustus Sallustius?

I speak to the astrologer of how I was walking with a friend the evening before, only an hour's distance from Yerushalayim, and that, as soon as my companion mentioned having recently caught a glimpse of Pilatus near the Imperial Theatre, a blazing star slashed across the violet dusk directly ahead of us, crashing through a grove of pines. 'We hurried after it,' I say, 'and found, to our astonishment, an owl whose wings had been broken by his fall, with an unusual silver ornament attached to one of his feet.'

I reach into my pouch and draw out the satyr given me by Lucius. He nods towards his throne, so I place it on the arm nearest him, and he studies it with arched eyebrows.

'I give it to you as a token of my esteem and goodwill,' I tell him.

He takes it in his fist, sits on his throne and gestures towards Ayin. 'Is that the owl that fell from the sky?'

'Yes.'

The astrologer summons one of his guards. 'Bring me the owl,' he orders.

I quickly snatch Ayin up and warn the guard away, since Augustus Sallustius likely intends to sacrifice him and read the future from his entrails.

Ought I to have given up Ayin up to help Yeshua? I see now that perhaps I made a fatal mistake by protecting him. But I also know that witnessing his slaughter would have shattered my composure – and made it impossible for me to maintain my assumed identity.

'Forgive me, noble Augustus Sallustius,' I say, 'but I dare not part with so sacred a messenger. He has been entrusted to me by the goddess Minerva, and she obliged me to vow that I'd care for him. She told me that unspeakable misfortunes would befall the Romans of Judaea if he were ever taken from me.'

'Why would Minerva speak to you?' he questions, as if the very idea is absurd.

'Because I have trained myself to hear the gods, even their murmurs and whispers – and I obey their commands.'

'Which gods have you trained yourself to hear?'

'All of them.'

'Including gods of the Judaeans?'

'They have but one.'

'So I have heard, though I do not entirely believe it. And do you speak your prayers to this lonely immortal?'

'Yes, my father was a Jew from the Galilee.'

He licks his lips as though he is about to use my revelation to trap me. But his keen interest in my story has excited my own potential for subterfuge and trickery. Indeed, living under a false identity seems a promising form of freedom. *I'd have saved myself a hundred damaging quarrels had I worn a mask since childhood,* I reason.

I am about to speak more of Minerva when he asks me to tell him more about my mentor, Demosthenes. 'I've heard of him, but we've never met,' he adds.

'He would rejoice to hear that word of his prowess has reached you here in Judaea, honourable Augustus Sallustius,' I reply, and I go on to speak of his most celebrated divinations.

As I am building to my climax – his prediction of a volcanic eruption on Thira that saved thousands of lives – my host cuts me off. 'And what demonstration can you give me of your own powers?' he asks.

'Demonstration? Here and now?'

'Where else?'

Panic makes me gaze down, and I hear a voice, and it belongs to Lucius, and I do not know whether it is Yeshua's intervention or my own reliable memory that rescues me, but my employer speaks the word *insula,* and, though it is one seemingly insignificant noun in a language that will never be mine, it is all I need to know.

I start towards the astrologer, and I do not stop when he signals for me to come no closer, since my impertinence will either impress or irritate him, and either reaction will make him easier to steer towards the destination I have in mind. 'You've asked me give you proof, and I shall find it inside your own eyes!' I declare to him.

'I forbid you to come any closer!' he snarls.

'It won't be necessary – I've already discovered all I need,' I assure him.

Who can say exactly where my courage comes from? And how I am able to subdue my terror that I am running out of time to save Yeshua? I hold the augur's gaze and speak in the confident, entranced voice of the oculomancer whose identity I have assumed. 'I see a boy who has been cursed by the gods of Rome. He is unimposing in stature and unsure of his place in the world. His clothes are rags, and his belly is hollow, and he must climb . . .' I close my eyes and grimace, as if interpreting what I saw in his dark irises is proving too difficult for me. 'I see that there are seven hills inside this young man, and the gods have decreed that he must climb up and over each of them in order to reach his home on the eighth summit.' I extend a trembling hand to reach out to the poor youth he once was. 'He makes his bed there each night, in a high wilderness where neither plants nor trees can grow, and he dreams of escape, but he –'

'Enough!' Augustus Sallustius shouts.

He points a menacing finger at me. 'Never speak of this boy or those hills again, or I'll have your tongue cut out!'

'Yes, noble Augustus Sallustius.'

He leans back in his throne. 'Now tell me what Minerva told you. And be quick!'

'She vouchsafed me a message for you. A man will be arrested and brought to this palace, but if he is killed his spectre will haunt its every corner, and no Roman working here will ever know a moment's peace again.'

'And who is this prisoner?'

'A magician. Far greater than Shimon of Samaria. Divine Minerva told me he is the most powerful since Shelomoh.' With my right hand, I make the abrupt slashing movement that indicates imminent catastrophe amongst the Ionians and other Greek-speaking peoples. 'She also told me that he is sure to avenge himself against you for being imprisoned. He must be set free without delay.'

'I have no fear of any man!' he says with an imperious expression.

'But this is no mere man,' I improvise. 'Minerva told me that he is the son of a god.'

'The son of a god? Which one?' He leans back, incredulous.

'Picus. Apparently Mars sent him to earth to impregnate a Galilean maiden.'

How Picus enters my mind at that moment, I cannot say, though I have confessed to you my deep fascination for birds, and a god with wings must have seemed the perfect choice to the nameless and unseen part of me that always seeks to guarantee my safety.

One moment a man has no memory of the bird-god who swooped and soared through his youth, and the next that creature of feather, air and light is the lord of all his hopes.

Augustus Sallustius combs a tense hand back through his long grey hair, which leads me to believe that I have convinced him of the truth of my words.

'What is the name of this son of Picus?' he asks.

I would not wish to display too much knowledge of Yeshua, for that might give away my motive, so I tell him that the goddess refused to grant me his name. 'All she would tell me is that he is a Jew from the Galilee. Apparently he is a sorcerer who has taken the guise of a woodworker – which is only to be expected, of course, since he is the son of Picus. I suspect that Minerva will honour only you, noble Augustus Sallustius, with his earthly name, which is why I rushed to you this morning. I beg you to heed the goddess's warning and order this magician escorted far beyond the borders of Judaea, for, if he is wounded or killed, he or his spectre will avenge himself against you and the Imperial Prefect and all your descendants for seven generations.'

He gazes up at the constellations as though to search for the reply his gods would want of him. After his lips move over an incantation or prayer, he snatches up the silver charm from the arm of his throne, gazing at it as though he has only just now grasped its meaning. 'What else can you tell me of this magician?' he asks.

'Nothing more. Minerva spoke to me as I gazed into the eyes of the owl she had sent me, but all too soon she withdrew into a silence so deep that I knew she had returned to Olympus, and I have failed since then to coax her back to me. Perhaps she will soon speak to you and give you the name she has withheld from me.'

'Eliezer!'

After I emerge into the daylight, and while I am confirming that Yirmi has obeyed my orders and gone home, a man calls my name. To my astonishment, Loukas and Shimon are hailing me from fifty paces away.

My attendant notices my unease. 'Do you know those men over there?'

'No, I don't recognize them,' I say, and I gaze down and away, so that they will understand that I want to be left alone.

Unfortunately, my two friends stride towards me, and Shimon calls my name again. Does he not see that my hair has been dyed and that I am wearing a stranger's clothing?

'Eliezer, what's happened?' Loukas calls out.

The attendant, overly curious – perhaps sensing my masquerade – rushes off towards him and Shimon. I gaze around the square to see which way I shall run. If I can make it to the jewellers' quarter, then . . .

'Do you know that man?' the attendant enquires, pointing back at me.

I dare not shake my head or make any other signal. Destiny has caught me, and I am paralysed by the irony of having my life menaced by well-meaning friends, here and now, in a place where I was certain I had rediscovered safety.

And this I decide: a sword shall set my soul free if Shimon unmasks me, for I shall charge the palace doors and curse the soldiers stationed there until one of them grants me a quick and merciful death. Need you ask why, Yaphiel? The torture of being nailed to a cross might very well make me denounce my most cherished friends and lament even my bond with Yeshua. What is more, my children are of a tender age, and I would not wish them to see me hanging from a cross or, even worse, turned to charred bones and ash by burning pitch.

But Loukas, who speaks Greek fluently, turns my destiny back towards life. 'No, I've never seen him,' he declares.

That single denial added at least another thirty years to my life, which is proof – if you needed it, Yaphiel – that each and every moment is a door.

Shimon is quick to catch on and adds an explanation. 'I thought he was my cousin, but as you know, we Jews look very alike, and that man over there . . . I see now that he is a full palm too small.'

Only after I am out of sight of Herod's Palace do I dare to pause. I am standing by a saddle-maker's shop, and, after I ease Ayin to the ground, I drop down on to the street, breathing heavily, my tears flowing freely.

If angels see with their eyes what we feel in our hearts – as I have been told – then they will recognize the glowing shape of my gratitude to the Lord for having helped me escape with my life.

A drizzle has started to fall, so my reprieve becomes the sound of that rain and the moist glory of it refreshing my upraised hands and face.

Yirmi runs to me and throws his arms around me while I am considering whether I have the strength to climb to the Upper Town and report back to Lucius on my audience with Augustus Sallustius. A stern part of me wishes to chastise the boy for disobeying me, but what father could turn away a trembling son?

Yirmi has bad news, however: 'Yeshua was led into the palace a little while after you entered. He was bound with ropes, just as Andreas described.'

'Were Loukas and Shimon with him?'

'No, he was alone.'

Yirmi suggests we go home so that I can dry off and put on a fresh robe. Although I am aware that Yeshua might remain a prisoner in the palace for months, I cannot leave. 'He may be released soon,' I say. 'We must wait.'

My son rests his hand on my shoulder. 'Maybe we should move closer to the palace, so we can see who comes out.'

He squats with me while alternatives circle inside my head. Soon my thoughts are drawn to Augustus Sallustius and his statue of Apollo. It's obvious now that they share the same hands and face – that's what I failed to see before. The astrologer must have served as a model for the Roman deity.

Let Yeshua bow before a false god just this once, I pray, though I know he will not.

42

Yirmi and I find an ideal place to keep watch on the square fronting Herod's Palace at the small marketplace on Jeweller's Street. We squat on our heels between the stall of a fruit-seller and workbench of a basket-maker, where we can remain largely hidden while following the movements of people and animals through one of the entrances to the square, which lies about two hundred paces west.

Word has spread of Yeshua's arrest, and hundreds of his followers have assembled in front of the palace over the last hours to await word of him. A phalanx of legionaries has crossed the square at least three times over the last hour, their swords drawn, ordering the crowd to disperse, which explains why we have occasionally witnessed waves of men and women fleeing into our street.

I question those who come down from the square to our marketplace, but no one has seen any prisoners released this day.

I ponder out what to do if Yeshua is not released by sundown and conclude that I shall visit his mother and brother Yaaqov, and we shall discuss the bribes we ought to pay. If they agree, I shall go to Lucius and prevail upon him to approach his friends amongst the Roman elite and tell him to promise my stocks of Parosian marble and Egyptian porphyry to the first of them who vows to intercede on our behalf. If more is required, I shall offer my scroll of *In the Beginning* and our silver candlesticks and all else of value that Mia and I possess.

Five days of light followed by dusk, then darkness . . . Over the past week, I have come to see how little time we are given to make a difference to the world, and if I must start all over again as a pauper, then so be it.

Close your eyes, Yaphiel, and imagine a naked man with gaunt, sun-darkened cheeks and a Galilean accent summoning you through a high gate that seems strangely familiar, and, the moment you step through, he takes your hand, and his secure grip now seems what you have always waited for, and when you look into his dark eyes you see the desert and snow-capped mountains inside not him but yourself, and you smell the rare blue-petalled flowers that open only under the moonlight, and you notice, as well, that your clothing has fallen away without you being aware of it, and you wonder how you will travel so far without a pack or even any sandals, and how long it will take, until he whispers in your ear that you must not expect to arrive any time soon, for *destination* has no meaning where you are about to go, and though that makes you laugh – and consider, too, that you have given your trust to a madman – it also makes you tingle in your belly, in the way that children do when they first sense that they must leave their parents' home behind if they are to find themselves.

I see now that I wanted only a quiet life – to have access to the writings of the Greeks and fulfilling work to keep my mind and hands busy, to chant and pray in the sunlight of Zion and grow powerful wings in my dreams.

I wanted to be free to express my affection for you and Leah and Yirmi and Nahara. And to plant a garden of *tsedeq* in which no one would ever go hungry.

I wanted to feel the praise of the flagstones in each of my footsteps – for what I helped you accomplish.

Perhaps, most of all, I wanted to awaken at *shepharphar* each morning and see the surrounding streets of our *eruv* paved with *racham*.

But I understand now that I asked for too much.

Voices from the square rise like the swell of the Great Sea, and I hear his name shouted a first time, then once again. My son and I look at each other, knowing that the time has come.

I tell him I must go this last part of our journey alone and ask his forgiveness.

'But you told me I'd protect you!'

'I can't risk what . . . what you might see,' I say. 'I'll return for you as soon as I can.' A purpose will lighten his burden, so I ask him to watch over Ayin for me.

And then I am gone.

I do not spot Yeshua amidst the multitude in the square, but near the palace doors two Roman horsemen and a burly centurion are leading a unit of eight legionaries, and they are clearing a pathway east for what appears to be a prisoner.

I fight my way towards them and, through the push and swell of the crowd, get a quick look at the naked, skeletal prisoner. The crossbeam of a crucifix has been tied across his shoulders. I have no chance to see his face, but I know that he cannot be Yeshua, for my friend has olive-coloured skin and this man's face and arms are the white of bone.

When the crowd parts again, I see that a fraying purple cape has been tied around the prisoner's neck. He wears a spindly crown of brambles and laurel leaves, which means that the Romans – who always value a chance to enact one of their ancient dramas – have dressed him as their legendary king of bandits, Laureolus, whose name means *crownlet of laurel*. Over the years, I have seen condemned men dressed as Attis, Prometheus and others who were made to endure unspeakable tortures.

As I thrust my way forward, I soon get another quick look at the condemned man. His ribs stand out like the bow of a ship, and a lash of dried blood extends from his right eye across his nose and over the left corner of his lips.

Why whip a man's face unless he has expressed – with convincing arguments – the right of every being to mercy and benevolence? So it is that I know that this devastated soul must have found the courage to challenge his persecutors, and I know, too, that he is articulate and intelligent, and I bless him for showing us that we must struggle against tyranny even if it might cost us our lives.

Continuing ahead, I pass a group of old women huddling together, and, when one of them catches my gaze, she seems to recognize me, and she speaks Yeshua's name, and tears are running down her cheeks, and all of me turns to ice.

Is it possible that my body understands before I do? Did my deepest soul forbid my eyes from recognizing the truth until that moment?

As I gaze again at the man dressed as Laureolus, he shifts his grip on the crossbeam, and . . . It is then that my heart collapses, for I recognize his hands.

And when I close my eyes, his fingertips brush against my cheek. *Has his spirit reached out to console me?*

Yeshua's eyes are circled by bleak ridges of bone. His look is distant and dull – as though he has been drugged.

I run to him then, and I push past everyone blocking my way, and I keep thrusting ahead even when the others shriek insults at me, and, before it seems possible, I am standing next to him.

His face has been lacerated by the strokes of a leather scourge, which the Romans tip with iron shards. The gouges on his left cheek are so deep that blood from them is dripping on to the street. His lips are swollen and also cut.

Tears gush from my eyes. *Take us from here!* I tell him, for, although he is broken in body, he is still who he is, and he can ask the Lord to deliver us.

But he remains where he is and does not turn to me.

'Yeshua, it's me . . . it's Lazarus,' I tell him.

Do I whisper these words? That is how it sounds to me, but I must have shouted his name then or soon afterwards – or perhaps I reached out to touch him – because one of the Roman soldiers comes to me and commands me in Latin to quiet down and keep my distance from the condemned man.

Yeshua shuffles forward, dragging his crossbeam. The muscles in his shoulders and arms strain. His hair is soaked, as if he has been dunked under water.

Onlookers behind me start jeering and ridiculing him. Some young men to the side of me throw stones and fruit, and a citron hits him in the face.

I notice then – why didn't I see it earlier? – that the skin of his sides and hips has peeled away from the bone and is bright with blood. To see such a violation of the body is to know that there is no limit to the crimes that men commit. Will we – the children of Adam and Havvah – ever be worthy of the gifts we have been given?

The world seems to tip to its side and fall as I study Yeshua's bloody hipbone, and I find myself sprawled on the ground, and I reach out to the ankle of a man striding past me, but he jerks his leg free of my grasp.

They flayed his body to destroy his soul, I think.

I get to my knees as a woman near me begins to wail. She thrusts her hands over her face when I look at her.

A large stone thrown from somewhere behind me crashes into Yeshua's shoulder and makes him stumble.

Others in the crowd reach out to him, but none dare come close enough to touch him. The human hand straining to give comfort but unable to do so . . . I have never seen so eloquent a representation of all that the Romans deny the men and women they conquer.

The buildings of the square and the sky grow very dark as I stand back up, and I think: *This life of mine has always been a dream. It's strange that it took me so long to realize it. I shall awaken soon in another world, and the Lord will show me that all I have lived – including this moment – passed in a single one of His pauses for breath. This life seemed like decades to me because He wished my soul to learn the lessons of physical form, and it can take many years to learn how to suffer so deeply for someone else that one would give up one's life to make that torment end.*

It seems to me now that I thought all these things in a single instant – between standing up and starting towards Yeshua – though I do not know how that is possible.

The Roman soldiers are now some seventy paces from me, and I am at the fringe of the crowd. No one tries to stop me as I fight my way to the front; perhaps it is obvious see that I have no choice in what I do.

Once I am in front of Yeshua, with the mounted soldiers just behind me, I raise my hand and bless him, and in the language of gestures that we have spoken since we were boys – shaking a fist with one finger pointing up – I tell him that the Lord and I are here to defend him.

It is the movement of my hand – a movement that only we understand – that gives me a plan. After all, has he not lifted me out of myself many times before? For him, it will be as easy as chanting our morning prayers.

This, then, is the reason why Yeshua summoned me back from death! I think, and the understanding in me is like the lifting of a frigid mist.

My old friend shuffles past without looking at me, which confuses me until I realize that he does not wish to give the Romans any excuse to take me prisoner.

I call his name and shout that I am ready, and he faces me, though our friendship remains hidden beneath the dull glaze of his eyes. It is now or never, so I rush forward and embrace him, and I press my cheek to his, so that he will know in his flesh who I am, and his skin is cold and damp, and I realize what ought to have been clear before – that he has lost so much blood that he may die. I know I have time for only a few words, so I say, *Exchange souls with me. I give my body to you freely. I see now why you gave me life again. Do it now, before . . .*

A blow catches me on the side of my head – from the haft of a sword?

My legs give way, and I drop down to the ground. Above me stands the centurion, his eyes small and black – beads of antipathy. He moves the tip of his sword into the hollow of my neck below my voice-box. If he thrusts, I will choke to death on my own blood.

Does he truly ask why he should spare my life, or is that what I imagine he growls at me?

'Your prisoner is my brother,' I tell him. 'I've every right to comfort him.'

The soldier eases the tip of his blade away, as though to show me mercy, but I soon discover that he is playing a game that never fails to make the Romans laugh: fool the Jew. Leaning over me, he takes out his knife and makes two quick slashes in the centre of my forehead, marking me for life.

'I'm going to kill you!' I shout in Greek.

He spits at me and strides away. As I clean his filth from my face, my fingertips discover that he has etched me with the letter *lambda*. I have no idea why he chose that marking. Indeed, I will never find out.

This need for ownership of other men . . . Is it a disease of blindness and faulty logic – an inability to see other people as real?

While Yeshua struggles onwards, I grip the calliper he has given me, and I chant to myself the secret names of the Holy One that he has vouchsafed to me, climbing up each rung of Yaaqov's Ladder on the sound of my own voice. *I have always belonged to you, so take me now,* I whisper to him.

But he does not come for me. Has his loss of blood diminished his powers? That must be why Caiaphas and Annas had him flayed so mercilessly.

Or perhaps he does not believe it is right for him to change places with me. But was that not why he tested me at the River Jordan – to make sure that I would sacrifice myself at this moment?

A thousand times since that day I have told him he ought to have summoned all his power in one final burst and sent his soul to take possession of me. I usually speak my condemnation of him for failing me in my secret prayer room, in a whisper of lost hope, but in dreams I say it with my arms and legs and chest, and I cling to him so tightly that when I wake it seems to come with the crack of stone splitting open.

43

I stand up and press my fingers to the cut on my brow because blood is seeping into my eyes. It seems criminal of me now to have spent my entire life in an imperial colony and not have a single friend or acquaintance amongst the Roman elite to whom I can appeal for help.

When a man calls my name, I turn around and discover Lucius hurrying towards me. His eyes are searching for answers. Abibaal is behind him.

'You're covered in blood,' Lucius says, grimacing.

I look down and see that hand-prints and smudges of dried blood have stained my tunic. 'A centurion cut me,' I explain.

Abibaal says that he will staunch the bleeding, but my well-being is of no import to me at that moment, and I wave him away.

'How did you get here so fast?' I ask Lucius.

'A servant I sent to the square alerted me to Yeshua's predicament. What's your plan?'

'We have to stall the Romans until help comes.'

'Help from whom?'

'I don't know!' I shout in desperation. 'Nikodemos or . . . Will Pilatus grant you an audience?'

'Me?' Lucius scoffs. 'Pilatus looks down his nose at me and calls me his big-bellied old *Garum*-Seller. He told me once there was no essence to me.'

'Meaning?'

'Meaning I am neither Jew nor Roman.'

'Then I'll have to appeal to Annas.'

Lucius shakes his head and tells me what I already know. 'Even if you accomplished the impossible and convinced the priest to make peace with us, you'd still fail to save Yeshua – Annas has no control over Roman executions.'

I sense it then for the first time – a hopelessness so massive that it will bury me alive. Does Lucius see that I need him to help me find the way forward?

'We'll catch up with Yeshua,' he says. 'We'll ask him what to do.'

'I don't think he'll be able to reply to us. He's lost a great deal of blood. He's been flayed with a whip.'

Lucius' eyes fill with tears. 'If he can't summon a voice,' he says, 'then he'll speak to us any way he can. He'll find a way.'

We find Yirmi back at the marketplace. The smoky scent of lamb being roasted for the Passover supper is everywhere now. It packs my nostrils and leaves a sour, sickening taste in my mouth.

An idea comes to me as my son stands. I face Lucius. 'Your elderly friend, Paullus – the one who was interested in my mosaic . . .'

'What about him?' he asks, but in his eyes I can see he has already glimpsed my plan and has passed an unfavourable judgement on it.

'He said that he wanted to meet Yeshua – which leads me to believe he might prove sympathetic to our cause. Do you think he might win an audience with Pilatus?'

'Paullus retired two years ago and has withdrawn from public life.'

I hold out my blood-covered hands. And I can see from his solemn nod that he has grasped their meaning: that what has befallen us gives me the right to ask a favour of even a man I do not know and who has withdrawn from the world. 'I'll ask you again,' I tell him. 'Will Pilatus grant Paullus an audience?'

'He might. Paullus used to organize all the Roman festivities in Yerushalayim.'

Lucius tells me that his friend lives outside the gates of the city, in the Roman enclave just beyond the pool of Breikhat Hashiloah. 'His villa has a turret modelled on the Phasael Tower,' he says. 'You won't have any trouble finding it.'

With my bad leg, I shall not be able to run, and it will take half an hour or more for me to reach so distant a location, so Lucius offers me the use of his horse and cart. But that is of little help, for I would first have to go to his villa, which would mean a long, uphill climb, and Abibaal would also have to bring the cart from his stables.

'I'll go on foot,' I tell him. 'You take your cart, and if you arrive before me, explain to Paullus that he must plead for an audience with Pilatus without delay. Say whatever you need to convince him.'

After Lucius agrees, I turn to my son and tell him he must look after Yeshua for me. 'You're my talisman,' I remind him.

'But what can I do?' he asks.

'Listen to him closely if he manages to speak. He might even speak to you within your mind. Just do whatever he tells you.'

'And if he doesn't say anything?'

'The Romans will take him to Golgotha or one of the other execution places. Look for friends in the crowd – Yohanon, Yaaqov or anyone else you recognize. Very likely, they fear for their lives and will be in disguise – or will seek to remain hidden. Tell any of them that you find that I'm on my way with an influential Roman. Tell them to stall the execution. They must be prepared to attack the soldiers – with swords and knives if they have them, if not, then with stones. Do you understand? If they permit Yeshua to be raised on a cross . . .' I do not end my sentence. Instead, I take my son's shoulders. 'Will you do this for me?'

'Of course.'

'But if you sense yourself in danger – if someone threatening recognizes you as my son – go straight home. Find Aunt Mia and tell what's happened. Are we clear?'

'I know what to do,' he assures me in an adult voice that chills me, since there is so much that he does not understand yet about life and death and everything in between.

He runs north. I head south, rushing along with my ludicrous cripple's gait.

My desperate knocking on the door of Paullus' villa draws no answer, but, when I step back from the high brick wall, I spot him squinting down at me from a window in his turret as if I am but the vaguest of apparitions. I call out my name to him. 'I'm the mosaicist you met at Lucius' villa,' I say.

He leans out his window with a puzzled expression. 'I remember who you are, but you're covered in blood. What's happened to you?'

'There was an accident. If you come down, I'll explain.'

He jiggles his gnarled old-man's hand in the air. 'I'll have a slave open the door. Wait there!'

Paullus awaits me in the colonnade that fronts his dining room. 'You look as if a chariot rode over you!' he says, holding an awning of hand over his wary eyes.

I stop several paces away so as not to frighten him further. 'I've come to you for help,' I begin, and I tell him that the dear friend of mine he wished to meet – the one who speaks with God – is about to be executed.

'For what reason?' he asks.

'He has quarrelled with our Temple priests.'

'Then it's a matter for the Jews alone.'

'Except that he was arrested by Roman soldiers.'

'Why was that?'

'Because the priests sought their help.'

He gazes down to consider what I've told him. In all probability, he has no grasp of why Jews would dispute amongst themselves.

'Does the Prefect consider your friend a rebel?' he asks.

'I don't know.'

'What's his name?'

'Yeshua ben Yosef.'

'I've heard of him. He's a well-known healer.'

'Yes.'

'Wouldn't he regard me – a Roman patrician – as his enemy?'

'Those who rule with swords are his enemies. You carry no arms.'

He looks past me, considering his options.

'You're my last hope,' I plead. 'I'll give you everything I own if you try to save him.'

'Me? But what can I do?'

'You can go to Pilatus and implore him for mercy.'

He laughs mirthlessly. 'My younger brother in Rome was disgraced three years ago, and Pilatus forced me to withdraw from public life shortly afterwards. He regards me as an embarrassment.'

Despair lowers my gaze, but Paullus steps to me and cups my chin in his hand. 'I ought to refuse you, and I'm not sure what good I can do, but . . .' His darkly shining eyes become those of a mischief-maker. 'I am so very tired of skulking around in the shadows because I'm no longer favoured by Pilatus, and I still have colleagues at the palace, and I'll go speak to them for you.'

Paullus summons his litter so that he can make an impressive arrival at Herod's Palace. Lucius ought to arrive soon, but something must have held him up, and I cannot risk waiting for him.

44

I have been counting on thousands of our supporters to have assembled at Golgotha, but, from a distance of a quarter of a mile, I already see that less than a hundred friends and concerned followers are there. Where are the throngs who cheered for Yeshua and called him our king as he entered Yerushalayim?

A prisoner already hangs on a cross, but I cannot make out his face. His screams reach me as I rush on. God forgive me, it is relief – and not horror – that makes me shiver, for his accent is unmistakably Judaean.

Although he is still only a tiny letter *tau* on the horizon, a favourable wind soon brings me the condemned man's appeals for the Lord's *gevurah* and *din* – divine judgement and justice. Over and over he cries out a verse from the prophet Jeremiah: '"Lord Almighty, you who examine the righteous and probe the heart and mind, let me see your vengeance on them, for to you I have committed my cause."'

His repetition of this verse becomes chant-like in its fervour, which gives me the idea that he is searching for a gateway out of the prison of his flesh. Yet vultures wheel through the leaden sky above him, waiting for the inviting silence that will come when he can speak no more.

After another fifty paces, my name is called. I turn to see Mia running towards me, her face flushed and bloated by tears. 'I was sure you'd been arrested, too!' she calls ahead.

I have not forgotten that she betrayed us to Caiaphas, but the little brother inside me apparently knows nothing of that, for he cries out her name as if she alone can change the direction of our destiny.

Mia stops two paces from me, afraid to come any closer. Does she see in my eyes that I am aware of her treason? 'I know,' I tell her, and, when she reaches out with beseeching hands, I add, 'No, only Yeshua can forgive you now.'

She raises her hands to her face and begins to wail.

In my dreams of that day, I often see the two of us backed by the hushed, reddened sky of a battle that has been lost in both the Throne World and Zion.

'Why did you go to Annas?' I ask.

'To protect our family,' she says with a moan.

'Protect us? Are you mad? Didn't you think I'd do everything to protect us? I even spoke to you of leaving for Alexandria!'

'The day you threatened Cousin Hannah . . . I could see you'd lost control of yourself. You were so . . . strange. And so angry. All of us could see you'd become someone else.'

I understand then that it had been fatal mistake to allow myself to express my true feelings – even in front of my own sister.

'Marta went alone to Annas,' Mia continues, 'but he insisted that both of us come to see him to plead for mercy or he would hurt you and your children.'

Now that I've ceased making excuses for Marta, I see the strategy she employed. 'Did Annas really say that, or is that just what Marta told you?'

'You think she lied to me? But if she did . . .' Mia turns away in horror, considering this revelation.

'Don't you see – Marta wanted *you* to betray me,' I exclaim. 'It was her way of destroying us. She must have known that Yeshua had spies watching the priest's house. She knew I'd find out that you'd gone to Annas.' I laugh bitterly. 'She's brilliant, and she's fooled the two of us yet again – and this time Yeshua is paying the price.'

A secret terror snakes through me as Mia acknowledges that I may have uncovered the truth: *Might Marta have been working with Yehudah of Kerioth for many weeks?*

I turn to leave because the crucified man is still screaming his prayer for vengeance, and his words tell me I have wasted too much time conversing with a woman who did not trust me enough to come to me with her misgivings.

'Annas promised me that he would not hurt you or your children or Yeshua!' my sister calls out as I start away. 'He swore it to me!'

If she comes after me, there is still a chance for us, I think. *And if not . . .*

'I know that what I did was unforgiveable,' she says with a groan. 'I'm sorry, Eli.'

She entreats me in a raw and desolate voice to stop, but I do not, and each step away from her is easier than the one before, and her voice is fading, and it will soon be gone. Something beyond the rage in me – something inseparable from our childhood – then turns me around. 'You should have spoken to me before seeing him!' I cry.

Mia runs to me. 'Eli, ever since your resurrection you've seemed a stranger to me.'

Do I take her back into my life? Even now, after decades of living with the memory, I do not know why I made the choice I did.

'Mia, there's no time for this,' I tell her, taking her hand and gripping it tightly. 'We can speak of the two of us later, but Yeshua is all that matters to me now.'

I already know, however, that I am lying: I shall never again talk of her betrayal of Yeshua. For if he lives there will be no need, and if he dies I shall never speak of this day to her or anyone else.

The pains shooting up in my hip force me to climb up the slope to Golgotha bent over, as though I were sowing this barren, miserable landscape with my panting breaths. Gusts of wind blow dust into my eyes and mouth, and, while I clear my throat, a small, frightful woman asks if I am the man whom Yeshua raised from the dead.

'I cannot help you – there's no time!' I say, pushing her way.

As I climb, my sister offers to help, but I must go these last steps alone, since the Lord may need proof that my own well-being and safety no longer mean anything to me. She reaches the top before I do. I see her pick a wild red poppy that's managed to poke its way out of the inhospitable soil. I expect her to hand it to me as a symbol of hope, but instead she crushes it between her thumb and forefinger.

It's not fair for there to be such beauty in his accursed place, her embittered expression tells me.

A small assemblage of men and women has gathered around the crucified man. Two additional uprights have been planted in the dry ground but have yet to receive their crossbeams, which means that three prisoners are to meet the Angel of Death today.

I call upon Hananiah, Mischael and Azariah to intercede on their behalf, for those three righteous young men were condemned to death by Nebuchadnezzar but were saved by an angel of the Lord.

I call on them three times in my mind and once more aloud.

Twenty Roman soldiers guard this benighted place. Four are on horseback. If any of our old friends tried to stall them, they obviously failed.

I see now that the man already hanging from his cross is small and muscular, with stiff black hair and a thick shadow of beard on his cheeks. A wooden sign has been posted at the top of his cross: *Lestes.* Rebel.

Fight Rome and you will die in agony! That is what the sign means in the language of tyranny.

The crucified man struggles at the ropes that bind his wrists to his crossbeam, cursing the Romans. The tendons on his neck stand out, and his grimace – defiant, savage, murderous – tells me that he is a man of uncommon strength, which is a misfortune under the circumstances, since it will take him a very long time to render his soul to God.

His thick, powerful wrists have been bound so cruelly that his hands have become limp and white. *I can no longer sense my fingers,* he must have already admitted to himself, and he has undoubtedly come to suspect by now that a crucified man vanishes from the outside in. *Soon my legs and arms will go numb as well, and then . . .*

His feet are so dark with filth that they look like roots just pulled from the soil.

Why do I notice all these trifles about him when here on the same hill must be the man with whom I have lived on an island in my mind since I was eight years old?

The spirit of a man who senses ruin and madness will sometimes flee into extraneous details. It is the only explanation.

Maryam of Magdala has kneeled by the upright furthest from us, her hands clamped over her mouth. She is surrounded by onlookers I do not recognize.

Two additional vultures now circle through the grey sky above us, making nine in total. Does this loathsome place rise up in all its foul-smelling, desolate glory at the centre of all their most nourishing dreams?

As we rush to the back upright where Yeshua must be, my sister and I pass by the central cross. The prisoner there is lying on his back with blood smeared across his face. He is elderly and bald. His lips are sealed tight. His eyes are open but not gazing at anything in our world.

I shall not beg, his expression tells me. *And I shall not give them any information they may want. Since the age of eleven, when my parents were both killed, I have made my own decisions, and I am fifty-seven years old now, and I chose the life of a rebel willingly, and I rejoiced each time I covered myself with the blood of a Roman, and I pray that I may meet death like a man.*

His executioner tightens the bindings on his wrists. The man has quick, decisive, skilful hands; he has probably made a good life for himself tying thick knots around the hands of Jews.

My son appears from out of nowhere and hugs his arms around me. His chin is soiled, but it is the bruising in his eyes that worries me. No one who is thirteen years old is ready for what he has seen.

'Are you hurt?' Mia asks him while I search desperately over his face and chest and arms for wounds.

'I'm all right,' he tells us.

'Paullus has agreed to help us,' I tell him, hoping to renew his strength. 'He's on his way now to Herod's Palace.'

'Then there's still a chance?' Yirmi says.

'Yes. What about you?' I ask him. 'Did you find any of our old friends?'

'I found Maryam of Magdala and Yeshua's mother. They're over there,' he says, pointing to the last upright. 'I spoke to them, and I told them to do anything they could to stall the Romans, and they tried, but –'

'And Yeshua?' I cut in.

Yirmi's eyes gush with tears, and that is when I start to run.

45

Yeshua lies on his back, bound to his crossbeam. His eyes are closed. His chest rises and falls in fitful bursts. To escape this time and place, is he dreaming of our childhood?

Runnels of sweat run down his hollow cheeks. His cape, discarded by the Romans, is now clutched in the arms of an old woman who sits on her heels beside him. She holds it over her nose, breathing in on the scent of him.

This woman is his grandmother, Channah, but I had not seen her in many years and did not yet recognize her.

The flies of Golgotha feed at Yeshua's eyes and lips and swarm greedily inside the flayed flesh on his side and back. A youthful executioner with surprisingly delicate hands tightens the bindings on Yeshua's wrists.

If you rip away enough flesh from a man or woman, the ribs become visible – white snakes in a moist sea of red. I had not known that.

Yeshua's crown of laurel still engenders baleful laughter amongst the soldiers, who seem to me a debauched caste – anxious to prove their manhood by showing their contempt for the tortured.

May those who are evil be destroyed before me – here and now! I whisper to myself, and I pray for Paullus to come quickly.

Yeshua's mother kneels on the bare earth two paces from the man who was once – not so long ago, it must seem – her newborn child, the swollen rims of her eyes so red that they might be bleeding. Her wan, forlorn face leads me so far down into grief that I must turn away to keep from shrieking.

A menacing pulse enters my ears and my legs tense, as though I am making ready to run.

Maryam of Magdala kneels behind Yeshua's mother, her eyes closed, her lips tracing prayers. Beside her stands Nikodemos, desperate hands framing his stricken face.

Yosef of Arimathea, another close ally of Yeshua's and member of the Sanhedrin, kneels in front of a centurion, beseeching him in his halting Latin. I recognize the word for mercy, *misericordia,* and perhaps the one for commandment as well – *praeceptum.*

Nikodemos, standing behind him, is the first to spot me. He nods at me mournfully, as if to say, *It is our destiny to witness his death in silence.*

But is it? I see a pulsing in Yeshua's jaw, which means to me that he is gathering his strength for one final effort.

Tear down this Philistine Temple! I beseech him. *Send it crashing down!*

As though to tell me that what I wish is impossible, Yeshua moans then turns his head to the side and coughs up blood. His mother calls for mercy from the Almighty, and underneath her words I hear her desire for Him to grant her son a quick death.

I find myself weeping. And a very strange thing happens . . . As I turn again to Yeshua, all movement comes to a halt and darkness falls, and I sense that Golgotha has fallen under the shadow of the outstretched wings of the Lord.

Yeshua and I are alone on the island we make from our words and flesh.

I answered you in the hiding place of thunder, I tell him in my mind.

As he licks his cracked lips, he answers me: *Shalom Aleikem, Lazar.*

I've come to help you, I tell him. *Just as I did when you were taken by the River Jordan.*

It's very good to have you with me, he says.

My heart is exploding with hope, because his voice is confident and sure, which means that he still possesses the strength to tell me what to do.

We have always been together, even when we did not know it, I say. *Even when we were miles apart. Even before we met.*

But . . . but I was lost, and I did not see you, and I grew worried. He speaks with the timid voice he had as a young boy, when he feared that his destiny would be a solitary one.

I went to see a Roman friend. He's on his way here. He's coming with help. You must fight to remain with us. You cannot leave us.

I cannot remain with you. This body is finished. Soon I'll have to discard it.

But there is still so much for you to accomplish here.

I shall do what I can in the time I have left to me. But I fear it won't be nearly enough.

Then there is no hope for your flesh?

No, none.

It takes me some time to make space for that sadness inside me – and to understand what it means. *Then you must grant me a favour,* I finally tell him.

What?

It will be your final gift to me, and it is what I have always most wanted from you.

Tell me, dodee.

His calling me *dodee* again sets me weeping.

Is this conversation truly happening or has my despair tricked my mind? I tell you this, Yaphiel, I heard his voice exceptionally clearly, speaking from inside me. And it made me certain that he could hear what I told him, no matter how weak he was.

I grip the gift of his that I wear around my neck and close my eyes and finish the sentence I was unable to end when I tried to make this request of him before. *Do not wait. Take me now. Use whatever force you have to put your soul in my body. I bequeath it to you freely and with no regrets. Once you are clothed in my flesh, you will have years to accomplish all that the Lord has asked of you.*

He replies with silence. Has he fallen back into dreams forced upon him by a body that can take no more pain?

I sit by him, and I touch his ankle to wake him, and the skin is frigid, and I tell him to take me quickly, but he does not wake, and a gruff voice speaking Latin draws my attention, and a legionary places the tip of his sword to my chest while four of his colleagues – two to a side – lift Yeshua's crossbeam.

They heave it on to the upright so quickly that all I can do is gasp.

And then a shattering scream rises inside me. But I do not let it out, for I know it will never end if I release it, and the Romans would drag me away from him.

He coughs up more blood on to his chest.

His eyes do not open.

Put your soul in me now! I order him. *I shall not mind suffering in yours if I know you will live.*

The executioner climbs a ladder to the top of his upright and nails a crude sign – written in three languages – above his head. On the way back down, he straightens the crown on Yeshua's head and says something in Latin to the soldiers that makes them burst into laughter.

Iesous Nazoraios Basileus Ioudaios, I read in Greek.

'He's not our king!' I yell at the executioner – for who else will tell these Romans the truth if I do not.

'Shut your face, Jew!' a young legionary shouts back at me.

'An important Roman is on his way here,' I tell him. 'He's certain to punish you if you don't set Yeshua free right now!'

The young soldier takes out his knife and starts towards me with his eyes already envisaging my burial.

I next remember being yanked backwards and falling to the ground so hard that the breath is knocked from me. A man with a scolding expression stands over me: Nikodemos.

'Do you want to be crucified, too?' he snarls. 'Is that what you want?'

I sit up.

'And if my last wish is for death, what right do you have to take it from me?' I shout.

I am surprised by my words; I had not realized that I'd wished to end my own life.

Mia is standing beside Nikodemos, and next to her is my son, and their worried faces confuse me. For a moment, I no longer even remember how I came to be here.

A man yells for divine assistance. Is it Yeshua?

His voice makes it difficult for me to breathe, so I turn on my side and pull as much air as I can into lungs. I pray for the Lord of Hosts to cut his ropes and fly us both so far from here that we shall never be found again.

Take us to the desert beyond Alexandria, I think. *Set us free.*

'Father, why have you abandoned me?' Yeshua cries.

Nikodemos and I listen for what he will say next. But we hear only a woman shrieking for mercy for her son Samuel, one of the other crucified men.

'What do I do?' I ask Nikodemos.

'Pray for his soul. And keep your distance from him.'

'I can't!' I declare. *And if you think I can, then you never understood anything about me!* I add in my mind.

Mia comes to me. 'Eli, we must leave here,' she says.

'No, just help me get up,' I tell her. 'I promise not to do anything reckless.'

Does she know I'm lying? She may, but she takes my arm when I reach out to her.

Yeshua's head has fallen forward, his chin against his chest, and his breathing is unsure. I imagine him in darkness, his soul gazing up, then down, no longer knowing which way leads towards life and which towards death. Blood is seeping from his right heel, which has just been nailed to the side of his upright, and the executioner, who kneels by Yeshua's left foot, has just raised his hammer again.

At the first crack of bone, I hear a scream louder than any I have ever heard before, but it is not from Yeshua.

'Stop!' I shriek again, and I keep crying it over and over.

But the executioner does not even look at me.

Mia clamps her hand over my mouth, and I fight her, but Nikodemos tackles me from behind, and I am on the ground again.

And then I am dizzy and sick.

Yirmi keeps his hand on my back as I lean over the ground and rid myself of all I was before this day. He fetches me a gourdful of water. As I study my son's crushed eyes, I imagine our thoughts meeting in the air between us, and his are pleading with me not to make him an orphan.

'I won't call out again,' I whisper.

Once I am standing, my son takes my hand and leads me forward towards the cross. How does he know what to do to help me?

I study the glistening flesh torn from Yeshua's side and the gouges in his cheek, confused as to why the Lord would make man such a fragile creature, so easily destroyed.

If I could I would hold out my hands and catch all the life dripping from him and put it back in him, and I would work so fast that he could never die.

A mad circle of flies feeds at his heels. The nails driven through his flesh are rusted.

They do not even waste new iron on the likes of us, I think, and the throbbing rage that creates in my head makes it manifest that his blood is no longer simply falling on to the dry soil at the base of his cross but rather on to every hope I have ever had.

Can it be that a small part of the Lord – exactly the size of a man – dies each time we do? All I see and hear seems to want me to believe that. For if it is not the case, then how can the Almighty feel compassion?

Maryam of Magdala stands behind Yeshua, shivering, her woollen mantle crumpled at her feet. *Perhaps,* I think, *she dares not stand in front of him, for she knows that she will faint if she sees his face.*

But I am wrong.

The tiny step she soon takes to her left, and the way she measures her distance from Yeshua, tell me that she has moved herself between him and the light from the cloud-shrouded sun so that the shadow of her head and chest will fall directly across his legs and feet.

He will feel that she is with him, I think, and I know then that she intends to follow the path of the sun as it descends to the horizon. In the holy language of shadows, she is telling him, *I shall remain with you for as long as it takes, and, in the end, I shall fall into the arms of death with you.*

And so I learn – too late, perhaps – that she loves him exactly as I do.

My son and I kneel. Mia comes around to the other side of me.

I study Yeshua's closed eyes and imagine my lips pressing first to one then the other. I take his hands in mine and squeeze them tight, then release them and trace the sloping curve of his hips with my palms and kiss the top of his head and neck and lips, and the scent of him is of wood and papyrus, as it always has been. I feel the weight of his sex in my hand and hug myself around his legs. I caress my cheek against his and rub his whiskers against mine.

I do these things because I need to know the beginning and the end of him, for only by knowing those things will the borders between us be erased, and I shall become the seer and the seen and the lover and the loved – and death will not end him, for he will for ever live in me.

I shall remember everything that has taken place this day, I vow to him, although I do not yet know why.

I take off my sandals and slip out of my tunic. Mia tries to stop me. 'You can't go naked here,' she whispers, but I tell her there is no other way.

'I shall shed all that might weigh me down,' I say.

Along with my clothes, I try to give up my fears, dreams, regrets and hopes, for Yeshua has always told me that the Lord greets us naked.

His mother understands the simple grace of removing all that would only keep me from her son, because she calls my name as I kneel again, and she nods her tearful comprehension of my motives while running her hand down her chest. And then she, too, removes her sandals and takes off her headscarf.

Could any of us send the person we most love to his grave – naked and defenceless – without wishing to accompany him?

The Romans point at my covenant with the Lord and yell rude comments about my manhood, but what they do not know is that I no longer fear them, for the Torah that lives and the Torah that dies are both on my side in this battle: *Naked I came from my mother's womb, and naked I shall depart.*

★

Eliezer ben Niscroch and Samuel ben Abdiou. Those are the names of other two men who were crucified with Yeshua. Both were Judaeans, and both were rebels.

Though they lived only at the fringes of this narrative of mine, they occupied the very centre of their own stories, of course.

Over the next hours, I stand only once, when Yeshua tugs at the ropes binding his wrists and groans. Blood has begun to seep from his brow, and his mouth hangs open. I take a step forward and speak aloud. 'Do not stay any longer than you have to. Finish what is most important, then leave us. No one will blame you for fleeing this miserable place.'

After a time, his groans cease.

Here are the last words I ever speak aloud to him while he lives: 'Were it not for you, I'd never have learned who I am and where I was meant to go. I would know nothing. I shall be for ever grateful to you.'

And then something unexpected stops my mind: his eyes open, and he recognizes me. As I gasp, he smiles encouragingly, as he nearly always does when we must part, and his right hand rises up, straining against its bindings, and he lifts two fingers to tell me that his work has come to an end – that he has done all he can do to heal our world, and the time has come for him to discard his earthly form and leave us. So I tell him in my mind that I shall join him as soon as he sends for me, and I thank him for transforming what could have been a bitter and lonely life into one of joy and gratitude, and I remind him to give counsel to the two holy warriors executed beside him, Eliezer and Samuel, for their souls will wish to have had more time and will become confused and anxious when they look back at their loved ones who are gathered here. And then his eyes close for the last time, and a sharp exhale of breath comes from his mouth accompanied by a trace of blood, and I hear a beating of wings so deep inside me that I perceive that a great mystery has taken place here and now, one that began with his birth and mine, and I know that I shall never fully understand what has come to pass this day, or why, and, when his chest no longer rises, Mia whispers his name, and she begins to chant a lamentation for our lost brother, and Yirmi adds his voice to hers, and I want to join them, but my voice is gone, and, after they fall silent, I embrace my son because he is weeping, and it is a blessing to be able to hold him against my naked flesh, and my sister hands me my tunic, and she tells me that she will take me back to Bethany, and I tell her, *'Let me embrace our brother one last time, when he is lowered from his cross, and then I will go home with you.'*

But this is another lie; now that Yeshua is gone I know that I have no home anywhere in this world.

46

Nikodemos carries Yeshua down from his cross, kneels and eases him on to the barren soil with the help of Yosef of Arimathea. After his mother and grandmother sooth his wounds and cry their laments and say their farewells, I sit by him and thank him in a whisper for leading me to the island that gave us shelter for so many years, and I apologize for not understanding so much of what he tried to teach me and for failing him, and I bury my face in his hands and breathe through them, but they smell nothing like him, and they are waxen and heavy and cold.

In death, we never much resemble who we were in life, for all the mystery is gone.

47

Maryam of Magdala stood for hours behind Yeshua's cross, so she could not have seen him open his eyes to me. Although I have no hope of raising her spirits – that is beyond the scope of any man or woman – she deserves to be aware of everything I know, which is why, after I say goodbye to the others, I tell her that Yeshua recognized me just before he departed.

She is no longer able to stand, so I kneel beside her.

She clamps her hands over her mouth and shows me glistening, hopeful eyes. 'Are you sure?' she asks.

'Yes. He raised two fingers in the way we used to do as boys – to tell me he had to leave us but that he would be all right.' I show her the sign I mean. 'And some time before that he spoke to me as well – in my mind, as he has many times before. He said that there still remained a few things he would try to accomplish before returning to the Lord. He said his body was failing and . . . and that he would have to leave it behind.'

Yosef of Arimathea has overheard our conversation and comes to me. 'I'm sorry, Eli,' he says, taking my shoulder, 'I never saw him open his eyes – and I was watching him the whole time.'

Three ragged waifs start fighting over one of the nails used to fix Yeshua's heel to the cross, for they know it will fetch a good price as an amulet. After Mia shouts at them to take their shameful quarrel elsewhere, I summon Nikodemos, who is talking with friends from the Galilee, and ask him to confirm what I saw.

'I didn't see him look at you or anyone else,' he tells me. 'And I know he didn't lift any of his fingers. In fact, the way his hand was bound, I'm fairly certain he couldn't have.'

I do not react with anger or resentment. I thank Nikodemos and Yosef for telling me the truth – *their* truth – but I also do not question what I saw. You see, Yaphiel, the mysteries of the world sometimes appear to each of us in ways that others cannot see, and there are experiences that are not meant to be shared. We have had them because they are right for us – and because we have been prepared to receive them by all we have ever seen and heard and touched. And suffered.

48

Yeshua must be taken to his place of rest without delay, since the Sabbath will be upon us at sundown. Yosef has offered one of his family's tombs for this purpose. I consider accompanying him and the others, but Mia will not hear of it.

'You've been through enough, and you'll only make yourself ill again.'

Mia leads me to Bethany and then to my room, and she washes the knife wound on my forehead and coaxes me into my bed, and she sits on my floor, by the window to our courtyard, and she watches over me.

Each time I awaken in the night, she is sitting beside me.

Over the next three days, I do not leave my alcove.

What would I do without the help of Erebos, the god of darkness? I keep the shutters closed. I cannot imagine ever allowing sunlight to reach me again.

When hunger overtakes me, I eat matzoh soaked in wine. It is the only food I can keep down.

I am able to keep tears away at times by telling myself that Yeshua's suffering is over. Still, when I am weeping, I am certain that the grief in my heart and eyes and belly will never leave me.

An irony: when Mia assures me that time will ease my pain, I grow frightened, for I would never want to diminish in any way the living hollow inside me. *Without my grief I wouldn't be who I am,* I think.

When I do not believe I can bear any more, I drink, for inside wine resides slumber, and inside slumber is forgetfulness.

*

Nikodemos sends a Greek servant to see me on the afternoon of the Sabbath, to assure me that Yeshua is in his tomb. I am too soaked in drink by then to retain much of what he recounts to me about the ceremony. His expression moves from disappointment to resentment over the course of our conversation. I know I ought to care, but I don't.

Paullus comes the next day in a litter carried by four slaves in saffron-coloured tunics. I am asleep when he arrives, and Mia refuses to wake me. Paullus tells her that he is sorry to have failed me and that when I am in better spirits he would like me to visit him.

When I am in better spirits? After Mia gives me his message, I am tempted to return to his villa for the pleasure of howling with laughter in his face.

In my reveries, I chop off Annas' wrinkled, shrunken old-man's head with an axe and carry it with me on a boat, far out into the Great Sea, and I toss it into the murky waters so that it will be eaten by cuttlefish and squid and all the scaleless creatures of the darkest depths, and he will be obliged to wander the earth for ever as a headless *ibbur.*

I am obviously not a generous drunk. No, I am more of the vengeful kind, which is why Grandfather Shimon is perfectly right to refuse me his sword when I ask if I may keep it with me.

White with a fringe of golden silk . . .

Those were the colours of Paullus' toga on the day he came to visit me. I missed his regal arrival at my door, but my neighbours were greatly impressed and apparently gossiped about it for days afterwards.

Sometimes I think that there are a vast number of episodes in my life that Mia and my children could tell more artfully and accurately than I could.

Mia tries to start conversations with me about trifles – the spring flowers, for instance – and I know I ought to play along and reply, *Yes, the plum blossoms are lovely,* but the words cling to my throat the moment I consider speaking them.

Although my children no longer have any reason to flee to Alexandria, my cousins Ion and Ariston suggest that I move my family there as soon as possible. 'We'd help you start over in Egypt,' they say.

I tell them I shall gladly consider their magnanimous offer once I feel strong enough to leave my room, but, the truth is, I have no idea what *start over* could possibly mean in this context.

When Lucius visits, I am asleep, and he has Abibaal dab warm water on my hands to rouse me from my fermented slumber and then proceeds to lecture me on how I must not give in to despair and that he wishes to stand with me at Yeshua's tomb so that our prayers might help his soul complete its journey. He seems to have decided that the way out of his own grief will be through usefulness, but I do not wish to be useful even to myself any more.

My children visit me sometimes, and the three of us play together with Nahara's top and wooden snake. Yirmi's worries about me prompt him to request that he remain with me at night, and Nahara wishes to share my bed as well, but I tell them that I snore when I am drunk and would only keep them awake. The real reason for my refusal – God forgive me – is that I do not wish to be touched by anyone but him.

Gephen comes to me as well, and I talk to him about the trifles that I am unable to discuss with Mia, because, when I listen to myself addressing a cat, my voice seems so silly and unlikely that I am occasionally able to imagine that nothing of what I witnessed on Golgotha was real.

It is such a glorious relief to give up on participating in my own life that I wonder why I bothered venturing out into the world for so long.

Once, while caressing Gephen's warm belly, I conclude that I would have fared better with my sisters and wife and parents if I had been born a pet cat.

My days are filled with such useless, wine-inspired revelations.

When I give in to weeping, I lie face down on my mat and cover my head with my pillow, since I would not want my sister or son hearing me and trying to comfort me.

Mia comes to sit with me on my third morning after Yeshua's death, before I have had a chance to dip my breakfast matzoh in wine, and she asks if she can open my shutters. It is a relief – in both body and spirit – to be able to reply with a simple but definitive *no,* and it is at that moment that I discover how much more secure and strong I would have felt over the course of my adult life had I said *no* every time I wanted to.

Marta does not come to see me. Yirmi tells me that she has been spending most of her time away from home. Did Mia and I fail her? Often, in my mind, I see an affectionate woman with Marta's face – quick to praise and laugh and a weaver of renown throughout Zion – who is the sister I might have had.

I visit my preferred brothel the first time I leave my house – late on the third night – but once again I am unable to find my manhood when the moment comes.

I almost wrote that I visited my preferred brothel *by accident,* since it was not my intention to go there when I closed my front door behind me, but instead to visit the stream where Yeshua and I used to go. But are there accidents? That is the question I begin to ask myself after I return home from the bordello, since that is when Yeshua comes to me and tells me more of what has taken place between us.

49

I awaken from drunken sleep to find myself lying on my side against the cold floor, my knees tucked up by my chest. Night has descended, and an oil lamp burns on my table. My shutters are open, and moonlight is streaming in.

It is a comfort to have solid ground beneath me, but my head is throbbing and my feet are freezing – proof, I conclude, that I need to drink some more. As I fill my cup with wine, a stirring on the other side of the room turns my head.

A figure there raises his hand to hail me. 'I answered you in the hiding place of thunder,' he says.

He is squatting on his heels underneath my window giving out on the courtyard. His hands are joined together and are glowing with a cool bluish light.

You will say, Yaphiel, that this uncommon radiance in my old friend's hands could not possibly have been produced by moonlight. So perhaps I ought to have realized that my shutters were not really open and that this was a vision.

What I believe now is that Yeshua opened my mind and showed me how the starlight of the Throne World was always shining inside him.

But I did not know that then.

'Shalom, *dodee,*' I tell him. 'How did you get here?'

'I walked, of course.'

'No, but . . . but what happened? Your hands were cold and limp. And . . . you were not breathing.'

'Your hands were cold, too.'

'When?' I ask.

He stands up and stretches his arms over his head, as he does after he has remained seated for hours, lost in chanting. The scourge-marks from his eye to his mouth have scabbed, but they will leave a long scar.

'Your hands were cold when I revived you,' he tells me.

'But what does that have to do with you?'

'I needed to make sure I could carry out my plan. So I summoned death to you first – to make sure it would work.'

'That what would work?'

'My plan.'

'So neither of us was really dead?' I ask.

'Our hearts were stilled, which brought us within reach of the Angel of Death. But, in both cases, I commanded him to leave us and brought us back to life.'

'Is this true?'

'Yes.'

'So you're still alive?'

'Yes.'

'Why didn't you tell me that your death was part of a plan?'

'I couldn't. Your sisters . . . I could not risk them finding out.'

'But you could've saved me all this pain and grief – and this ocean of wine I've been drinking.' I hold up my cup.

'That's why I'm telling you now.'

'But why do you want everyone to think that you're dead?'

'I need to leave this place. I don't want everyone waiting for me to return or to try to find me. That's what the Father . . . that's what He has asked of me.'

The slight hesitation in his voice gives me the idea that he is not telling me the *whole* truth. When I confess that to him, he says that it isn't important at the moment for me to believe him or understand everything. 'We're together now – that's all that counts,' he says.

He stands up and smiles, and when we embrace, my tears begin to flow. 'None of this makes any sense,' I tell him.

'There was no other way,' he whispers.

Panic makes me hold him away from me. 'We can't let the Romans know that you've survived. We need to return to the Galilee right away!'

'No, I must leave the Land of Zion.'

'Have you decided where you'll go?'

'Yes,' he says.

When he caresses my cheek, I notice that his hand is still glowing. Yet it is cool.

'Listen, *dodee*,' he says, 'I need you to go somewhere for me.'

'Where?'

'To Ge Hinnom.'

'Why there?'

'I've left something there for you.'

'What?'

'You'll find out when you get there. Go at dawn. Do you promise?'

'Yes, of course.'

'He touches his fingertip to the crusted blood on my brow. 'What happened here?'

'A Roman cut me – to mark me.'

'Didn't he see you were already marked?'

'What do you mean?'

'I marked you when we were only eight years old.'

'You did?'

'Only a few people could see it. Most people can't see what's right in front of them.'

He smiles as if he would not have had it any other way. I touch the crusted scars on his cheek. 'Do they hurt?' I ask.

'No.'

'Your disfigurement means you'll never become high priest.' I say that with an ironic smile, since it is not a post he would ever have wanted.

I expect him to laugh, but he starts as if he has heard pursuing footsteps. 'I must go,' he whispers.

'Already?'

He nods. 'I'm sorry.' He hooks his arm in mine and leads me to the door, where he places his hand on my brow and blesses me, and I feel his glow entering me as a thought: *I am the fire that does not burn.*

He leaves me before I have a chance to bless him in return. As I watch him running away, I realize that he may never come back to me, and my legs give way, and I reach out to the wall of my home to keep from falling.

From the end of my street, Yeshua turns back to me and holds up two fingers and . . .

Then I awaken to find I am lying face down on my mat. When I turn over, I discover that my shutters are closed. *His higher soul found a way to come to me,* I think. *And it was clothed in flesh so I would not be blinded by its light.*

I realize then that I am gripping the calliper he gave me, and the scent of him is in my hands as if I have been holding him all night.

I reach the valley of Ge Hinnom just after sunrise. It is the monstrous refuse heap that serves all of Yerushalayim. We consider it an accursed place because children were sacrificed here to the gods of our ancient ancestors.

At this hour, the only other visitors are four pauperous children searching together over mounds of smouldering filth for shreds of food and remnants of clothing. They seem to have no trouble with the stench, but I must keep my hand over my nose and breathe through my mouth.

The Romans and wealthy Jews often discard their dead slaves here, and as I walk the valley's eastern perimeter – searching for what Yeshua has left me – I am forced to climb high up the stony hillside to avoid two slavering mutts gorging on the corpse of what was once a woman. Beside a myrtle bush in flower, poking out from underneath a rusted coulter, is a soiled but charming puppet of a flower-seller. His roses are made out of red glass beads.

Might he be what Yeshua meant me to find?

After I put him in my pouch, the convulsive wailing of a child – far off and muffled – reaches me. I follow it to a rush-work basket hanging from a high branch of an oak tree on the hillock where infants are often left for rescue by mothers unable or unwilling to raise them. Inside is a baby in foul-smelling swaddling clothes – a girl, I soon discover. She has downy black hair and a squashed little face.

The baby girl is cold and wet and stained by her own filth, but I find that her fist around my finger is strong and purposeful – a favourable sign. Her urine, which slides warm over my fingers as I unwrap her, is neither bloody nor viscous, and its scent is sour, as it should be. I wipe her bottom with oak leaves and a towel I pull from my pouch and ease her inside my tunic.

I lay her belly down against my chest, where she will soak up my heat.

As I continue my search around Ge Hinnom, she begins to wail and my inability to nurse her becomes a torment – a form of injustice. Men are such limited creatures when it comes to children.

Ilana – that is what I decide to call her for the time being, since I found her in an oak tree. 'You are in luck,' I whisper to her as I jiggle her in my hands. 'Mia will bring you to her orphanage and the women there will find you a wet nurse and a new home.'

I make a second complete circle around that pestilent valley, and, since I find nothing else of interest, I start calling out to Yeshua, but he neither appears nor shows me a sign.

A young woman dressed in an old robe and thick-soled shoes suddenly hails me from the steep ridge in the west. After she descends the rocky path to me, I recognize her as Salome, one of the orphanage's child-savers. She wishes to relieve me of Ilana, and I am well aware that it would be for the best, but the child clings so desperately to me with those strong hands of hers that I cannot give her up.

Only when I have her inside my tunic again do I realize – as though jostled out of a deep sleep – that Ilana is what Yeshua left for me.

It will be many years, however, before I understand the reason why he wished for me to find your dearest mother, Yaphiel. Indeed, it will take me until after your birth.

50

I keep Yeshua's visitation a secret from my family, since I need time to consider what he told me about his death – and mine. That means, of course, that I cannot tell Mia and my children that he intended for me to find the baby I bring home. Instead, I say that I found Ilana by accident while walking past Ge Hinnom.

Does my sister find it odd that I insist on bringing a baby into our family at the worst possible time? Her tense, brooding looks tell me that she fears that my grief may have severed my hold on reality and trapped us with a child she neither needs nor wants. She undoubtedly hopes that I shall soon discover that I am in no condition to serve as father to a newborn.

I am quite aware that a reasonable man would conclude that there could not be any occult meaning to my finding an exposed infant in Ge Hinnom. It is, after all, where mothers leave babies they wish to see rescued, and someone else – probably Salome – would have heard Ilana crying sooner or later and delivered her from danger.

A wet nurse and friend of Mia's – Rachel – stays with us all that first day of Ilana's new life in my home. I keep the baby with me when she is not nursing. She sleeps nearly all the time, exhausted from her ordeal, unaware that she was chosen for me.

I show off her astonishing grip to Yirmi, who laughs with admiration.

To see my son holding Ilana so tenderly is to believe that we have a future together.

I wait up for Yeshua all night, expecting him to return to see that I have carried out his wishes, but I receive no visitation or vision. At sunrise, after Rachel has had a chance to nurse Ilana, I decide to take her to visit Maryam of Magdala; she deserves to know that Yeshua's soul clothed itself in his body and told me where to find the baby.

Neither pilgrims nor residents of Yerushalayim await me on my street; my week of notoriety has apparently ended. And so, as in times past, I do not lock the door behind me when I start for Yerushalayim.

Now that Yeshua is gone, I think, *everyone must see the truth – that I never had any control over the workings of the world.*

As soon as I reach the road west out of Bethany, I realize I must turn around; I cannot risk Maryam disbelieving what I had intended to recount to her and judging me mistaken or mad. I do not want her or anyone else to explain to me where Yeshua ends and I begin.

In such ways I have learned over the course of my life that there are experiences that I do not fully understand but do not wish to have explained to me. Who, after all, would permit his most cherished inner disputes to be settled by someone else?

The morning sun has risen by the time I start back towards Bethany, and it seems a much better idea to take Ilana into the countryside, where I shall begin to teach her the names of the trees and flowers of Judaea. You see, Yaphiel, every father is Adam, just as every mother is Havvah, and Yeshua has made it my joyful obligation to name the world for my new daughter.

51

I shall never know every detail of the plot against me and my family. Still, a man who has spent decades placing tiny fragments of stone together to tell stories that hold some meaning for him has his own peculiar needs and most especially a desire – ingenuous though it may be – for everything in his past and present to fit together neatly.

One thing is certain, Mia had only a sliver of time to decide between trying to save herself and my son.

It surprised me at first that the intruders wore slippers or soft-soled sandals, but then I realized that they must have had years of experience at such work. I suspect that Mia only detected their cushioned steps because the floor tiles in front of my alcove were in need of fixing and made a clinking sound when stepped on.

We are not generally aware of it, but if we are fortunate, I think, then our lives are redeemed by a few moments of deep and sacred understanding, when there is almost no time to think, and what we do is decided by forces unseen inside ourselves that know – somehow – what must be done.

The intruders did not need to break the hinges on my door because, as I have told you, I had left it unlocked that morning.

From twenty paces away, I already see that my front door is wide open. Gephen is seated inside the threshold, licking his right front paw. Only when I step to him and spot the red stains on his forehead and nose do I realize what it is he is cleaning from himself.

I grip Ilana tightly, step inside and call out to my son and sister.

My ears are tingling, listening for the slightest movement, but my house returns only silence. A sense of slowly falling tells me I ought to turn around and go for help. But if my children are in danger . . .

I find Grandfather Shimon lying on his back at the base of the ladder leading up to his room. His old sword has fallen from his hand, and a rose of blood has blossomed on his chest. His dull, unseeing eyes remain open.

At first I believed that an assassin had killed Shimon on entering my home. Later, I came to understand that my grandfather must have come downstairs from his room only *after* hearing Mia call out for Yirmi to run.

I ease my knife out of my pouch and take it in my fist. My grandfather's brow is cold.

Yeshua gave me Ilana, so I must protect her before I go any further, I think, so I step as silently as a fawn into my alcove and slip the sleeping child into my clothes chest. She fusses, but she does not wake.

When the killers entered my home, Mia would have heard their footsteps and assumed I had returned. She would have been anxious to know if I had kept Ilana or come to my senses and left her at the orphanage.

What I later learned was that she had been with Yirmi in Marta's workroom. They were studying her latest weaving. When Mia heard the steps coming in my front door, she smiled at Yirmi, then stepped through the doorway into her own bedroom and from there into the courtyard. Perhaps she held herself back for a moment before coming to greet me, to feel her relief at having me home more fully.

Mia told me once that I changed her life when she first held me in her arms. 'As I cradled you, you giggled, and you kept on laughing while I made faces for you, and that sound was like finding a reason to be alive, and my heart became the exact shape and size of you.'

Everything small and fragile was sacred to Mia.

I had not known that butterflies will feed on blood. Two ivory ones flex their wings at the edge of the thick bloodstain spreading from my sister's neck. Her head sits on the wooden table where she kept our ladles, tongs and other kitchen tools.

Mia, who took me aboard Noach's Ark and rescued me from the Flood, who taught me that we need never be ashamed of love, who was always trying to make her long arms seem shorter, who sang to me whenever . . .

I cannot keep the tears away. And I cannot leave her like this.

How long do I look into her dead and filmy eyes?

So this is the way you and I end. The unfairness of that is a heavy stone in my gut, and already I know I shall never rid myself of it.

What she and I never knew on all those thousands of occasions when we ate together and played with each other's children and conversed about our parents was that we were always on the road to this violent end.

She was barefoot when she heard the intruders in my house, and her hair was down. In her left hand she still grips a woollen cat she made from felt. Its body is white and eyes are blue. It is styled after Gephen, of course. She had probably finished it this morning. I am certain it was to be her first gift to Ilana.

Her body was left where it fell, between the table and her cooking tripod.

A bird whose wings have been cut away.

That is the image that steals into my mind after I study what was done to her.

I step around her into her bedroom. It is empty. In Marta's workroom, however, is a surprise that makes me jump back – a wounded man whom I recognize. He sits slumped by my sister's loom. He is immense and powerful. Blood oozes on to the floor from a wound in his thigh.

'I'll kill you if you move!' I cry out.

Did Mia stab him with the blade that she was using to shape her felt cat?

With the injury to his leg, he cannot possibly chase me down, but I make my knife ready in case he should make a desperate lunge.

Two much smaller men lie dead behind him. Only one of them still has his head. Both are drenched in blood. I do not recognize their faces.

'I saw you outside Herod's Palace on the day Yeshua was crucified,' I tell him.

'I . . . I see you there, too,' he replies.

His voice is heavily accented – as it was on the day we first met. He sits up and grips a leg of Marta's loom with his right hand, while his left presses against his wound.

His sword lies by his side, covered in blood.

'I've called you Goliath,' I tell him.

'Not so original,' he says, but he smiles to soften his criticism.

'What's your real name?'

'I see what you think, but I not kill your sister,' he says.

I do not believe him. Any hope I might have in finding peace resides in my next question. 'What about my children? Where are they?'

'Children safe. When Yirmi come racing into street, I go to him. He tell me that Mia shout at him to run. She say that two strangers are in courtyard . . . that they have swords. I tell him to take sister Nahara and run away – go find friend.'

'He took Nahara away?'

'Yes, she play with hens on street. Yirmi take her arm and they run.'

'How do you know my children's names?'

'I study you. It helps.'

'Helps what?'

'It helps to know a man – to know his habits – if we want to defend him.'

'What are you talking about?'

As he holds my gaze, tears squeeze past his lashes. 'I fail to protect you. I sorry – very sorry. If you wish to take my life, I not fight. In any case, I die soon.'

'I don't understand.'

He wipes his face with his sleeve. 'We have friend together.'

'Who?'

'Yeshua.' While holding my gaze, he nods for me to accept his affirmation, but I cannot.

'Friend is wrong word,' he continues. 'I do not know him so well. I envy you. You and he so close. His brother come speak to me on day when you return to life. They ask me make certain you not killed or injured.'

'Why?'

'They know people want you to heal them and bless them. They know you important now – you sure to make enemies.'

He breathes in deeply, fighting to control the pain. 'I call you Eliezer or Lazarus?' he asks.

'Either.'

'Which Yeshua call you?'

'He preferred Lazar.'

'Then I also call you Lazar. You not mind?'

'No.'

'I am bodyguard for many years, Lazar. For rich Romans. My strength give me advantage. I train much with sword. I good. But this time . . .' He points a finger to his eye and nods. 'You see me following. I tell Yaaqov I make mistake. He asks other man to guard you – a smaller man. Yaaqov tell me to protect your children and sisters.' Goliath coughs and struggles to breathe. Tears slide down his cheeks. 'Lazar, I not expect men from Annas to enter your door. That my mistake. I am sorry.'

'How did you know Yeshua?' I ask.

'He help my sister two years gone. He take demon from her.' He splays out the fingers in his left hand. 'Five years the demon stay in her – from birth of first child. I pledge my service to him then.'

'And who are these men behind you?'

'Annas send them. Or maybe Caiaphas. They kill sister.'

'And also my grandfather,' I tell him.

He grimaces. 'I am sorry. I not know. When I enter house, they searching for Nahara.'

'And the wet nurse . . . what about Rachel?' I ask. 'Have you seen her?'

'No, you ask Yirmi when find him.'

Could he still be trying to fool me? 'You haven't told me your name,' I say.

'In Aramaic, my name is Ehud.'

'We can speak Greek if you prefer,' I tell him.

He laughs. 'Greek more difficult than Aramaic!'

'Where are you from?'

'Near Masis.' He designs a curve with his hand. 'Near mountain you call Ararat.'

'Why didn't the men come for me instead of my sister? I don't –'

'They no come for sister, they come for you!' he cuts in, raising an emphatic fist. 'They enter through your door. I not expect that. That is why I not save Mia.' He cups his hand by his ear. 'She yell – I hear. But I come too late.'

'And the man who was supposed to guard me – where is he?'

He shakes his head. 'I not know. Maybe he go away. I not ask Yaaqov – he not well. So I watch your sisters and children. I make vow to Yeshua that I guard sisters and children. I keep that vow.'

'What did Yeshua tell you about me?' I ask, hoping his reply will prove that his story is true.

'He say I guard you with life, since you beloved friend. And he tell me you save him in River Jordan.'

Thinking of my boyhood with Yeshua reminds me of my children, and panic seizes my spirit. I kneel by Ehud and thank him. The touch of my hand to his cheek sets him crying again 'I'm sorry to leave you, but I must find my children now,' I tell him. 'They must be terrified.'

'Wait just a moment,' he pleads. 'I need to tell you more. Your sister Mia . . . she go to see Annas today. She must say something that scares him.' He clears his throat. 'Annas not rest until you are dead. He send other killers.'

To my next questions, Ehud replies that he followed Mia that morning and that my sister may have terrified Annas by telling him what happened to Maryam of Magdala. When I say that I have not heard anything about Maryam of late, he tells me that she found Yeshua's tomb empty on the morning after his death.

'His body had vanished?' I ask.

'Yes.'

Did I see Yeshua in the flesh, after all? I wonder.

'Might Yosef of Arimathea have had his body taken away?' I ask Ehud. 'Or perhaps Annas had it removed to keep Yeshua's followers from gathering at his tomb.'

'Maryam hear Yeshua speaking in body of caretaker who watches execution place.'

'One of the caretakers on Golgotha?' I ask.

'Yes.'

'His soul passed into another man?'

'That what we think.'

'Where can I find this caretaker?'

'I not know. But soul of Yeshua no longer in him. Maryam say that after Yeshua speak to her, caretaker . . . he fall down, and when he awake he not remember.' Ehud shakes his head. 'You not hear this?'

'No, I've hardly left my house since the crucifixion.'

'Mia maybe hear of it and go to Annas to tell him. To tell priest Yeshua not dead.'

In that case, she withheld the news from me, I think. *She must have known I'd try to find the caretaker and question him, which would have put me at risk again.*

'What about my sister Marta?' I ask. 'Have you seen her?'

'She leave house at first light and not return. I not know where she go.'

A disquieting possibility makes me start.

'What is it?' Ehud asks.

'Maybe Marta knew that Annas would send killers after us. She didn't want to see all our blood. That's why she has only spent a few hours here since Yeshua was crucified.'

In that case, I think, *she must have been the person who sent a note for me to meet Yeshua at a tavern. She needed to make sure I would not go home and catch her meeting with her conspirators – or at some other evil work. Or maybe she hid outside the tavern to observe me and my son from afar, anxious to watch us one last time.*

Ehud has a fit of coughing. Afterwards, his face pales and his eyes go dull. Unless I act fast, his soul will depart from his body for ever.

I help him ease back down and lie flat on his back. 'Why your hair black?' he asks.

'I dyed it for a role I was playing. Wait here. I'll be back in a moment.'

'No, go find your children!' he says.

'I must do one more thing first.'

I return to my room, check on Ilana and take an old robe from my chest. Back with Ehud, I tear it into strips. Though he tells me he is beyond my help, I bandage his wound tightly. As I help him drink some water, he takes hold of my wrist. 'You leave Zion,' he says as if it is the Lord's command. 'You take children and go.'

'I'll get help for you first.'

'No, too late. But I ask one favour.'

'Anything.'

'I selfish man,' he says with an apologetic smile. 'I want know something about Yeshua that only you know.'

And so I tell him that my old friend came to me in a vision and told me to find Ilana. When I hold the girl up to him, he caresses a bloody fingertip across her chin and up her cheek with such good-natured tenderness that I understand immediately why Yaaqov chose him to guard me. 'I'm certain that Yeshua sent her to me for a reason,' I say, 'but I've yet to find out what it is.'

'You think he still with us?' Ehud asks.

'I don't know. Perhaps he staged his death, as he told me in my vision. Or maybe his higher soul has remained amongst us and will now move through the world in different guises. There are things he could do . . . I'm not sure we can even imagine what is possible for a prophet.'

Goliath tells me again to leave Zion. He speaks of a friend of his who lives near Yeriho and who will hide me until I can make my way safely out of Judaea. 'Change name,' he tells me, holding up a hand of warning. 'Speak only Greek in public. Go to place where you never are – where no one expect you go. Never mention Yeshua. Make believe you are not from Bethany.'

I am impressed by his logic. And his struggle to make himself understood in Aramaic creates an ache of fondness for him in my chest. I know immediately that I shall follow all his instructions. 'If only you'd told me that you were sent to protect my family,' I tell him. 'I might have been able to save you.'

'I not important. Yeshua needs *you* to survive.' He wipes away his tears roughly. 'Please, Lazar, you must not fail him!'

'But why was I so important to him?' I ask.

He shakes his head. 'Only he can tell us.' He laughs and points to the baby. 'Maybe she is the reason. And maybe she tell you why when she grow up.'

Before I leave, I rend my collar and chant a quick lamentation over Mia and my grandfather: *Daughters of Israel, weep over Shimon and Mia, who . . .*

After extolling their virtues, I thank them for all they have done for me, and I apologize to them for being unable to see their defiled bodies safely into the ground.

I have spent nearly my entire adulthood in this house and yet there is almost nothing I wish to take with me. In addition to a small secret stash of silver, I grab only my scroll of *In the Beginning*, a drinking gourd and my stones from Alexandria.

Ayin is standing at the window of Grandfather Shimon's eyrie. After I tuck him gently into my pouch, I go up to the roof and call out to Gephen, but he does not appear. *Come to me now or I shall have to leave you behind,* I warn him in my mind.

When I climb back down, I find that the flow of blood from Ehud's wound has nearly stopped. The colour in his face is better as well. 'I'll get you a physician,' I tell him.

'I too . . . too afraid to hope,' he confesses.

'You tell the Angel of Death to bother someone else or you'll cut him to pieces!'

With a grin, he assures me that he will do what he can to live.

'I have four children,' he tells me, and he kisses my hands, and I know it is to thank me for helping to save them from orphanhood. It is a moment I shall never forget because it proves to me that there is still a chance for me to make a small difference to the world.

'Ehud, there is one more important thing you can do for me,' I say. 'Tell all those you meet over the coming days that I've fled south. Tell them that I intend to go to Egypt.'

'South to Egypt,' he confirms with a nod.

'And if you see Marta or any of my nieces or nephews or cousins, tell them in a conspiratorial tone . . . as if you're confiding in them . . . that I'm on my way with my children to Alexandria but that they mustn't reveal that information to anyone.'

'Lazar, do you not hear me?' he growls. 'You known in Alexandria. You go to other place, where –'

'Ssshhh, dear Ehud,' I cut in, and I kneel beside him. 'I'll do exactly as you say, my friend. I won't go anywhere near Alexandria. I intend to head north into Phoenicia. But I shall be much safer if you tell my sister and everyone else who asks that I am on my way south.'

52

After prevailing upon Weathervane and two other neighbours to help the wounded man that they will find in my house – and to summon a physician – I gather up Ilana in my arms and search for Yirmi and Nahara. At the edge of Bethany, I find Alexandros on his millstone. When he sees me, he starts humming and twitching. I grip his shoulders hard and ask him if he has seen my children.

With a grunt, he thrusts out his arms and pushes me away – towards the east. Might he be helping me the only way he can?

I call out to Yirmi and Nahara as I go. After half a mile, by a house in ruins, I spot them running to me through a grove of date palms. After I make sure they are unhurt, I ask them if they have seen the wet nurse.

'She went home after you left with Ilana,' my son tells me.

The knowledge that I shall never return to Judaea – that this phase of my life has ended – is what I see in my son's grieving eyes when I take him aside and tell him of the murder of his aunt and great-grandfather.

Once we reach Ehud's friend in Yeriho, I cut Nahara's hair short and dress her as a boy; no emissaries of Rome or the

Temple will be searching for a man with two sons and an infant girl.

On our journey, I speak only Greek with Yirmi and keep my conversations in Aramaic with Nahara to a minimum. When I am obliged to speak with her in public, I pretend an Ionian accent. To those who seem too curious about our mixture of languages, I explain that Nahara, whose name has now become Nahor, is more comfortable with Aramaic because he is the son of my youngest sister who died giving birth to the infant who is also in my care. My sister's husband is also recently deceased, so my adolescent son and I are taking the orphaned children to Halikarnassos, where my parents make their home.

I have always preferred to be clean-shaven, but I have no choice but to let my beard grow, and Nahor makes a game of finding the grey hairs amongst the brown. I introduce myself to those we meet along the way as Erebos of Miletus, and I ask them to call me Eri, which is close enough to Eli for me to always respond when summoned.

Yirmi becomes Irenaeus, which I find the most beautiful of Greek names.

Why Halikarnassos? It is Yirmi's choice; his beloved Herodotus was raised there.

So you see, Yaphiel, you were born in the Roman province of Asia thanks to your uncle's devotion to the greatest of Greek travellers!

We consider heading to Persia instead, but I do not speak any of the local languages and know almost nothing of the customs of the various peoples living there. It would seem prudent to remain under the dominion of an enemy we know, at least for the time being.

I carry the ponderous weight of two ever-present worries on our journey out of Judaea. The first are the spies that Annas may have sent after us and who may learn somehow of our true identities. The second is Ilana, for every morning and evening I must find her nourishment. Though I cannot begrudge the wet nurses I approach their insistence on a modest payment, the expense soon leaves us with little silver. It becomes only too clear that I ought to have taken with me the jewellery belonging to my sisters, so that I might sell it in the villages and towns we visit.

Often, lying with my children at night, I picture Gephen on our rooftop, scenting our sudden departure and wondering where we have gone. They say that cats can track their families over hundreds of miles, but I am not of the opinion that we shall ever see him again. Who now will care for his wounds when he fights his rivals?

I pray each morning for Ehud. I hope that my neighbours were able to find him a capable physician and that he has returned to his four children.

Ayin proves a pleasant travelling companion, though fearful of our unfamiliar lodgings. We spend as much time with him outside as possible and stand him on the branches of trees, since he always feels at home when he is looking down from a perch.

Yeshua . . . Whenever I see something of beauty – an ivory-coloured egret feeding in a brook or an apple tree in blossom – I think, *He ought to be with us; it would cheer him to see the wonders of the earth at springtime.*

When tears overwhelm me, I go off by myself. At my worst moments I am certain I shall never be able to make a new life and that my children would be better off with someone else. And yet, each morning I lead us closer to Halikarnassos. This is how I discover that I am the kind of man who continues walking even when he does not know if he has chosen a worthy destination.

I breathe the warm air of safety again only when we cross the border into Samaria, where Annas is unlikely to have any spies.

The threat from bandits and brigands forces us to travel only during the day, and we are always careful to sleep within the walls of a town or perimeter of a village. All the same, thieves ambush us on the coastal road leading to Tripolis a little over a fortnight after our flight from Bethany. The swaggering leader of the ragged band takes Nahara's amber necklace and puppet of a flower-seller and forces me – his dagger pressing into my cheek – to surrender Yeshua's calliper. I fall to my knees and explain that I cannot give it up, since it was a gift from my dearest friend, who was recently murdered, but he laughs and recommends that I find myself a new best friend.

He permits me to keep my scroll of *In the Beginning*, however, since I tell him that I am a scribe and that it is holy writing.

I try to sell it in Tripolis, but the booksellers there scent my poverty and offer me but a fraction of the manuscript's true value, so I keep it. That proves a mistake; two days later, as we are trudging through waist-high weeds towards a small pond where we can bathe, six marauders ambush us and carry off the scroll and all that is left of our provisions.

In consequence, for more than a fortnight, we survive on guile and what I can beg. Never – not even during our years of hardship after my father's death – have I been so aware of the generosity hiding in each crust of bread and the sweet and precious solidity of each bean that we are able to scrounge.

Then, unexpectedly, good fortune hails us one morning on the road north during a cold drizzle.

A cheerful old man in a donkey cart asks if we need shelter. When I explain about my starving baby, he asks for a look at her and tells me, smiling benevolently, that all-merciful Eleos has brought us together so that she might live.

He explains that the daughter of the farmer for whom he works has milk enough for Ilana, since her own infant girl died in childbirth just a few days earlier.

The farm belongs to a wealthy Sidonian named Lycophron. Soon, thanks to his daughter, Dido, Ilana regains her health and joy.

We are so tired of trudging down the backroads of Zion by then that we decide to ask Lycophron if we might work for him for a time. And so it is that Yirmi becomes his house servant while I labour in his fields from sun to sun, all the way through to the autumn.

Just after my fellow fieldworkers and I have harvested Lycophron's generous horizon of barley, he informs me that he will have no work for me over the winter. He is eager to employ my son permanently, however, and his daughter would like to keep Ilana. But I cannot give away my little girl, of course, and I have not laboured since I was sixteen years old to see Yirmi spend his youth scrubbing walls and floors.

When I give Lycophron my decision, Dido grows so blustery with recriminations and curses that we dare not spend even one more night with her for fear she will have me murdered and steal Ilana. I have bought myself a new vine-knife, and I make ready to use it, but Lycophron disregards his daughter's pleas and issues us grudging permission to set out again for Halikarnassos.

*

It is a wonder that Ilana and I survive the final portion of our journey, since there are days when I can find her no milk, and she fusses and shrieks all night. In one accursed hamlet, the inhabitants refuse me a single day's supply of ewe's milk even when I offer my sandals and cloak as payment.

We live mostly on bread, leeks and wild greens that we gather on riverbanks. On every Greek grave mound we pass I place a stone and pray for the Lord to protect and preserve my children, and, once, I sketch Yeshua from memory on a discarded square of papyrus I find in a dungheap, and every contour and line is a prayer for my old friend to show himself to me again, but he does not.

As a result, perhaps, I develop the habit of speaking aloud to him as we walk. Do my children regard me as having lost my mind? Very likely they realize that I have no other choice.

At one terrible moment on our trip, Ilana grows so weak that she is no longer able to cry. Though I coat her lips with olive oil, they bleed. And her neck grows swollen from some foul vapours or spell that I do not know how to combat.

By this time, I have sold everything I own except for my tunic, so I go everywhere barefoot. I am begging in the square beside the Temple of Athena in Tarsus, in the corner where the mendicant eunuchs come to ask for alms, when a kind-hearted and spritely Phoenician girl named Selene takes pity on us and leads us to the home of her sister-in-law whose name is Europa. That graceful young mother holds my starving infant to her breast without hesitation and whispers encouragements to her as she suckles. Healthy colouring returns to Ilana's face after only a few hours, and within three days she is smiling again and sleeping through the night.

Europa, may she be blessed for ever, asks for nothing in return, but Yirmi and I pay for our lodgings and our meals by labouring in the vineyard and orchard that belongs to her and her husband. Even after Ilana is fit for travel, we end up staying with that generous young mother for another several days, because she returns our sense of trust to us.

And now you know, Yaphiel, why your two sisters are named Selene and Europa.

A disagreeable surprise greets us when we finally reach Halikarnassos, for, instead of the lustrous and cultured city we have expected, we find a musty and provincial town cursed by clouds of flies, with emaciated, flea-infested dogs snoozing in every shady spot and feral cats hissing at us from the tops of walls. I imagine all the luckless residents whom we pass thinking what Tiresias asks of Odysseus: *What brings you here, forsaking the light of day to see this joyless kingdom of the dead?*

The home belonging to Herodotus is, by local tradition if not actual fact, next to the shambling wreckage that was once the city's theatre, and, to pay our respects, we climb to it over fallen columns and broken statuary. Only one wall remains standing, etched with licentious graffiti in both Greek and Latin.

One lesson that our journey to Halikarnassos teaches me: no matter what their religion or geographical origin, young men will nearly always be eager to engrave comments about how mighty their phallus is and with whom it was last put to use.

We spend only a few hours in the abominable town, and, because of its pestilent vapours and mists, spend that night sleeping in the surrounding hills beside a shepherd's hut. Mosquitoes keep me cursing the gods of Olympus most of the night, and, in the morning, a representative of the town council tells me that there have been complaints about our trespassing on Roman-held properties. He demands that we leave as quickly as possible.

That morning, a fisherman with an ulcerous ear, speaking the hard-to-fathom local dialect, ferries us to the island Rodos for a small payment. We decide to try our fortune there because we have been told that the island's winds are always fresh and health-giving and that a modest Jewish community has flourished there for centuries.

We find the island blessed with turquoise waters and enterprising citizens. The fish are so plentiful in the bays that no one goes hungry. The public gardens are planted with beds of colourful flowers and magnificent sycamores.

That same week, a Jewish stonemason named Nikas – whose family, he says, came from the Galilee three centuries earlier – offers us two long-neglected rooms at the back of his house. Just next door lives a wealthy family that has made their fortune cultivating fields of the local *orkhis* plant, whose roots are used to make a frothy drink that Yirmi in particular grows to appreciate. They take to my children straight away, and the elder daughter in the family – Zoe – watches over Nahara and Ilana when my son and I are working.

At this time, I permit Nahara to become a girl once again.

After seven months as Nikas' assistant, I receive my first commission for a mosaic from a local aristocrat. With my profits, I rent my own storeroom and workspace near the port.

During my first weeks in my new place of business, my loneliness becomes a stalking presence, standing beside everyone I speak to, even my children. As a result, perhaps, I begin to write down everything I can remember about my final week with Yeshua. Over the next two months, I make more than three thousand notes and commentaries on papyrus. Indeed, compiling a corpus of details, impressions and speculations about what has happened seems a *mitzvah* I must fulfil or I will not be able to rejoin my life.

Over our first five years on Rodos, Yirmi studies with a youthful rabbi named Georgious who has a deep knowledge of Greek philosophy but who understands it from right to left, so to speak, since he insists – comically at times – on giving the works of Antisthenes, Zenon of Kitieus and many other Greek luminaries distinctly Jewish interpretations. Did you know that the Fallen Angels are none other than the Greek Titans? And that the Babylonians who built their prideful tower were simply copying the Aloadae?

Three years after our arrival, I purchase a small home on a graceful sun-blessed hillock overlooking the bay. It requires extensive repairs and smells of the urine of the abundant feral cats living in the vicinity, but a jasmine vine has taken over the roof and pink mallow bushes grow amongst the weeds in the garden, and all that beauty seems a very favourable omen.

Ayin grows ill shortly after we move in and, one chilly autumn day, he closes his golden eyes for the last time. We bury him in our garden, and I spend my week of grief soaking in wine, as is my wont, though neighbours tell me that it is improper for me to weep over what they call a *mere bird*.

It has long astonished me that so many Jews and Greeks alike reach adulthood without coming to see that we have the same capacities and traits as all the creatures of the field and forest and sea and sky. Is that not, after all, the unspoken message of the animal-headed gods that the Egyptians worship?

Do our new neighbours and acquaintances believe me when I tell them that I am an Ionian born in a secluded hamlet half a day's walk from Miletus? In general, the inhabitants of Rodos ask few questions of foreigners, since they consider themselves far superior to all visitors. When anyone does try to take my lyre from its locked case, I tell them that, just prior to reaching the island, I suffered the death of both my wife and a sister and that I am incapable of discussing my past without weeping.

Nahara is only seven years old when we reach Rodos, and over our first three or four years there she occasionally reveals more than she ought to about our lives in Judaea, but, by the time she is twelve, she has learned to keep our past in a secret hiding place.

I vow never to return – or permit my children to return – to Zion.

During our first years on our island, I keep to myself and make no close friendships. When loneliness threatens to drive me screaming from my prayer room, I visit the quietest and most comfortable of the brothels by the port.

To compare every man and woman you meet to your dead loved ones is a particularly seductive curse. Indeed, I have been able to make only one true friend over the course of nearly thirty years on Rodos. I shall call him Agapetos. He is a talented ceramicist and also wise and amusing and exceedingly kind to me and my children. I have confided my true identity only to him and his widowed younger sister, who shares his home.

Yaphiel, it occurs to me now that you may not know that our neighbours used to call your mother Thetis, the Nereid who was mother to Achilles. Indeed, she spent entire months of her childhood playing in the gentle waves of our coastline with her little friends and elder siblings, and she swam like a dolphin by the time she was nine or ten. In the summer, the sun browned her skin to the colour of cedarwood.

How many times I had to tug her from the summer waters even after the sun had been swallowed by sea!

She always shared my bed at night when she was small, and to this day I sleep better if there is a fragrance of sand and salt around me.

If you ever become a father, dearest grandson, as I hope you will, then you will know the amaranthine joy of holding a tiny daughter in your embrace and feeling the unstoppable growth of the world working through her.

I also wish you to know your mother saved me from the life of bitter and angry recrimination, for she was Yeshua's last gift to me and to gaze at her was also to gaze at him – and to know that he still wanted something from me.

When Ilana was small, she and I would often walk by the sea, and, with her little hand in mine, I would wonder how everything had changed so completely in my life. One moment I was living with my sisters in Bethany, without any expectations of having another child, and the next I was in Rodos, seated in the sand with a five-year-old, telling her all that Grandfather Shimon had taught me about the constellations.

Sometimes, seated in my prayer room, facing Yerushalayim, I would speak to Yeshua about Ilana. Once he told me that I had always been meant to be a grandfather to many children, which was a shock to me.

Do other men hear the voice of the dead as plainly as I do? There are times I think I have been blessed by having only the slenderest borders – the width of a night-time whisper – between my thoughts and those whose souls have ascended. .

53

Your father's parents first broached the possibility of his marriage to your mother when she was eight years old. Unfortunately, they spoke to me as if they were granting me a monumental favour by considering Ilana for their son, since she and I were of dubious lineage. And yet they patronized me with such eager and seething delight in their eyes that the patient birdwatcher in me couldn't help but admire them as perfect examples of the tiny provincial finches one encounters the whole world over.

I concealed a far more serious doubt about them, however, for although your grandfather Heracles had studied philosophy and was a successful exporter of the Rodian wine that is flavoured with pine resin, I was quite certain that he had never read anything more insightful than his own marriage contract. I apologize if that sounds unkind to you, but it is the truth, and, as you now have reason to understand, I have always been overly protective of your mother. I would never have permitted her to marry into a family in which learning was held in contempt.

I gave Heracles to understand my doubts, and straight away he countered by ridiculing my foreign ways then proclaimed in a smug, censorious voice that he would never come to the home of so insolent a labourer again, which was confirmation that my strategy had been . . . a perfect success!

Some four years later, however, your father introduced himself to me one day near the Temple to Athena and asked permission to converse with me. Under the shade of the beneficent sycamores shading the nearby square, sitting on one of the marble benches, he vowed that he would never prevent Ilana from continuing her study of philosophy and mathematics, even if his parents disapproved.

At this time, your father was a strong-willed youth of sixteen years and already a renowned musician. Indeed, he never left home without his *cithara*, and he kept it on his lap as we talked, which charmed me. He was a tense and vibrant young man, quick of speech and movement, and I was struck immediately by his unusual face, with its large and magnificent Dorian nose, which made him look like a proud young hawk.

As you know, Yaphiel, you resemble your father quite closely – with your glorious beak-like nose and quick sunlit smile – though you have also been blessed with Ilana's soft physical grace and comical gifts. If you will permit me a more intimate tone, you also have something of your mother's need for solitude. Often, I have seen you walk away from your cousins when they are keen to include you in a game – as though you had to safeguard your loneliness.

How I greatly respect you for not running from silence!

On my initial two visits to your grandparents' home, I was moved and impressed by the jubilant melodies that your father coaxed from his cithara and the bee-like swiftness of his fingers. When I invited him to my home, he spoke to Nahara, Ilana and me about the career as a musician that he envisaged for himself. At the time, Ilana was a twelve-year-old Nereid with slender hips; she had not yet stepped into the sunrise of womanhood. She told me that evening that she found your father endearing but odd, and, when I asked for a more fulsome assessment, she giggled as though embarrassed by her own feelings. That seemed a sideways admission of interest, so I invited him to journey with me to Ephesus to visit your Uncle Yirmi, since you can learn much that is hidden about a person when you travel with him. Also, I wished to have my son's opinion of him.

Kassandros proved himself a cheerful and considerate companion, and, in each town we visited, his cithara made him the friend of one and all. We stayed mostly at modest inns on our journey, and on each night he played me to sleep with tender-heated Lydian melodies, which proved the cure to my lifelong insomnia.

I decided to give my consent to the marriage while staying with Yirmi, who became an older brother to your father over the course of that week together. All that was left was Ilana's agreement, since I had long ago vowed to my sister Mia that I would never force a husband upon my first daughter, and I saw no reason to change that wise policy with my second.

Yirmi, who had already journeyed into the hinterlands of Parthia, had introduced in Ilana his wanderlust, and, since she knew that she would not be able to spend more than a few days away from home while her children were small, she asked to be able to put off her marriage until she was fifteen and to travel with me whenever possible over the coming three years. With that agreement in hand, all the marriage details were settled quickly with your father's parents, and, over the next three years, I took your mother with me on trips to as far as Cemenelum in the west and Babylon in the east. Just before her wedding, we invited Kassandros and his mother along with us to Alexandria, so that he might get to know Ion and Ariston and my aunt Esther.

On our journey, I revealed to Kassandros my true name and told him of my past. I explained why my children and I had been forced to flee Bethany and take on new identities. My confessions shocked him, of course, but he reassured me that he understood our reasoning and agreed to keep our past a secret – even from any children that he and Ilana would have.

'We will explain to them as they come of age,' I assured him.

Just prior to our first supper in Alexandria – of the Egyptian-style lamb stew for which my aunt is renowned – I enquired after our friends and enemies in Zion, and my cousins gave me the glorious news that both Annas and Caiaphas were dead.

Never again would I have to lock every door and window in my house and wonder when and where my children might be confronted by an assassin.

As for Pilatus, he had been called back to Rome a few years after my departure. My cousins knew nothing more of him or his astrologer Augustus Sallustius. To my tearful relief, however, they assured me that Ehud had survived his wounds and was living in the Galilee with his family.

As I had long expected, Yehudah of Kerioth had come to a sad end; my cousins informed me that he had hanged himself in the garden of Gat Smane shortly after Yeshua's crucifixion. Though they could not say whether he had chosen one of the trees he had helped us plant twelve years before, I felt certain that he must have.

I could find no one in Alexandria who knew anything of the fate of Lucius, so I sent off correspondence to him without delay and asked him to reply to me care of my cousins, and after I returned to Rodos I received a letter that Abibaal had dictated to a scribe. In it, the old slave told me that my former patron had died several months after my flight from Bethany. Apparently he had taken ill after a festive supper one summer's evening – at which there had been a great many aristocratic guests, including several Roman dignitaries – and had died in his sleep. Poisoning? Abibaal made no speculations in that regard, but I read into his words that Annas might have discovered Lucius' allegiance to Yeshua and had had him murdered.

Abibaal also told me that, subsequent to my escape from Bethany, Lucius had investigated the failure of our scheme to win Yeshua's release. It seems that my old friend had indeed been brought before the court astrologer, Augustus Sallustius, as we had hoped, but he had refused to demonstrate any of the powers I had ascribed to him. In addition, he had shown contempt for his host as an idol-worshipper and had accused him of using his talents for evil.

I cannot vouch for the accuracy of this account, but, if it is true, then – just as I'd feared at the time – Yeshua was unwilling to bow down to a false deity, even one who could have spared his life.

Aunt Ester took me aside on my first night in her home and informed me that my sister Marta had blossomed after my departure and Mia's murder. Her renown as a weaver had spread across Judaea, and she now employed four other women in the small factory she had set up in my house.

Was Marta flourishing now because her life's work had been accomplished? After all, Mia was dead and I was living in a faraway province.

That possibility loosened my tongue, and I told Ester of a speculation that I had never dared share with anyone: that Marta had informed our father's murderer where and when to find him alone. I added that it had long seemed as if my sister had consumed our family like a snake swallowing a lamb – serenely, quietly and expertly, one limb at a time.

Though Ester dismissed my speculations as impossible, I read in the way she stood up to leave me, her hand clutching at her neck, that her suspicions of my sister for the death of her younger brother were far older than mine.

Yaphiel, your parents were married on our return to Rodos, and you were born two years later, a little more than a year after your sister Tamar. By then, your family had relocated to Ephesus.

Twelve years have passed since then. In less than a month you will be thirteen. You are on the verge of manhood – and very nearly the same age as Yirmi when we fled from Judaea.

On the day of our departure, I did not dare look back to see my home in Bethany vanishing in the distance, but I have searched the town every day since then for all I might have done differently.

A history made of *ifs* – such is the life of mortal men.

54

Dearest grandson, I know I have tried your patience with this serpentine story. I imagine that you have been asking yourself for some time, *Why has this ancient grandfather of mine written so extensively of the past to me?*

A little more patience, *dodee;* you are, in part, to blame for this flood of ink, so, before I make my request of you, I must tell you how you yourself summoned it forth from me!

Four months ago, you visited me here on Rodos and stayed for two Sabbaths. Near the end of our time together, I heard odd noises coming from my secret prayer room, and I was certain that one of the island's playful dormice had slipped inside and, having little regard for learning, was nibbling away at one of my papyrus scrolls. I fetched my broom, intending to sweep him flying into my garden, but, when I eased the door open, I discovered a creature far larger and more troublesome than I had expected.

You were seated with your legs crossed, holding a cup of wine. My blue ceramic jug – only half full, as I recall – stood beside you. With a horrified grimace, you erupted into tearful apologies. So concerned was I to allay your fears that I fumbled my words, but what I meant to say is that it is natural for a boy your age to sneak across the border of adulthood now and again, either alone or accompanied by companions. There is no shame in it.

You were stunned that I fetched another cup and asked you to fill it to the brim rather than give you a reprimand. I confess that seeing your shocked countenance made me do a brief victory dance inside my head. Confounding the expectations of others is often so great a joy that I tend to indulge in it whenever I can. And now that I am an old felucca with six decades of wind in my sails, I need not even apologize for the eccentric turns of course I choose.

I lit a second oil lamp and dropped down close to you. We were seated on the first mosaic I made in my new home, *The Living Torah Greeted by Bee-Eaters*. You had positioned yourself next to Yeshua, and I made myself comfortable under my terebinth tree. I always sit there to welcome the Sabbath to Rodos. Indeed, it is the perfect spot for me to send my soul on its travels, for, when exhaustion summons it home, my eyes are welcomed back by my cerulean-blue bee-eaters speaking to Yeshua in their opalescent language.

As I have already had reason to mention to you, the Lord Most High manifests Himself in limitless guises, appearing in the form most appropriate to each of us, and in my case – as you have guessed by now – He has nearly always made his presence known to me while wearing feathers.

You asked me about the naked man in the mosaic, so I told you his name, and I spoke of the dream of an eagle that I had had when I was a boy and how, as I recounted it to Yeshua, he decided to join our paths together.

To speak to you about Yeshua, I was forced to reveal to you my true name and tell you of my parents and sisters – and swear you to silence about such matters. I spoke only superficially about my friend's special nature, however, because my memories of him began to blaze as I told you of our Torah studies, turning my inadequate words to ash.

You went on to question me about the black flames in the *menorah* in the mosaic that covers my south-facing wall, which, as you now know, is a small copy of the one I did years ago in Lucius' swimming pool. I answered you hesitantly, since I am not permitted to speak to a young man your age about how we may open and close its gates. Also, I have lost the habit of discussing Yechezkel's Chariot and Yaaqov's Ladder in any meaningful way; on Rodos, everyone except my friend Agapetos and his sister are certain that I am just an illiterate Ionian mosaic-maker.

Once you knew that I had spent many years in Judaea, you encouraged me to speak to you about the wonders of Yerushalayim. I started with the Temple, explaining how its successive courts represent the different levels of our soul, but, when I spotted a request in your eyes for a more familiar story, I told you again about how I was threading my way through the foul-smelling filth of Ge Hinnom when I heard the desperate cries of a baby girl coming from a basket dangling from an oak tree. Now you understood, of course, that I was not a traveller in Judaea when I found your mother but instead a resident of Bethany.

'Ilana called to me and no one else,' I told you, and, since I could see you needed to hear more, I spoke for a time of our escape from Judaea.

Like you, it comforts me to know what is coming next in your mother's story. In this case, however, I could not have predicted what would follow my recollections.

'*Pappous,* I'd like to see where you found my mother,' you chirped.

Shock made me turn to face the wall, as though someone had died.

You smiled innocently when our eyes next met, unaware of the terror that was now crouching behind me. And then you sent me crashing through the foundations of my mind. 'Is Yeshua still there?' you asked. 'You could take me to meet him.'

I left you without a word. And did not reply to your calls. You see, the gap between the life I had made for myself in Rodos and what it might have been was staring out at me from your eager brown eyes, which are also your mother's, and this distance was so wide and deep that it held all I had done since fleeing Bethany twenty-nine years earlier. Indeed, at that moment, it also held everything I would ever do.

As I stared out across that expanse, I knew I could not fulfil your request.

I hope you can understand now why I was unable to remain with you that day or even speak of why I had fled. All lives, dear Yaphiel, have their sorrows and regrets, and we sometimes require time to ourselves if we are to keep from drowning in them.

That evening, I tried to make up for my rudeness by requesting that you play your cithara and sing for me. But I have studied you closely since you were no bigger than a squirrel, and I am familiar with all your different forms of silence, and I knew you were on the verge of tears the entire time.

I am sorry to have failed you so miserably.

I started to write this scroll to explain myself to you and to make the apology that I have just made. At first, I intended it to occupy no more than an hour of your time, but I soon discovered that the point of my calamus was, in truth, the entrance to a memory palace, giving me access to events of my past that I had long forgotten.

It was then that I fetched my strongbox from its hiding place and began to look over my notes about my last days in Zion. I realized straight away, of course, that I ought to use them to guide my writing. And I finally understood why I had stood before Yeshua on his cross and vowed to remember everything that had taken place that day.

The words and sentences grew and multiplied, and, to give them the honest and useful form that all living things deserve, I was obliged to rewrite them myriad times in my mind before giving them the permanence of ink, until what you now have in your hands became a great deal more than a compendium of disparate recollections, though what it is exactly I cannot say.

You are the first of my grandchildren to sit with me in my prayer room, since I was certain I would feel cornered if I allowed one of you inside. After all, it is there that I make concessions to no one about what I ought to be. And it is there that I study Torah with Yeshua. Yet once I discovered you hiding inside the room – a tipsy little mouse! – I felt graced.

Dearest Yaphiel, had I had not found your mother you would be the grandson of another man. But for Yeshua, you and I would never have met.

A door opens and we step through, and we are for ever changed.

Did you know that a thousand such doors appear before us each day, and behind each of them is a different world? Can you imagine how it makes me shudder to think that Ilana might never have called out to me?

But she did cry out. And my sister Mia warned Yirmi in time for him to save his life. And Yirmi gathered up Nahara and told Ehud about the killers in our house, and that righteous giant raised his sword . . .

All my children are safe. And they now have sons and daughters of their own.

We are all still here. Often, lying awake at night, that seems inconceivable – as though it is simply too generous a destiny for a mosaic-maker who failed at the most important task he was ever given. Sometimes I stop in the middle of a walk through the forest near my home and gaze around me at the congregation of life going about its business under the immense, heartbreakingly blue sky, and I think, *Despite the bottomless misery and oppressive solitude I've known, I've been blessed with nearly impossible good fortune.*

At your young age you walk beside a thousand different Yaphiels whom you might yet become. You have told me of a few of them that you have envisaged: the musician, the wine exporter, the ship's captain, the magician, the sculptor . . .

Will you ever see Natzeret, the town where I lived when I was your age? And, if you do, how will it change you?

Each turn you make along your journey will move you closer to the single Yaphiel who will finally take form. And one day, when you are as old as I am, you will have all but lost every chance of becoming any of the other *yous* you might have been.

Life is sad in that way. And the hard, brittle, ever-diminishing contours of identity are still something that moves me down to the sea on many nights to ask the moon and stars if they, too, have ever wished to be other than what they are.

On several occasions, I have met other grandfathers and grandmothers limping along over the warm soft sand, looking out towards the horizon with their leaky eyes, as though in search of a lost love, and we have spoken of our insomnia, punctuated by that sorrow-tinted laughter that comes so easily to people who have seen their most cherished friends turned to dust, and so I have become aware that most of us never fully accept that we walk beside an entire host of selves we might have become.

Indeed, when I cede to feelings of sorrow about the way life traps us inside one mind and body, I wonder if I ought to have tried out dozens of other lives while I still had the chance.

It often seems to me that youth is one kingdom and old age quite another. And death a mysterious third.

Is affection the bridge between them? That is another of the many questions I pose to the moon on occasion.

I shall tell you two secrets that have helped me understand this important link: when I taught you my old game of Noach and the Ark, it was really my sister Mia who was speaking to you through me; and when I climbed with you to the top of the highest hillside near my home and showed you the Archer and all the other constellations, it was my Grandfather Shimon who named them for you.

When we are together, I am an astronomer, teacher, poet and actor and all those other men I might have become!

And know this: when you were first presented to me by your mother, at least three other people carried you in their arms with me and bathed you and sat you on their belly: Yeshua, Mia and Leah. Even today, when I embrace you before bed, they do, too.

You have been watched over by all the men and women who have loved me.

After you requested I take you to Yerushalayim, I pondered such connections on many a morning and evening, and I came to believe that if I did not consider your request I would fail to honour what you have meant to them – and to myself.

And yet for weeks I slept with a talisman around my neck and chanted Psalms to chase away the doubts assaulting me. Often, while working on my mosaics, I would find my hands trembling, which seemed to be the Lord's way of saying: *I shall give you no peace until you have given your grandson an answer.*

And then, as I was casting my gaze over the sea from my rooftop, imitating my old friend Ayin, a flash of insight made me climb back down with the knowledge of what was keeping me from answering you: the mystery of why Yeshua brought you into my life.

I realized I could not reply to you until I had an answer.

This, then, is the second reason why I started to write this scroll – to search the past and discover why he gave you to me.

Just half a day after I began to write to you, during the first watch of night, a disturbing, trance-like dream descended upon me. In it, I caught a glimpse of another Yaphiel – the one who will exist ten or fifteen years from now, after my death. I saw that you had become a strong and purposeful man with the tender light-infused eyes of your mother. You were seated by the palm tree in my garden, and you were playing a Lydian melody on your cithara that your father had taught you. At length, I noticed a figure behind you listening with a rapt and grateful expression – Yeshua. When our eyes met, he smiled as if to say that he was proud of you, which was when you spotted him. You ran to him as if you had known him your whole life.

This dream gave me to understand that you asked me if you would meet Yeshua in Judaea because your soul has realized that you will need to know the man who gave you to me if you are to live the life you were meant to have.

Of course, I wish he could sit with you and speak to you himself.

Or has he? Men such as Yeshua can accomplish feats far beyond our comprehension, and I would not be surprised to learn that he has written this scroll through me, though I would swear to any judge or daysman that I wrote every word of it myself.

Over the last fifteen years, I have heard a handful of different accounts of Yeshua's life and work. Three were told to me by acquaintances here in the Jewish community of Rodos, and they focused almost exclusively on the physical nature of my old friend's miracles, including – in one case – my resurrection.

I found the two other accounts quite troubling, however. In fact, they struck me as misleading and dangerous and, in one case, left me pacing my prayer room and cursing.

I heard the first of these narratives in Alexandria a decade and a half ago, on the journey I took with your mother and your father to visit Aunt Ester and other relatives. On my very first morning there, my cousin Ion informed me that Yeshua's mission had splintered into several different sects in Judaea and the Galilee and that their adherents had spread word of his activities west to Rome, east to the Parthian border, south into Egypt and north to the Greek settlements on the shores of the Hospitable Sea.

Ion and I were eating breakfast when he gave me this news, and hearing that Yeshua's teachings had spread far beyond the borders of Zion so stunned me that I cut the palm of my hand with the knife I'd been using to slice open an Egyptian melon, so that even today, whenever I receive some unexpected news, I see the heavy fruit breaking open on the floor and scent its sweet yellow pulp.

While I staunched the blood, Ion responded to my questions about old friends, and I was particularly relieved to hear that Yohanon and Yaaqov were not only still alive but amongst those teaching Yeshua's precepts far and wide. They had apparently founded two synagogues in Judaea and one each in the Galilee and Samaria.

I realized how sorely mistaken I had been to believe that Yeshua's dreams had vanished from our world, and I spent my first night in Alexandria chanting and praying – giving voice to my profound gratitude.

The next afternoon, Aunt Ester told me that a charismatic follower of Yeshua's lived in the main Jewish quarter of the city. He was a preacher and healer who had adopted the name of Theophanus ben Netzach, undoubtedly intending to communicate the idea of victory through the Lord's intervention.

As you may know, *theophanus* is Greek for the appearance of the Almighty, and *netzach* is Hebrew for victory, often with the connotation that it has been won through considerable struggle.

Ester had once spoken with this Theophanus, whom she referred to as a man of considerable magic. He had told her that he had seen Yeshua preach in the Galilee on three occasions when he was a young man, and he further avowed to her that my old friend had initiated him into the mysteries of Yechezkel's Chariot in Capernaum. Since that seemed entirely possible, I slipped out of the house that evening to hear him preach, going in secret because I feared that emotions long dormant might overwhelm me.

As might to be expected – after so long an absence from Alexandria – I promptly lost my way in the labyrinthine streets of the main Jewish quarter. I questioned several passers-by to no avail, but a young woman, noticing my despair, came to my aid.

I studied her with curious attention, for not only did she possess the dark enigmatic beauty one often sees in Egyptians but she was missing the tips of three of the fingers on her right hand.

When I told her of my destination, her luminous green eyes opened wide with surprise, and she informed me that the Lord had guided me well, since she herself was a member of Theophanus' congregation. After I introduced myself, she told me that her name was Melitta and that she had been born and raised in Heliopolis.

Our destination proved to be close by, and, since it was too early to go inside, I invited her to sit with me on the outdoor patio of a tavern in a nearby square. When I offered her wine or posca, she gazed down at her feet and hugged her arms around her chest, as though fearing my anger, and she said – in a diffident voice – that she would be happy with just a cup of water.

If anyone had asked me for my assessment of Melitta at that instant, I would have said that she was giving me tacit proof that she had been brutalized at some time in her life.

When I asked how she had come to meet Theophanus, she told me that he had saved her from what she called *a vagrant life,* and, by way of explanation, she said that she had been orphaned at the age of ten and had turned to begging and thievery.

By that point in our conversation, Melitta had already proved so articulate that I found it hard to believe that she had received no education, but she assured me that she could neither read nor write and that she had made her home in the forests and fields until she first heard Theophanus preaching shortly after her twenty-first birthday. She was now twenty-four.

To explain her extensive vocabulary, she told me that Theophanus and his disciples read aloud to those who studied with them. 'I have heard all of Mosheh's scripture,' she told me with pride. 'So if I can speak sensibly now, it's because I have listened closely to his words.'

Melitta went on to tell me that she never stayed in one place for more than a week until she met Theophanus. 'I moved around more than most thieves,' she told me, 'because I even stole food from the altars in the Greek temples – from Zeus and Athena and all the other divinities. And, although I told myself I believed in nothing and no one, I feared their revenge and always hurried away to the next town or village. Sometimes I even risked travelling at night.' She laughed mirthlessly. 'Perhaps I wanted the gods to take revenge on me by sending bandits to chase me down and hurt me.'

She shook her head in judgement at the reckless waif she'd been, then smiled while shrugging, as if to say that her difficult times no longer mattered. Curiously, her fleeting smile seemed a cry for help more than anything else.

'Were you ever caught by town officials or the people you stole from?' I asked.

'Yes, and I was flogged and beaten many times.' She raised her disfigured hand. 'A bailiff in Berea chopped off the ends of my fingers so that everyone would know I was a wicked girl. Then he bound me with rope and left me for dead in the mountains to the west of the city.'

'But you survived even that.'

'Yes. The Lord guided two peasants to me – elderly sisters – and they took me in.' She shakes her head again. 'I ended up thanking them by stealing all their silver.'

'Was it Theophanus who put an end to all that?'

'Yes, he fed me and clothed me,' she said with a solemn nod, 'and he spoke to me of the flame of the Lord that, despite all the terrible things I'd done, was still flickering inside me.' She took a long, pensive sip of her water. 'On my request, his followers taught me a trade as well. I'm a midwife now, Lazarus.' She was silent for a time, gazing inwardly, considering the turns in her journey, I speculated. 'Since meeting Rabbi Theophanus . . . How can I explain to you? Only now do I realize that it was my own shame that led me around for eleven years.' She looked around, this way and that. 'My shame pursues me now – every moment of every day. I can't even imagine myself entirely free of it.'

Her intelligence and honesty made me feel as if I had stumbled upon a woman I was meant to meet. Still, I wondered why she trusted me enough to tell me her story, and, after speaking to her briefly about my life on Rodos, I managed – hesitantly and awkwardly – to ask her.

'Theophanus has counselled me to let my shame reveal itself on occasion. In that way, he says, I will get to know it better, and, when I do, it will stop clamouring for my attention all the time.'

As if to obey his words, she opened her sack to me. Beneath a jumble of beans and gnawed chicken bones was something round and brown that might have been a withered pomegranate. 'I still hoard my food,' she told me, 'like I did when I was just a girl.'

Her sack smelled of decay, and the sour face I made prompted her to close it again and clutch it tightly to her chest. Her eyes were moist when they looked at me.

'I'm sorry I've made you uncomfortable,' she said.

'No, please, don't be. You didn't do anything wrong. The bad smell . . . it surprised me, that's all.'

She nodded her understanding, but I sensed something hard in her now – that she'd reached a wall inside herself beyond which she would not go. At least, not with a stranger.

If Theophanus has such a brave and sensitive young woman as a follower, then I will like him, too, I thought. Still, I dared not confess to her my true identity.

To my questions about what she had learned about Yeshua from Theophanus, she replied that she had come to regard him as the *Christos.* When I asked what she meant by that Greek term, she replied that the Lord had taught Yeshua the secrets of creation and anointed him as our future king – and asked him to help us create an age of peace and justice.

She added that she was certain that – with the aid of her beloved mentor and other courageous men and women – Yeshua would soon achieve that goal.

'And yet, he is no longer with us,' I told her gently.

'Perhaps not, and yet he speaks to me.' She brushed some crumbs off the table between us, as though needing to put confusing thoughts in order, which reminded me – achingly – of my sister Mia.

'In truth, I think that he . . . he speaks to us all,' she said reticently. 'Though most of us are too deaf to hear him.'

'And what is he trying to tell us?'

She deliberated while gazing at a troupe of acrobats preparing their performance across the square. 'I don't know what he wants to tell the others, but whenever I think I can't go on . . . when I feel my life has been wasted, he tells me to keep walking. He says that a journey well-travelled is a worthy – even glorious – accomplishment in itself.'

That insight set a warm rain falling inside me, for I remembered a spring shower in Bethany and Yeshua telling me much the same thing – which made it seem as though Yeshua had brought Melitta to me. Though I did not yet know why.

'You believe me – I see it in you,' she said, as if it were a great surprise.

'Yes, of course I do!'

'And yet sometimes I think I'm not hearing him but only myself,' she confessed in an embarrassed whisper. Her need for help prompted her to smile again in that strange way of hers. 'Do you . . . think I'm mad?' she asked.

'What I think, Melitta, is that Yeshua has chosen you,' I replied, and, raising my hand over her, I blessed her as he would have.

To comfort her silent weeping, I spoke to her then of my admiration for Yeshua and his teachings. Unfortunately, my longing and affection for him entered my voice while I was discussing how he would embrace the lepers who came to him for help, and she cut me off to ask if I had known him.

'No, though I wish I had,' I replied.

'The way you talk of him . . . You never even saw him preach from afar?'

'Never.'

'You're certain. Perhaps he –'

'I think I would have recognized him if I had ever seen him,' I cut in.

'You can't be sure of that.'

'I don't understand. What do you mean?'

'I was told that Yeshua sometimes appeared in different guises to different people. When he was with the Father, he was able to transform himself into all sorts of things.'

'Such as?'

'Rabbi Theophanus told us that Yeshua once came to him in the form of a bird – a royal ibis. And that they spoke together.'

That news hit me hard, and I began to have second thoughts about accompanying Melitta to the synagogue to hear her teacher preach, and as we walked there I envisaged each step leading me back to Bethany and all that I was not yet prepared to revisit.

Melitta wished to sit with me in the synagogue, but I asked to be able to stand at the back by myself. Two hundred followers were soon seated on the marble flagstones of the room. Another twenty or so stood beside me.

Theophanus entered after the crowd had settled. He was perhaps fifty years of age, strong of build, with thick and unruly brown hair and intensely aware dark eyes. He wore long scarlet robes and a jewelled *hosen* around his neck, as if he were the high priest of his own temple.

After striding to the front, he turned to face Yerushalayim and spoke the Shema aloud, whereupon we in the audience echoed his words. When his assistants placed lanterns around him in a circle, I was able to see the impressive fresco of Mosheh and the burning bush behind him.

Mosheh will summon the Lord of Sinai to join us this day! I told myself, and the expectancy that gripped me was so sudden and overwhelming that I was forced to chant calming prayers to myself.

After a brief chorus of Psalm-singing accompanied by harp, flute and sistrum players, Theophanus began to preach. He spoke first of the tyranny of Rome that had reduced many amongst us to abject poverty, and his parables – delivered in a slow, commanding rhythm – entered me with such force that my hands and face began to tingle. I sat with my head down, so stunned by his eloquence – my chest banging out a message about homecoming – that I dared not look at him.

Keep listening to him closely! I heard Yeshua tell me.

Indeed, Theophanus soon proved he could inflame those of us in his synagogue with both his poetry and his calls for justice.

And that he knew Torah as well as I did.

And that he could shape silence to his purpose.

Just after he reached a particularly dramatic cadence in his evocation of Yeshua's teachings, he paused, as if waiting in the shadow of my old friend, and I think that all those assembled before him listened to the night sounds outside the temple in the certainty that the Holy One was telling us of the wonder of all of creation through the screeching cry of a nightbird and rolling of wooden carriage wheels against stone.

And then . . .

Then he lost me with a single word, and the word was *anax*, the Greek term for king.

Theophanus avowed that the man who had shown him the light of truth – Yeshua ben Yosef – had been our rightful *anax*, the inheritor of the sceptre of Shelomoh. 'Yeshua was not only our king but also the direct descendant of David,' he told his congregation.

With a moan, I realized that he seemed to have no deeper an understanding of Yeshua than the Romans who had murdered him. Yet the crowd cheered his claims.

How could so many adult men and women believe that Yeshua's goals had been so trivial? Did they think he rebelled against the priests of the Temple and Emperor in Rome simply because he wished to wear the robes of royalty and collect our taxes?

'My Kingdom is not of this world,' he had told us many times. Did they think he was lying?

Theophanus went on to describe Yeshua as the *Mashiah* who had come to us to strike down our enemies with a sword – to cast them from Egypt and the Land of Zion. In Greek, he referred to Yeshua as the Christ, as Melitta had, though, unlike her, he seemed to understand this term only as an unschooled peasant might – as a general bent on military conquest.

You are turning Yeshua into a Jewish Alexandros of Macedonia! I would have cried had I believed I could make it out of the synagogue with my head still on my shoulders, but an armed bodyguard stood at each of the doors.

Did anyone in the room but me know that Yeshua had asked us to cherish the Romans as our brothers?

When Theophanus told the crowd what now seemed inevitable – that he was Yeshua's rightful heir – I felt the ground beneath me shiver.

My gaze sought out Melitta – she was seated near the front – and I implored her to turn to me so that I might see what she was thinking. I waited for some time, but she would not face me.

He may be a man of understanding and wisdom, and I know that he has helped you, but he has reduced Yeshua to the size and shape of his own desires, I told her in my mind, and, knowing that she and all the other good people in this synagogue deserved far more, I prayed that Theophanus would lose his ambitions for kingship over the coming years.

Then I gathered up my disappointment, covered my head with my hood and rushed away.

Near the end of our month-long sojourn in Alexandria, I was able to re-establish contact with Yaaqov and Yohanon, who were both living near Yerushalayim. I also began a correspondence with Maryam of Magdala, who had moved years earlier to a place that she wished to keep secret.

Over the past three decades, Yohanon has anxiously recorded the development of the many new sects competing for the hearts of the people of Zion. He tells me that most are composed of Jews who have modified the sacred laws to include beliefs based on their understanding of Yeshua's teaching. Others, like the congregation presided over by Theophanus, welcome members who had previously worshipped the Greek, Roman, Egyptian and Phoenician divinities.

Maryam of Magdala has asked me never to reveal to anyone – not even my children –where she makes her home because some of these sects show unqualified scorn for women and have threatened her life at meetings where she has spoken of her years of association with Yeshua and her understanding of his teachings.

Several of these new faiths condemn those Jews who refuse to renounce their traditional beliefs as traitors. The most sanctimonious amongst them claim that Yeshua had abandoned Judaism long ago.

Why would he have abandoned his faith? And, if he had, would he not have sought to teach us the tenets of his new religion?

Unfortunately, a number of branches of this divisive and imprudent movement are growing in strength. Yirmi told me recently, for instance, there are now two synagogues in Ephesus for a Greek-speaking sect whose members refer to themselves as Christians and who have abandoned certain traditional commemorations and celebrations, including Yom Kippur. Furthermore, and to my immeasurable outrage, they have added prayers to Yeshua to their liturgy.

Just six months ago, I met one of their emissaries, a rabbi born in Elephantine by the name of Kalev ben Enoch. My friend Agapetos – who has studied Torah with me – met Kalev at our small synagogue and invited me to dine with him as a way of welcoming him to our island.

It was a risk to meet him, of course. After all, if he questioned me about my beliefs about Yeshua, I might once again reveal too much affection for him in my voice – or accidentally mention some facet of his life that only a friend could know. But I was too curious of him and his movement to refuse my friend's invitation.

Kalev had a fox-like face and vibrant green eyes that charmed me right away. With his affecting smile and whirling hand gestures, he looked as if he might have made a convincing and popular actor, which made me think fondly of Lucius. In a cheerful voice, he told us of how he had overcome the severe trials he had suffered on his long trip from Egypt, always – and to our delight – emphasizing the amusing details. His beautiful Judaean accent returned my spirit to my home in Bethany.

The silver broach of a dove he wore around his neck was of exquisite workmanship, and he told me that he had commissioned it from a master jeweller working in Caesarea. It symbolized, he said, Yeshua's purity of spirit and the freedom from death granted to those who believed in his words, which caused a surge of excitement in me.

Might Kalev help me with my own continuing doubts about the afterlife?

Before I dared give voice to my old worries, he asked me about my adaptation to the culture of Rodos, and we laughed together about the misunderstandings that invariably occur when we live in a place whose customs are not our own. As we talked, the moon slipped into the open window of my friend's cluttered but comfortable dining room, as though to offer our conversation its luminous blessing.

Our words turned sour, however, the moment that he told me that his intent was to establish a synagogue in one of the coastal cities of Thracia. His eyes took on a wolf-like intensity when he spoke of the obstacles some local authorities had put in his way, and, as he leaned over our table, his voice gained an arrogant, abrasive edge.

I thought it best to return to safer ground, and, to my questions about his knowledge of Yeshua's mission, he told me he had studied with two of his disciples, Andreas and Didymus, whom he described with eloquent and moving affection.

Again we seemed to be moving in the right direction, but when I asked after the fundamental beliefs and requirements of his sect, Kalev started by telling me that Yeshua had been born to a *parthenos*. Since that merely meant *girl* in the dialects of Greek that Agapetos and I spoke, we remained confused until he clarified his meaning by confiding – behind the awning of his hand – that Maryam had been a virgin.

Why the shameful whisper?

When I asked him, he told us in a definitive tone that a woman's body was a vessel for evil.

No one had dared speak such slander in my presence in decades – owing perhaps to my well-known pride in the accomplishments of my daughters – and my shock made me realize I would have to be even more careful about what I revealed to him about my life. As to how a virgin had come to be with child, Kalev told me that the Lord of Hosts went to Maryam's bed and lay with her, to which I said, 'You mean, of course, that God gave her a child through the person of her husband Yosef.'

'No, that's not what I mean at all!' he snarled, which made the hairs on the back of my neck stand up. When I took a long inquisitive look at him – to see if he truly wished to offend me – he showed me a defiant look.

I longed to reveal to him I had known Yeshua's father very well, and that he had been devoted to his wife in both spirit and flesh, but I could not.

After he had finished his explanation of Yeshua's birth, I leaned back in my chair – to seem less threatening – and likened his story to the legend of the virgin birth of Alexandros of Macedonia that is told throughout the Greek-speaking world. I told him that it is generally only believed by small children.

Kalev glared at me and gripped his silver dove. In a haughty voice, he assured me that Yeshua had been a far more powerful king than Alexandros. 'And if you do not believe in Yeshua's divine birth,' he added in a threatening tone, 'eternal life will not be granted you.'

Divine birth? I realized then that I had chosen the wrong comparison; Kalev and his friends had not turned Yeshua into Alexandros but rather into Pharaoh!

I was pleased that he threatened me, however, since that enabled me to be give voice to my growing resentment and frustration.

'But if Maryam was pregnant, then why did Yosef marry her?' I demanded.

'The child did not yet show in her womb,' he replied confidently.

'So she tricked Yosef?'

'No, she confessed to him that the Almighty had impregnated her.'

'Which she knew because she had gone to the bed of the Lord and permitted Him to enter her, so to speak?'

'An angel appeared to her,' Kalev told me, 'and he explained to her how she had come to be with child.'

'And how did this angel come to learn of her condition?'

'The Lord told him.'

'And Yosef believed Maryam's story?'

'Yes, of course.'

'For what reason?'

Kalev jumped up and banged on our table. 'Because he trusted his wife!' he shouted in frustration.

'But she was not yet his wife,' I pointed out.

'No, but she was betrothed to him.'

'Betrothed and pregnant . . . So why wasn't she stoned to death as an adulteress? Or, at the very least, sent away by her parents as a common whore?'

'Because she wasn't any of those things! I told you – the Lord had placed *His* child in her!'

'How old are you, Kalev ben Enoch?' I asked, knowing then that I was about to give in to my own worst impulses but unable to stop myself.

'Thirty-seven,' he said.

'And were you ever dropped as a baby? Or perhaps hit on your head by your father with a mallet?'

Kalev turned to our host. 'Why does this friend of yours insist on provoking me?'

'Because', I replied, 'you have expressed the single most childish understanding of the way God works through men and women – and all the creatures of the woodlands and meadows – that I've ever heard. My daughters, by the time they were seven years old, understood more than you do – and simply from watching the insects that crawl and rabbits who hop and all that participates every day in the Lord's creation.'

To my astonishment, Kalev made his hands into fists. 'You're a heretic!' he shouted. 'And if you persist in your ways, the Lord will punish you!'

I never spoke another word to Kalev. After offering a quick apology to Agapetos, I rushed out of his house and made my way home.

As I sat fuming in my prayer room, it was Melitta's face that came to me, and I saw again that idiosyncratic smile of hers that seemed to reveal so much of her despair and shame.

After a time, my memories of our conversation reminded me that she and her fellow Christians were clearing a new path forward, and that it was inevitable that they would occasionally find themselves steered on to dangerous byways by leaders with selfish objectives – arrogant men eager to charge those who disagreed with them with heresy.

Perhaps the first Galilean Jews had seemed as wrongheaded to their brethren as these Christians now seemed to me.

Listening again to my conversation with Melitta also reminded me that those men and women who believed in

Yeshua's divine birth were – like all of us – looking for the doorway out of their suffering, and they therefore deserved my understanding and empathy.

If you'd have remained calm, you could have tried to help Kalev see a different way forward, Melitta now told me in my mind. *If not for his own benefit, then for me.*

This wise counsel now seemed the reason why the Lord – or Yeshua – had brought us together. And that night, while sitting on my roof and searching out the constellations, I even began to consider that I had lost my way in Alexandria's Jewish quarter precisely so that she could help me overcome my outrage and resentment.

I sent a letter the next day to Yaaqov about my troubling conversation with Kalev, confessing my own intolerant and rude behaviour, and he informed me in his reply that entire communities – tens of thousands of adherents in Zion alone – hold Yeshua's virgin birth as a fundamental belief. 'Worse,' he wrote, 'they have come to worship my mother as a goddess – the wife of the Lord – which is why they refer to Yeshua as the son of God.'

Yaaqov added that he would not have been surprised now to learn that they believe that what dripped from the nail-wounds in his brother's heels was not the red blood of mortality but golden ichor.

While writing of his mother, he informed me that she had had to move a number of times over the previous decade and now lived far beyond the borders of Zion. She has taken an assumed name, because the moment her identity becomes known hundreds of pilgrims appear at her door wishing to worship her as if she were an idol.

'How can they really believe I'm a goddess when my beloved son was crucified in front of me and there was nothing I could do?' she wrote to me recently through a cousin of hers who has become our go-between. She fears for her life and never leaves her home during the day – and never without a bodyguard.

I have invited her to stay in my home as long as she likes, for I am convinced that her worshippers will not discover her in so isolated and unexpected a refuge, but she told me that for the time being she will remain in her chosen hiding place.

Of course, I wrote to her that if these sectarians had once seen Yeshua and Yosef together they would have immediately noticed their resemblance, but she and I both know that their insistence that her beloved husband was not her eldest son's father is but a minor flaw in their reasoning compared to their veneration of Yeshua as a Jewish Pharaoh of divine birth. Such a ludicrous belief proves that they understand very little of the man I knew. Indeed, if they are like Kalev, they cannot even comprehend that when Yosef put his seed in Maryam the Lord of Benevolence was working through him, just as He is at work in all acts of creation!

They have eyes unable to see. And ears unable to hear.

And here is something that I ought not tell you, Yaphiel, but my fear that they may one day try to move you to join them keeps me from stilling my calamus: if we employ the poetic language favoured by Mosheh in his Torah, then we may indeed say that Yeshua is the son of God, but then, to be fair, we must also say that I am also His son, as is every man who has ever been born – just as every woman is His daughter.

We are all of us children of Havvah and Adam. God does his work on earth with our hands and eyes and lips.

Let me make my point even clearer: Kalev and his friends believe that the Almighty is not manifest in His creation – not manifest in each of us. They hold that He lives apart from us in some far-off Eden.

Presumably, this distant paradise lies somewhere near the Cloudcuckooland that Aristophanes describes in *The Birds,* but you will have to ask them about its exact location, since I would prefer not to know.

When Yeshua told us all that the Kingdom of Heaven was within us, were they too busy counting heretics to hear him?

I doubt you have ever met anyone who could see three decades into the future, Yaphiel, but believe me when I tell you that there are men who can. On occasion, they are born amongst us, and they look exactly like us, but their higher soul lives a part of each day in the *Hekhal ha-Melekh.*

I think now that it is just possible that Yeshua saw across the length and breadth of his life – following a thread of destiny too slight for the rest of us to see – until he glimpsed how his message would one day become distorted and betrayed.

Now, nearly thirty years after his death, he is counting on my help.

Even if this speculation is madness, I have to defend him against those who would sculpt him into an idol and worship at his feet. What other choice do I have?

If I am right, then he did not bring me back to life to save him on Golgotha, as I used to believe. Instead, he resurrected me in flesh and spirit because he knew that he would need me one day far into the future.

Our greeting was always *I answered you in the hiding place of thunder.* It took me until after his death to realize that he chose those words because I would one day need to remember the very next verse: *I tested you at the waters of Meribah!*

Yes, I am convinced that he put me on trial in the River Jordan to see if I would be willing to risk everything for him now.

Twenty-nine years ago, a wounded man named Ehud told me that your mother – then a baby – might one day tell me why my life was of such importance to Yeshua. It seems now that he was almost right; it was not your mother who told me but you!

Only you could force me to return to my past.

Only you could bring me back to Yerushalayim.

So, my answer is *Yes, I will take you there.*

I must go, in fact.

It was the Angel Raphael who told Tobit to write down all that had happened to him. And, like that righteous Naphtalite, I have written what I know of Yeshua and all that happened to us over the days prior to his death.

I shall tell you much more about him along our journey. And I shall initiate you into the mysteries you will need to know in order to understand why I refer to him as the Living Torah.

Yirmi will want to return with us to the city of his birth. And Nahara and Ilana may wish to come as well.

Once we are there, I shall go to Yohanon and Yaaqov, and I shall ask them to help us. Perhaps Maryam of Magdala will join us as well.

Of late, Yaphiel, I have begun to feel a potent vibration inside me in the morning – as if the world is singing through my body. It is, I think, a kind of silent ecstasy and gratitude – for Yeshua's having chosen me.

I sense, too, that hope is beginning to stir again – to flex its muscles and renew its strength. Both inside me and in all the myriad creatures who inhabit our world. And even in the sun and moon.

Life takes us places we could never have expected. And only one man could have predicted what I would need to request of you at this time.

As you know, I dwell now in the kingdom of old age, and it happens that I have been deliberating about my mortality of late. I have come to understand, in fact, that I have neglected an important duty: I must select a man or woman to inherit my knowledge of Yeshua.

I hope you will not be frightened to learn that I have chosen you.

Will you come to find this an onerous inheritance? I hope not.

I ask that you occasionally reread what I have written for you and heed what I shall tell you on our journey. It will be an immeasurable comfort to me to know that you will guard and protect all that I am able to tell you of Yeshua.

It may be the greatest sadness of all to think that we shall be unable to pass on what we have learned to those who come after us, but we can try.

Show this scroll to those whom you can trust. If you come to be threatened, then pass it around in secret. Some day – whether five years from now or five thousand – men and women will want to know that Yeshua was neither a king nor Pharaoh.

Yes, this will undoubtedly be a burden to you at times, but it will also be, I think, a source of joy and comfort.

And, when the time comes, when you find yourself as stooped and frail as I am now – when you sense the end of your individual journey approaching – choose a worthy man or woman or child to take on this responsibility.

Ask me any questions you like as we talk of these days gone by and the mysteries that informed them. Doubts are good; they are proof that our minds are sojourning in lands far from home.

Perhaps I knew a Yeshua that the others did not, and the man I have described to you is vastly different from the one they would sketch and paint for you. That is as it ought to be, of course; we are each wide and deep enough to be many things, and we change shape and colour any number of times over the course of our lives, and we are often contradictory. Sometimes we have wings and at other times two arms and legs.

I would not expect my Yeshua to be the same man who appeared to Yohanon, Maryam or anyone else. Let them write of him if they want, and we shall put all our accounts together.

I do not know what we shall find in Zion. At times, you may hear me reviled and cursed for what I plan to tell Yeshua's followers. That will be hard for both of us. Still, we shall keep on walking, remembering always the teaching that Yeshua once gave Melitta – that a journey well travelled is a glorious accomplishment in itself.

A warning: I would not be entirely surprised to find Yeshua in Yerushalayim or Natzeret or somewhere along a hidden byway, either as himself or in the body of another man or woman. If he is alive, then he must be hiding where none of us would expect him to be. And waiting.

We shall look for him and call to him in our thoughts. And he will answer us any way he can.

The oak where I found your mother must be a towering giant by now, if it has not been cut down by the Romans. We shall thank it for keeping your mother safe until I could find her.

A second warning: if we come to be threatened or menaced by Roman soldiers or other men with swords, I shall send you and the rest of my family back to Rodos without me. I vowed long ago not to risk the lives of my children and grandchildren, and I shall not go back on that pledge.

This is Yeshua's final test for me, and I do not intend to fail him.

But do not worry about me. If my life must end at the tip of a sword, then so be it. My journey has been blessed with more affection and friendship than I could ever have hoped for.

And I shall not be alone, for he will be with me.

55

Dearest Yaphiel, I have been looking for a way to introduce the first of the mysteries to you – of what is often called the Sacred Treasure – before we set out on our journey. Last night, while seated in my prayer room, under my terebinth tree, a brief story came to me. It is not true – in the sense that Yeshua never greeted the visitor I write about. Yet it is true enough, for it will tell you about the Sacred Treasure in a way that is consistent with his teachings.

What I write here might very well have happened – indeed, it has taken place many times in the world that exists beyond the one we see. Through it, I hope you will begin to understand that, although we are certain we are creatures of a particular time and place, we are nothing of the kind. We are, in fact, a great deal more than that.

Will Yeshua come to you as you read my words? I hope so, because I know he would wish to tell you this particular tale himself.

A young sandal-maker from Isfahan once dreamed of jewels and gold hidden in the walls of the City of David in Yerushalayim. In his dream, a strangely familiar voice coming out of a thick mist told him that he would only be able to find happiness by taking possession of this treasure, so over the course of three months he travelled across desert and mountain to reach Judaea. When, at last, he found himself by the walls of the City of David, he realized he had not had any notion of their grandeur. He understood that it might take him many years, if ever, to locate the treasure.

And even then, how could he claim it as his own?

Yeshua was passing by at that very moment, on his way to have supper with me and my family in Bethany. After introducing himself to the Persian, he asked him the reason for his grim countenance. The young man decided it would be best to tell this humbly dressed but kind-hearted resident of Yerushalayim the truth; perhaps he could locate the treasure and they could divide it equally.

After he had heard the sandal-maker's story, Yeshua said to him, 'I have often had a similar dream, but in mine the treasure is hidden in Isfahan. It is in a house on a street near the Temple of the followers of Zarathustra.'

Yeshua and the Persian discussed the appearance of the houses and shops in this dream. By making use of clues that the young man unwittingly gave him, Yeshua was able to contrive a detailed description of the visitor's own street.

'The treasure . . . it's on the street where I live!' exclaimed the Persian excitedly.

'I suspected as much when I saw you,' Yeshua replied. 'Tell me more about the house where the treasure is hidden.'

'I saw flowers in the courtyard – pink oleander, or perhaps they were some other flower that I mistook for –'

'Might they have been roses?' the man interrupted.

'Yes, I think you might be right,' Yeshua told him, and he closed his eyes tightly, feigning deep concentration. 'They were lovely – a certain shade of . . . is it red? Or perhaps the colour of fire, or maybe even . . .'

'Fire-coloured – that's what they are! My friend, you saw my house in your dream! And I understand now who you are and why you came to me. You're a sorcerer, aren't you?'

'All I can tell you is that I am who I am,' Yeshua replied.

'I could have encountered a hundred thousand other men but it was you I met. It cannot be an accident.'

Yeshua closed his eyes and said, 'I remember other details now – in my dream the treasure was hidden under the bed of the owner of the house with fire-coloured roses.'

The man smiled, but then – sensing that this Jewish sorcerer might be trying to fool him – took a step back. Might he be lying in order to keep the treasure in the City of David for himself? 'But if you have dreamed so clearly of a magnificent treasure in Isfahan,' he asked, 'why didn't you go there to find it? All my neighbours would have recognized my house from your description and directed you there.'

'It was only a dream and not a prophecy,' Yeshua replied. 'Can you really believe I would travel all the way to Isfahan, risking scorpions and snakes and bandits and desert-demons and tyrants, for a treasure that might or might not be under the bed of a man I have never met? Especially because if jewels and gold are indeed hidden there, they will belong only to the owner of the house and not to me.'

Impressed by Yeshua's reasoning and encouraged by his story, the sandal-maker started back for Isfahan that very day. Three months later, when he reached his house, he lifted away his bedding and the jumble of possessions he always kept beneath his mat, including the bronze hand mirror he used to groom himself each morning. Since nothing resembling a treasure was immediately visible, he removed the mosaic floor with a hammer and chisel. Still he found nothing. So, over the next six weeks, he dug away at the cold, never-sunned earth below his bed. He did this work alone, since he was unwilling to share the treasure that he expected to find.

After all those weeks, however, he discovered nothing of value in the pit he had dug.

In despair, he concluded that he might have failed to notice a small jewellery box or purse in so many thousands of shovelsful of soil. He searched through the two enormous piles of earth he had made in his courtyard, but he discovered only the personal possessions he'd kept under his mat, including his mirror.

It was then – lost and exhausted – that he began to weep.

And he knew he must give up his quest.

Seated in his courtyard, he polished the mirror's surface with his tears and the sleeve of his cloak. When he beheld his face, he realized for the first time that, in truth, a great mystery was looking back at him. *Who am I, and what is the 'I' in my head to do with the journey I have been on?* he wondered.

And then he laughed, for he suddenly understood why the Jewish sorcerer had sent him home.

You see, Yaphiel, what I need to tell you before you visit me is that our treasure is always with us, and it is a treasure meant for us alone, but only a sage who understands our deepest dreams can tell us where to look for it.

Lazarus ben Natan
1st of Sivan, Year 124 of the Roman Conquest

POSTSCRIPT

Dodee, if you are alive, or if your soul is amongst us, then perhaps you are reading these words as I write them. Have you intended all along to meet me in Yerushalayim?

We shall sit together by our stream and converse about all we have seen and done since we last parted company. I shall tell you all you wish to know about Ilana and Yaphiel. You will be proud of them, I know.

We shall become our island once again.

'Love is as strong as death,' we learn from the Song of Songs, and, if I stand on tiptoe at my bedroom window here on Rodos, I am reminded that it is true, for I can see your family home in Natzeret, and you are often chopping wood in the side garden with your father's old axe, and when you espy me watching you, you smile and raise two fingers.

I still have questions about why and how you tested me – though perhaps I fear your answers. Not because they may change my ideas about you. No, it is simply that after all these years my doubts have become a part of you – a garment meant to protect me from forming too fixed an image of you in my mind.

Even in death, a man deserves room to change and develop.

If I met the Lord today, I would ask him only one question: Why did You not send a host of angels to rescue Your chosen one from the Lion's Den?

Though perhaps I already know the answer: God wished to tell us that we are nearing the end of our era – and maybe even the end of time. Was that why you cited Daniel so often over our last days together?

If you prefer to have your secrets, then you need not reply. You do not need to give me answers or tell me what you have done over these past twenty-nine years. I shall not be overly inquisitive. I shall accept you as you are, just as you have always accepted me. And, when we grow tired of conversation, we shall return to Bethany and sleep in my old room together, side by side, as when we were boys.

There, in the grateful and final silence that comes to all those who have reached the journey's end, I shall give you my dreams and you will give me your prophecies.

Know this: I shall never again let you face your fears alone. And should you ever grow uneasy at the descent of night, I shall curl up behind you and hold you in the hiding place of thunder, as I always have.

GLOSSARY

All words and phrases in Hebrew transliteration unless otherwise noted

Atman	Sanskrit for the spark of God in each person according to Hindu theology
Aleph	First letter of the Hebrew alphabet: א
Anax	Ancient Greek for king, lord or leader
Ar-garizim	Mount Gerizim, the mountain in Samaria where the Samaritans constructed their temple
Apotropaios	Ancient Greek for protective magic meant to ward off curses and spells
Aureus	Latin for golden
B'tselem Elohim	In God's image; a reference to the Lord having made human beings in the divine image, as related in Genesis 1:26–28
Baal Nephesh	Master of the breath or soul; a holy man
Book of Names	Ancient name for Exodus, the Second Book of the Torah or Old Testament
Book of Words	Ancient name for Deuteronomy, the Fifth Book of the Torah or Old Testament
Caldarium	The hot room in a Roman bathhouse
Caseus	Latin for cheese
Chasidah	Stork
Chesed	Kindness
Cloaca Maxima	Latin for the principal sewer in ancient Rome
Derash ha-Torah	Hebrew for Torah study (*derash* = to seek to fulfil the Torah)
Din	Divine justice
Dodee	Beloved
Dupondius	Roman brass coin

Ehyeh-Asher-Ehyeh	I Am Who I Am, one of the names of God in the Torah
El Elyon	The name of the Lord, traditionally translated as God Most High
Elohim	One of the most common names of God in the Torah
El Roi	Literally the God Who Sees, a name of the Lord used in the Torah that first appears in Genesis
Etrog	Citron
Eruv	A ritual or spiritual enclosure
Garum	A fermented fish sauce used as a condiment in ancient Rome and its colonies
Ge Hinnom	Literally, the Valley of Hinnom, an area outside Jerusalem's walls believed to have been the great rubbish dump for the city. Also, very possibly, a place for human sacrifice in ancient Israel. In medieval times, it was often the name given for hell in folk tales and kabbalistic texts.
Gephen	Grapevine
Golgotha	Ancient Greek for the place outside Jerusalem's walls where, according to the Gospels, Jesus was crucified
Gevurah	Divine judgement
Havvah	Eve
Hametz	Foods which Jews are forbidden to eat during Passover, especially leavened bread
Charoset	A mixture of fruit, nuts and spices traditionally prepared for Passover; at the Seder meal, it represents the mortar with which the Hebrew slaves constructed the buildings of the Egyptian Pharaoh.
Hekhal ha-Melekh	The Palace or Sanctuary of the King
Hosen	Breastplate traditionally worn by the High Priest of the Jewish Temple in Jerusalem
Ibbur	Ghost, spirit or spectre, especially the wandering soul of a deceased person that possesses a living person
Iesous Nazoraios	Ancient Greek rendering of 'Jesus of Nazareth, King of
Basileus Ioudaios	the Jews'
Ilana	Oak tree
In the Beginning	Ancient name for Genesis, the first book of the Torah or Old Testament

Insula	Latin name for the huge apartment buildings in ancient Rome
Kakiaphas	Ancient Greek for evil or what is to be avoided
Kethoneth	A coat or robe
Kerioth	A town in the southern part of Judaea, near present-day Hebron; the follower of Jesus known today as Judas was probably from there, since Iscariot is now believed to mean Kerioth.
Ketubah	Marriage contract
Kesilim	Trickster spirits
Kinnamomon	Ancient Greek for cinnamon
Kittim	The name for the Romans used in the Book of Daniel; elsewhere in the Torah it generally refers to the inhabitants of Cyprus.
Koheleth	Preacher; the Book of Koheleth is the original Hebrew name of Ecclesiastes
Kore	Ancient Greek for girl or daughter, as well as the pupil of the eye
Kuklos	Ancient Greek for wheel or cycle
Lambda	Eleventh letter of the Greek alphabet: Λ
Lapis specularis	Latin name for a variety of gypsum that forms near-transparent crystal sheets; in Roman times it was mined in Spain and used to make windowpanes.
Lestes	Latin for rebel or revolutionary
Lethe	One of the five rivers that flow through Hades, the Greek Underworld; all those who bathe in it or drink its waters experience complete forgetfulness.
Malach Hamavet	The Angel of Death
Melekh ha-Mashiah	The Anointed King
Mashal	Parable master
Matzoh	Unleavened bread baked by the Israelites during the Exodus from Egypt and eaten during the holiday of Passover; the only ingredients are flour and water.
Mastuma	The Angel of Lies
Megillah	Literally scroll, but also a common name for the Book of Ester
Menorah	In ancient times, a six-branched candelabrum that was kept in the Temple; modern versions used to celebrate the festival of Hanukkah generally have eight branches plus a separate holder for the special candle used to light the others.

Mithras	Originally a Zoroastrian angel and divinity, Mithras later became the principal god of a mystery religion in ancient Rome.
Mitzvah	Commandment; it generally refers to the duties of each and every Jew and, by extension, any good deed.
Morah	Bitter trouble or grief
Moreh	Teacher
Moretum	A cheese paste made from curds, olive oil, garlic and vinegar that the Romans and those who adapted their eating habits generally ate with bread
Moria	Ancient Greek for stupidity or foolishness
Neshamah	The divine spark of God in man; the soul.
Netzach	Victory
Nissan	The month of the Hebrew calendar that falls in March or April of the Gregorian calendar
Ochlos	Ancient Greek for rabble
Ophel	A darkness that is gloomy or oppressive
Orkhis	Ancient Greek for orchid
Phasael Tower	One of three high towers in the north-west corner of the city walls of the Upper City of Jerusalem; the others were called the Hippicus and Miriamne towers. Built by Herod the Great, They were situated close to where the Jaffa Gate is today.
Philoromaios	Latin for a foreign supporter of Rome – literally a Rome-lover
Posca	A popular drink in the ancient Roman Empire made by mixing vinegar or sour wine with water
Poikiliphron	Ancient Greek for multi-coloured mind
Qalat	Deformed
Qelalah	A curse
Pappous	Ancient Greek for grandfather
Passover	The Jewish festival commemorating the escape of the Hebrew people from bondage in Egypt; traditionally celebrated for eight days during the spring
Peshar	Word for interpretation used in the Book of Daniel
Racham	Tender compassion
Reka	Empty-headed
Sanhedrin	The ruling council in each city of Judaea
Sappir	Sapphire

Seder	The traditional ceremonial meal eaten on the first and sometimes second nights of Passover
Sefer	Book
Sekel	Insight or, in a negative sense, cunning
Sha'ar ha-Rahamim	Golden Gate, one of the ancient gates of Jerusalem; the original meaning was Gate of Mercy.
Shalom Aleikem	Peace be with you
Shed	Demon or devil
Shema	The prayer that serves as the centrepiece for morning and evening prayers; it begins: 'Hear, O Israel, the Lord is our God, the Lord is One.'
Shepharphar	Aramaic for dawn
Shofar	A ram's horn; it is sounded for certain festivities, including New Year. Joshua's 'trumpet' was actually a *shofar*.
Shohet	A butcher trained in the techniques governing the slaughter of animals
Sivan	The month of the Hebrew calendar that begins in late May or early June of the Gregorian calendar
Sofer	A scribe and notary responsible for drawing up legal documents
Sukkot	Seven-day Jewish holiday beginning on the 15th of the month of Tishrei. The Hebrew word *sukkot* is the plural of *sukkah*, which means booth or tabernacle, a small structure covered with plant material such as palm leaves. Jews traditionally build a *sukkah* for the holiday, and it is meant to commemorate the fragile dwellings in which the followers of Moses dwelt during their forty years of wandering in the desert. Throughout the holiday, meals are eaten inside the tabernacle, and many people sleep there as well.
Sunkope	Ancient Greek for the onset of dizziness and loss of strength that can overwhelm worshippers
Tallit	A rectangular prayer shawl
Tau	Nineteenth letter of the Greek alphabet: T
Taw	Last letter of the Hebrew alphabet: ת
Tekhelet	Turquoise
Theophanus	Ancient Greek for an appearance or manifestation of a god (or God) to a mortal person
Theta	Eighth letter of the Greek alphabet: Θ

Torah	The Pentateuch or first five books of what Christians refer to as the Old Testament; in a broader sense, it can refer to the entire canon of sacred Jewish books or even all of Jewish teaching. For thousands of years, Jews ascribed the Torah to Moses.
Triclinium	Latin for the formal dining room in Roman-style homes
Tsalmaveth	Deep, penetrating shadow
Tsedeq	Justice
Tzitzit	The tassels or fringes at the corners of the prayer shawl; they are to remind us of the commandments of Deuteronomy 22:12 and Numbers 15:37–41.
Yamim Nora'im	Literally Days of Awe, this is the ten-day period of festivities and reflection starting with *Rosh Hashanah* (New Year's) and ending with *Yom Kippur* (Day of Atonement).
Yaqad	To set ablaze
Yod	Tenth letter of the Hebrew alphabet: י
Yeshua	A cry for help; also, Jesus' name in Hebrew
Yom Kippur	The holiest of Jewish holidays, on which Jews fast to atone for their misdeeds and sins
Zadok	Zadok was a patrilineal descendant of Eleazar, the son of Aaron, the elder brother of Moses and first High Priest of the Israelites. The high priesthood remained in the control of his progeny for many centuries.
Zeman	Time or temporal
Ziz	The king of the birds in Jewish tradition and lore
Zonah	Whore

9 781909 954496